The Distance from Normandy

Also by Jonathan Hull

Losing Julia

The Distance from Normandy

Jonathan Hull

ST. MARTIN'S PRESS ❧ NEW YORK

www.stmartins.com

ISBN 0-312-31411-6

First Edition: September 2003

10 9 8 7 6 5 4 3 2 1

In memory of my father,
who showed me the wonder of books
and the wisdom of kindness.

Morton D. Hull
1927–2003

Sorrow makes us all children again.

—*Emerson,* Journals, *1842*

Part One

Chapter 1

They were late. Mead peered out the living room window again and checked his watch. Already an hour late. That was Sharon for you. It was, he'd decided long ago, a genetic flaw like baldness or myopia, only more irritating. Even as a child she'd been chronically late—pleading for a ride after missing the school bus, lingering dreamily on the jungle gym long after the school bell rang, prancing down the stairs to the dinner table at the very last moment, her sunny round face disarming his anger. She'd even been two weeks overdue at birth as Sophie swelled like a manatee and finally had to be induced. Mead dropped back down into his dark blue overstuffed chair, shuffled through the paper, then stood back up and peered out the window again.

After realigning the magazines and books on the large oak coffee table, he gave the brown sofa pillows a few dutiful whacks, then adjusted the gray dustcover draped over the telescope that sat on a tripod in the corner. Crossing the light blue carpet again he entered the kitchen, wiped down the counters one last time, then refilled his coffee mug and held it to his lips, taking small sips as he surveyed the empty sink and the neatly folded hand towels that hung from the oven door handles and the tidy row of spices and medicine bottles on the windowsill. So damn many medicines. He tapped the fingers of his right hand against the tip of his thumb, counting off the last dosage: next batch at 4 p.m. (A complete waste of money, he suspected, hating the frailty they implied.)

He set his mug on the counter and walked down the short and dimly lit hallway to the first bedroom on the left, peering inside. Sophie's room, the 1960s Singer workhorse still sitting on a small white table, waiting. "Just give me one little teeny, tiny place where I can make my mess," she'd said when they began looking for their first house in 1954. And finally, after Sharon went off to college and they purchased their third house in 1974, he'd been able to oblige. "It's *perfect,*" she said as they surveyed the small extra bedroom. "Just wait until I'm finished with it." Once they'd fixed it up with some new carpeting and paint she'd disappear for hours to sew and hum and iron and do her decoupage and putter—or just sit like a queen in her hand-painted rocking chair by the window, gazing proudly at her small vegetable garden, now untended, overgrown and reclaimed by nature. Like Sophie.

For the first three months after she died Mead kept the door closed, unable even to set foot in there, as though afraid he might see her, afraid that she'd have to go through it again. The unbearable thing. So he kept the door closed and walked quickly past, some days wondering whether he had heard a sound, a sigh or rustle of fabric.

When Sharon visited that first Thanksgiving—nearly three years ago now—she tried to clean things up, making big piles of her mother's clothes to give away. But while she went to the grocery store to restock his refrigerator, Mead quickly rescued several of his favorite items and returned them to Sophie's closet, where her best shoes still hung from a pink wire rack on the left. And her slippers. Her worn, old yellow slippers, which still bore the impressions of her narrow size-six feet. Mead could never bring himself to throw out her slippers.

He listened to a car pass, still standing in the doorway, then checked his watch again. He'd spent three days trying to ready the room for his grandson, removing some of the pictures on the dresser—but leaving enough to remind the kid of his roots, of where he was. He stored all the plastic boxes of thread, pins, fabric samples, knitting needles and patterns beneath the twin bed. And buttons. There were jars and jars of buttons stashed everywhere, like acorns for winter. Sophie loved buttons. She adored the shiny, small, matching cuteness of them. Whenever Mead lost a button, a look of singular purpose shone on her face as she'd snatch off his shirt or coat and whisk it away to her room. "I can match it *perfectly,*" she'd say as she foraged noisily through her button jars.

When he tired of trying to organize the room he'd sit in the rocker thinking of her sitting in the rocker and he'd steep himself in as much of her as still remained in the room. There was plenty. Enough, he thought, to survive on. At least for a few years. He didn't think of it as a memorial or a mausoleum—nothing quite so morbid; it was simply the place where she was more present than anywhere else, where her scent was the strongest. And so he'd gotten into the habit of spending a few minutes each day in the rocking chair, telling her things and imagining what she'd say and how she'd laugh or scold him, or just give him that look of hers where her eyebrows came together. After three days of moving things back and forth he'd finally made what he considered adequate space for his grandson. Just enough for a few weeks, then he'd put everything back exactly as it was.

He smoothed down the bedspread one more time before returning to the kitchen where he finished his coffee, washed out the mug, dried it and re-shelved it before wiping down the counters once again. Then he checked the refrigerator: plenty of sandwich meats, orange juice, milk (whole, as well as Mead's one percent), two flavors of Gatorade—terrible stuff, he thought, after a taste—two packs of all-beef franks, several pounds of lean hamburger meat, Swiss cheese, eggs, bacon, sausages in both links and patties. Even ice cream bars with nuts, which he'd selected after much consideration. (He'd been off ice cream for two years after noticing a certain softness around the midriff.) Plenty to get started. Who knew what the boy would eat?

He went back into the living room and peered out the window, then sat back down in his blue chair and waited.

A knife. A goddamn pocket knife.

. . .

Andrew sat in silence next to his mother, arms wrapped around his backpack. Crazy stupid thing. Crazy stupid world. And now this. He tapped his toe against the floorboard. And the thing was, he'd do it again if he had to. He'd push back again. He squeezed his backpack to his chest. *Push, push, push.* That's what it was all about. Getting pushed and pushing back. So he'd finally pushed back. Hard. And now everybody wanted to destroy him.

They always had.

It wasn't hate he felt, not the usual hate that seemed to pressurize everything until his ears ached. More like a sort of burning in his pimpled, freckled face. He kept thinking about what his best friend Matt used to say, about how sometimes it felt like life was gonna bust his head wide open. And then one day Matt decided he couldn't take the pain anymore;

he'd had enough. *How could you leave me like that?* Now Andrew was no longer sure that he could take it either.

He stared out the window at a passing silver Porsche convertible, watching the middle-aged driver talk smugly on a cell phone. Sixteen, and still the fucking helplessness of it. Can you will yourself into someone else's skin? But who'd want to switch with him? No one. He watched the driver, one hand resting lazily on top of the steering wheel, world by the balls. Probably talking dirty to his horny girlfriend. And with a silver Porsche convertible hauling his rich ass anywhere he wants to go. Andrew couldn't imagine the freedom of it, the absolute independence; doing only what you want to do, going wherever you felt like going. Just being able to pick up and *move.* Was it just a matter of waiting long enough? Learning when to push? But he'd always been waiting. He was tired of waiting. He slipped on his headphones and turned up the volume on his CD player. Fuck waiting.

They'd left the house at nine that morning for the flight from Chicago to San Diego, landing just after lunch. But his mother took the wrong bus to the wrong car rental agency and it was another forty-five minutes before they arrived at Thrifty, where they were given a tiny, white two-door with the smallest tires Andrew had ever seen. Typical, he thought, squeezing into the front seat and putting his headphones back on. The cheapest everything.

He looked quickly over at his mother, then back out the window, forwarding to the next song. He'd have to wait a lot longer now. Maybe forever. Okay, so he'd wait forever. What did it matter, really? What did anything matter? Because the thing that he could never stop thinking about was: *nothing* really mattered. The vast stupidness of everything was always there laughing at him: when he took a test, when he studied, when he stood before the mirror in the bathroom for twenty minutes each morning struggling to conceal his acne with his mother's makeup. It was all so amazingly pointless. All of it: grades and sports and theorems and diagramming sentences and always having to pretend to be what you weren't, and—most of all—the way everybody worked so hard trying to impress everybody else. *Pointless.* Yeah, he understood that. He understood a lot of things. That's what made it harder: *knowing.* And no one thinks you know. They don't have a clue that you can see through it all. Or maybe they've forgotten that they could once see through it all, too. (Is that it? He was never quite sure what happened to adults, how they became so pathetic.) He turned up the volume on his CD player. But still he'd have to get through the next three weeks. Twenty-one days with his grandfather. Mr. D-Day himself. The great Nazi slayer. Just thinking about it scared him, knotting up his stomach. And Andrew hated being scared more than anything. He was tired of being scared.

His mother tapped him on the shoulder. "How are you doing?"

Andrew shrugged.

"We should be there in fifteen minutes."

Another shrug.

"But you'll try?"

Andrew remained silent.

"Please?" Her features drew up with concern, which always got to him.

"Yeah, I'll try."

He didn't hate his mother. He never could, not like some guys hated theirs—a deep, primal sort of hatred. His mother was simply too stupid to hate. Nice but stupid, always losing things and leaving the car lights on and forgetting to pay the phone bill and dating the biggest jerks in the world. And then there was all her crying, which seemed to get worse and worse so that her mascara was always smearing, which drove Andrew nuts. She cried over everything: television shows, his grades, boyfriends, burning dinner, being poor. No, he didn't hate her. She was too fragile to hate. But he couldn't tell her anything. No way. There was a time when he wished he could, when he wanted her to understand what was happening to him, when he desperately needed her help. But not anymore. Who wants their mom to know the truth, to know that their son is silently drowning—that every morning when he goes to school and walks down those cold, echoing corridors with the jeering faces and the impenetrable circles, he just *dies?*

He changed CDs.

And that was the worst thing: hurting her. He still couldn't shake the look on her face when she arrived at the principal's office and saw him sitting there with the knife on the table and the cop and the flushed angry faces and the accusations. Like he was crazy, one of those wackos on TV in combat black, taking the whole fucking football team down with them.

No, he wasn't the crazy one. It was the rest of them that were crazy. All he wanted was for the pushing to stop.

Just please stop pushing me.

. . .

Sharon had called her father that night.

"Oh God, Dad, you'll never believe what's happened . . ."

"Try me."

"Andrew's been expelled. He brought a *knife* to school. He pulled it on a classmate. He didn't hurt him but—"

"Now slow down a minute. A *knife*? You sure they got the story straight? Andrew hardly seems like—"

"Of course I'm sure. He's been expelled. Andrew's been *expelled.*" She burst into tears. "I can't handle him anymore, Dad. I know he's a good kid inside but I can't handle him."

"How long is he out of school?"

"At least three weeks, which is all that's left until summer break." Sharon's voice wavered. "I don't know what's going to happen in the fall. There's a hearing. They could press charges."

"Just back up a minute. What kind of knife?"

"A pocketknife. The one you gave him when he went to that camp you sent him to."

Mead recalled the small buck knife he had engraved for Andrew's tenth birthday, just like the one that his own father had given him and that he'd kept all through the war. Did he still have it somewhere? "And you're saying he *pulled it* on somebody?"

"An older boy named Kevin Bremer. All I know is that he's on the football team."

"Maybe Andrew was just trying to show it off, impress the guys." He couldn't imagine his grandson trying to hurt anybody. Being hurt, yes.

"No, he was going to . . . stab him. That's what all the other kids said." She tried to stifle another sob. "I just can't believe it. I've completely failed. I'm just a mess, Dad. I don't know what to do anymore. Ever since the suicide, Andrew's been . . . oh God, Dad, what am I going to do?" She cried even harder.

Six months earlier, Andrew's best friend had killed himself by overdosing on alcohol and a bottle of his mother's tranquilizers. Mead had offered to send Andrew away to a boarding school, thinking it might give him a new start, but Sharon wanted to keep him close by.

And now this. Mead shook his head. To hell in a handbasket. And he'd seen it coming for years. The riots, race problems, drugs, violence, promiscuity. Christ, the filth on television. Pure pornography at family hour. At least all those young soldiers who never came home didn't have to see what became of the country they died fighting for. Freedom? More like anarchy. But he'd be gone soon enough. And frankly, that was just fine with him. He'd seen plenty, thank you.

"It's the goddamn television," he said finally. "That and the music and those computer games they play and the general lack of respect. You throw your TV out the window and tell that boy to straighten up and mind his Ps and Qs, or I'll do it for him. Better yet, tell him he'll go to military academy and I'll spring for it."

"This is Andrew we're talking about," said Sharon. *"Andrew."*

Mead looked over at the photograph on the coffee table: Sharon and Andrew at the boy's middle-school graduation. A nice enough kid, Mead thought, but shy and small and underfed-looking, with oily skin and a droopy, introverted face. A disappointment, frankly. Four-F. And as for teenagers, Lord, Mead could hardly bear the sight of them lurking in the malls, the girls dressed like hookers and the boys with their pants practically at their knees, cracks showing for all to see. "Pull up your trousers, sonny," he'd mutter to himself, never quite able to figure out how they stayed up at all. Every Christmas he made sure to give Andrew the finest belt money could buy. But the kid never wore one. None of them did.

Still, he'd always had a soft spot for Andrew, the only child of his only child. How Sophie used to dote on the boy, making him little outfits, buying him more presents than he could ever need, puddling up at the mention of him, as if having a grandchild was her life's crowning triumph. And Mead knew it hadn't been easy for the kid, whose father, Carl the Creep, ran off with some floozy when Andrew was just eight, and hardly bothered to call except when he was crocked. Mead had felt something funny on the back of his neck the first time he met The Creep, and he had sat distraught during the wedding wondering what in God's name he'd done wrong to cause his daughter—his sweet, precious Sharon, the only child Sophie had been able to have—to seek out a lazy son of a bitch like that. (Though she'd always had terrible taste in men, like the color-blind choosing a wardrobe.) Oh yes, he'd been onto The Creep from the start, and every time he was forced to talk to his son-in-law he'd find himself fantasizing about where on that big, mushy, arrogant face he might plant a decisive punch.

"Why'd he do it? There must have been some reason."

"How do I know why?"

"You ask him, that's how."

"He won't tell me. He won't tell me *anything.*"

"Well then you lock him up in his room until he will tell you."

"You don't know him, Dad. He'd stay there until he starved. He's . . . he's changed. He's just boiling inside." She paused to blow her nose, making a loud honking sound. "I know he hasn't had it easy—I'm doing the best I can—but this?"

"Wasn't he seeing some sort of therapist?"

"He went for a while. Then he wouldn't go anymore."

"You don't give him a damn choice."

"Dad . . ." her voice broke. "I just can't handle him anymore. I took tomorrow off from work but I just started the job and . . ." She began to cry again.

Mead winced at the sound of her tears. What had happened to her? How had she become so beaten down and overwhelmed by life that he feared what each phone call might bring? Without thinking, Mead said, "Why don't you let me take him for a few weeks?"

There was a long pause. "You?"

"Why not? Maybe I can knock some sense into him."

"You know you'd go crazy in about five minutes."

"Give me some credit."

"Let's just say that teenagers aren't exactly . . ."

"Aren't exactly what?"

"You're serious?"

"Sure I'm serious."

Was he? Already Mead wondered whether it was too late to retract the offer.

There was another long pause. "Maybe it would be good for him. God knows, he needs a man around. But you're really serious?"

Mead swallowed hard. "Of course I'm serious."

· · ·

Mead was on the front walkway of his small, white, one-story ranch house when the car pulled up. Three years in the service and the one lesson that stuck with him was: never volunteer. But Sharon needed him. Frankly, she needed a lot of things. Poor girl, always reeling from one disaster to another. Sophie had been right, their daughter just wasn't a natural when it came to motherhood. Or men. But did I really say three weeks? You're getting soft, old man. The thing is to lay down the law from the start. State the rules and consequences. And there would be consequences.

But exactly what consequences? He'd given that question considerable thought over the past few days. He couldn't just take the boy over his knee and smack him (though it might do him some good). He could always ground him, but ground him from what? It wasn't like the boy had any friends in the area. And what the hell would they *do* for three weeks? He was stumped on that one. At least there was the basketball hoop he'd purchased in a panic the day before and spent four hours assembling in the driveway. So—he could take away the boy's basketball privileges. And no Gatorade. Any back talk and down the drain goes the Gatorade, which is where it belongs anyway.

Across the street his neighbor Evelyn came out to water her flowers, stopping to wave enthusiastically. He waved back politely, hoping she wouldn't bring him over another batch of her nefarious raisin cookies. He wasn't quite sure what to make of Evelyn. A few years younger than Mead, she'd been widowed ten years previously and seemed to spend most of her time tending her garden and cooking raisin cookies or brownies or muffins, which she'd leave on Mead's doorstep in little decorative tins, returning every so often to collect the empties and chat. She and Sophie used to gab about gardening, sharing tips and an occasional recipe, but they'd never been close. Mead always suspected that it was because Sophie thought Evelyn was excessively attentive to him. (She didn't miss a thing.) It probably didn't help that Evelyn's bougainvillea scrambled enthusiastically up her trellis while Sophie's seemed paralyzed with a fear of heights. Indeed, Evelyn's flower garden put the entire subdivision to shame, exploding in riotous reds and yellows and oranges and blues long after every other garden—including Sophie's—had expired in the summer heat. "I think she *uses* something," Sophie would say accusingly.

She wasn't at all bad-looking—for her age (no small qualification). But Mead certainly didn't think of her *that* way. Indeed, he was careful always to be extremely circumspect in her presence, not wanting to give her any encouragement. The thought of Sophie rolling jealously in her grave was

simply unbearable. Besides, Mead had little confidence in his ability to cor-
rectly interpret the subtle signals that guided male-female relations. Years
earlier he'd been the unwitting and mortified subject of a vigorous pursuit
by a chain-smoking, six-foot-three divorcée named Frances who worked
in the accounting department of his engineering firm. At first he thought it
a mere unfortunate coincidence that she always appeared at the coffee
machine whenever he went for a refill, but when she goosed him at the
Christmas party after imbibing too much punch he knew he was in trouble. The next day he went out and purchased his own coffee thermos, and
from then on he took elaborate precautions to avoid being in the same
room with her. Yet two months later an envelope with no return address
arrived in his office mail. Inside was a one-page poem, which, as far as he
could tell, had something to do with the different shades of light on a Sunday afternoon—though he suspected it might be some sort of coded
proposition. He received three in all, and though he shredded each one on
the spot, they left him feeling sullied and traitorous (despite a flawless
record of fidelity). Should he tell Sophie? But how could he? *You must
have been leading her on.* And yet if he didn't, he'd have something to hide.
A secret. He never did tell her—despite several aborted attempts—and
thankfully the pursuit ended as suddenly as it had started. Still, the experience convinced him that one could never be too cautious in dealing with
the opposite sex. He glanced over at Evelyn across the street, then quickly
looked away, pretending to be busy adjusting his sprinkler.

Finally a small white car—so small he thought it might be electric—
turned the corner and came down the street, popping the curb as it pulled
into his driveway.

"Hi, Dad." Sharon jumped out and gave him a big hug. He'd forgotten
how familiar she smelled. Even with her lotions and shampoos and the
awful perfume that always made his and Sophie's eyes water—*are you sure
it's not tear gas?*—he could still trace her original scent, the one that drifted
into his being the day he first kissed her fuzzy little scalp at the hospital in
Tampa, where they had lived for three years after the war.

"You're late."

"Sorry. We had a small problem with the rental car."

"Mom went to Hertz by mistake," mumbled Andrew. "This is from
Thrifty." He pointed disgustedly at the car. "We should have gone to
Hertz. Everybody else goes to Hertz."

What a punk, thought Mead, studying his grandson, whose enormous jeans could easily have fit on the biggest man in Mead's old rifle company. He wore dirty, unlaced sneakers, walking on the flattened back heels as though they were slippers, and a large and rumpled black T-shirt with some sort of Satanic omen painted on it. He had a small, gold hoop earring in his left earlobe and his hair—once brown but now streaked with yellow along the top—looked like it had been cut with shears, then fermented under a helmet for several weeks. In short, the boy looked like a refugee or drug freak.

Mead felt a chill of repugnance. My own grandson. And a hooligan as well. He reached down and tapped the roll of antacids in his front pants pocket. What the hell was Sharon thinking, letting him travel dressed like that? It was no wonder so many friends had retreated into elderly compounds over the years, safe in their snug little time capsules, oblivious to their irrelevance. Mead would never do that. He wasn't about to hide behind some damn guard and gate. Finally he stepped forward and put out his hand. "How are you doing, son?"

The boy shrugged and took his hand, offering a limp, moist grip, so that Mead feared he might break the boy's bones if he squeezed too hard.

"Well, get your things and come inside."

Andrew returned to the car for his backpack, duffel bag and skateboard. Sharon stood staring at Mead, her eyes moistening. "Thank you," she whispered. "I don't know what else to say."

Mead watched the boy for a moment, wondering if he should help—naw, let him carry his own load—then turned and went inside, hoping Sharon wouldn't get weepy.

"Well, this will be your room," Mead said, standing awkwardly at the doorway to Sophie's room.

"It was Mom's," said Sharon.

"You guys had separate bedrooms?"

"Of course we didn't have separate bedrooms," Mead said with a scowl. "This was her . . . workshop."

"Mom loved this room."

"What did she make?" asked Andrew, eyeing the room suspiciously.

"What didn't she?" said Sharon. "She was incredible with her hands. I think I must have been adopted."

"Your grandma made half the stuff in this house," said Mead proudly.

"Take that mirror with the shells, for example. She found every single one of those shells herself."

"When they lived in Tampa," explained Sharon. "Mom loved beach-combing."

"And look how she glued each one on just perfectly," continued Mead. "You could get some money for that one. And those curtains, made them herself, and this quilt . . ." Andrew eyed the bright orange and brown bed-spread. "And that plate on the wall."

"Decoupage," said Sharon.

They stood in silence, shifting from foot to foot.

"So, why don't you unpack your things and your mom and I will be in the living room," said Mead finally. The moment they walked away Mead heard the door close.

After stopping in the bathroom to down two antacids, he offered Sharon a soft drink—Fresca, his favorite—then took a seat in his blue, overstuffed chair and looked closely at her. She looked thinner than usual, with a puffi-ness around her large hazel eyes and lines on her oval face that he didn't remember seeing before. Even her hands looked thinner, veins showing. *Where did you go, Princess?* It broke his heart to see what had happened to her, how she never seemed to get her footing, going through jobs and men like tissue. What had they done wrong? Nothing. Sophie had even offered—much to Mead's horror—to move out to Chicago to help with Andrew after The Creep first walked out. (Thank God Sharon wouldn't hear of it.)

She had a big enough heart; maybe too big. It was common sense that she lacked. He looked at the gray roots of her thinning, dark brown hair, remembering how full and shiny it once was and how Sophie loved to braid it into all sorts of designs before sending Sharon skipping off to school in the morning. "Look at me, Dad!" And what a beauty she'd been, beauty that gradually had been washed away by heartbreak and circum-stance. Mead took a deep breath, fighting back a tightness in his chest.

"How have you been, Pumpkin?" he asked softly.

"The truth? Awful." She sat on the sofa across from him, leaning over her knees. "I just don't know what to do about Andrew. He's . . . he's not a bad kid, Dad. You know that. But he's got so much stuff inside and I don't know how to get it out. Ever since Matt's death he's been . . ." She raised her hands into the air, eyes welling up.

"Any more word from the school?"

"I'll find out more next week. They're considering whether to let him back next fall."

"How are his grades?"

"Terrible. In the last couple of years he's just stopped trying. And he's such a smart kid. I know he is." She wiped her eyes.

Mead leaned forward and took Sharon's hand. "Are you taking care of yourself?"

"Oh God, don't worry about me."

"But I do. You look thin."

"I've never been thin."

"Baloney. You getting any exercise?"

She shrugged. "I was working out a couple of times a week until I started this new job. I've just got to get a routine going."

"You're not still smoking?"

"I stopped—for *good*."

Mead raised his eyebrows.

"It's been a month. Promise."

"You two could move out here. Get some sunshine." Mead surprised himself with the offer, half hoping she'd decline.

"Dad, I *like* Chicago."

"Can I give you some money?"

"You just sent me a check."

"I have more than I need."

"I'm not your charity."

"You're my daughter."

She leaned toward him and kissed him on the cheek. "So how are you?"

"Fit as a fiddle."

"I hope I have your genes, but I'm starting to have my doubts."

Mead considered inquiring into the latest developments of her tumultuous love life, but then thought better of it. "So, uh, how does Andrew feel about . . ." he gestured around the room, "this?"

"Coming here? Well, it wasn't exactly his idea. He's a little nervous."

"Of course."

"I don't know how to thank you. With this new job and—"

"Don't think about it."

She wiped her eyes, smudging her mascara. "I think you'll be good for him. He needs a man, Dad. I really think he needs a man to reach him."

Mead took a deep breath and finished off his Fresca. "Well, we'll see." He heard noises coming from Sophie's room. Christ, was the boy rearranging things? Mead wouldn't stand for that.

Sharon glanced at her watch. "Yikes, I'm supposed to meet Cindy in half an hour. You remember Cindy? She's letting me sleep at her place tonight and I've got a flight home first thing in the morning."

Mead tensed. "You could have slept here," he said, trying to keep the hurt from his face.

Sharon looked around the living room, simply furnished with a dining room table at one end, and at the other a sofa, two chairs and a coffee table set around a small gas fireplace with three artificial logs.

"I would have slept on the couch."

"You're sweet, but I haven't seen Cindy in years." She got up and gave him a hug. "Thank you for paying for the tickets. I'll pay you back. Promise."

"You know I won't let you do that."

Sharon tried to smile, then gestured toward the hallway. "I'll just go say good-bye."

Mead nodded.

"He's really a good kid, Dad. He's just . . ."

"We'll be fine."

Mead stood on the front porch watching Sharon drive off, waving until the car turned down the block, then waving to the memory of her being there. He lingered for another moment, making a fist at his side to keep hold of himself, then pulled the mail out of the box and went back inside, bolting the door before returning to his chair where he sat leafing through the bills and catalogs and wondering what to fix for dinner. He heard more noises coming from Sophie's room. What the hell's going on in there?

When Andrew failed to emerge after half an hour Mead finally got up, walked down the hallway and stood outside the door listening. Not a sound. Was he taking a nap, for Christ's sake? Mead would have to put a stop to that, put the boy on a firm schedule. He returned twenty minutes later and listened again. "You want some Gatorade?"

"What?"

"I said, do you want some Gatorade? Got orange and red."

"No thank you. I don't like Gatorade."

Mead stood at the door for a moment. "Neither do I," he grumbled, heading back to the kitchen where he removed both jugs of Gatorade from the fridge, opened them and poured them down the sink.

An hour later he returned to the door and listened again. "You coming out of there sometime?" No response. Mead knocked. "I said, are you ever planning on coming out of there—or shall I just slide the food under the door?"

"I'm sorry, I was listening to music. Sure, I'll be out. When do you want me out?"

Mead stared at the door, noticing how faded the paint looked. Come to think of it, the whole house could use a fresh coat. Mead remembered how he and Sophie had spent weeks repainting it themselves, using the savings to go to Hawaii. Must have been fifteen years ago. "When would you want to come out?"

"Whenever."

"When's that?"

A minute later the door cracked open and Andrew peered out, all the shyness gathered around his eyes. Damn if he doesn't have the saddest eyes. Mead took a step back. "Well, I'll be in the living room. Dinner's at six. *Sharp.*" He turned and headed back down the hall. The door closed behind him. Three weeks, Mead thought, shaking his head as he settled back down in his blue chair and shuffled through the newspaper. Better restock the bourbon.

• • •

First, the orange and brown bedspread would have to go. Pathetic. It was like rooming with an orangutan. He folded it up and stuffed it onto the top shelf of the closet. After contemplating the layout of the room for several minutes, he switched the rocking chair with the dresser, then back again. Maybe the bed should go against the window. He tried four different arrangements, finally settling on the bed in the corner by the window, next to the dresser, with the small rattan desk at the foot of the bed and the rocking chair in the opposite corner. He considered unpacking his bag, but all but two of the drawers were full, crammed with sweaters and bracelets and earrings and balls of yarn and socks and shawls. Grandma's stuff. He picked up a yellow sweater and held it to his nose, then put it back and closed the drawer. Creepy. So he'd just keep his things in his bag. No need to unpack anyway. Only three weeks. Any luck and he'd go home early. The thing was just to get through it.

He sat on the bed wondering whether to take down any of the photographs and cheap-looking artwork, the kind sold at garage sales, then drummed his fingers on his kneecaps. Day one. Should he make a scratch on the wall? At least he'd finish *The Two Towers* and maybe even *The Return of the King*. But man, three weeks with GI Joe? He got up from the bed and stood at the dresser studying the framed photographs of his grandparents that were neatly arrayed in rows. As he looked closely at them he realized for the first time that both his grandfather and grandma had once been okay-looking, at least in black and white. He picked up a photo of his grandfather in uniform, surprised by how young he looked, like he barely shaved. Definitely good-looking: powerful eyes—deep blue in real life, which always made Andrew wonder why his own were dirty brown—good nose, all-American face. Frankly, way better looking than me. And the thing was, there was no similarity at all. He tried to see himself in his grandfather's eager young face but couldn't. Not even a trace. Grandfather the Kraut killer. Probably killed dozens of them. He'd seen plenty of shows on late-night television about the big war, the German dive bombers screaming downward and the guys jumping into the water and wading to the beach and then the grand finale with the mushroom cloud and then all those white crosses that went on forever. *Saving Private Ryan* was definitely intense, especially the scene where the Jew gets knifed by the German. Nasty. But he could never place the old guy in the green, button-down sweater sitting in the living room with those battles in Europe. That was like, *fifty* years ago.

He carefully placed the photograph back on the dresser, then knelt over his bag, opened a side compartment and pulled out the extra large Ziploc bag containing Matt, or what was left of him. He'd been surprised that the ashes weren't exactly ashes—not like what's left from a campfire—but more like little coarse white and gray pieces of ground shells from the beach. He had spent hours imagining Matt's body being placed on a big grill and then slid into a hot furnace and cooked to a crisp. (Heat for two hours at up to 1,800 degrees Fahrenheit, then pulverize—according to a

Web site he checked out.) Even dead, how could that not hurt? And how did they catch the ashes and keep them from being mixed with other people's ashes? What if it wasn't Matt at all that he was holding but some big-butted Bertha from the South Side? He carefully opened the Ziploc and put a finger in, stirring the little pieces of bone. Was it a crime to transfer stolen ashes across state lines? He didn't care—stealing Matt's ashes was the single best thing that Andrew had ever done. Once he heard that Matt was going to be taken to some family plot in Indiana he knew he had to do it. Matt *hated* Indiana, where he had to spend every Thanksgiving and Christmas on a farm visiting relatives, all of whom were seriously religious. Everyone suspected him, but they couldn't prove it. *The perfect crime.* He smiled and placed Matt in his lap.

Actually, he didn't really think of the ashes as Matt. He figured Matt had already been reincarnated into something else. He was always on the lookout, scrutinizing cats that rubbed against him and dogs that licked him and babies wailing at the grocery store and any stranger who gave him a second glance. He knew that Matt was out there somewhere; it was just a matter of time before he made the connection.

He put the Ziploc on the dresser and pulled out a smaller baggie containing three joints, which was all he could scrounge up for the trip. Would his grandfather search through his things? (Didn't everybody?) He looked around the room, then went over to the closet, chose one of his grandma's shoes at random and stuffed the baggie containing the joints into the toe, smiling to himself at his cunning. Then he gently flattened Matt's ashes and placed them under the mattress near the head. When he finished he sat back down on the bed and checked his watch. Is the old man expecting me in the living room? But what the hell are we going to do sitting in the same room?

He'd never felt comfortable around his grandfather (it was never *grandpa*). Not the way he had with Grandma, who played hours of cards and checkers and Parcheesi with him and always brought him homemade cookies and brownies when they came to visit. He hardly knew his grandfather, who always seemed to sit watchfully in the largest chair like the teacher during an exam. Sure he respected him, at least in the reflexive way you admire an astronaut or Olympic athlete, or show reverence for the dead. But he felt more intimidated than anything, hating the sweaty smallness he felt in the great man's presence. GI Joe's generation saved the world and there's been nothing but riffraff ever since. And basically, hero or not, the guy was wound up tight as an asshole. It was like having a cop, a priest and a principal all wrapped into one. And what's with the big American flag out front? It's like staying at the fucking post office.

He got up and looked at the photographs again, trying to figure how the young man in the uniform mutated into the cranky old headmaster sitting in the living room. What the hell did he do for kicks? Fondle his medals? Andrew tried to imagine his grandparents having sex but the idea made him cringe like he'd just sucked on a lemon. He sat back down on the bed, feeling edgy. Oh man, three weeks.

• • •

Mead settled on hamburgers. Top-grade, mixed with his own special seasoning. He scrubbed his hands, dried them, then carefully laid out a sheet of wax paper on the kitchen counter and began to knead the meat, shaping the patties until they were just so, plump but not too thick in the middle. Four patties should do it. These kids could eat entire livestock. He added a bit more pepper, then another dash of Worcestershire. Nothing like Mead's juicy burgers. (To hell with doctors.) After putting on his apron—the black one with the white chef's hat on it that Sophie made for his sixty-fifth birthday—he grabbed a box of Ohio Blue-Tip Matches from the top of the refrigerator, opened the screen door and went out to the side of the house to light the grill, suffused with a rare sense of contentment.

Once the burgers were on, he sliced up some onions, tomatoes and lettuce, then readied the condiments—ketchup, French's, Grey Poupon and horseradish spread—as well as cheddar cheese. He'd make two cheeseburgers and two plain. The boy could take his pick. But where to eat? Mead usually had his breakfast at the small table in the kitchen, then ate lunch and dinner on a TV tray in the living room. *Hmm.* They could eat at the table outside, enjoy the evening air. But it might be buggy. He stared at the little kitchen table, imagining them sitting face-to-face. Not a chance. There was always the dining room table; certainly plenty of elbowroom. But no, too formal. Besides, Mead never ate at the dining room table. As far as he was concerned, that was for entertaining, and he most definitely was not entertaining. Well then, they could eat from trays in the living room, keep it casual. He glanced down at the condiments, imagining his grandson dribbling ketchup and mustard all over the sofa and carpet. To hell with the bugs, they'd eat outside. He went back out and checked on the burgers, delighting in their freshly-singed smell. As he flipped them one last time—nearly perfect—Andrew appeared.

"What are those?"

Mead looked down with pride at the sizzling patties, adding cheese to two of them. "Well now, cut off my leg and call me Shorty, but in these parts we refer to them as burgers. *Hamburgers.* And they happen to be my specialty."

"Are they meat burgers?"

"I don't think I follow you, son."

"Are they made of meat?"

Mead put down his spatula. "Now what do you think?"

"I mean, *real* meat?"

Mead sized up his grandson, wondering if the boy was on drugs. It would explain a lot of things. But his eyes were clear enough and he seemed steady on his feet. "Yes, you're looking at real, honest-to-goodness hamburgers. Top grade. Ol' Daisy herself gave up the ghost so that we might eat." He picked up his spatula again. "Grab a plate."

"I thought they might be veggie-burgers."

"Now why would you think a thing like that?"

"Because I don't eat meat."

Mead stood motionless. "You don't eat . . . meat?"

"I'm not like a total vegan. I like cheese and tuna fish. But no land-based animals. It's been almost a year now." Andrew shoved his hands into his front pockets. "Farming's like the biggest polluter in the country," he mumbled. "And the energy that goes into raising one cow could feed thousands of people. Cows are even considered holy in India. Did you know that? They're practically rock stars. Man, if I was a cow I'd definitely want to live in India."

Mead looked down at the burgers, then back at the boy. "You don't eat meat?"

"Nope. But with tofu—"

"By God, it's no wonder you're so damn scrawny. You're not getting any protein."

"Beans have tons of protein."

Mead stared at the boy, then down at the grill. The burgers were now overcooked. Nothing Mead hated more than overcooked burgers. He grabbed a plate and took them off.

"I figured Mom would tell you."

Mead considered forcing his grandson to eat a cheeseburger on the spot, double time. Might be just what he needs. "You come with some sort of instruction manual?"

"I'm not that hungry anyway," Andrew mumbled.

"And for God's sake, stop mumbling." Mead carried the hamburgers to the kitchen while Andrew held open the screen door. "I've got some tuna fish. You said you like tuna fish?"

"Yeah, I guess I'll have some tuna fish."

Mead set the burgers down on the counter. They'd be cold by the time he ate. Tough and cold. He thought of all the meat sitting in the fridge. Enough for a platoon. *Damn.* He'd have to freeze some or it would spoil. Or was it too late to freeze meat that had been in the refrigerator for two days now? Better freeze some anyhow, give it the sniff test when it thaws. He looked back down at his burnt burgers. *Patience.*

"I make great tuna fish," he said finally, trying to sound pleasant. "Your grandma taught me the secret. Gotta mince it up real fine with your fingers. Then a squeeze of lemon, some Grey Poupon, mayonnaise and relish."

"I just like mayo, thanks. If that's okay . . ."

Mead stood looking at the boy, who was a good five inches shorter. (Mead was six-foot-one, or liked to think he still was.) "Fine. You make the tuna. It's there in the cabinet." Mead pulled out a bowl, a can opener and the mayonnaise, then covered the hamburgers with tin foil. "I'll be in the living room."

"You can go ahead and eat," said Andrew.

"I'll wait," said Mead, heading for the bourbon and feeling his stomach growl. He could hear Andrew rummaging through the cabinet.

"There should be a couple of cans right there in front, second shelf," Mead called out, knowing full well there were five cans of Starkist stacked right between the jar of Prego pasta sauce and the two cans of sliced Dole pineapples.

"I was just wondering if you had any packed in water?"

"Excuse me?"

More sounds of cans and jars being moved. Damn it. Mead rose from his chair. "Is there some sort of problem with my tuna fish?"

"It's just that it's packed in oil."

"It's Starkist, for Christ's sake."

"You can get it packed in water—but that's okay."

Mead sunk back down into his chair wondering if he should just call Sharon and tell her the whole thing had been a mistake; that Camp Mead was closed for the season and that little Sad Sack would be on the first plane home in the morning with a bag of carrots to see him through.

Several minutes later Andrew appeared in the living room. "I'm ready to eat when you are."

After Mead toasted a bun he slathered his hamburger with condiments, touched up his bourbon, then sat down at the small, white kitchen table across from Andrew and ate in silence.

Midway through his burger the doorbell rang. The raisin cookie lady, thought Mead, shaking his head.

"I'll get it," said Andrew.

Mead rose to stop him but Andrew was already halfway to the door.

"You must be Andrew," he heard Evelyn say. "Every bit as handsome as your grandfather." Who is she kidding? "I hope I'm not interrupting . . ."

"No, please come in. Hey Grandfather, you have a *visitor.*"

Mead quickly wiped the mustard from his mouth and grabbed the three empty tins from the top of the refrigerator. "Hello, Evelyn."

"Hello, General."

"General?" Andrew looked at his grandfather with a grin. "I didn't know you were a *general.*"

"I'm *not* a general."

"But he seems like one, don't you think? Must be that commanding presence." She winked. "Anyway, I've brought you some muffins." She took the three empty tins from Mead and handed him a full one. "I would have made more if I'd known your grandson was in town."

"This looks like plenty," said Mead.

"How long are you visiting for?" she asked Andrew, who was still grinning.

"A couple of weeks—maybe." Andrew took the tin from Mead, popped it open and selected a muffin. "This is *good,*" he said, taking a bite. "And I love the raisins."

Oh, God, thought Mead, she'll bake up a storm. She gave him a big smile. He had to admit she had a nice smile, which after so many years had been etched into her face as a kind of testament to her pleasant nature.

Taller than Sophie, she had warm hazel eyes, sun-freckled skin—a bit wrinkled but not yet lifeless—and good posture. Her gray hair was cut short and styled simply and she wore khakis, sneakers and a plain lavender shirt. Either good genes or healthy living or maybe even both. (How quickly Sophie had aged those last years, shrinking so fast that he had the illusion he was getting taller.)

"I try to keep your grandfather from wasting away," she explained to Andrew as he stuffed the remaining half of the muffin into his mouth.

"Delicious," he mumbled.

"Evelyn lives in the white house across the street," said Mead.

"Oh, I see," said Andrew with a knowing smile, which made Mead blush. "Well, it's really nice to meet you."

"I'll leave you two to finish your dinner," said Evelyn, sending Mead another one of her smiles, which wafted toward him like an enormous smoke ring. Sophie would have had her neck, he thought.

"Thanks for the muffins," Mead said, walking her to the door.

"Yeah, they're *awesome*," Andrew called out from the kitchen.

• • •

Mead always took a walk after dinner—it kept him regular as a Rolex—but he wasn't keen on leaving Andrew alone in the house. Nor did he especially want his grandson to join him for what was his favorite time of the day, watching the colors change and feeling the heat finally break and in the winter being able to look in the windows of his neighbors and glimpse little snapshots of solitude and chaos. After clearing their plates—at least the boy cleaned up after himself—Andrew retreated to his room while Mead returned to the living room. Jesus, it's like rooming with a monk, he thought, giving the paper a final once-over while listening to the tick of the silver clock on the mantle above the fireplace. Sophie's parents had given them the clock as a wedding gift along with the brass nameplate that still hung just above the doorbell beside their front door, though Mead always felt it belonged on a much larger house (which was why he kept it hidden in the back of the closet for years until Sophie insisted they put it up shortly after their last move). "Seems a bit showy to me," he muttered as Sophie marked off with a pencil exactly where she wanted it mounted.

"Everybody has one," she said, handing him the drill.

"They do?" Mead looked around at the other houses. "Looks like someone better tell the neighbors." But it was worth it just to see the glow on Sophie's face when she stood back and admired it.

"Now isn't that the homiest thing you've ever seen?"

He listened as Andrew emerged from his room and headed for the bathroom, closing the door quickly behind him. The kid goes more than I do.

He looked back at the clock. The thing was to have some sort of talk. Man to . . . juvenile delinquent. What the hell business have you got bringing a knife to school? Don't you know who you are, son? Oh, the things he could tell the boy. Goddamned vegetarian, worrying about cows when you're pulling knives on classmates. He took another sip of his bourbon. You know the kind of work I was doing when I was your age? Have you any idea what work is?

"Good night," said Andrew, appearing in the hallway with his Sad Sack face again.

Mead looked at his watch. "Hell, it's only eight o'clock," he said. "Thought we might play a few darts." He gestured toward the dark wooden cabinet that hung above the small bar. Sophie had bought it for him with her first couple of paychecks after she got a job working at a fabric store once Sharon went away to college. Mead loved the way the cherry cabinet doors swung open to reveal the board and the little drawer beneath that held his six high-density tungsten darts with solid aluminum shafts and feather flights. There was a small blackboard for scoring on the inside of the left cabinet door and a second drawer for chalk and the eraser. Mead had carefully mounted the board so that the bull's-eye was exactly five feet, eight inches from the ground, and he had adjusted a table and chair until he could draw a visual toe line across the carpet precisely seven feet, nine and a quarter inches from the board. Regulation.

Mead walked over and proudly opened the cabinet.

"I'm tired," said Andrew.

Mead hesitated. "Sure. Traveling and all." He closed the cabinet back up again. "Well—got everything you need, toothpaste and all that?"

"I'm fine."

"I keep a light on in the bathroom. I'm always up by six."

"Good night."

"Good night. And don't forget to brush your teeth." Mead listened as Sophie's door clicked quietly closed, then went out front, took down the

American flag, carefully folded it and placed it on the top shelf of the hall closet. Then he freshened up his bourbon, opened the dartboard cabinet again and selected three darts.

It felt strange having someone else in the house. After Sophie died he hated the quiet, which was so enveloping that he soon found himself tip-toeing about. Then one evening he dropped a glass in the kitchen and it shattered with such a loud noise that he ran from the room in a panic. For the next few months he left the radio tuned to a classical station, even at night, and when that wasn't enough he hummed to himself. Then one afternoon the power went out and the silence swept over him so suddenly and completely that he could almost hear his grief, as if loneliness was an audible thing. But he had faced it, and when the power came back on three hours later he kept the radio off, gradually acclimating himself to the hushed timbre of widowerhood. Still, he couldn't shake the awful feeling of being left behind, like a child who loses his parents at a carnival and can't remember the meeting place. Every room seemed so desolate and hungry for her presence that he even considered moving. But when the perky young realtor with a long tear in her nylons suggested that the house would show better if they rented some *happy* furniture he'd gone cold on the idea, thinking that anywhere else would just be farther from Sophie.

Mead carefully took aim and threw the darts one by one, clustering well below the bull's-eye.

Even dying she'd been stronger. As soon as she knew she wasn't going to get better she started worrying about how he'd manage.

"Now, Peanut, don't concern yourself about me."

But she had. If she could have she would have cooked him ten years' worth of meals and frozen them in labeled Tupperware containers. *Monday dinner, preheat to 325. Tuesday lunch, thaw overnight.* She'd even left him a list of simple recipes, writing everything out as clearly as possible with smiley faces drawn here and there. *No, you can't cook it in half the time by turning the oven up to 600!* (He'd tried, and sure enough she'd been right.) The last thing she'd done before she was bedridden was to make and freeze a large batch of her special pasta sauce, which he loved. But he never could bring himself to eat it. When he thawed it out two months after she died the smell was simply too much. But he couldn't bring himself to throw it out either, not until it got moldy. *Sorry, Peanut.*

After putting the darts away he turned off the living room lights and sat in the dark, thinking he'd wait until he felt a little more tired before heading to bed.

He looked over at the burgundy sofa, remembering how he'd slept there that last month when Sophie was in the hospital bed they'd set up in the living room with the IVs and oxygen.

"I've been having the most lovely dreams," she said one night as they lay in the dark talking.

"Don't keep any secrets."

She started coughing, almost a choking sound, then caught her breath. "You'll just laugh."

"Try me."

"If you insist." She coughed again, then cleared her throat. "This afternoon I dreamed that you and I were having a wonderful picnic—on the roof of the Duomo in Florence."

"On the roof? We've never even *been* to Italy."

"But I know what the Duomo looks like." And that she did. She had dozens of coffee-table books about Italy and France and Spain, planning for the trip that they never took.

"You see, we'd just gotten married in the Sistine Chapel and—"

"The Sistine Chapel? Not by the Pope, by any chance?"

"Actually, yes! It was Paul."

"John Paul?"

"No, the first Paul. Saint Paul."

"*Saint* Paul? Geez, that's some wedding, especially for a couple of Unitarians."

"It's just a dream, silly."

"Go on."

"Anyway, it was a beautiful service but your stomach kept growling."

"Probably just nerves."

"And so I decided to have a picnic on the roof of the Duomo in Florence."

"Good thinking. But isn't it a sloped roof?"

"That's why the grapes kept rolling off!"

"It's the medicine, my dear."

They lay in silence listening to a large plane rumble overhead, then suddenly Sophie let out a laugh.

"Now what?"

"I was just thinking about the night you asked me to marry you. Remember how you kept getting up from the table to use the restroom? You must have gone four times."

"Must we really—"

"To tell you the truth I thought you had . . . you know, problems."

"I was rehearsing my lines."

"You never told me that."

It was true. Mead had gone to the restroom four times to practice in front of the mirror. But it hadn't done any good. Once he took Sophie's hand and began to speak, the words had derailed right in his mouth and Sophie had to finish his sentence.

"I must be the only girl who proposed to herself," she said.

"I would have gotten to the point eventually."

Mead listened to the sound of her turning in her bed, then more coughing, which made him wince. "Can I get you anything?"

"No no, I'm fine." She coughed again. "I'm sorry to be such a bother."

"Peanut, please."

"I really don't want a big fuss made at my funeral."

Mead opened his eyes and stared at the red blinking of the monitors by her bed. "Let's not talk about it."

"I just don't like big fusses."

"Okay, no big fusses."

"You'll keep going to church?"

"Sophie . . ."

"I need to know."

Mead hesitated. "I'll keep a foot in the door."

"Promise?"

"I said a *foot*."

"That's good enough." She sighed. "I just worry about you so."

"Come on now, I'm a tough old bear."

"Oh no you're not. You're a big Pooh." She laughed again. "I'll never forget the look on your face when you walked Sharon down the aisle. Goodness, you had the whole place in tears."

It was true. Even though he loathed his son-in-law, the sight of Sharon in her wedding dress had completely undone him. There were other times, too, when he'd suddenly find himself full of more emotion than he knew what to do with: anniversaries, Christmas, New Year's Eve when Guy

Lombardo and his band played. He always fought it, disliking the feeling of being out of control. And yet every year it got worse.

"I don't know how you're going to get through my funeral," she said, her voice suddenly squeaking.

"For Pete's sake, Sweetie Pie, let's talk about something else."

But she'd been right. For when he sat there in the front row looking at her casket he thought he would drown.

Her final wish was to die at home and yet he hadn't let her. When she couldn't catch her breath one evening and the monitors started flashing he simply couldn't bear it and had called an ambulance. *Hurry!* They'd resuscitated her all right, yanking her back to life despite the D.N.R. orders she'd drawn up months before and granting her one more hideous week, which she spent behind the curtain of a small, semi-private hospital room.

"I'm so sorry," he told her over and over again, bent over her bed and trying to keep away the pushy nurse who pumped the fluid from her lungs twice a day.

She just squeezed his hand.

He used to visit her grave twice a week, bringing her yellow tulips—her favorite—and making sure the gardeners were keeping things up. But no matter what time of day he went, he always ran into an enormous widow who parked herself in a little beach chair right on the adjacent plot and yacked nonstop to her dead husband Henry.

"Should have been at the races today, Henry. All the long shots were placing. And did I tell you about the trifecta? My God, Henry, we almost won the trifecta! Five thousand dollars, Henry!"

Thousands of headstones and not a visitor in sight except the big, loud psychotic sitting three feet from Sophie and chewing the ear off her dead husband.

"Excuse me, I wonder if you could keep it down a bit," Mead finally said one sweltering afternoon.

A look of hurt came across her big, juicy face, which was heavily powdered. "I'm just talking to Henry here." She fondly patted the top of Henry's gray headstone.

"Yes, well you see I can't hear ..." Mead started to gesture toward Sophie's grave, then dropped his arm, feeling foolish.

She winked at him. "You too? And my daughters think *I'm* crazy."

"Now wait a—"

"Not to worry." She leaned over and gave his forearm a knowing squeeze, then turned back toward her husband's headstone. "Hey Henry, you want to meet the neighbors? I mean we *are* practically neighbors." She gave Mead a big, lusty smile.

He placed the flowers on the grass beneath Sophie's name, silently apologizing for the short visit, then turned to go.

"Maybe we could go to the races or have dinner or something?" the widow whispered. "Seeing as we're neighbors."

Mead looked at her in horror. "I don't think Henry would like that," he said in a loud voice. Then he walked quickly to his car.

• • •

Andrew lay in the dark listening to his headphones for a while, then placed them on the table next to him, pulled up the sheets and rolled onto his stomach, digging his fingers into the pillow. It had him again, grabbing him in its claws and tearing at his skin. Tossing and turning, he couldn't escape the awful, cold emptiness of everything.

That was what he feared most about silence. At least the music could chase it away, scattering all the thoughts and images like a hurricane flattening trees. But silence? He dreaded silence. In bed at night in the dark was always the worst, stranded there with all the fears, squirming and batting at them, feeling embarrassed just being alive.

He could never figure how other people managed. How could they be so calm, even cheery? Were they clueless? I mean, fuck me, fifteen years of homework just so you can get a job kissing up to some asshole? (All his mom's bosses were major assholes.) *Please.* And then after putting up with all the bullshit—years of it—what happens? You croak.

Very funny.

Ever since puberty Andrew had been haunted by the conviction that he had been born into a primitive and brutal stage of human evolution. The older he got, the harder he found it not to dwell on the mounting evidence that life was, in a nutshell, ridiculous; a big tease in which you could imagine and hope for wonderful things—constant sex, being able to live forever, world peace—only you couldn't have them. (Not even close.) So what was the point? (And what kind of God would invent a creature with needs it had no hope of fulfilling?) And yet other people didn't seem the least bit fazed. Truckloads of bullshit every way you turned and nobody else seemed even remotely freaked out. Was he just wired differently? (Sometimes he imagined himself as one of those huge radio dishes, able to suck in all the bad vibes in the cosmos simultaneously.) Was he the only one who *was* wired?

He sat up and opened the window a few more inches. When he lay back down he could just hear the soothing murmur of a neighbor's TV, then down the block the groan of an automatic garage door. As he closed his eyes he felt the anger backing up in his veins.

He used to cry. At night when his parents would yell at each other— mostly his dad—he'd sit in the far back of his closet under a pile of clothes crying with his hands pressed against his ears.

"Goddamn it, Sharon, can't you even balance a goddamn checkbook?"

"I thought I'd—"

"Twenty-five bucks every time you bounce a goddamn check!"

"Please, Carl."

"Where's your checkbook?"

"I told you I'm not going to talk to you when you're drinking."

"Give me your purse."

"Please lower your voice, Carl." Crying. The screech of a chair being pushed aside.

Andrew pressed harder against his ears.

"Give it to me now, you dumb bitch!"

Crash.

And then the day in third grade when he came home from school and his dad was gone. At first he thought they'd been robbed. The TV and stereo were missing and the house was a mess, with all the dresser drawers in his parents' room opened. In a panic he called his mother at work.

"Oh my God," she'd said. "Your father's left us."

He didn't believe it at first. Not until he went into his room and saw the note on his bed.

Andy,
I'm not sure how to explain this to you, but your mother and I haven't been getting along too well and I've decided to move out and get my own place. You're just going to have to trust me that it's better for all of us. Sorry I didn't have a chance to say good-bye, but

I'll call you when I get settled and you can come and visit, all right? So be tough and take care of your mother, okay Tiger?

Dad

But he didn't call. Not the first week. When Andrew's mom finally handed him the phone nine days later the voice on the other end sounded distant and slurred. "Now don't start bawling on me, Tiger." He called again three days later, then once a week, then once or twice a month, always promising things that never happened.

Andrew stopped going into his closet after that. Instead he'd just lie in bed and cry, not even meaning to or knowing when it would start or how he could ever stop it. But one night he couldn't cry anymore. He was *empty*.

He rolled over on his back, watching the light from a street lamp press through the curtains. He tried to imagine Grandma sitting in the corner sewing those curtains, working her wrinkled fingers over every stitch. He could recall her hands perfectly: the large brown splotches, the green veins snaking between the knuckles, the way her fingers curled this way and that like they'd all been broken a dozen times.

He put his headphones back on and turned up the CD as loud as it would go until his body rocked back and forth beneath the sheets. They understood. He could tell by the sounds and lyrics that they'd been there. That's how he knew that he wasn't alone; that there were others out there. Man, thank-fucking-God for that.

Music was basically the only thing that wasn't bullshit. It said *everything*. Ever since he got his first radio when he was eight he could hardly get enough of it. He loved singing, too. Sometimes when he was in the shower he'd sing so loud that his mother would bang on the door. "Time for school, Pavarotti." He spent hours strutting around his room with his stereo cranked, howling into his hairbrush and hitting the notes just perfectly. He knew he had a good voice; maybe even a great one. When he was little he'd been in the choir at church and sweaty Ms. Swanson frequently complimented him. "You have a gift, young man," she'd say, pinching his bright red cheek.

Only there wasn't much he could do with his gift. He quit the church choir in sixth grade after blowing his debut solo at the Christmas concert—he'd been so paralyzed with fear that he began hyperventilating—and he wasn't about to sing at school, where being in the choir was not only seriously uncool but infested with sexual implications. He thought about trying to start some sort of band—Matt played the clarinet when he was younger and could keep a beat—but Andrew couldn't imagine getting up in front of people—not unless he was drunk. (Going to the blackboard was misery enough.) Besides, he didn't have enough friends to form a band. So instead he sang in the shower and in his room and on the way to school—if no one was around—and at Matt's prodding he began keeping a notebook in which he wrote lyrics.

He'd been singing the first time he really got beat up. It was the second week of fifth grade and he was walking home from school while slowly working his way through "Sunshine on My Shoulders" (his mom was a huge John Denver fan and Andrew had Denver's entire playlist involuntarily embedded in his brain). He'd scanned the block for pedestrians, but somehow he got so caught up in the lyrics that the Laffley brothers, who were several years older and ruled a four-block area between Andrew's house and school, managed to creep up behind him. Just as he was hitting the high notes—*makes me crrryyyyyy*—they pounced, locking his left arm up behind him before flagging down every kid for miles and demanding Andrew sing.

"Take it from the top, Sunshine," they said with hoots of laughter, thereby creating the nickname that would haunt him for years.

"Let me go," he cried as a swelling crowd of kids formed an expectant semicircle.

The Laffley brothers lifted his arm inch by inch until he was fighting tears.

"Sing it, Sunshine."

Andrew searched all the faces, looking for help. But he only saw smiles.

After that he seemed to get picked on more and more—mostly with words, sometimes with fists, until he felt like a target every time he passed by a group of classmates. He didn't tell his mother. Years earlier he stopped telling her things like that, not wanting to upset her any more than she already was. Even as a child he could sense that she had her hands full just fending for herself—she always seemed to be getting fired and he figured it was because of trying to take care of him, making her late for work—and he was determined to show her that he could look out for himself just fine. He didn't want her to leave too.

He'd always been a loner, keeping such a low and cautious profile that he often thought of himself as a Special Forces commando slithering through each day. But it wasn't until sometime in the middle of fifth grade that he realized he'd been ostracized; that he'd always be alone, that he could no longer pretend he was a loner by choice. As far as he could tell, it was like, one day when he wasn't looking everybody in the school had a secret meeting and paired into lifelong cliques, passing out various codes and inside jokes. Once, when he was younger, he felt like part of the class; invited to all the birthday parties, included in games at recess. Then suddenly it was nothing but tribes and packs and clans and he couldn't find anywhere to squeeze in, not until he met Matt, and even then he still felt alone because their friendship was based on loneliness.

For a couple of years he pretended that he didn't care, that when he headed down the hallway at school or crossed the yard he was going somewhere important; that he had other plans and friends. But once he went to Montrose High there was no more faking it. You can't hide your status in high school. People know just by looking at you. At first all the unspoken rules and rituals of high school completely baffled him. Just figuring out where among the bike racks an unpopular freshman should park in the morning was trauma enough; running the gauntlet between classes was almost unbearable. Can I piss safely at the urinal if flanked by two juniors? If a bunch of jocks are blocking my locker (to his horror, his locker was situated right in the middle of a hallowed stretch known as football row) should I attempt to politely squeeze through and get my books, or is it better to go to the next class unprepared, but unmolested? He spent hours trying to figure out exactly where the boundaries were, where he could and could not set foot. Then one day he got it; he cracked the code. It all came down to numbers.

It was breathtaking to suddenly see everything so clearly, to understand exactly what high school was really all about. And yet it depressed him enormously too. Because from then on, there was no escaping the *stupid fucking numbers.* Every day when he stood with his lunch tray at the cafeteria wondering where to sit he could see them; the all-important rankings that were updated hourly and written right on the calculated expressions of every student from number 1—Sue Richards, the prettiest girl in the school—to 3,000—Bill Humphrey, who at two hundred and eighty buttery pounds was the undisputed social caboose of the entire student body. The kids in the top thirty sat at one table while those from roughly thirty-

one to sixty sat at another. Once the higher numbers sorted themselves—
and it was an effortless, almost instinctual process—the lowest-ranked
kids, the untouchables, shared whatever empty tables were left. And so
every day as Andrew stood holding his lunch tray, he'd anxiously scan the
tables to see where he belonged, which meant first eliminating all the
tables where he didn't belong.

For years he worshipped the most popular kids, trying desperately to
imitate everything they did and said, hoping that someday, somehow, he
would be initiated into the elite. He studied what they wore and how they
walked and even the way they laughed and scowled. But it was a joke trying to be like them. Because no matter what he did he never could. Not
even close. And then he started hating them. Every time he saw them clus-
tered at the best tables having all the fun he hated them. He hated their
expensive clothing and their perfect hair and teeth and their beautiful
faces and trophies and cars. But most of all he hated them for making fun
of people like him.

One to three thousand, plain as day right on every student's face. There
was no hiding from the numbers. Maybe you could keep it from your parents, but not from other kids. For some reason Andrew always thought of
himself as number 2,888, well below Matt—not that it really mattered
once you were anywhere below five hundred, which was social oblivion—
but above complete losers like Phil Lubman and Beth Rodriguez and Stuart Smith, whose nervous ticks and physical deformities were surpassed
only by Bill Humphrey's endless rolls of smelly fat. Yes, everyone could see
Andrew's ranking just by looking at him. Even Andrew could see it.

He could still remember the morning, standing before the mirror in the
tiny bathroom with the peeling yellow ceiling that he shared with his
mother, when he first realized he was ugly. It was as though one day he
was just this kid like every other kid, shy and quiet, but physically average,
and the next he was ugly. *So that's why they don't like me,* he thought, standing there at the mirror with tears coming down his stupid ugly face. He
looked at his ears from different angles, wondering why he'd never noticed
just how *obvious* they were, like they belonged on a much bigger head.
Then he studied his teeth, which were all bunched up in the front of his
small mouth (braces in sixth grade would straighten them, but not
improve the overbite that made him look like a braying donkey when he
smiled). He stood back and looked at his face from one side, then the other.

No matter how he tried to push out his jaw, his chin just sort of disappeared into his neck as if he was wearing a muffler. In a panic he leaned into the mirror and examined his nose. Straight enough, but a bit short, so that the nostrils looked slightly flared. *Jesus, have I always looked like this?*

He switched the bathroom light off, then on again and reexamined his face. *Ahhh! I can't have morphed overnight.* Yet everywhere he looked the proportions were wrong. His muddy brown eyes seemed a little too far apart and lacked any of the power he'd started noticing in other people's eyes; his shoulders were small and severely sloped, like a broken hanger; his skin was getting greasier by the day. In short, he was one ugly fuck. He turned off the light again, then sat on the toilet, dropped his head into his hands and cried, feeling as if a terrible mistake had been made and he'd been assigned the wrong face. And that's when he realized that there'd be hell to pay for *years*.

Some days, standing there before the mirror after school, it was all he could do to keep from trying to peel his face right off. He came to think of it as a mask behind which he was imprisoned. People could look at him, but they couldn't see him, and that explained almost everything. *Nobody picks on you if you're good looking. It's like* armor. *Good-looking people are practically celebrities. They get* everything. But if you've got an ugly face, it's just flies to shit.

Sitting in Spanish class, he couldn't decide which was worse: having Cori Fletcher (a genetically perfect goddess he'd been tracking since fourth grade) look at him—especially when his face was all broken out— or being ignored by her. He tried to sit right behind her and he would spend the entire period staring at the back of her neck and bartering with the devil. (One minute of free reign with the soft flesh just behind her ear—oh, to bury his face in there and never come out!—for five years in burning hell. What do you say, Satan?) If she could only see him for what he could be—what he *would* be—instead of what he was! *Look at me, Cori. No, not my face, at* me. *Look all the way inside me.* But she didn't see him. None of them did. And that right there told him that God was a big, fucking joke.

He rolled back on his stomach, remembering the feel of the knife in his hand and the power that he felt shaking it right in Kevin Bremer's stupid face. *Now who's scared?* Wasn't even like it was him holding it. And yet everything in his whole life seemed to lead up to that moment; being pushed around on the playground and on the way to school, pushed in the hallway, pushed during P.E. Then one day Sunshine pushed back.

Surprise.

First he just started sleeping with it, like for good luck, wanting its power to rub off on him. He loved the smoothness of its handle and the shiny brilliance of the blade, sharp and deadly as anything. It wasn't until Matt died—until after they'd killed him with all their taunts—that Andrew started carrying it in his front pocket, desperate for the companionship. Just knowing it was there made all the difference when he set off to school each morning, bracing for blows. *If only you knew,* he thought. *If only you knew.*

He lay listening to the CD for a while, still watching the light from the street lamp creep around the edges of the orange curtain. Gradually the volume faded. He checked the dial: still on full. Must be the batteries. That's what he'd forgotten to pack: the adapter. *Shit.*

He took his palms and pressed the headphones against his ears, desperate for sound. *Why'd you leave me, Matt? Why?* And then closing his eyes he saw the whiteness of Matt's face again and felt the coldness of his cheeks as he shook his head back and forth trying to wake him. *Wake up, Matt! Please oh please wake up.*

He held the headphones to his ears until the music died, then curled up on his side and rocked himself to sleep.

Chapter 2

By 9 A.M. Mead was worried. What if the boy had sneaked out the window or done something crazy? He thought of a red-haired fellow from Pittsburgh—ammo carrier for a BAR team, strong as an ox—who wandered off into the woods near their bivouac in Germany just after mail call, let out a bloodcurdling roar, then pulled the pins on two grenades and blew himself up, after learning that his fiancée had run off with a musician. And three weeks later Hitler was dead.

Mead listened again at the door, paced the living room a few more times, then decided to knock.

No answer.

"You alive in there?"

Silence.

"Andrew?"

Finally the creaking of the bed frame, which reminded Mead of Sophie rising from one of her afternoon naps. The only time she slept there was during her naps, dozing off for half an hour after lunch, then longer and longer in the last years, until he'd wait longingly for the sound of the creaking that signaled that she was awake. And then he'd hurry into the kitchen and make an iced tea with a wedge of lemon and sprinkling of sugar and bring it to her, sitting next to her on the edge of the bed and admiring whatever she'd made that day, until finally her gnarled hands could no longer make anything.

"Yeah?"

"You still sleeping?"

Pause. "I was."

Mead looked at his watch. "Well, I'd say it's high time to get up. You eat cereal don't you? Got Cornflakes and oatmeal. Might even have some Product 19."

"Yeah, cereal's okay." Another pause. "Do you have soy milk?"

"For crying out loud." Mead leaned his forehead against the door, trying to calm himself. "We'll go shopping after breakfast, how's that?"

"Sure, whatever. I don't have to have milk. I'm not even hungry."

Mead hesitated, staring down at the door handle. "I'll be in the living room."

Andrew was polite enough during the trip to Vons, pushing the cart and offering to carry everything. But he didn't talk. On the drive to and from the store Mead couldn't get more than single-sentence answers from him, and they were barely audible. And the thing was, there was nothing to talk about. Mead racked his brain trying to think of topics. Sports, of course. But the boy wasn't interested in sports. He didn't seem to care about the Lakers or Bulls or Cubs or Cardinals. And that was a big warning light right there: a sixteen-year-old boy who didn't care about sports. Mead tapped his fingers on the steering wheel.

Girls? Mead wasn't about to go down that road with his grandson, though it was certainly the primary preoccupation when he was sixteen. He remembered the first time he saw Sophie, no sweater girl but cute as all get out in her bobby socks and skirt, with a softly waved shoulder-length bob of blond hair framing her warm and open face. Mead smiled to himself as he remembered the first time he ran his hand under her blouse, his fingers trembling at the unbearable softness, afraid he might hurt or scratch her. He slammed the brakes at a stop sign, just barely avoiding the car in front of him. Jesus, watch the road. His grandson gave him a funny look.

So what else was there? Hobbies? The boy didn't seem to have any, aside from knives. He glanced down at Andrew's small soft hands, still the hands of a child, no veins showing. Boys not much older were hurled against Fortress Europe, rolling it back one stubborn German at a time. (And those sons of bitches could fight.) Mead always thought of the war as a sort of kiln in which his generation had been fired—at least those who survived. But today? Seems like they take forever to grow up, still babies at nineteen and twenty, expecting handouts. By God, he thought, it's going to be a long three weeks.

As they pulled into the driveway Evelyn was out front watering her flowers.

"I get the feeling she likes you," said Andrew.

Mead glared at him.

Andrew smiled. "You have to admit she's nice."

"That'll be enough."

Evelyn waved as they got out of the car, then signaled for them to wait and dashed into her house. Moments later she emerged with a large red cookie tin.

"Great, I'm starving," said Andrew, trotting across the street.

Mead watched as Evelyn and Andrew chitchatted like a couple of old hens. It was the first time he'd seen his grandson so animated. Was it a raisin thing?

"These are even better," said Andrew as he returned triumphantly with the tin. After they unpacked the groceries Andrew asked if there was anything else Mead wanted him to do before he went to his room.

"Come to think of it, the grass could use a trim."

Andrew nodded without expression. "Where's the mower?"

"In the garage." Mead gestured toward the door off the hallway that led to the garage, then stopped Andrew. "It can wait another day." He forced himself to smile. "I've got a basketball hoop out front. Brand new. Ball's in the garage. I thought maybe you'd like to throw a few hoops?"

"Maybe later."

"Sure, later."

They stood facing each other.

"Listen, I know this wasn't your idea to come here. . . ."

Andrew stared down at his feet, one hand fiddling with his earring.

"I just want to say that . . . well, I'm pretty damn upset about this whole business."

"Sorry." Andrew started for his room.

"Where are you going?"

"I was going to read."

"I'm *upset*, you got that?"

"Yes."

"And I don't like you moving things around in there too much."

"I'll move everything back."

Mead hesitated. "Well, hell, you might as well not move them back now if you've got things set up the way you want them. Just don't do any more moving. Be careful with things, you got that? It's your *grandmother's* room."

"Yeah, I got that." Andrew turned and headed down the hallway. "Thanks for getting the veggie burgers," he said before closing the door.

. . .

Sixteen. Mead tried to remember what he felt like when he was sixteen but there was no comparing it. He slumped down into his chair and closed his eyes, recalling his sixteenth birthday. June, 1940—a downpour in Akron and somewhere beyond the fields and factories the world was catching on fire. Less than two years later his brother Thomas would be dead, his cruiser sunk by two torpedoes in the Pacific. After that all Mead cared about was getting into the army. He remembered heading proudly down to the recruiting station on his eighteenth birthday, destiny all over his boyish face. *I'll get 'em back, Thomas.* And then the physical and the swearing in and that first time he looked at himself in the mirror wearing his crisp new uniform, feeling a part of the biggest thing ever, ready to save the world, hometown girls falling at his feet.

He listened to the sound of Sophie's door opening, then the bathroom door closing, then the loud rush of urine.

Sixteen. Mead had killed sixteen-year-olds. Even younger. Because at the end, that's all Hitler had left to throw at them. Children.

"They're coming!"

Mead peered over the top of his foxhole in horrified fascination as two dozen screaming Germans emerged from the woods and charged across a snow-covered field. Mead began on the far left, aiming and firing at chest level. One down, then another, then a third, who tried several times to get back on his feet until Mead shot him again. But the rest were closer now. Forty yards, then thirty, then twenty. Mead heard a shout from the foxhole to his right and then cries for help. He kept firing frantically as the concussion from a grenade ripped off his helmet and momentarily blinded him, blood streaming down his nose. He blinked several times as he struggled to reload, then aimed again at another German, hitting him in the shoulder. Another concussion snapped against Mead's eardrums but he kept firing, this time at point-blank range.

And then it was over. Two dozen Germans dead and wounded on the snowy field, their bright, red blood seeping into the downy whiteness. Hitler's boys.

The toilet flushed, then a minute later the bathroom door opened and Sophie's door closed.

He'd spent years trying to forget the faces, their little bodies twisted this way and that where they fell, as if part of some enormous Aztec sacrifice. Sometimes he'd be in a store or at the beach and he'd see a face that would stop him in his tracks; a face that accused him, even in its ignorance. He particularly remembered one young German boy who looked just like a kid who lived down the street when he was growing up. He was lying in the snow on his back bleeding from his gut and crying, and Mead briefly caught his eye before hurrying on because there simply wasn't time to help. When he passed back that way the next day the boy was frozen solid, arms still reaching for the sky.

By January the Ardenne was littered with frozen bodies, some still at their guns so that you'd shoot them to be sure they were dead. Mead felt himself shiver, the memory of coldness biting through his overcoat and gloves and his double-sole woolen socks and wool-knit cap and the bed-sheets he'd wrapped around himself like a scarf. Coldest winter in years, so that you didn't dare breathe on your weapon for fear it would freeze up.

Bitte, hilf mir.

He could recall the German boy's frozen face perfectly, the way the frost gathered around the eyes and nostrils and mouth and the bluish tint of the lips and ears. There were dozens of faces that he could never forget; faces that hounded him over the years like unwelcome visitors pounding at the door. And Mead had spent his whole life leaning his shoulder against the other side, praying the locks would hold. *Just leave me be.* For years he'd managed to keep them out. By piling everything he could find against the door he'd kept the faces from breaking in and overwhelming him. But he always knew they were out there; faces of friends and enemies and the living and the dead pressed against the door, demanding to be seen.

Mead massaged his temples with his two forefingers, then got up and walked over to the couch, figuring he'd stretch out for a few minutes. Just not used to being around teenagers. Or maybe it's the new thyroid medication. He carefully removed his wire-frame glasses, folded them and placed them on the coffee table, then clasped his hands over his belly and closed his eyes. He tried to think of the latest American League West standings and then congratulated himself on how nice the lawn looked, thick and dark green. Then he remembered his retirement party and how embarrassed he'd been when he fell apart during his little speech. Finally he tried to recall in correct order the winning teams of the first ten Super Bowls. Okay, that's better. Take it nice and easy. Now let's see, was it Green Bay or Oakland in 1968? But he felt it coming. No matter what he tried to think of he felt it coming, and before he could stop himself he was suddenly back in the well-furnished chalet in Berchtesgaden, Germany, May 1945, reaching for his pistol. And then he saw him. For the first time in years he saw the young German with the brown eyes and the large forehead and small chin standing there looking at him in disbelief. *You wouldn't would you? Oh yes, but I would.* How long had they stared at each other in stricken silence? Thirty seconds? A minute? And then in a momentary fury, it was over.

Hans Mueller.

Mead could still see the angular scrawl of the German's signature on the inside page of his worn *Soldbuch*—military pay book. And he remembered the Luger and the medals and the wristwatch and the black leather wallet filled with photos; treasured little snapshots of mother and father and sister and girlfriend all waiting for Hans Mueller to return. And he could have returned. Yes, Hans, you could have returned.

Bang.

Mead opened his eyes and sat up, feeling his heart going so fast he wondered if he was having a heart attack. He took several deep breaths and rubbed the bridge of his nose before putting his glasses back on. Jesus, get hold of yourself. He got up and walked back to the kitchen and took four medicine bottles down from the windowsill, trying to still the tremors in his hands as he struggled with the tops. After parceling out his dose he poured himself a glass of water and swallowed the pills before replacing the caps. Then he rinsed the glass, dried it and placed it back on the shelf before heading out to the backyard to scrub down the grill. But no matter how hard he worked his hands he couldn't stop thinking about the chalet in Berchtesgaden and the final expression in the young German's face.

Please, just leave me be.

• • •

At least he had batteries. His grandfather had bought him an eight-pack and Matt had taught him that if you boiled the batteries in water they'd recharge a few times. (So long as they didn't explode.) Of course, he'd have to wait until Sarge was out of the house. Did he ever go out? What did he do all day besides read the paper and play darts and clean the barbecue? Talk about needing a life.

Andrew was horny and debated masturbating. It seemed a little weird to do in his grandparents' house, even potentially sinful. But three weeks? He couldn't remember the last time he went three days, except when he had the flu. (After forty-eight hours the first symptoms of an imminent nervous breakdown would appear, requiring immediate action.) Maybe later. He shuffled through his CDs, put one into the player and flopped down on the bed, wishing he had his PlayStation.

He checked his watch and thought of his classmates sitting in school. He'd be in Spanish now, staring at Cori Fletcher and thinking that if she wouldn't even bother to look at him then what was the point of existing? They'd all be talking about him still, laughing at what a mental case he was, pulling a knife on Kevin Bremer and getting expelled. He felt the burning in his face again and turned up the volume on his CD player.

Would they let him back to school next year? What if they sent him to prison, or worse, reform school? Or maybe they'd punish him by keeping him back a year? He'd kill himself, right on the spot. He wondered what kind of pills Matt had taken and where he could get some. In a way it was comforting to know that Matt was always there waiting for him; that any time he wanted to he could join him, like having a secret escape hatch. But he didn't want to join him. Not yet. He kicked his shoes off, wondering what the school would decide. No matter what, they'd always be watching him; he'd be under scrutiny forever. He clenched both fists and closed his eyes tight, wanting to smash something. Did his dad know yet? He wondered if his mom had called him. What would he say? Or would he even care?

He thought of their last conversation three months earlier when his dad had called from Texas.

"Your mother says you're failing at school."

"I'm not exactly failing."

"You don't call two Ds failing?"

"I got a C in—"

"Listen, buster, I want those grades up by next semester, you got that?"

"Okay."

"Good. You bring home some As and Bs and we'll go fishing. How 'bout it?"

He was always offering to take Andrew fishing, only they never went. Not since Andrew was a kid. He could still remember the one trip they took to Wisconsin, setting up the little pup tent and cooking the fish they'd caught right in the campfire wrapped in tin foil. It was the greatest feeling in the world, waving good-bye to Mom and sitting in the front seat of Dad's red Jeep Cherokee with his new tackle box on his lap, heading off on an adventure, just the two of them. But then he'd ruined it, thinking he'd heard a bear the first night—*something* was snorting around the tent—and getting so hysterical his dad took him home the next morning, saying he wasn't man enough to camp. "Hell, you're still a damn baby."

Fuck him too. Fuck all of them. He put his palms together and pressed as hard as he could while clenching his jaw. Anyway, none of it matters. Even the whole planet hardly matters when you think of how big the universe is, which was the best thing about getting stoned because you could really *feel* the bigness.

Matt understood that. He understood everything. They'd been best friends ever since a winter afternoon in seventh grade when Andrew discovered that his book bag had been filled with snow and Matt helped him empty it out and dry his homework, thereby destroying any chances of his own social rehabilitation. But Matt figured he'd never be accepted anyway. He had too many demons to really belong. Yeah, Matt understood all about the demons, maybe even more than Andrew, and knowing that he understood made everything bearable again.

Retaliation had been swift. Andrew and Matt were walking home together the next day when they were both hit by a fusillade of ice balls. Matt fell to the ground crying with a bloody nose while Andrew scrambled to gather ammunition and prepare a defense. Only he never saw who threw them or where they came from. The enemy was *everywhere.*

"We'll get them back," said Andrew, helping Matt to his feet. "I swear we'll get them back."

Matt was slight like Andrew, only shorter, with curly black hair and dark green eyes set close in his thin face. He was smarter too, always reading all sorts of books to see if things were really as desperate as they seemed. Whenever they got stoned together Matt would quickly pare their options in life down to two rather bleak choices.

"Look, you and I know that life is basically a lot of bullshit, right?"

"Right."

"So the way I see it, we've got two choices."

Andrew held in a chest full of smoke, then let out a loud exhale. "I remember that part, I just forget what the choices are."

"It's simple: either we pretend we don't realize what a big joke everything is, which means we've got to be total fakes like everybody else, or we don't pretend."

"So what happens if we don't pretend?"

"Then we're fucked."

"Pass the joint."

Matt's dad was as unpredictable as Andrew's. Sometimes he was the nicest man Andrew had ever met, building a model rocket with them—it blew up midflight, which was depressing but still kind of cool—and taking them ice skating and to the auto show, and other times he'd be sitting in the living room watching TV and if anyone so much as made a peep he'd start throwing beer bottles. Twice he gave Matt a black eye and by eighth grade Matt no longer invited anybody to his apartment. Instead, they hung out either at Andrew's where they could play video games and listen to music, or in the forest preserve near the freeway where they had a stash of stolen cigarettes, liquor, firecrackers and dirty magazines that they kept buried in a plastic container. That's where they'd been: the forest preserve, tucked into their sleeping bags and knowing nobody could find them.

Wake up, Matt.

They lived only five blocks apart in nearly identical ugly brick apartments with graffiti covering all the Dumpsters and scowling old ladies perched on their little patios monitoring every movement. You didn't belong in certain circles when you lived in an apartment. No one said anything, it was just understood. Matt could draw almost anything and he would spend hours sketching floor plans of great big houses with dens and TV rooms and sunken Jacuzzis and saunas and pools and patios and rec rooms with pool tables and air hockey and Ping-Pong and the latest arcade games. To Andrew, there was nothing better than sitting in the forest preserve on a warm afternoon sipping from the bottle of Southern Comfort that Matt stole from his father and arguing over plans for the houses they would build, houses that would sit side by side on a cul-de-sac in Holly-wood or South Beach or Aspen.

"We're talking total soundproofing," Matt would say, putting the finishing touches on his living room. "Built-in speakers *everywhere*."

Andrew imagined himself walking room-to-room in a house full of built-in speakers, the guitars and drums and lyrics welcoming him everywhere he turned, like he was strolling around inside his own head. *Someday.*

Matt was the only person Andrew had ever met who was even more sensitive than he was, like he was always walking barefoot across gravel. Though not quite as ugly as Andrew, Matt was picked on for being short and for being different, wearing nothing but black and dying his hair green and wearing a stud in his tongue. He never fought back. When the bullying started he'd just curl up into a ball and plot his revenge. His theory was that people either went through total hell as kids or as adults, so he figured they were just getting the bullshit over with early. "You'd better be right," said Andrew as they lay side by side on their backs in the forest preserve getting stoned after school.

For a while they tried to hang out on the fringes, like stray dogs seeing how close they can get to the barbecue without being kicked. But they quit even trying after they were beaten up one afternoon by a group of jocks in the parking lot of the McDonald's where everybody hung out after school.

"Here come the Beanie Babies," said a voice as they approached.

Matt looked over at Andrew, pain in his face.

"Just ignore them," Andrew whispered, hoping for a glimpse of Cori.

They tried to casually meld in, hands shoved deep into their pockets and feet shuffling back and forth. Matt wore a black knit cap and lit a cigarette with a flick of his Zippo, which had a skull and crossbones on it. Andrew saw Cori huddled in a cluster of girls and tried to catch her eye. Jesus, she was absolutely perfect. What was it like being so perfect? He imagined kissing her right on the tip of her adorable little nose and then scooping her up into his arms. *Argh* . . .

"Hey Sunshine, what's with the Salvation Army shoes?"

Andrew pretended he didn't hear, slowly trying to move away from a nearby pack of jocks without triggering the chase instinct. But it was true, they were dorky shoes. No matter how many times he begged his mother, she wouldn't buy him the right brand.

"You think I'm spending eighty dollars on a pair of sneakers? Dream on." So he wore the cheap imitation ones, and every morning when he slipped them on his feet he felt the shame running right up his legs.

"Are you like, in mourning or something?" said another jock, gesturing toward Matt's black clothing. "Or is your mother some kind of vampire?"

Andrew and Matt backed off a little more, dropping their heads low between their shoulders and trying to look at nothing. All the girls were watching now.

"Hey Shorty, how about a couple of bucks for a burger?" said Bremer, who was an enormous junior and easily the biggest prick on the planet.

"Fuck off," said Matt.

Oh shit, thought Andrew. "Come on, let's go," he whispered.

"I think Shorty here wants to get his ass kicked," said Bremer, walking up to Matt, who was half his size.

"Leave him alone," said Andrew.

"You shut up, Sunshine." He turned back to Matt. "So how about it?"

"I said, fuck off."

Bremer shoved Matt backward a few times, then hit him in the stomach, causing him to double over. Matt didn't fight back. Instead he just buckled and fell to the ground as Bremer kept punching him. Andrew wanted to run. He wanted to run and never stop running. But as all the fear and hatred welled up in him he suddenly lunged at Bremer, swinging wildly. Instantly he was in a headlock being slowly twisted to the ground, finally dropping down like a calf, barely breathing as he caught a glimpse of Cori out of the corner of his eye. He hardly even felt the blows.

Two days later Matt called Andrew to announce that he had the perfect plan. First, they'd need lots of weed killer, which they purchased from several hardware stores in different neighborhoods to avoid suspicion. The following Saturday night Matt stayed at Andrew's for a sleepover. Once Andrew's mom went to bed they quietly played PlayStation in the living room until 2 A.M., then dressed, turned off the lights, crept outside and rode their bikes to the school where they'd stashed ten jugs of weed killer in green garbage bags they'd hidden in the bushes near the football field.

"Just do what I say," said Matt, pulling out a large diagram and tape measure from his pockets. He had also brought along a bottle of Coke heavily spiked with Bacardi, from which he took a large swig before handing it to Andrew.

"Why won't you tell me what it's going to say?" asked Andrew, carefully pouring out another bottle of weed killer as he crouched on the grass beside Matt and followed his instructions.

"You'll just have to wait and see. Now make a sharp ninety degree turn there and go down another three feet." Matt crawled along on his hands and knees, the diagram between his teeth. "Perfect!"

The next Saturday Matt and Andrew attended their first high school football game. "We are ass-deep in enemy territory," whispered Andrew as they waded through the crowds of jocks and wannabes. Cori passed right by him but he couldn't catch her eye. He stared at her butt, hugged tightly by her jeans, and tried to imagine her in just her panties. *Marry me.*

"Come on." Matt led the way up the bleachers, stopping at the last row and letting out a whoop. Andrew turned and looked out over the field where large letters of dying brown grass spelled *Home of the cocksuckers.* It was their finest moment.

Bremer pegged them right away, nearly knocking out one of Matt's teeth the next week after school and then taking a crowbar to Andrew's bike, which his mother had given him for his fifteenth birthday.

"I still say it was worth it," said Matt, lisping through his swollen lips as he helped Andrew carry the pieces of his bike home.

"I'm going to kill him," said Andrew, quaking. "I'm going to fucking *kill* him."

Andrew and Matt spent hours fantasizing about precisely how they'd kill Bremer, how they'd torture and humiliate him before throwing his big hairy ass to the sharks or crocodiles or a pack of hungry pit bulls. (Each Christmas they begged their parents for a pit bull—or at least a rottweiler—to no avail.) It was the one thing they talked about almost as much as sex: ways to kill Kevin Bremer.

Big, tall and unbearably arrogant, Bremer looked about five years older than he was, with huge arms and a dark beard always just about three days old. He was not only the star fullback of the football team but he held the school record at the bench press—320 pounds—and drove a brand new blue-and-white Suzuki SuperSport motorcycle, which everyone figured was stolen. Andrew and Matt were in study hall with Bremer both their freshman and sophomore years—they couldn't believe their misfortune—and somehow Bremer singled them out the first day of school. "The Beanie Babies," he called them. "Shorty and Sunshine." And the girls loved Bremer. They got giddy over his big, stupid shoulders and his stupid jokes and the way he swaggered onto the football field after half time like he was going to save the whole fucking season. Andrew never understood why the nicest girls, the ones he fantasized about night after night until he was sore, could be attracted to a fuckhead like Bremer. And if it had to be that way, why couldn't that be enough? Why did Bremer still have to pick on *them?*

"The important thing is that he feels a lot of pain before he dies," said Matt as they sat in the forest preserve getting stoned. "We can't just shoot him in the head."

"Maybe we could poison him?"

"I still say the best thing would be to shoot him in the balls. That way we don't even have to kill him. It wouldn't be homicide." He passed the joint back to Andrew.

Matt had a point. They both lay back on the leaves imagining Bremer without any balls, then Andrew pushed aside a small log and dug out the plastic container that held their stash.

"I'll take the *Hustler,*" said Matt. Andrew tossed it at him.

"Careful!"

"You're the one who drools all over the pages." Andrew flipped through their tattered copy of *Penthouse,* then glanced through two issues of *Playboy* before settling on *Gallery,* which had a memorable scene on page forty-three. The stash also contained two packs of firecrackers, six bottle rockets, three M-80s, two Bic lighters, four packs of Marlboros, two Garcia y Vega cigars, a quart of Southern Comfort, rolling papers and a small baggie of pot.

"Jesus, check this out," said Matt, handing the *Hustler* to Andrew.

"She's too skinny," said Andrew.

"Skinny? Are you crazy? She's *gorgeous!*"

Andrew stared intently at a photo of a redhead bending over a desk, trying without success to place himself in her immediate vicinity.

"Oh God, this one kills me!" howled Matt.

"Quiet, I'm trying to concentrate." Andrew looked at a photo of the redhead slipping into a hot tub. *Come take me, Big Boy. All of me.* Finally he put down the magazine, relit the joint and handed it back to Matt, feeling utterly depressed. "I got a D on my science report," he said.

"Don't worry about it. I haven't even turned mine in."

"But you're good at science."

"I refuse to dissect a pig."

"You have to," said Andrew.

"No way. What are they going to do, kick me out of school because I won't butcher Piglet? What am I, a sushi chef? I mean, that just blows my mind."

"Everything blows your mind."

Matt took another hit, then coughed. "Especially this stuff."

"Speaking of mind-blowers, didn't I see you talking to Megan yesterday?" Matt had been madly in love with Megan Wynn for three years running, despite the fact that she wouldn't have anything to do with him. He spent hours talking about her, describing her lips and nose and ears and knees and the way she tossed her head to the side. "God, that kills me," he'd say, frequently collapsing into despair at the thought that he'd never get to so much as touch her. Unable to contain himself, he had even started writing her poems and letters, anonymous at first, then open declarations of his love because that was just the way Matt was; shy, but gutsy as hell at the same time. She was the one part of the world that he couldn't let go of, and Andrew sometimes thought that the only reason Matt even bothered to get up in the morning and shower was in case he ran into Megan.

Matt shrugged.

"I know I saw you talking to her." He elbowed Matt. "You didn't ask her out, did you?" Andrew burst into laughter, not meaning to but unable to deal with the idea of Megan and Matt on a date, which was a *real* mind-blower.

"Actually, I did," said Matt.

Andrew sat up. "No shit. What did she say?"

Matt shrugged again.

"Tell me. Tell me what she said."

"She told me I was a creep and to leave her alone."

"She said that?"

"And she said if I didn't stop writing her letters she'd call the police."

"No kidding?"

Matt's face twisted up as he tried not to cry. "She said I was stalking her."

"*Stalking* her? Jesus, that's bullshit."

"That's what she said, that I'm a creep and to stop stalking her." He dropped his head into his hands.

"Oh shit, buddy, don't listen to the crap. She couldn't have meant it."

"But she did. She meant every word."

Two weeks later Megan started going out with Bremer. A week after that Matt killed himself.

Wake up, Matt.

． ． ．

Sharon called that evening after getting back to Chicago.

"How are the boys?" she asked nervously.

"Just peas in a pod," said Mead, sitting on the edge of his bed and working polish into his shoes.

"Honestly, how is everything?"

"You didn't tell me he was a vegetarian."

"Oh jeez, I thought you knew. And he's terribly allergic to strawberries and bee stings."

"Anything else I should know?"

"It's not going well, is it?"

"We're just . . . getting reacquainted, that's all."

"Are you sure? Because if—"

"Of course I'm sure."

"I can't tell you how much I appreciate this, Dad. I don't know what I would have done."

Mead held his shoe up to the bedside lamp, admiring the gloss. "No trouble at all. You know your mother and I would do anything to help."

"I miss Mom. I keep thinking she'd know what to do, that this wouldn't have happened if she was still alive."

"I miss her too, Pumpkin."

"Has he told you anything yet?"

"I've learned quite a bit about tofu."

Sharon tried to laugh.

"You'll have to give us a little time."

"I'm so worried about him." She started crying again.

"Now, you just take care of yourself."

"He's not a bad kid, Dad. I haven't raised a bad kid."

"Of course you haven't."

"I don't know what I'll do if they decide to press charges."

"One thing at a time."

"He hates me, Dad. Andrew hates me."

"He doesn't hate you."

"But he does. He's never forgiven me for his dad leaving."

"Good riddance, if you ask me."

"And he's just horrible to the men I date."

Perhaps the boy's got some smarts after all, thought Mead.

"I don't know how to talk to him anymore. I can't even find him behind all that anger."

"He's a teenager. You can't talk to teenagers."

She took a deep breath. "I love you, Dad."

"I love you, too."

"Don't forget to remind him to work on his homework every night. His teachers gave him a big packet of assignments."

"I'll get on him. Now listen, you take care of yourself, you hear? And no cigarettes."

"I promise."

After he hung up Mead finished shining his shoes, then carefully replaced the wooden shoe trees before returning them to the floor of his closet, lined up from light to dark. Then he undressed, put on the light blue pajamas Sophie made for him and went to the bathroom, filling the sink with warm water. Once the temperature was right he leaned forward, cupped his hands and gently lifted the water to his face.

• • •

Andrew cut the lawn the next morning, stopping several times to talk with Evelyn. Mead peered cautiously out the window. What the hell could they be yacking about? After sending Andrew to his room to put in an hour of homework Mead gave the lawn a once-over, hitting all the spots his grandson had missed and getting the rows in nice neat diagonals running left to right.

"Evelyn's a real hoot, don't you think?" said Andrew over lunch.

"What do you mean by *hoot?*"

"She's cool. She cracks me up."

"I'm glad someone does."

"Her husband's dead, huh?"

Mead nodded.

"Do you guys ever like, do anything?" An annoying grin crept across the boy's face, smearing his features.

"What is that supposed to mean?"

"I'm just wondering if maybe you guys ever went to a movie or dinner or something?"

"The answer is no." Mead ate quickly, trying to avoid Andrew's inquisitive stare.

"Just asking."

After lunch Andrew shot baskets while Mead vacuumed, which gave him an excuse to inspect Sophie's room. As soon as he opened the door he felt a sense of panic. Andrew's things were heaped in a pile on top of his duffel bag, and the bed had been pushed into the corner where the sewing machine used to be and the rocking chair had been moved to the opposite corner near the door. The framed photographs were still there, but rearranged, and in the closet one of Sophie's dresses—the flowery blue-and-yellow one she made for their last trip to Hawaii, getting all dolled up for their anniversary—had fallen off its hanger and lay crumpled on the floor. Mead bent down, picked it up and carefully rehung it, then ran his fingers slowly along the row of dresses like a harpist. When he finished vacuuming he sat down briefly in the rocking chair, then went out and closed the door behind him.

Andrew was still out front throwing baskets. Mead watched him through the bay window in the living room, enjoying the rhythmic sound of the ball striking the cement. Yet his grandson obviously had no talent for the sport: he rarely made a basket and he threw with a sort of flailing of his arms, so that it was painful to watch.

Andrew missed a few more baskets, then put the ball away and came inside.

"Have a seat," said Mead, catching him before he could retreat to his room.

Andrew looked around nervously, finally settling on the edge of the sofa, ready to spring back up.

"Nice hoop, huh?"

"The hoop? Yeah, it's all right."

"Put it together myself."

"It's nice."

Long silence, both looking at anything but each other.

Mead swallowed and sat forward in his chair. "So, I'd say it's high time you and I had a little talk."

"A talk?"

"About this trouble you've gotten yourself into."

Andrew seemed to shrink into his T-shirt. "Not much to talk about."

"Oh, I think there is. I mean, it's a goddamn stupid thing you did." Mead hadn't intended on getting so angry but suddenly he couldn't help himself. "Pulling a knife on somebody? Who do you think you are, for Christ's sake, Marlon Brando?"

"Who's he?"

"An actor."

"I wasn't acting."

"I didn't mean *acting.*" Mead rubbed his forehead. "Pulling a knife at school?" He made a snorting sound and leaned back in his chair, then forward again. "By God, they can lock you up for that kind of thing."

"I'm sorry."

"Sorry? That's all you've got to say?"

Andrew sat immobile.

Mead slammed his fist against his armrest. "You know the only time you ever pull a weapon on somebody? When you're going to use it. *That's* when you pull a weapon on somebody. You understand that?"

"Okay."

"What the hell do you understand?" Mead fell back into his chair again.

"I'm sorry."

"Do you have any idea what this is doing to your mother?"

"It has nothing to do with her."

"Like hell it doesn't. She's worried *sick* about you."

Andrew fidgeted nervously. "Can I go now?"

Mead felt flushed in the face, wondering what else to say. "I want you to do another hour of homework, you got that?"

Andrew rose to his feet. "Yes, I've got it," he said meekly as he crossed the living room and headed down the hallway.

.   .   .

Mead sat stewing in his chair after Andrew left. Shouldn't have lost my temper. But damn the boy. Who the hell does he think he is? Mead got up, straightened out the brown sofa pillows, then sat back down. Sharon had been far too soft on him. Sure it was hard without a father around, but still, she'd been too easy on him. Discipline, that's what he needs. They should never have done away with the draft. Of course, even the army isn't what it was. Hell, you could probably sue your D.I. for slander. Five guys died when Mead was at Benning. But then they were training to fight Germans and Japs.

Mead got up again and walked over to the mantle and picked up the wood-framed glass case that held his Purple Heart, his silver jump wings, his Bronze Star and his European Campaign Medal. Sophie had purchased the case for him, insisting he display some of his decorations. (She was so proud of them.) He carefully opened the case and pulled them out one at a time, placing them in his palm. On the back of the Purple Heart was the inscription FOR MILITARY MERIT, which always bothered him. Merit my ass, I got in the way of an 88.

He placed the decorations back in the case and closed it. Sophie had always had a certain awe for what he'd done. They all had, his family and friends and neighbors. Even if they couldn't really understand where he'd been and what he'd been asked to do, they honored him for it. But they were mostly gone now. And it wasn't a thing he ever talked about anyway. During all the hoopla for the fiftieth anniversary of D-Day Sophie had tried to get him to go back to France but he wouldn't. He hadn't set foot in Europe since 1945—and he'd be damned if he ever would.

For the first few years after he returned she tried to pry stories out of him, hoping to get her arms around what he'd been through so that she could understand him better. But she couldn't. Nobody could. Sure, he had lots of stories. Just none he wanted to tell. For years he privately slugged it out with the war, jabbing and weaving and bobbing and punching at all the images and sounds and faces that came howling back at unexpected moments. And then in the sheer exhaustion of it he'd found a sort of truce: you leave me be and I'll leave you. That was the deal. He'd kept his side of the bargain ever since, avoiding reunions and politely fending off inquiries. And nothing, absolutely nothing would change him now. He could never understand how other veterans could sit around at cocktail parties retaking every ridge and hedge over and over again. It was dishonest, he thought, reducing it to vignettes, as if combat had a story line. And they never told the whole truth anyway. Not nearly.

He gently rubbed his sleeve over the glass case, then pulled out his book of crossword puzzles, took a pencil from the silver holder he kept on the end table—always stocked with fresh, sharp pencils, tip down—and dropped into his chair, reaching into his breast pocket to pull out his bifocals. The first two words came easily enough, and then on the third he pulled out his crossword puzzle dictionary. But no matter how hard he tried he couldn't stop thinking about the faces at the door.

There was a time right after the war when he wasn't sure he could take it anymore. His mother had been the first to notice.

"I knew you wouldn't be the same," she said softly one evening during dinner a few weeks after he came home. "God knows, your father never was. But I always thought . . ." She struggled to maintain her composure, pushing her shoulders back and sitting up straight in her chair. "I always thought I'd still recognize you."

And then he'd started drinking too much, cutting back only after Sophie poured all the bottles down the drain one night in 1948 and threatened to leave him. "I won't live with a drunk," she'd said in tears. At her coaxing he began meeting with their minister once a week.

"I know exactly what you're feeling," said Reverend Hadding, who had been a chaplain with the Big Red One in Sicily, losing three fingers on his left hand. "I have my days too. We all do. It's a part of our lives. An unforgettable part, no doubt about that, but by golly we've got to keep living."

And that's what Mead had tried to do, aiming only for a simple and honest life; comfortable enough to assure Sophie's happiness. He worked hard at his engineering job—rising slowly up the ranks but never displaying a flair for management, in part because he had no desire to manage people. And he saved and he made sure to help Sophie with the church's annual canned food drive and he gave blood at least twice a year *(There's no more plasma, Captain)* and he always emptied his pockets for the Salvation Army and anyone else who seemed in need. Yet no matter how carefully he tried to walk in the shoes of a decent man, no matter how hard he tried to emulate the other veterans and put the past far behind him *(just let bygones be bygones),* he still caught glimpses of the faces over the years, glimpses that left him silent and shaken for days.

Mead and Sophie had been sitting by the pool of their hotel on their first trip to Hawaii when a group of German tourists came and sat next to them. There were three couples, all of them young and sunburned. Mead tried to ignore them at first, but the guttural sound of their voices soon made him perspire. And then he looked at the young man closest to him—maybe twenty, with a high forehead—and he saw the resemblance.

"What's wrong, Sweetie?" asked Sophie, looking over at him.

"I . . . nothing." Mead stared back down at his newspaper, trying to quell the shaking of his hands. The German youth said something to his girlfriend and then erupted in laughter.

"Are you feeling okay?"

"I'm fine." By now Mead's whole face was flushed.

Sophie got up from her lounge chair and sat on the edge of his, putting her hand on his forehead. "Why, you're burning up. Do you think it's something you ate?"

"Maybe I'll just go up to the room for a minute." He tried to block out the string of German phrases coming from his left. *Nicht schiessen!*

"Let me help you. Should I get a doctor?"

"I'll be fine."

He'd spent the rest of the day in bed trembling with Sophie there holding him, and no matter how many times she asked he couldn't tell her why.

Mead put down the crossword puzzle and took off his glasses, feeling unusually tired. He considered taking a nap, yet he always felt guilty sleeping during the day. Better fire up Mr. Coffee again. Just half a cup. He'd only closed his eyes for a moment when he felt himself falling. He reached out to grab hold of something but it was too late.

· · ·

Just getting into the plane was difficult, weighed down with more than 120 pounds of gear and already groggy from the airsickness pills. His jump suit was stiff and itchy from the chemical treatment intended to protect against poison gas and he kept nervously checking to make sure that his equipment was properly tied down beneath his parachute harness and the yellow Mae West life preserver. Unable to sit comfortably in the bucket seat, he fell down to his knees on the floor and let his gear and chute rest on the seat behind him, fear coursing through his insides. For the third time that evening he mentally itemized everything: M1 rifle disassembled and secured in a padded gun case strapped under his reserve chute; two bandoleers; a cartridge belt; a 45-caliber pistol; two cans of machine-gun ammo; one Hawkins mine; an entrenching tool; a coil of rope, in case he had to lower himself from a tree; an escape kit containing French francs, a small hacksaw, a compass and a cloth map of France; a brass cricket; a gas mask strapped to his left leg; four blocks of TNT; two first-aid kits; a French phrase book; a jump knife, buck knife and trench knife; one canteen; two smoke and four fragmentation grenades; a Gammon bomb; clothes; two cartoons of cigarettes; *The GI Prayer Book* bound in imitation brown leather; toiletries and rations; Sophie's letters.

Again he felt the need to relieve himself. Too late now. Must just be nerves. He struggled to pull out and light another cigarette as they circled endlessly above England getting into V formation. Must be a thousand planes. How many would be shot down, maybe twenty, thirty percent? Just get me out of this plane alive—give me a fighting chance.

They'd spent the last days studying maps and aerial photos and three-dimensional models of Normandy, eagerly memorizing every road and gun emplacement. The briefings lasted hours, interrupted by the best meals they'd had in months—even ice cream with seconds—and they had a laugh saluting the men who strolled around the marshalling grounds wearing different German uniforms and carrying various weapons to help familiarize the troops.

Two hours after taking off they finally headed out across the Channel. So this is it. Everything comes down to this night. Mead lit another cigarette, a habit he'd only picked up weeks earlier, and began to itemize his gear again, starting with his rifle.

Once he satisfied himself that everything was secure and in place, he looked across the aisle at Jimmy Smith, but couldn't catch his eye. Known as Jimbo, the lanky Kentuckian came from a proud line of moonshiners and once made a thousand dollars in a single night of poker, which he promptly sent to his mother. He and Mead had become friends immediately when both realized they suffered from an intense fear of heights, which they desperately tried to hide from the others. "It's like I don't trust myself more than ten feet off the ground," Jimbo had whispered in his heavy drawl as they nervously climbed up one of the 250-foot towers at Benning for a practice jump.

Mead tried not to look down. "So why the hell did you volunteer for the airborne?"

"To get girls, why else?"

"Stupid question."

"What about you?"

Mead clung to a railing, hoping his knees wouldn't buckle. "I figured it would cure me of my fear."

"Has it?"

"Not yet."

During a final practice jump in Britain, Jimbo had crashed right through the glass panes of a country manor greenhouse, cutting himself in several places. (Another paratrooper died making a similar landing, the glass shards severing his carotid artery.) Despite stitches in his chin, forehead, hands and shins, he refused to be left behind, saying he'd be laughed right out of Kentucky for such a stunt. "You gotta understand, I *can't* go home without a good story," he explained. "I need a *real good story.*"

Jimbo was frequently teased by the men for his lack of education and extreme superstition—he once feigned sickness to avoid a live fire exercise on account of a warning he'd seen in his scrambled eggs that morning—yet he had more common sense than just about anybody in the company and a sense of intuition that had proven uncanny. Two men died that day. Just before D-Day word spread that Jimbo knew who would and who wouldn't be coming back.

"So what about you and me?" Mead had asked nervously.

"Oh, I could never say a thing like that," Jimbo had responded, avoiding Mead's eyes.

As the plane bounced Mead looked over at Jimbo, who sat in silence, eyes cast down, arms crossed over his reserve chute.

Behind German lines. That's where they'd be soon. Same thing as being surrounded. And those helpless moments floating down, no protection at all. Mead tried to ignore a sharp pain in his bowels. Landing in a lake would be the worst thing. They'd all agreed on that. He looked at his harness and gear and tried to figure how quickly he could get it off if he was sinking. No way. Not in time. Or would he land in a tree or on top of some building or straddling a wrought-iron fence? Jesus, it was just a crap shoot. No saying you weren't going to land right on the turret of a Panther tank.

He looked down the row of sullen faces lit only by the dim glow of a blue light. Mother of God, get me through this night.

Then more turbulence as they descended, everybody wincing at the sound of antiaircraft fire, which grew louder and louder until some men were covering their faces. Jimbo started vomiting all over his gear. "I can handle anything but this fucking bouncing," he moaned.

Looking out the open door near the rear Mead could see the red, green and blue tracers streaking past. The plane heaved as shells burst above, then below, and when flak raked the wings *smack smack smack* like hail against a tin roof they were ordered to stand up. Sixteen snap fasteners clicked as they hooked their static lines to the steel anchor cable running above the aisle, all eyes on the red light near the rear doorway. *Just get me out of the plane.*

"I'm dying," said Jimbo, trying to keep on his feet as he vomited again. The plane rocked hard to the left, slamming Jimbo against Mead, who clung to his static line for balance. "What the fuck are we waiting for?"

Finally green *Go! Go! Go!* and Mead was in the air, smacked by the prop blast *one-one thousand* as the chute crackled open overhead and the suspension lines and connector links hissed past his ears *two-one thousand,* then bracing for the opening shock of the canopy—*POP!* He looked up. *Thank God.* Then falling toward the angry sound of machine-gun and antiaircraft fire, desperately using his risers to steer away from the orange flashes and trying to make himself small and raising his knees up to cover his groin when he thought he was going to get it. *What if I land right on top of them? Oh, Jesus. Stay with me, Lord. Please stay with me.*

He was still trying to make out the ground when he landed, skidding briefly before frantically collapsing his chute. After unsnapping his reserve and harness he quickly rolled his canopy, stashed it in the underbrush and crawled behind a tree, straining to make sense of the shadows as he assembled his rifle. A bush? A cow? And that sound over there? Then more fire, much closer this time. He felt his pockets. Where's the goddamn cricket?

Above, the sky moaned with the low drone of planes. He stared in awe at the colored tracers and flak bursts and burning pieces of planes floating to the ground. He counted two planes with their engines on fire, then watched as another ran right into a flak burst, tearing apart. Jesus, what if the landings are repulsed? What if we're left here?

More small-arms fire on his right. A German burp gun. He recognized the sound from training, just like burping. He squinted and made out a figure sitting on the ground next to his chute and groaning.

"Broke my fucking leg."

Different company. Mead promised to tell a medic, then grabbed his gear, discarding his gas mask, and moved on, crawling through the brush on his knees. Where is everybody?

Across a small clearing he saw a figure hanging from a large tree. He crept closer until a white flash bounced off the clouds and illuminated the expressionless face of Louie Lathrop, a quiet but powerfully built college boy from California. His boots dangled just six feet from the ground.

"Louie, you okay?" Mead shook one leg, causing the body to sway. "Louie?"

And then the sound of German voices—*Amerikanische Fallschirm-jäger!*—as Mead quickly crawled back into a thicket. A short burst of machine gun fire slapped across Louie's body, causing it to sway again. *Bastards.* Mead aimed his rifle at one of the dozen figures running past, fingering the trigger. Should I shoot? No way I can get them all. But I could get at least two of them. Two for one. Enough to win a war over time. He'd be expected to shoot. Certain death perhaps, but that's what he trained for, right? *War.* Only, his whole being recoiled. He raised his rifle, trying to blink the sweat from his eyes, then hesitated. Too late. The figures hurried down the road. How many Americans will they kill?

Mead remained hidden in the underbrush for several minutes looking at his compass and trying to figure out how far he was from the assembly point. He tried to recall every feature of the sand table model back in England as he searched the horizon for landmarks but nothing looked familiar. Damn it, where is everybody? Looking up, he saw another paratrooper floating to earth with what looked like coils of rope hanging down below him. Mead watched the American descend. Jesus God, entrails. Once the paratrooper hit the ground Mead ran over to help. The man was dead.

Then he heard cries from across the field. He ran toward the noise, crouching as he went and dropping to his stomach every few minutes to check for enemy movement.

"Help me," cried out a hoarse voice.

Mead ran the last few yards until he came upon an American lying on his back and cradling one arm to his chest. "Is that you, Jimbo?"

"Jesus, Mead. I lost my hand. I can't find my fucking hand!"

"Okay, just take it easy and let's have a look." Mead quickly removed the first-aid kit from his cartridge belt and leaned over Jimbo. Gently lifting Jimbo's good arm he saw that the other arm had been severed just above the wrist, exposing splintered bone as blood streamed out.

"It's gone. My hand is gone."

"You're going to be okay. I'm going to get you some help." Mead looked around but saw no one. Got to think. Okay, first stop the bleeding, then find a medic. Damn it, where is everybody?

"I think I'm dying, Mead. No kidding, I really think I'm dying."

"Hell, it's just a million-dollar wound, ol' buddy." Mead tried to steady his hands as he opened the first-aid kit and pulled out the cloth tourniquet, which he carefully tied two inches above the wound. Was it tight enough? He tried to remember the first-aid lectures but couldn't think clearly. Why hadn't he been given more training? He checked the tourniquet again, then opened a sulfa packet and sprinkled it over the stump, trying not to gag.

"I don't even have a story." Jimbo was crying now.

"Sure you do."

"I do?"

"Darn right, and it's a hell of a story. Now you just rest."

Jimbo looked confused. "I'm thinking so many things. You don't know all the things I'm thinking."

"How about thinking about that warm bed back in England while the rest of us sorry asses are over here."

"I hope my mother's not alone when they tell her. Since my father died she—"

"*Shh.*" Mead took off Jimbo's helmet and then put his hand on his forehead, which was still blackened with linseed oil. "Just think of all those nurses, you lucky bastard." Then he tried to bandage the wound, wincing as he wrapped gauze around the flesh and bone.

"I don't feel so good. I can't even move my legs."

Mead looked down at Jimbo's legs but saw no wounds. "You're just scared." Then he pulled out a morphine syrette, using his knife to cut an opening through Jimbo's clothing before jamming the syrette into his good arm.

Jimbo kept moaning, slowly rocking his head back and forth.

"You'll feel better soon." Mead opened his canteen and held it to Jimbo's lips. "You're going to be just fine, ol' buddy."

Jimbo stared up at him, his eyes still wild with fear. "I'm telling you, I really don't feel so good."

"Just give the morphine a minute. You won't feel a thing." Mead looked around again, suddenly wondering if any Germans were approaching. He reached for his rifle. "You just stay here a minute while I get some help."

Jimbo gripped Mead's arm with his good hand. "Don't go. I don't want to be alone."

"I've got to get help." Mead noticed that Jimbo's face was now draining white. Was the tourniquet tight enough? He undid it and tied it again, making sure the bleeding had slowed.

"I always figured it would be you," Jimbo whispered, now slurring.

"What are you talking about?"

"I always figured you'd get it, not me."

"Thanks a lot."

Jimbo tried to laugh, then started crying again. "I don't feel so good." His eyes rolled up toward the back of his head, then down again, trying to focus on Mead.

"You want some more water before I go?" Jimbo didn't answer. Then Mead saw the blood seeping into the ground beneath his head. *Oh no.* Mead gently rolled Jimbo onto his side and saw the piece of shrapnel protruding from the back of his neck.

"What is it?"

"Nothing, it's nothing," said Mead, trying to stop the quivering in his voice and using Jimbo's gear to prop him up on his side. His hands shook uncontrollably as he tried to think of what to do. Can't compress the wound because of the shrapnel. Should I try to pull it out or just bandage it?

"I can still feel my hand."

"Just be quiet, save your strength." Mead sprinkled sulfa powder on the neck wound, pulled out another syrette of morphine, opened it and shot it into Jimbo's arm.

"I want you to make sure my mother gets the insurance money, you got that? Tell her to pay off the house." Jimbo now struggled for breath. "And don't let Uncle Frankie touch a penny."

"You can tell her yourself."

"I'm thinking so many things, Mead."

"I'm going to get you some help, okay?"

"I've never thought about so many things before in my life."

"You just hold on for a few minutes and I'll be back."

"Ah Jesus, this is just gonna kill my mother."

"Quiet." Mead scanned the horizon for signs of movement.

"It's ten thousand bucks, right? Ain't she gonna get ten thousand bucks? She could sure use the ten thousand, maybe paint the place and fix the roof. Goddamn roof's been leaking for years. . . ."

And then as Mead held Jimbo's face in his hands, he knew he was dead.

●   ●   ●

Andrew sat on the bed listening to his headphones and singing, keeping one ear partially uncovered to make sure he wasn't being too loud. Maybe he could save up for a Karaoke machine and make some demos. He imagined top music executives in Hollywood sitting around a large shiny conference table listening to him, their jaws dropping. *Who is this kid?*

He got up on his knees and looked out the window, squinting in the bright sun as he watched a small bird land on the edge of a little gray cement birdbath that stood in the middle of an overgrown vegetable patch, the one part of the narrow side yard that wasn't perfectly tended. The bird turned its head side to side, then looked over at Andrew.

"That you, Matt?"

The bird cocked its head quizzically, hopped a few times along the edge of the bath, then flew away.

Andrew turned the latch and opened the window, examining the screen. It would be easy enough to climb out without being noticed. But where would he go? There seemed to be nothing but old people in the neighborhood. It was like the quietest neighborhood in the world, as though everybody had slipped into a coma and it was just a matter of waiting for the relatives to show up and let out a scream.

He started to pry off the screen when a loud knock startled him.

"Thought we might go for a drive," said his grandfather from the other side of the door. "Maybe hit the beach."

Andrew quickly closed the window and sat at the desk. What would he do with his grandfather at the beach? "I've got a lot of work to do."

"There'll be plenty of time for that."

Of course it *would* be nice to check out the beach. He'd only been to the ocean once, and that was on the East Coast in the winter. (His grandparents had always visited them in Chicago on their annual tour of Midwestern relatives who were scattered across Michigan and Ohio.) A Southern California beach was a different thing entirely. But with his grandfather?

"Yeah, I'll go. Should I put my suit on?"

"You bet. I'll bring the towels."

Towels? Would he swim too? Great, I'm going surfing with gramps.

Mead was standing in the kitchen wearing navy blue trunks, a white button-down short-sleeve shirt, white socks and white leather sneakers like the kind that nurses wear, all shiny and new. On his head he wore a fancy-looking white straw hat with a black band around it and he'd placed large clip-on sunglasses over his gold-rimmed glasses, the shades tilted up. It was, thought Andrew, one of the more pathetic sights he'd ever seen.

They were both quiet on the drive, Andrew staring out the window taking in all the palm trees and cactus plants and trying to memorize how to get to the strip mall with the 7-Eleven they passed. They got to the beach in thirty minutes. Mead paid extra to park close and carried a small canvas tote bag as well as two towels he hung around his neck. Andrew carried the jug of water and two folding chairs they'd placed in the trunk.

As they passed a concession stand Andrew eyed a tanned and disinterested teenager who sat next to a row of boogie boards for rent. Now that's my idea of a job.

"I'm happy to rent you one of those if you like," said Mead.

Andrew shrugged. "Maybe later," he said.

"You *can* swim, can't you?"

"Of course I can swim." Actually, Andrew was only a so-so swimmer. He'd taken a few lessons at the local Y but stopped going after being towel-whipped in the locker room one day by a couple of Hispanic gang-bangers. He'd never swum in the ocean and the waves looked huge.

After they set the two chairs in the sand Andrew stood wondering what to do as he checked out the other teenagers, envying their tans and muscular bodies and sun-streaked hair. He couldn't get over how happy they looked, big, confident smiles on their faces as they ran past with their boards and lunged into the water. And the girls were unbelievable; the prettiest he'd ever seen, so that he knew there'd be no chance of getting through the day without jerking off big-time. He felt stupid and white as a snowman standing there next to his equally white grandfather, suddenly realizing that his bathing suit was way too short. He tried to slide it down lower, then kicked at the sand and took a few more steps toward the water.

"You going in?" asked his grandfather, pulling a book from his bag.

"I might."

"You're mumbling again."

"I said I *might*."

"Water's about sixty-seven degrees. Current's to the south so keep an eye on the lifeguard tower behind us or you're liable to wind up in Mexico."

Andrew looked up at the tower.

"And watch out for riptides. You know what to do in a riptide, don't you?"

"Sure I do."

His grandfather eyed him doubtfully. "You don't fight it, that's what you do. Swim parallel to the shore until you're out of it. And don't panic."

Andrew stripped off his shirt, pushed out his chest and headed toward the water, walking first, then trotting. A real California beach. He couldn't help but smile, feeling the warm sand between his toes. Two girls his age walked past as he reached the water, both ignoring him. They wore skimpy bikinis and laughed and swiveled their heads so that their long perfect hair swayed in the wind. *Shoot me.* He quickly memorized their predominant features, adding them to an extensive collection of mental images that he consulted almost nightly. He'd jerk off to them, too, and to the girls sitting up near his grandfather and the blonde up ahead in the water playing in the waves. All of them. He'd jerk off to every single one of them so they'd wake up in the middle of the night just knowing that someone out there was jerking off to them.

He waded further into the water, letting the waves pound against him and promising himself that one day he would build a house near a California beach.

．　．　．

Mead watched his grandson enter the water, wondering if he really did know how to swim. That's why he'd parked them right in front of the lifeguard station. He turned and looked up at the tower where two lanky teenage boys in bright red bathing suits reclined in their chairs, their hands clasped contentedly behind their heads. Not exactly vigilant. Both wore mirrored sunglasses and Mead wondered if they were asleep. Probably on drugs. Hell, the whole country was pretty well pickled, as far as he could tell. Dopers and pedophiles. He put his book down, deciding to keep an eye on Andrew himself.

Up until a few years ago, Mead had tried to come to the beach once a month and prided himself on the fact that he could still fend for himself even among the bigger waves. It was the air that he enjoyed the most, the clean dampness filling his chest. And yet he'd always found something a bit melancholy about beaches. Sitting there looking out at the waves, he couldn't help thinking how small and insignificant his life was; the same waves rolling in long before he was born and sure to be pounding the sand long after he was gone, oblivious to his passing. He looked out over the horizon, trying to visualize the curvature of the earth. What impact had he had? Little that you could trace. (He never counted the war.)

Sophie had made an impact. She'd changed people's lives. Two hundred mourners showed up at her funeral, all of them full of stories about the kind and selfless things that Sophie had done for them, things he'd never even heard about before because that was Sophie for you, never boasting. Some of them tried to keep in touch in the months after she died, inviting him to parties and sending him cards now and then. But gradually the phone stopped ringing. He knew it would. There was his friend Marty, who tried to talk him into moving back to Florida to some retirement community, which he refused to do. (He couldn't bear the thought of sitting around listening to people tell their stories over and over—the trip to Kenya and Tuscany and Machu Picchu, and the time that Milly was propositioned by the gondolier, and of course The War, as though it was the greatest damn thing that ever happened.) He still saw Bob and Angela Wright now and then and played an occasional golf game with Harry Braxton, but that was it. The truth was, he'd never been very social. Not like Sophie, who always did most of the gabbing at their dinner parties. (And that girl could gab.) Mead preferred to tend bar and man the grill, offering up a witty remark now and then. Still waters, Sophie would say with her smile.

He watched Andrew wade into the surf, the boy's movements awkward and hesitant. Scrawny little thing.

What went on inside a kid like that? Mead couldn't imagine. Sophie would know how to reach him. She'd know exactly the right approach. But Lord, it would have broken her heart to see what her grandson had become. She wouldn't understand it at all. And neither did Mead.

It was the insanity of the times, all the youth being spoon-fed nothing but garbage and raised in broken homes because marriage wasn't even expected anymore. And the crime! Ought to string up a few in the mall; bring back the road gang. They'd never mess with Mead, though. He still kept his Belgian Browning—lighter and more accurate than the standard issue Colt .45—right there in the drawer by his bed, ready for bear. Harry

Braxton's house had been broken into twice and a neighbor had her bicycle stolen right from her front yard. You couldn't trust anybody anymore. That was the damn sad truth of it. It was dog-eat-dog and let the last man turn out the lights. But they'd never get him. He'd make sure of that.

Andrew was now up to his waist in the water, diving beneath the waves or letting them topple over him.

Perhaps Mead could take him to church, arrange a little chat with the minister. Mead himself had been slacking off a bit since Sophie passed. Every time he went it just reminded him of her funeral until he couldn't stand sitting there listening to the organ and looking at Jesus up on the wall, patiently awaiting the rest of his flock. The truth was, he hadn't set foot in church for over a year now. *I'll keep a foot in the door.* He adjusted his hat and took a drink from the jug of water. Actually, a lot of things had been slipping. He tried to remember the last time he'd played golf or gone bowling. Must be six months. But he just didn't feel like getting out as much as he used to. The place he felt best was sitting in his chair with a good steak and a bourbon and working on his crossword puzzles. It wasn't happiness he sought. No, he'd given up on that the moment Sophie's hand went limp and they'd left him alone with her for another hour before wheeling her away. It was the brief absence of pain that he cherished.

He looked up and watched a seagull swoop down and skim low over the water, rising and falling with the waves.

Sophie loved to walk on the beach. He'd take her to Hernandez's for an early dinner—once a week they'd both get a craving for nachos and chicken tacos—and then they'd drive down to the beach and walk it off, she with her big white hat and scarf that she wrapped around her chin and the oversized sunglasses that she wore like Jackie O. Maybe it was being Midwesterners that made them appreciate the beach so much. Back when they first started dating they talked about how they planned to live within driving distance of the ocean, and that before neither of them had seen anything but the dreary shores of Lake Erie.

"So you see, you have to come back from the war because you've promised to take me to the ocean," she had said on one of their first dates.

Mead smiled to himself, remembering how nervous he'd been sitting across from her at the hamburger joint not far from his father's hardware store where Mead worked after school, and thinking she must have made some sort of mistake agreeing to go out with him.

"I'll do better than that. I'll get us a place near the beach. We'll go every day."

She laughed. "Don't you think we should get to know each other first?"

"I've seen all I need to see," he had joked. And he had. It was written right there in her small, smooth face: her humor, her easy manner, her honesty and through and through goodness. Mead knew right away that he'd found just what he wanted; that he'd do just about anything to wake up next to that smile each day. He just couldn't believe she'd want him.

He was good-enough looking, tall and strong with expressive, if a bit serious, dark blue eyes; but he'd always been reserved, never quite thinking of what he wanted to say until it seemed too late. When he wasn't in school he was usually working in his father's store, so socializing never came easy to him. He wasn't much for drinking or carousing with the guys and he rarely took part in their pranks and posturing, preferring to spend his free time tinkering with one of his three homemade radios.

"The truth of it is, Mead, you're a bit of a square," Sophie had said, leaning toward him with her chin propped up on her hands.

"I'm not so square," he'd said defensively.

"Of course you are. But that's what's so charming about you. You're not the least bit cynical. You're all right there. You're just ..." she held her hands up, *"Mead."*

From the moment he first saw her when they were both in their junior year of high school he'd been acutely aware of her, smitten not just by her emerald-green eyes and oval face and sandy blonde hair but by the effortless way she carried herself, her confidence and poise making him feel clumsy and inadequate. For months he watched her, feeling himself change in her presence like a pointer on a hunt. And then one day she showed up at the hardware store to buy some gardening tools and gave him a smile that seared him like a cattle brand.

He'd never been smiled at in that way before. He never knew that such smiles existed. That night he'd lain awake in bed deciding that he'd never be happy unless he could be around such a smile. And since he figured she'd never want to be around him, he assumed he'd always be unhappy. He'd never felt such sweeping sadness before, finding it almost unbearable to see her at school, like a shipwrecked sailor watching a mast recede on the horizon. He lost interest in everything: food, baseball, his studies. He even stayed for the second sermon one Sunday because he wasn't done asking God if there wasn't some way He could intervene.

And then she'd appeared at the hardware store again, just browsing the aisles and giving him that smile.

"How come you never talk?" she said suddenly, coming up to the counter when no one else was there.

"Talk? I talk. I'm talking." He felt himself blush.

"At school. You never talk in class but I know you're thinking faster than anybody."

"Guess I'm not a big talker."

"I don't like big talkers," she said, toying with a display of work gloves. "But you've got to talk at least a little bit to get to know somebody, don't you think?" She stood there looking at him until he felt the sweat gathering on his brow. Finally she said, "I'm Sophie," and extended her hand.

And right then without thinking he'd asked her out and she'd said yes, which floored him so completely that he did five hundred jumping jacks that night after dinner.

"Did anything unusual happen today, dear?" his mother had asked, watching him from the porch.

Leaving Sophie was the hardest thing about enlisting. He struggled over his letters, never quite capturing what he meant to say and never quite believing that she'd be there when he returned. But she wrote him almost every day; long, tightly-spaced letters that sometimes arrived in packs of six or ten.

I'll always wait for you.

And she had. The greatest miracle of his life came when he stepped off the train and her smile burst from the crowd gathered on the platform. *You waited.*

They married right after the war, skipping their honeymoon to save for a house. Once he'd gotten his degree in engineering at Ohio State—the GI bill was bar none the best damn thing the country ever did—they'd driven down to Florida where he'd found a job with an aerospace firm. But the heat was too much for them and three years later he applied for an opening in San Diego, taking the job sight unseen.

He watched a young couple—mid-forties—walk by holding hands, keeping one eye on his grandson.

Sophie. God, what a girl. Always finding the best in everybody, knowing just when to give him a little room and putting up with his dark moods—happy with the simple things. *Oh Peanut, I had so much more I meant to say.*

Mead stared out at the ocean watching the horizon blur. Then he rose to his feet, took off his hat, shirt and glasses, placing them neatly on his chair, and walked toward the water.

• • •

"How is it?" Mead called out as he waded into the ocean.

Andrew turned and winced at the sight of his grandfather approaching, the skin on his white chest all droopy and covered with a small tuft of even whiter hair, like one of those mummies at The Field Museum. He'd never seen his grandfather shirtless before and it seemed so weird that he felt like he ought to close his eyes. "Great."

"Look at that one coming." Mead pointed to a large wave swelling in the distance.

Andrew looked to his right at the blonde bobbing in the water not far away. *Look at me,* he commanded, only she wouldn't, not once since he'd been out there. He took a few steps away from his grandfather, scooting his feet until he was up to his chest, then turned and looked back toward the beach.

The wave knocked him right under, hitting him so hard in the back that he breathed in before he realized that he shouldn't. Then he was spinning in the dark, knocking hard against the bottom, then rising, then being pulled under again. He struggled for the surface, not knowing which way it was, but the wave kept rolling over him.

He felt a hand grab him under his arm. Finally he burst through the surface and retched and fought for air.

"I've got you."

Andrew felt his grandfather's body pressed against him but he could only cough and heave, then another wave hit him and the grip slipped, then held him again. When he got his feet on the bottom he stood and gasped.

"You never turn your back on the ocean," said his grandfather, pulling him toward shallower water. Andrew kept coughing, feeling an acidic burning in his throat. *"Never."*

Out of the corner of his eye Andrew could see the girl looking at him. Right at him. There was concern on her face, then a hint of amusement before she turned away and slid gracefully under. When Andrew finally caught his breath he turned away from his grandfather and headed quickly to the beach, his limbs filling with anger.

· · ·

He stayed in his room the rest of the afternoon, coming out only for dinner. They ate in silence at the green plastic table in the small backyard. The mosquitoes were bad and Andrew got bitten twice on the leg and once on the cheek.

"I get my hair cut tomorrow," said Mead, finishing his rib eye. "Every other Saturday. Thought maybe they could clean you up a bit, too."

Andrew slapped at a mosquito that landed on the back of his neck, but missed. "I just got mine cut."

Mead looked in disbelief at the boy's tangle of ratty brown, yellow-streaked hair, which had no identifiable part. "Well, I'd say they missed a spot or two, wouldn't you?" He stood and picked up his plate. "We'll leave at nine forty. *Sharp.*" Then he headed inside and finished his potato in his chair in the living room.

· · ·

Andrew lay in bed that night listening to his headphones and wondering what to do. No way he'd get his hair cut, he knew that. If he did, it was only a matter of time before GI Joe had him walking around in a tie saluting and selling bibles. But he had no idea how to refuse him. It was . . . inconceivable. He got up and walked to the window, pulled aside the curtain and examined the screen. He could just pack up and leave, load up at the 7-Eleven with the forty dollars he'd brought and make for the beach. Or he could head down to Mexico and bum around for a couple of years, let the whole thing blow over; maybe even get a job at one of those cool resorts with all the swimming pools and waterfalls and gorgeous girls sprawled out everywhere. He imagined himself driving triumphantly back over the border on his eighteenth birthday in a brand-new, red Dodge Viper with a wad of cash in his pocket. *You should have waited, Matt.*

But then he thought of his grandfather discovering his empty bed and the frantic call to his mother and her crying until her makeup ran down

her cheeks. That's what he hated: how every time he tried to free himself
a little he had to go face-to-face with other people, like they were surrounding him in a circle and he couldn't break free without knocking
somebody over.

Fuck.

He crawled back in bed and pulled the sheets over him.

Then he thought of the girl at the beach and her wet breasts pushing
out of her bikini top and the way she looked at him when his grandfather
was holding him, like he was just a child. He reached down and took his
limp cock, trying to push away all the shame he felt. He thought of the
other girls he'd seen that day—their flat stomachs and smooth perfect
thighs and especially their delicious round asses churning as they walked.
He felt himself harden quickly as he closed his eyes, lining up in his mind
every hot girl he had seen that day. Just the word *girls* made him horny.

Girls. The male body was basically disgusting; both he and Matt had
agreed on that. But girls?

As he started stroking himself faster the headboard began to knock
against the wall and the bed springs squeaked. He slowed down and
changed positions until he was lying at an angle on the bed, but that only
increased the squeaking. He peeled off his T-shirt and placed it between
the headboard and the wall, then tried again. Still the bed squeaked.
Finally he lay completely sideways with his legs hanging over the bed, but
as soon as he started the bedsprings shrieked. He stopped for a moment,
listening for sounds, then got up, put a chair against the door—it wouldn't
lock—and lay down on the light green carpet, which itched his back like
crazy. Then he took hold of himself and lined up the girls again one right
after the other and jerked off faster and faster until he came in a blinding
spasm, his back arching up off the carpet. After cleaning himself up with
his underwear, which he stuffed under the bed, he crawled back beneath
the sheets, rolled to his side and tried not to think about the girl in the
water and the look of amusement in her eyes.

• • •

"I'm not getting a haircut," said Andrew, standing in the hallway the next
morning.

Mead was flustered. "Nonsense. Now if we don't get a move on we're
going to be late."

"I don't need one. I just *had* one."

Mead thought he saw fear in the boy's face and wasn't sure how to respond. "By God, I told you we're getting haircuts today. You look like a . . ." He couldn't think how to finish.

"Please." The boy said it so softly Mead had to watch his lips. He felt his face redden, not knowing what to do. Sophie would know what to do. And the boy would never challenge her this way, standing there like he was preparing for the gallows. Mead wished he could go and sit in Sophie's room and think it over. He wanted to see and smell her things and pull open the drawers of her dresser and run his hands through her sweaters. *I don't know what to do, Sophie.* In a way she was lucky, not seeing what the boy had become, no longer the shy little child who loved to play checkers and fly kites when they traveled to Chicago to visit, always bringing him an extra suitcase full of presents.

Mead stood looking at Andrew, feeling suddenly lost. "I'll be back in an hour," he stammered, grabbing his car keys off the hall table and heading for the front door. "I want you working on your studies, got that?"

Andrew nodded.

•   •   •

After Mead locked the door behind him Andrew stood in the hallway waiting for the sound of the car pulling out of the driveway, then took out his soiled underwear from beneath the bed, gathered up his other dirty clothes and carried them out to the garage and put them in the washer. Then he went into the kitchen, found a medium-sized pot, filled it with water and placed it on the stove, turning the range up to high. After collecting his used batteries and dropping them into the water he took an ice cream bar from the refrigerator, peeled off the wrapper and slowly walked through the house.

He started in the living room, working back toward his grandfather's room as he opened drawers and examined all the things on the shelves—mostly books and photographs, with a couple of figurines and fancy little painted jars and teacups. He opened the dartboard and pulled out one of the darts, surprised by how heavy it felt. He tested the tip with his finger, then ran the feathers of the end along his nose. Serious darts. He backed up a few steps, aimed at the board and threw the dart. *Shit.* The dart buried itself into the wall above the dartboard. He carefully pulled it out and pressed his finger against the small hole, trying to flatten the edges, then put the dart back in the drawer and closed the cabinet. He examined the hole again, wondering if his grandfather would notice. But how well could someone that old really see anyway?

He walked down the hallway, stopping to check out the closet, then continued on to his grandfather's bedroom, hesitating at the doorway. The bear's lair. He felt nervous as he leaned his head in and looked around. The bed, queen-size with a cheesy blue and gold comforter, was perfectly made while the items on the large dresser—a comb, a silver shoehorn, two pairs of glasses—were arranged in tidy little rows. On the walls and matching bed stands he counted nearly a dozen photographs of his mother and grandma along with several of himself as a much younger boy.

The first thing he noticed when he entered was the smell, like cologne and baby powder mixed together. He cracked open the closet and looked at the shoes all lined in a row and the sport coats at one end and slacks hanging at the other. A class-A neat freak. He sat on the bed, testing its softness, then walked back to the dresser and opened the two top drawers. Three old watches, more combs, a little box of gold and silver tie clips, a compass, one of those pocket odometers that count your steps and a neat stack of white handkerchiefs with his grandfather's initials on them. He opened more drawers holding neatly folded shirts and rolled socks and white jockey underwear—Jesus, even the underwear's folded—and then a drawer full of nerdy sweaters. He went back over to the bed and sat down, picking up a gold-framed photograph of his grandparents together on a beach, maybe even the one he'd been to. They certainly looked happy. Were they still like, in love? He tried to imagine what it was like for his grandfather when she died after all those years together. Had to be tough. Was it harder than losing a friend like Matt? But nothing could be worse than that. He looked at another photograph of his grandma on a balcony with the ocean behind her, a huge smile on her face. *Hi, Grandma.* Then he reached down and opened the large bed stand drawer. Pushing aside several bottles of pills and a little packet of tissues he saw the gun.

Bingo.

He sat staring at it awhile, uncertain whether to pick it up. Before finally slipping his fingers around the handle he memorized its placement in the drawer, then gingerly drew it out and held it in front of his face, turning it one way, then another, careful not to finger the trigger. Of course it would be loaded. That's why his grandfather kept it by his bed. The real fucking thing. He felt a tingling sensation as he switched it from one hand to another, mesmerized by its weight and coldness and don't-fuck-with-me authority. Probably from the war. Maybe even used to kill Germans. Man, think of that. He touched his finger to the tip of the barrel, imagining a bullet tearing out and slamming into the chest of a German just about to toss a grenade. *Pow pow pow!* He tossed the gun into his left hand, then back into his right. Then he held his arm out straight and aimed it at the mirror above the dresser, wondering what kind of kick it had, then turned it and touched the tip of the barrel to his right temple. That's all it would take. Bammo. Brains everywhere. He listened to an approaching car and checked the time on his watch. The car continued on. Then he stood and aimed at different objects in the room, pretending to fire. He sat back down and stared at it again, practicing different kinds of grips. The real thing all right. Fuck me. He sat there for a few more minutes holding it, then gently returned it to the drawer, careful to put back the medicine bottles and pack of tissues exactly as they were. Then he got up and went to his room and started on his homework.

· · ·

Mead always enjoyed getting his hair cut. He liked the ritual of it and the easy banter with Rick Moreni and the off-color jokes and then the fresh restorative feeling after Rick brushed him off and shook out the apron, spinning him back to face the mirror. "Just right," he'd say, reaching into his shirt pocket for the five-dollar tip he always left on the counter. Rick understood all about what was happening to the country. He'd served in Korea and knew a thing or two about the world. Yes sir, Rick understood. And damn few people did.

But Mead was distracted today, not even following Rick's jokes or his withering analysis of yesterday's game. He'd let the boy stand up to him. Worse, he'd backed down. There'd be a price to pay for that. His hands tightened on the sides of the barber chair. He never should have let it happen. Either he shouldn't have insisted on the haircut, or once he had he should have stuck to his guns. But how? That was what stumped him. How could he *make* the boy obey? He couldn't just seize him by the collar, though it was damn tempting. He could always force the kid to eat a big juicy steak. Grill him some prime rib. (Like to see him live on shit-on-a-shingle for months.) Or maybe demand a few sets of push-ups. Mead must have done a million push-ups in basic. *Drop down and give me thirty, now!*

He thought of his own father. Veteran of the Argonne. Strict as a war-den. The only time he ever remembered his father touching him—beside the two occasions when he got himself whopped—was when they shook hands before Mead boarded the train for Camp Toccoa. "You come back in one piece," his father had said sternly, as though it was just another one of his orders. And Mead had. By the time he returned his father was four months dead, felled by a heart attack in the stockroom of the hardware store he'd owned for thirty years.

"You feeling all right today?" asked Rick, brushing off Mead as he rose from the chair.

"Just a little tired, that's all."

"I know that one. Didn't sleep well myself. Rita's veal parmigiana. Always gives me the worst gas. 'Course, if I don't eat it there's hell to pay. Can't win, know what I'm saying?"

"I know exactly what you're saying."

Mead placed a five-dollar bill on the counter, then paid for the haircut up at the cash register.

"Two weeks from today then?" said Rick, as he always did.

"Put me down," said Mead, as he always did. He was walking to the car when he felt Sophie hovering just above his right shoulder.

You know what day it is tomorrow, don't you, Pooh?

Let me guess.

It's Sunday.

Oh.

You promised, remember?

But—

A foot in the door. That's all I ask.

Chapter 3

Mead didn't invite Andrew, thinking maybe he'd break the ice by himself and take the boy along the following week. He felt guilty as he parked outside the church and checked his tie once more in the rearview mirror, like a drunk returning to AA after several months' absence. *We were wondering what happened to you,* they'd say, all the widows hovering like buzzards over carrion. *Won't you come for dinner? How handsome you look. Did you hear what happened to poor so-and-so?* And then the look he'd get from the Holy Joe, a comically young minister—what could he possibly know about life?—who seemed to sense that Mead wasn't buying in.

And he wasn't.

Because it wasn't God that Mead sought when he slipped into the very last pew next to the aisle just as the service began. Rather, it was the comfort of seeing hope ritualized; of witnessing how many other people sought God, desperate for something that would right all the wrongs. He liked the hymns too, and the sense of community when they all stood shoulder to shoulder and belted one out. (He remembered a service in the ruins of a church in Belgium just hours after the last German sniper had been killed, and how all the townspeople sang so beautifully that soldiers were in tears.) But he wasn't seeking God. No, he hadn't done that since he saw Jimbo bleed to death in Normandy. *Praise the Lord and pass the ammunition.* He looked down the row at another man about his age. Pacific theater, he guessed. Destroyers. Ordnance. Mead had a sixth sense when it came to that, though others frequently mistook him for a Marine. (There were worse things.) After the service ended he socialized just long enough to be polite and then excused himself and walked quickly to his car, suddenly fearing that when he got home Andrew would be gone.

But he was there all right, standing out front in the driveway shooting baskets. As Mead pulled up to the curb he wondered again how in the world his grandson kept his pants halfway down without them falling completely to his ankles, as though he was just about to relieve himself and suddenly changed his mind. Tape? Some sort of string and hook apparatus? Love to see him run a few laps.

"Game of horse?" asked Mead.

"I'm kind of tired," said Andrew, setting the ball down on the grass.

"Maybe some other time," said Mead, noticing the cookie tin on the front stoop. "I see we've been resupplied."

"Yeah, isn't she great? Ah, I hope you don't mind, but I invited her for dinner. I was telling her about my tofu hot dogs and—"

"You invited her for *dinner?*"

"At seven. I'll cook . . ."

"*Tonight?*" Mead could hardly contain himself.

Andrew fiddled nervously with his earring. "It's just that she seems kind of lonely, you know, and she was interested in trying one of my hot dogs. I didn't think—"

"Jesus, who the hell do you think you are?"

"Sorry."

Mead glanced across the street at Evelyn's house. "From now on, I'll make the social engagements around here, you got that?"

Mead felt unusually tired as he sat in his chair eating a B.L.T. and wading through the Sunday paper, which, it seemed to him, was really nothing but lingerie ads with a murder and a molestation here and there. He put the paper down and tried to imagine the three of them sitting around a dinner table. Good Lord. He felt his pockets for his Tums, popping two in his mouth. And yet he was slightly excited, too, which made him feel guilty. Of course, it hadn't been his idea. He felt his whiskers, wondering if he should shave again, then debated between steaks or pork chops. At least he had plenty of meat. Hell, might as well invite the whole neighborhood over.

He picked up the paper again and read about a mother who drowned her two kids in a bathtub, then about a teenage boy in Los Angeles who shot his driver's-ed instructor twice in the head. He put the paper back down and listened for Andrew, wondering what he was doing. He tried to pretend he wasn't there—oh, for an hour of peace—but he felt bad thinking of the boy holed up in his room like a hermit. The point was to make some impact on him; to spend a little time together. Suppose I could always drive him down to the mall, maybe spring for a real pair of trousers. Mead glanced at his watch. What the heck, the day's shot anyway. He rose from his chair and headed toward Sophie's room.

· · ·

They walked through the mall together at first, but when Mead sensed Andrew's growing discomfort he volunteered to meet up at the food pavilion on the second level in half an hour, figuring he'd let the kid off-leash for a bit. Mead watched him disappear into a music store, then walked slowly to the far end of the mall hoping he wouldn't run into anybody he knew. Some of the wives went to the mall just about every day, using it as an enormous lap pool for their daily exercise, back and forth, back and forth, with a rejuvenating purchase here and there until they were weighed down like pack mules. Mead never cared much for malls himself. Not like Sophie did. She could spend all day in a mall, ohhing and ahhing over things and getting ideas for the dresses she made. Malls felt too lonely to him, a sterile imitation of the bustling street life he remembered growing up, sitting on the bench in front of the variety store after working in his father's stockroom and seeing just about everybody he knew pass by. And then there were the packs of teenagers who prowled the malls like rabid hyenas, once nearly knocking Sophie over as they ran up the escalator.

Mead passed two particularly loathsome-looking specimens strutting and posturing like a bunch of Baby-Faced Nelsons. Ah, to make them drop and give me fifty right on the spot. Bet they couldn't do twenty. So many fat kids these days, atrophying in front of that damned TV. Had German boys gone fat too? The Japs still looked plenty slim and they were the ones who made all the TVs. (Guess who won *that* war.) Mead prided himself on the fact that he'd never gotten fat. He'd slowed down all right, just barely squeaking out ten acceptable push-ups a day (he could do forty up until about five years ago). But he'd never let himself get fat.

He stopped in a bookstore and browsed, repeatedly checking his watch, the Hamilton that Sophie had bought him for their thirtieth. He'd buy Andrew lunch and then take him to Nordstrom, get him something decent to wear, maybe even something he could wear to church. That would be something, telling Sharon that Andrew had come to church with him—voluntarily. He had to make some sort of headway with the boy, enough to give Sharon something to work with. But where to start?

He purchased a cup of coffee and sat at a small table in the corner sipping it and people-watching and checking his watch. He used to sit in that same spot waiting for Sophie to return from one of her shopping expeditions, scanning the passersby until he saw her bright face and the colorful bags in each arm, though she always went for bargains, keeping a file of coupons in the kitchen drawer and waiting months on certain items until it was the right time to strike. *Gotcha!* He finished his coffee quickly, then tossed the cup into the garbage and headed back down the mall thinking he might run into Andrew. As he approached the music store he noticed a group of gawkers gathered around the entrance. Mead slowed as he passed, and then as he looked through the window he saw Andrew by the store counter being held by a large security guard.

No.

He pushed his way through the crowd. "That's my grandson. What the hell's happening here?"

Andrew wouldn't look at him.

"I said, what's going on here?"

"I saw him slip this under his shirt." The security guard kept one hand on Andrew and with the other picked up a CD sitting on the counter. "We're calling the police."

Mead stiffened. "I'm his grandfather."

"Yeah, well you're going to have to deal with the cops on this one. We don't screw around with shoplifters."

"Andrew, did you do this?" Mead's voice was quaking.

"Of course he did it," said the security guard, whose stomach bulged out of his light blue uniform. "I *saw* him."

Andrew still refused to look up.

"Please don't call the police," said Mead. "I'm his grandfather. I'll pay for anything. He's . . . he's had a hard time and I'd like to handle this. *Please.*"

The security guard frowned and looked over at the young woman behind the counter, who held the phone in one hand and shrugged uncertainly.

"We can't just let him go. He was stealing."

"I'll punish him. You can count on that."

"I don't know," said the security guard.

"I'm his *grandfather,*" said Mead, standing as straight as he could.

The guard looked over at the cashier, then turned back to Mead and sighed. "I don't want to see his face in this mall again, you understand?"

"We understand."

The guard let go of Andrew, who remained immobile, shoulders hunched and head bowed down, his hair covering his eyes.

"Come on, son," said Mead, taking him firmly by the shoulder. With one arm on Andrew, Mead made his way through the crowd still gathered in the doorway, then hurried to the nearest exit and across the large parking lot to the car.

"Goddamn you, boy," he said, as he fumbled for his keys and unlocked the door. "Goddamn you."

• • •

Andrew sat in the backseat stunned. He hadn't meant to do it. It wasn't even on his mind. But then, he'd forgotten his wallet and there was the CD he'd been looking for and suddenly without thinking he just sort of slipped it under his shirt. Fuck, he hadn't even noticed the fat-assed security guard.

He looked at his grandfather up in the front seat driving, his silver hair neatly trimmed and the skin on the back of his neck splotched with old-age freckles, or whatever they were called. The car smelled of cologne and baby powder.

This was it. It was all over now. As he sat there feeling the hotness in his face and palms and fighting back tears he knew that it was finally all over. Even after pulling the knife at school he thought that maybe in a few years things would be okay again, that he could eventually recover. But not now. He'd be sent off to some institution somewhere and locked away. He looked out the window at a couple on a motorcycle, the girl hugging her arms around the guy, thighs splayed. *Why not me?*

"Do you want to tell your mother or shall I?" said Mead finally.

"I don't know," said Andrew softly, his fingers digging into the sides of the seat. It was unbearable thinking of his mother finding out what he'd done. And while he was staying with his *grandfather*. She wouldn't be mad, she'd be *crushed*. That was the worst thing, how she'd always start crying when he fucked up, not even yelling at him. If only she'd just yell.

"Stealing," said Mead under his breath. "It wasn't enough pulling a knife on someone at school. Now you're a goddamn thief as well." He glanced at Andrew in the rearview mirror. "My own *grandson*."

• • •

Mead had to concentrate on his driving, remembering his turn signals and keeping the car within the lanes. God help me on this one, Sophie. I am out of my league. *Stealing*. At least the police hadn't come; Mead still had control over the situation. But what to do now? And how would he explain it to Sharon?

As soon as they got to the house Andrew peeled off for his room. Mead stopped him. "You sit right here and wait for me," he ordered, gesturing toward the sofa before continuing down the hallway. He stopped in the bathroom to splash cold water on his face, staring in the mirror at the lined grayness of his features, which looked increasingly like someone else's. After wetting his comb and running it through his thinning hair he went into his room and sat on the bed, taking off his glasses and rubbing his temples. Was the boy just plain evil? A born loser? But he didn't look evil. Just shy and miserable. No confidence at all. It saddened Mead to see how little confidence his grandson had. He had hoped to boost him up a bit, find things to compliment him on. But the fact was, he hadn't found a single thing so far. The kid could walk into the room and you'd hardly know he was there except for the sulky face and baggy pants and the dyed yellow hair. He had no presence at all.

Well, the pants would be the first to go. No more of this saggy butt business. And there'd be chores. A whole long list of chores. That's it, Mead would draw up a list of rules and requirements. Start the day off with a few sets of push-ups and jumping jacks, get the blood flowing, then water the lawn, mop the kitchen floor, that kind of thing. He'd make a list that very night. But first it was time for a little talk.

He paused to look at the photograph of Sophie on the bed stand, the one where she was standing on the balcony of their hotel room during their last trip to Hawaii, then rose from his bed, straightened his shirt and walked back to the living room where Andrew sat meekly in the blue overstuffed chair.

"That's *my* chair," said Mead.

Andrew jumped up and moved to the couch.

Mead remained standing. "Well, what have you got to say for yourself?"

Andrew stared down at the carpet. "Nothing, I guess."

"*Nothing?* I'm afraid that doesn't quite cut the mustard."

"It was a dumb thing to do. I wasn't thinking."

"Seems like you haven't been doing much thinking at all lately, wouldn't you say?"

"I'm sorry. Did you call Mom?"

Mead paused briefly before responding. "Not yet."

"What are you going to do? Are you going to have me committed?"

Mead studied the boy, thinking how pathetic he looked sitting there like a condemned man. No starch at all. "It's worse than that."

"*Worse?*" Andrew looked up briefly, as if trying to assess the implications.

"First thing you're going to do is to sit down and write a letter of apology to the manager of that store. Then you're going to work on your studies until you can't see straight and by tomorrow I'll have a list of things for you to do. And rules. I'll be drawing up a list of rules which you will follow to a T."

"Okay," Andrew said quietly. "Can I go now?"

Mead stood looking at him, wondering what else to say. "You can go."

The boy rose to leave.

"And no music. You bring me that music player of yours. Leave it on the kitchen table."

Andrew hesitated, then headed down the hallway. Mead heard him set the music player down on the table, then the click of the bedroom door. He stood in the living room another moment, trying to slow his breath, then went and fixed himself a bourbon. He was just sitting down with pencil and paper to draw up a list of rules when the doorbell rang.

"Am I early?" It was Evelyn. She was wearing a teal blue dress with a white sweater slung around her shoulders and her face was dusted with just enough makeup to sharpen her pretty features.

"No, I . . . come on in." Mead felt his face redden as he gestured for her to enter. *Son of a bitch.*

"Are you okay?"

"Me? Fine." He closed the door behind her, distracted momentarily by the scent of her perfume, which was more subtle and pleasant smelling than the flowery stuff most older women seemed to soak themselves in. "It's just that . . . well," he let out a sigh, "it's been one of those days."

"Andrew did tell you that he invited—"

"Oh, yes."

"Good, I was afraid he might have forgotten." She stood in the center of the living room smiling and looking at Mead expectantly.

He rubbed his hands together nervously. *Stay calm.* "Can I offer you a drink?"

"I suppose one glass of white wine wouldn't hurt."

Hell, he hadn't even gotten to the store. He tried to recall if there was any of Sophie's Pinot Grigio left in the cabinet. "I'll have to chill it a moment," he called from the kitchen. And he hadn't even set the table. *Damn damn damn.*

"No hurry."

He grabbed the last remaining bottle, dusted it off and shoved it in the freezer. Then he knocked on Andrew's door. *"Evelyn's here,"* he growled in a low voice.

"Oh."

"You've got *two* minutes." Mead hurried into the bathroom to fix himself up. How could I have forgotten? He sniffed the armpits of his dark green polo shirt. Should he change? But then she'd know he hadn't been prepared. (And he had laid out his best shirt and slacks on his bed before going to the mall.) He quickly combed his hair and brushed his teeth, then hurried back into the kitchen. Broccoli and steaks, and maybe some cheese and Triscuits to start. He grabbed the matches from the top of the fridge, then dashed out the back door to light the barbecue.

"Are you sure I can't help with anything?"

"It's all under control," said Mead, cutting off the moldy edge of an old square of cheddar he found at the back of the refrigerator. "Just make yourself comfortable." He put down the cheese and ran to Andrew's door. *"Now."*

They ate at the dining room table, Mead and Evelyn at each end and Andrew in the middle. Evelyn loved Andrew's tofu hot dogs, eating two of them and leaving her steak untouched, much to Mead's chagrin and Andrew's unending delight. Despite her good-natured charm and quick humor, the conversation was so strained that Mead's face began to sweat.

"I think it's wonderful that young people are so concerned about the environment," Evelyn said after Andrew finished reciting a grisly series of charges against the cattle and poultry industries. "My husband George was a real meat-and-potatoes man. I sometimes wonder if that wasn't what killed him."

"Don't mind me," said Mead, jabbing his fork into his last piece of steak, which was grilled to perfection.

"You have to admit that Andrew has a point."

"I do?"

"Well, we really don't know what all those growth hormones are doing to us, do we?"

"I for one have no intention of living forever," said Mead.

"If you don't care about yourself maybe you could think of the rest of the planet," said Andrew. "Do you have any idea how much toxic waste a single chicken farm creates? Arkansas is basically a cesspool. And have you seen the machine they use to kill cows?"

"His dinner manners need a little work," said Mead in a steely voice, giving Andrew the eye.

"I don't mind," said Evelyn. "My family never talked about anything interesting. In fact, I'm not sure we talked at all." She smiled at Mead, who smiled politely back, then cleared his throat with a stretching motion of his neck and drummed his fingers on the table. Andrew stared sullenly at his plate.

"So, what did you two gentlemen do today?"

"Well," said Mead, scooting his chair back from the table. "Uh, let's see. I guess we stopped by the mall."

"What fun. Did you buy anything?"

"Not *exactly*." Mead searched the room for an innocuous place to park his eyes while Andrew sank lower in his seat.

"It's none of my business," said Evelyn finally, "but is anything . . . wrong?"

Andrew glanced nervously at his grandfather.

"Wrong?" asked Mead gingerly.

"I just thought that maybe—"

"I guess we're a bit tired," Mead said quickly. "Big day. *Big, big* day."

"I understand." She looked them both over with such a kind and searching expression that Mead suddenly wanted to tell her everything and ask her for advice. *Help!* "You two haven't had a run-in by any chance?"

"No—"

"More like a collision," said Andrew, standing up and taking his plate into the kitchen.

"I see."

"It's nothing really," said Mead. "Teenagers," he whispered with a thin smile. He heard Sophie's door close.

"Are you sure you two are okay?"

"We'll be just fine."

"He's a nice young man."

"One of a kind." They traded awkward smiles.

"I wish my daughter would have kids before it's too late but she doesn't seem the least bit interested."

"They're not for everybody."

"But grandchildren are. All the fun without the responsibility."

"In theory."

Evelyn dabbed her lips with her napkin as Mead ate in silence. "I just want to say that I know how hard it's been for you since Sophie died."

Mead didn't respond.

"After George passed away there were days when I thought that time had come to a complete standstill."

"I've managed."

She leaned over and gave him a quick squeeze of the hand. "It's good to see you looking better. I was worried about you for a while there. You looked so . . ." She didn't finish.

Mead stared down at the table, spotting several smudges and wishing he'd remembered to give it a good polish. And the two silver candlesticks were looking a bit tarnished too. Why hadn't he noticed before?

"I'd drop by more but I know how you like your privacy." She laid her silverware neatly across her plate and then adjusted the embroidered place mat that Sophie had made during her frenzied place-mat phase. "I bring you food because I don't know what else to do for you."

"Nothing you need to do." Mead cleared his throat again, feeling her eyes against the side of his face like the heat from an oven.

She leaned closer. "I'd love to be of help."

"I don't need any help."

"But if you did . . ."

Mead looked at her briefly but couldn't hold her gaze. "I'm just *fine.*"

She sat back. "I didn't mean to put you on the spot. It's just that, well, I wouldn't want you to hesitate to ask, I mean if you did need someone to talk to or if there was anything I could ever do." Mead nodded as she rose and began clearing the table. "Thank you for dinner. I don't get out much."

"My pleasure." He stood and tried to help but she swatted his hands away.

"The least I can do is return the favor," she said.

"There's really no need to trouble yourself."

"But I insist."

Mead followed her into the kitchen, trying not to look at her backside, which held her dress surprisingly well. Exactly how old was she? "Can I get you some coffee?"

She looked at him and smiled. "I think I'd better leave you two to patch things up." After helping him load the dishwasher she took her sweater off the couch and wrapped it around her shoulders.

Mead looked down the hallway, wondering if he should get Andrew to come out and say good-bye. Nah, to hell with him. He turned back to Evelyn, sensing that she was reading his thoughts. "He just gets a little moody. Nothing I can't handle."

"Do you remember being his age?" she asked.

"They didn't have his age when I was growing up."

She laughed. "Well, I remember. I felt so full of life that the world couldn't contain me. I thought I would just *burst* with desire."

"I see," Mead said, avoiding her eyes.

"Of course, I knew I'd never have time for more than a tiny slice of all the life I wanted. Oh, how I used to lie awake at night thinking of all the places I'd never see and all the people I'd never get to meet. It drove me *crazy.*" She paused, a wistful look on her face. "The truth is, it still does. I suppose that's why I garden."

"You're a heck of a gardener, if it's any consolation."

"Why thank you."

He flicked on the front lights, opened the door and walked her to the curb. "Well, good night," he said.

"Good night, General," she said, bunching up her nose and giving him a wink before crossing the street. When she reached her door she turned and waved. He waved back, then waited until she had unlocked her door, closed it and turned off her porch light.

Forgive me, Peanut.

. . .

It seemed like the quietest night of his life, lying there in the dark with the silence pressing against him so hard he heard a ringing in his ears. He must have lain there for two hours trying to sleep, and when he finally did he was right back in the forest preserve screaming for Matt to wake up.

At first he thought Matt was just sleeping off the alcohol. But by ten the sun was glaring. Andrew finally pulled himself part way out of his sleeping bag and rolled toward Matt.

"Wake up, buddy."

He shook him once, then twice.

"Come on, we gotta get going."

Matt didn't move.

Finally Andrew got up on his knees and pulled aside the top of Matt's sleeping bag. "Jesus, you don't look so good." He shook him harder. "Wake up."

And then he knew. From the sickly cast of Matt's face and lips and the coldness of his skin he knew. *Wake up!* And then he couldn't stop screaming.

Andrew bolted upright in bed, the sheets wet with sweat. *Damn you, Matt.* He rubbed his face, took a sip of water from the glass he kept by the bed, then lay back down and looked at the light from the street lamp leaking through the edges of the curtain, wondering if Matt could somehow see him. He always thought he'd see some sort of sign. If anybody could come back from the dead it was Matt. Andrew figured he'd raise hell, too. But there was never any sign, nothing that Andrew could be sure of.

"Do you think dead is dead?" Matt had asked as they lay side by side in their sleeping bags drinking from a bottle of Southern Comfort. "Like, that's it?"

"How would I know?"

"Just wondering." Matt was always talking about death and ghosts and suicide, especially when he got drunk. A few months earlier he'd completely redone his room with posters of dead rock stars, and it amused him to no end that his parents didn't get it. "Would you want to come back?"

"Not if I have to wait another sixteen years to get laid."

"More like seventeen or eighteen years." Matt took another swig. "I wouldn't mind being a bird or something; but I'll be seriously pissed if I have to dissect another pig."

"Maybe next time you'll go all the way to the state science fair."

"Very funny." Matt lay back and clasped his hands behind his head. "I've decided I'd rather come back as a ghost than a real person."

"That's just so you can hang out in the girl's locker room."

"We could both be ghosts. Think of the stuff we could do."

"But you couldn't get laid. I don't even think ghosts can jerk off."

Matt frowned. "I hadn't thought of that."

"Anyway, I don't think we're going to get a choice."

Matt didn't respond.

"Okay, tell me what happened." Matt had been acting strange all day and Andrew figured he'd had another fight with his dad.

"Nothing happened."

"Bullshit." Andrew reached for the bottle and took a sip, then stretched out and watched the moon rise through the trees while Matt blew large smoke rings.

"We're never going to have enough money," Matt said finally.

"So that's what's bugging you." For several years they'd talked about going in on a car once they were old enough and then heading down to Mexico to get jobs at one of the fancy resorts. Matt had read *On the Road* twice and figured he might write a book about their experiences, thinking maybe they could get some kind of movie deal.

"I'm just facing facts. There's no way we'll ever have enough money." Matt had worked at Taco Bell over the summer while Andrew bagged groceries, but most of their savings went to buying pot, which they got from Matt's older cousin, and beer, which they bribed panhandlers to buy for them from 7-Eleven.

"Sure we will."

"Not soon enough."

"What's that supposed to mean?"

"That I can't wait any longer." Matt's voice squeaked.

Andrew sat up and looked over at him. "You okay?"

"I'm just su-fucking-perb. Pass the bottle."

Matt sat up and took another drink, then fell back down again and hiccuped. "You're a really great guy, Andy. Did I ever tell you that? I mean it, you're going to do great things. Just don't let the assholes stop you."

"You're drunk."

Matt sighed loudly, then burped. "God, there's a lot of bullshit. Don't you think there's a lot of bullshit?"

"Nothing but."

"Well, I've had it with bullshit. Finito."

"Lucky you."

"I'm serious, Andy. I can't take it anymore."

"Don't start that *I'm going to kill myself* shit again or *I'll* shoot you."

"Would you really shoot me if I asked you to?"

"Don't tempt me."

Matt smiled and looked up at the sky, his face lit by the moon. "You know the funny thing? For the first time I can remember I feel *great.*" His words were heavily slurred.

"Boy, are you moody."

"Seriously, I feel fucking *great.*"

"Good, then stop complaining. I'm going to sleep." Andrew rolled over and buried his head in his sleeping bag, feeling woozy.

"I hope you make it, Andy, I really do."

"Would you shut up with that?"

"Hey man, you oughta take a look at this moon. I mean, it's *huge.*"

"Would you *shut the fuck up?*"

"No kidding, I've never seen the moon so big. I think it's gonna pop."

Andrew buried his head deeper into his sleeping bag, feeling the pot and alcohol take him.

Matt was silent for a minute, then said, "I can see the man in the moon. I've never seen him before but now I can make out his features *perfectly.*"

"Shut up."

"Sorry, it's just that . . ."

Andrew let out another groan. "Okay, tell me. I'm dying of curiosity."

"I thought he'd be smiling."

"Who?"

"The man in the moon. I always thought he'd be smiling."

"Oh, *please.*"

Another minute passed.

"I'm going to miss you," Matt whispered, sniffling now.

"Would you stop with the weepy stuff?" Hard liquor frequently reduced Matt to unintelligible blubbering.

"I'm serious, Andy."

"Fine, go kill yourself. What the fuck do I care?" Andrew crossed his hands over his head, starting to feel seasick.

And those were the last words that he ever spoke to his best buddy in the whole world.

• • •

After finishing up in the kitchen Mead sat in the living room long past his normal bedtime of nine-thirty, a notepad on his lap and the small stereo tuned to a classical station, volume low. One hell of a day. He looked over at the dining room table, wincing as he recalled the long silences. That ought to scare Ms. Raisins away for a while. And yet despite the tension she seemed to enjoy herself, always smiling and trying to draw Andrew out and even getting him to laugh once or twice, which was the closest thing Mead had seen to a miracle in quite some time. He thought of the way she had winked at him and how nice she smelled and the way her dress hung on her hips (and the fact that she had hips at all). Ah hell, I'm too old for such nonsense. Besides, it just didn't seem right.

He stared down at the notepad in his lap, wondering if Andrew was asleep yet. Time to get serious with the little hoodlum. As he started drawing up a list of calisthenics he suddenly thought of Sergeant Fisk at Camp Toccoa screaming at him, his face just inches away. *Give me another forty, now!* As much as he hated the s.o.b., he was always thankful for the training he'd had, first stateside and then in England preparing for the invasion. They'd made a soldier out of him all right, tough enough to take just about anything life could throw at him (except, perhaps, his grandson). But how do you raise a boy nowadays? What's the rite of passage in a world of drugs, sex and violence? He thought of a shooting that occurred a few years back at the high school not three miles away. One kid dead and another paralyzed. American boys, luckiest in the world. And what even made them Americans anymore, except for having the freedom to do just about any goddamn thing they pleased? Hell, in California you had to press "1" to continue in your own language.

He picked up his pencil:

Two sets of twenty push-ups each.

Fifty jumping jacks.

Forty sit-ups.

Could the boy do forty sit-ups? He scratched out the number and wrote down thirty, then rose from his chair and walked over to the stereo, his knees cracking as he squatted down and thumbed through the old records neatly shelved beneath. He hadn't played them in years. Not since Sophie passed. He pulled a few out at random: Harry Belafonte: *Calypso*; Edith Piaf; *Porgy and Bess*; Judy Garland: *Judy at Carnegie Hall* (Sophie wept when Judy died); The Glenn Miller Band. He smiled to himself as he ran his palms over the covers, which were taped in places by Sophie, the tape now yellow and peeling. She always loved her records, forcing him to dance at every opportunity. (That girl could cut a rug.) Finally he settled on Piaf and carefully slid the record from the cover and placed it on the turntable, fiddling with the knobs and levers until he remembered how to work the thing. Then he turned the volume up a notch and sat back down, putting his feet up and listening to the pop-pop-pop of the scratches as the first song began.

· · ·

Roy Rokowski was a Polish meat packer from the South Side of Chicago whose family sent him care packages full of smoked sausages that he proudly shared. Tall and gangly with a pronounced accent, he had fine black hair, extremely pale skin and large brown eyes sunk deep and underlined with permanent dark bags, as though he'd been brooding for years. Though well liked for his simple and uncomplaining nature, he preferred to keep to himself—as much as anyone could in the army—and spent hours whittling animal figurines with his jump knife, especially ducks and fish. His dream was to own a fishing cabin up in Michigan and after a few beers he often got misty-eyed describing his favorite rivers and lakes and explaining exactly where he planned to build his cabin. "What I'd give to be fishing right now," he'd sigh.

Rokowski's reputation grew considerably during the nine months training in England when several of the men began frequenting an ice rink not far from the base. Word had spread that the rink was crawling with lonely English girls and it was only a matter of bumping into them to make an introduction. Unfortunately, Rokowski was the only one who could skate.

"Well, son of a bitch," said Tony Bertucci, clinging to the rail next to Mead as they watched Rokowski glide backward across the ice. Mead couldn't believe how graceful Rokowski looked, nimble and assured as he zigzagged between the other skaters. The English girls were soon lining up for lessons and within days Rokowski and a small brunette with curly hair and a pretty mouth had fallen madly in love, much to the envy of the rest of the company.

"Jesus, the fucking Polack's getting laid," said Bertucci, tossing in his cot one night. Bertucci was a talkative amateur boxer from the Bronx with curly black hair—later shaved into a Mohawk for the invasion—a thick neck and a flat nose, thus earning the nickname Punchy. He was renowned for his acute and nightly bouts of squirrel fever, so that nobody wanted to sleep in the same bunk. "I'm stuck with you bunch of fruitcakes and Rokowski's out on maneuvers."

Rokowski volunteered for the paratroopers because he loved planes but couldn't qualify for flight school. On D-Day he nearly landed on top of the burning wreckage of a C-47, singeing all the hair on the left side of his head and burning the skin on his neck so that it was covered with blisters. Still, he'd been so certain that he'd land in a lake and drown that he was delighted just to be alive. "All this time I'm thinking I'm going to drown and what happens? I just about get my goose cooked," he laughed after he and Mead met up a few hours after the drop, both completely lost and Mead still so shaken by Jimbo's death that he couldn't form the words to tell Rokowski.

"Shh," said Mead, crouching next to a hedgerow and gesturing for Rokowski to get down.

"We must have missed the drop zone," said Rokowski.

"No shit," whispered Mead. "I think we're too far north."

"I was thinking we need to head west."

After some debate they decided to walk west following a narrow road, but soon retreated into the underbrush at the sound of approaching vehicles. They watched in horrified silence as two German trucks filled with soldiers passed by.

"Where the hell is everybody?" said Rokowski.

"I think we have to go south," said Mead, looking at the brass compass strapped to his left wrist.

"What I'd give to be sitting by a river in Michigan fishing right now," said Rokowski. "I know this spot—"

"Would you shut up?"

They waited several minutes, then crawled forward, keeping to the side of the road.

"I gotta take a crap," said Rokowski after they'd only gone a few hundred feet.

"Oh, Christ, make it fast." Rokowski squatted against a tree while Mead kept watch.

"What was that?"

"What?"

Silence, then they both heard a metallic sound coming from a clump of bushes off to their right. Rokowski yanked his pants up and crawled back to Mead. "See anything?"

Mead shook his head and tapped his forefingers together, gesturing for Rokowski to use his cricket.

Click-clack.

No response. They both kept their rifles aimed at the bushes, straining to see.

"I don't wanna kill no Americans," whispered Rokowski.

"Think we should use the challenge?" asked Mead, trying to suck some saliva into his mouth.

"If they're Americans, yes. If they're Germans, definitely not."

They heard a rustling in the bushes.

"Flash?" Mead called out in a loud whisper.

No response. They looked at each other again.

"Flash?"

The first bullet hit just in front of Mead, throwing dirt in his face. The second hit the first-aid pack he kept strapped to the right side of his helmet, jerking his head to the side. They both emptied their clips into the bushes, then slid backward into a shallow ditch and reloaded. "It's too far for grenades," said Rokowski; peering over the edge and firing again before sliding back down.

"Yeah, but what if they're coming closer?"

They both crawled forward and fired off several more rounds, then pressed down into the earth as bullets splattered dirt around them. "We've got to get closer first," said Rokowski, nervously snapping his teeth together. Mead tried to stifle the waves of fear that churned his stomach. "I'll try to crawl through that hedgerow and go around. Count of three, you toss a grenade and cover me."

"You're crazy," said Mead.

"Staying here's crazy. They're probably flanking us right now."

Mead felt a rising sense of terror as he imagined several German soldiers crawling toward them. Or maybe they'd already gotten behind them and were preparing to attack. Mead quickly turned his head and stared into the darkness, trying to make out shapes.

"You ready?" whispered Rokowski, rising to his knees.

Mead reloaded and pulled the pin on a grenade, wondering whether it was common to be feeling as shaky as he did or whether he wasn't going to be able to handle actual combat. Jesus, fighting until someone dies? But he had to handle it. Everything was irrevocable. "Okay, I'm ready."

"One, two, three . . ." Mead hurled the grenade as far as he could, then flopped down on his stomach and squeezed off five rounds as Rokowski scrambled off through the hedgerow. The grenade exploded, then silence, broken only by the sound of distant gunfire.

Mead held his breath, listening. Nothing. A minute passed, then another. Was Rokowski dead? What if they'd knifed him? Then they'd be coming for me. *Just let me go home.* He slid forward again and fired off three more rounds, then pulled out another clip and reloaded as bullets cracked overhead.

So this is it. Only nineteen, just like Thomas. Hardly a life. He remembered the smell of his father's hardware store and the way the worn floor planks creaked and the jingle of the cash register. How will Mother take it? He thought of the day the telegram came informing them that Thomas's ship had gone down, how his parents went silent for weeks. *Gonna miss you, big brother.* Then he thought of Sophie and all the letters she had written him, letters promising more than he ever deserved. Would she really have married me? Would our children have had blue eyes or green eyes? How long before she falls in love with another guy?

Suddenly he heard an explosion followed by rifle fire. He raised his head and saw a figure zigzagging toward him. *My turn.* He aimed and squeezed off a shot but the figure kept coming. He fired another but missed again. After the figure cut right Mead aimed just to the left and began to squeeze the trigger.

"It's me, you stupid son of a bitch!"

Mead lowered his rifle. Jesus, Rokowski.

"Who the fuck are you firing at?"

"I . . . I thought I saw someone behind you. I was covering you."

"Like hell you were." Rokowski collapsed down on the ground next to Mead and gasped for air.

"You all right?"

"I don't know." Rokowski checked his body. "Nothing missing."

"Did you get them?"

"Yeah, I got them."

"How many?"

"Four."

"No shit? That's great."

Rokowski pulled out a cigarette, trying to hide the flame as he lit it. Mead noticed his hands were shaking. "I've never done anything like that before," Rokowski said, rolling over on his back. His blackened face glistened with sweat.

"I didn't think you had." Mead wondered whether he could have done it. No, not a chance.

"Can't believe I really did it, to tell you the truth."

"You're a born killer."

Rokowski looked back where the dead Germans lay. "Wonder how long it will be before their families find out?"

"What the hell are you bringing up a thing like that for?"

"Well, it's strange, don't you think? Four dead Germans and nobody knows yet but us. I'm just wondering how long it will take for the families to find out."

"I could care less."

Rokowski took a long drag of his cigarette. "Guess they'll never know what really happened. Heck, they'll probably be wondering about it for years." Rokowski was like that, always mulling over things other people didn't even pause to think about.

"Just be glad it's not our families."

They lay in silence for several minutes listening to the various gun battles off in the distance and the constant rumble of artillery both in front and behind them, so that it sounded as if they were in a vast echo chamber. Then Rokowski said, "I don't think I could ever kill anybody with my bare hands."

"Hopefully, you won't have to."

"Could you?"

Personally, Mead had strong doubts and desperately hoped he could keep the war at some sort of distance. "If I have to."

They both watched a bright white flare rise in the distance and hover, followed by more small-arms fire. "Crazy world, isn't it?" said Rokowski.

"Crazier every minute," said Mead, getting up and standing cautiously against a nearby tree to piss. "Now let's go find the others."

They wandered in cautious confusion through darkened fields and along hedgerows until daylight, shooting at shadows and hiding from German troop convoys until finally they heard the *click-clack* of a cricket on the far side of a hedgerow. Rokowski answered with his cricket and they slowly raised their heads to see Punchy and Jay Goldberg leading five German soldiers at gunpoint.

"Look what we caught ourselves," said Goldberg, who was from Long Island and once got to throw out the first ball at a Yankees game. Like other Jews, he'd removed his dog tags in case of capture. "Whose brilliant idea was it to put an H on them?" he'd complained repeatedly. "I mean, is that supposed to be for *Hebrew* or *Himmler*?"

"What the hell are we going to do with them?" asked Rokowski, gesturing toward the Germans. They all knew they weren't supposed to take prisoners the first twenty-four hours. It wasn't official policy, but it was understood.

"That's what we've been wondering," said Punchy.

Mead studied the Germans with fascination, feeling slightly self-consciousness when they returned his stare. The enemy. Face to face. Two of them smiled and seemed happy to be finished with the war while the other three looked either frightened or sullen. Behind them the sun was just rising through the trees, stretching shadows across the road.

"Our panzers will be here soon," said one of the Germans, who spoke excellent English and carried himself with enormous dignity. The tallest of the five, he had a long thin scar along his chin and was missing part of an ear. "They will throw you back in the sea."

"Like hell they will," said Rokowski.

Mead studied a short, muscular-looking blonde whose eyes were full of anger. He looked at the insignia on the German's dirty uniform: *SS*. So this is Hitler's finest. Hardly superhuman. Yet the arrogance is still there. All those years the swaggering conqueror. The German caught Mead's eye, his face filled with disgust. Taste of your own medicine, eh? When the German edged closer Mead raised his rifle, motioning for him to back away.

"I've been to Minnesota once," said the oldest German, who looked middle-aged and spoke with a thick accent. "My uncle lives in Minneapolis."

"You should have stayed in Minnesota," said Rokowski.

"We both know that the real enemy are the Russians," said the taller German. "Why fight each other?"

"For starters, because I'm a Jew," said Goldberg. "See, we're basically one big Jewish army. Millions of angry Jews. Isn't that so, guys?"

Mead and the others nodded, trying not to laugh.

"This here is a lead element of the Goldberg Division," he continued. "You have heard of the famous Goldberg Division, haven't you?"

Two of the Germans nodded obediently.

"And off course we got the Schwartz Division on our right and the Cohen Armored on our left, though frankly, neither have quite the reputation of the Glorious Goldberg."

More nods as Punchy, Mead and Rokowski howled with laughter.

Goldberg put his face up to the tall German. "You like matzo ball soup? Good, because our cooks make a fine matzo ball soup. Hell, you probably won't be eating nothing but matzo ball soup from here on in: breakfast, lunch, dinner . . ."

The German took a step back and raised his hands in appeasement.

"That's right, you stupid fucking Nazi," said Goldberg. "We're going to stuff a few matzo balls right up Adolf's big fat ass."

Suddenly the short German lunged at Rokowski, who was standing nearest, and ripped the pin from one of two grenades hanging at chest level from the metal D-rings of his suspenders.

Rokowski stared down at the grenade in disbelief.

One-one thousand . . .

"Throw it!" yelled Mead.

Rokowski dropped his rifle and tried to grab the grenade but the German wrapped his arms around him, locked his wrists behind Rokowski's back and held him in a bear hug, the grenade between them.

Two-one thousand . . .

"Jesus Christ, get him off me!"

Mead grabbed the German by the back of the coat and yanked, then took his rifle butt and struck it against the side of the German's head as hard as he could. The German held on, saliva hissing between his clenched teeth. Mead struck again.

Three-one thousand . . .

Blood poured down the side of the German's head but still he hung on, almost lifting Rokowski into the air.

"Somebody help me!"

Mead hesitated, looking straight at Rokowski. *I can't help you, Roy. Can't you see that there's nothing I can do? I've got to save myself, Roy. You can understand that, can't you?*

Four-one thousand . . .

"For God's sake, Mead, get out of there!" cried Goldberg, who had taken cover along with Punchy. From the corner of his eye Mead saw the remaining four Germans making a dash for the woods.

I'm so sorry, Roy.

Mead turned and started for the ditch along the side of the road just as the grenade went off. He felt it against his back, the concussion lifting him and then a strange sensation of wetness. There was a moment of silence, then Mead heard Goldberg firing at the fleeing Germans. "You bastards!"

"You all right?" said Punchy, crouching beside Mead.

Mead couldn't talk.

Punchy inspected his back, which was covered with blood and bits of flesh. "I don't see any wounds. For a moment I thought it was . . . you."

Mead slowly sat up, resting his head between his knees.

"Crazy fucking Kraut, huh?" said Punchy.

Mead nodded.

"Poor fucking Rokowski. What a way to go. And Christ, you almost got yourself killed too."

Mead started to raise his head.

"I'm telling you, you don't even want to look."

But Mead knew he had to look. He owed it to Rokowski to look. *All I want is a nice little fishing cabin in Michigan.*

Slowly, very slowly, he raised his head.

• • •

Mead remained perfectly still in his chair as the record began to skip, his shirt soaked through. He took another sip of his drink, his eyes fixed on a needlepoint pillow Sophie had made during her furious needlepoint phase, then pulled himself up, walked over to the stereo and turned it off. After closing down the house and checking the doors twice he paused outside Sophie's room, listening for sounds, then cleaned himself up for bed. Before turning off his bedside lamp he went back to the living room, took his list from the notepad, then got a piece of tape and stuck it on the refrigerator.

• • •

This has got to be a joke. Push-ups? Andrew stood in the kitchen staring at the list. His grandfather was out front weeding the lawn. Jumping jacks? *Fuck me.* The old fart was right, it was worse than being committed. They didn't make you do jumping jacks in the nut house.

No telephone calls.

No music.

Mop kitchen floor each morning.

Prepare room for daily inspection at 8 A.M.

Inspection? Was he out of his mind? Andrew read further down the list.

Homework: three hours a day.

Reading: at least one hour a day. Books to be assigned.

Assigned? GI Joe had cracked. Alzheimer's for sure.

"Good morning," said Mead, entering the kitchen and pouring himself a cup of coffee.

Andrew grunted.

"The mop's in the hall closet. I'll inspect your room in twenty minutes. Then we'll do some calisthenics."

"But I . . ."

"Questions?"

Andrew stood there in his oversized T-shirt and underwear looking up at his grandfather in horror. "I guess not."

"And don't *ever* come out of your room in your underwear."

The obvious thing to do was to get stoned. *Really* stoned. Cleaning could even be fun with the right buzz. Sometimes, after smoking a joint on the way home from school, Andrew would spend the whole afternoon rearranging his room and organizing his CDs and putting his magazines into perfect piles. He went to the closet and searched through his grandma's shoes, trying to remember where he'd hidden his dope. Finally he found the small resealable baggie in the toe of an orange dress shoe. Man she had tiny feet, he thought, sniffing cautiously at the shoe. He pulled out the red

Bic lighter and one of three joints he'd managed to scrounge before the trip and carefully slipped them into his pocket.

"I thought I might warm up with a quick jog around the block," he told his grandfather as he headed for the front door.

Mead looked surprised. "Not a bad idea. Just don't get lost. All the houses around here look the same. Mine's the one with the name plaque."

Andrew walked until he saw a small park with a playground at one end and a small wooded area at the other. He looked around quickly, then crawled into the bushes and lit the joint, deciding to smoke half and save the rest. He preferred drinking to getting stoned because alcohol usually made him feel bigger while pot could make him seriously paranoid if he wasn't careful. But he loved the way weed cranked up his imagination so that he could really appreciate all the poetry in *The Lord of the Rings* and sometimes even feel the deadly pull of the one ring. He took a long hit, keeping the joint cupped in his left hand. He'd gotten stoned before classes a few times but stopped when he realized that it made Kevin Bremer seem even more intimidating than he was, exaggerating all his features until he looked like a huge fucking troll. Besides, pot gave Andrew the giggles, sometimes so bad that he got heartburn. He held in the hit another few seconds, then exhaled loudly, immediately feeling the lightness in his head. Truly, everything was pretty fucking funny when you thought about it. He let out a giggle, then another. Some days sitting in class he felt like his head would burst from trying not to laugh at the hilarity of everything. He giggled again as he thought of how he and Matt used to spend months building model cars, agonizing over every little piece, which they sandpapered down until the fit was just right. And then as soon as the last coat of metallic paint dried, they'd hurry down to the lake, strap firecrackers to the cars, add a sprinkling of gas, then light the fuse and push them down a hill. Now that's funny. He took another hit, then carefully tapped the joint out and slipped it back into his pocket before climbing out of the bushes and brushing himself off.

Hand me the mop and bucket, Sarge, and step aside. I am a cleaning machine!

He sang "Rocky Mountain High" all the way back.

· · ·

"Do you have any Cheetos?"

Mead looked up at his grandson, who had just finished sweeping the back patio and still held the broom in one hand, a silly look on his face. "Have a raisin cookie."

"I did."

"Then have some pretzels. There's a bag in the cabinet just to the left of the oven."

"Do you have any Doritos?"

"No, I don't have any Doritos."

Andrew seemed to mull the matter over for a moment. "Guess I'll have pretzels."

Twenty minutes later Mead got up and went to the kitchen to make sure Andrew had resealed the pretzel bag. First he checked the large tin of cookies on the top of the refrigerator. Empty. After searching through the cabinets for the pretzel bag he found it in the garbage pail beneath an empty can of smoked almonds, which Mead had purposely hidden behind the soup bowls. *Christ, the boy's going to clean me out.* He quickly grabbed a jar of Skippy Super Chunk peanut butter from the shelf along with a box of Melba Toast and took them to his room, hiding them in his closet.

At least the kid could clean. Mead peered into the bathroom where Andrew was furiously scrubbing the toilet while humming loudly to himself, reminding Mead of a smart-mouthed guy from Mississippi who was twice forced to clean an entire latrine with a toothbrush. The odd thing was that his grandson actually seemed to enjoy cleaning. He had the same look on his face that Sophie used to get when she sewed on a button, all radiant and purposeful. Several times Mead even heard laughter coming from the bathroom. *Strange kid.*

That afternoon Mead went to the library and spent an hour looking through the history collection. He had always shied away from books and movies about the war because he didn't see the sense in going back to a place that he hated the first time. But it would be good for the kid. *Give him a little education. And I am his grandfather. He should know who he's dealing with.*

But what book to start with? *A Bridge Too Far? The Longest Day? The Rise and Fall of the Third Reich?* (That would keep the boy out of the malls for a while.) Then he saw it there on the shelf: *Brave Men,* a collection by Ernie Pyle. *Yes, that was the place to start. Brave Men. We'll go from there.*

· · ·

They ate dinner that evening at the kitchen table, both silent. Andrew had some sort of tofu hot dog, piling on the relish, while Mead ate pork chops and baked beans. As Andrew pushed the last piece of hot dog into his mouth Mead got up, retrieved the book from a bag on the counter and slid it across the table.

"I think we'll start with this one."

"Start . . . what?"

"Teaching you a few things."

Andrew glanced down at the book, then back up at Mead. "Did you tell my mom yet? Is she coming to get me?"

Mead paused, taking his time. "No, I haven't told her yet."

"But you're going to?"

"I'm thinking about it."

"You mean you might not?"

"I mean I'm thinking about it."

For the first time Mead saw the hint of a smile flash across Andrew's face.

•   •   •

Andrew hadn't even considered the possibility that his grandfather wouldn't tell, that she might never have to know. It made him want to laugh and cry at the same time, knowing that she wasn't at that very moment sitting in the living room with her head in her hands weeping and wondering what she was ever going to do with him. Would his grandfather still tell her? But why wouldn't he? He didn't seem like the kind to keep secrets or bend the rules. But maybe he wouldn't. And so Andrew would do everything he could to please his grandfather until the twenty-one days were over. Anything would be worth keeping his mom from finding out.

After taking a long shower he sat on his bed rubbing his sore shoulders—I'm way out of shape—then got into bed with the book. He set the timer on his watch for an hour and began to read.

Chapter 4

The house was looking damn tidy, no doubt about that. Mead even had his grandson hanging the flag each morning—it was a sight to see—and folding the laundry and washing the windows and waxing his old blue Chevrolet Caprice, which guzzled gas like a Sherman but had the heart of a squad car. But the morning exercises were an embarrassment. The boy could hardly do ten push-ups without his back swaying like an old horse. Mead tried to supervise at first, but soon found it unbearable to watch as Andrew gasped and struggled.

"You've got to *push!*"

He still hadn't said anything to Sharon. Part of it was his reluctance to cause her further pain and part was Mead's own embarrassment that Andrew had gotten into further trouble. And then he started thinking that maybe he and Andrew would work it out themselves. And they *would* work it out. Mead was determined now. After three years in the service he ought to know a thing or two about dealing with delinquents.

Mead sat in the kitchen finishing his oatmeal and watching as Andrew bent over to rinse the mop in a bucket. Mead slammed down his spoon. "For God's sake, I can see your undershorts, and even they're falling off."

Andrew stood and tried to hoist his pants up but as soon as he let go they slid down again, exposing exactly four inches of underwear. "Sorry."

"I can still see them."

"That's kind of the way the pants fit."

"But they *don't* fit. I know a good tailor—"

"They're *supposed* to be this way."

"Well you ought to get a good look at yourself from behind. Takes away a person's appetite."

Andrew rinsed the mop and then pushed and pulled it slowly across the floor.

"Listen, I know the budget's kind of tight back home. Heck, I'm happy to buy you some decent clothes. If you hadn't gone shoplifting the other day, I was going to take you to Nordstrom and—"

"I don't need any clothes."

And there Mead was right on the edge again, wanting to say, *To hell you don't, boy. Pull your goddamn trousers up.* It was like keeping your boots shined to a spitting polish as you trained to take on Rommel's panzer divisions. Mead hadn't understood the connection at first. It seemed like more chickenshit to him. But then after a few weeks in Europe he got it. The whole psychological machinery made perfect sense to him. If you let one thing slip then another thing would. You couldn't afford any slips. You needed absolute *perfection.*

He got up and carried his bowl of oatmeal into the living room, vowing to revisit the matter later.

"Looks like we got an invitation," said Andrew excitedly, coming in with the mail and dropping a handwritten note into Mead's lap. Mead cautiously opened the beige unstamped envelope, which was addressed to Andrew and the General.

> Might you two gentlemen do me the pleasure of honoring me with your company for dinner tonight, say around six? I happen to have good intelligence that you are both available so regrets will not be taken kindly!
>
> Evelyn
>
> PS: Vegetarian fare only.

Vegetarian fare? Mead looked at Andrew. "How does she know we're not busy?"

Andrew squirmed. "I might have said something."

Mead gave him the eye.

"So we're going?"

Mead reread the invitation, impressed by the flawless cursive. "I'll think about it."

"Great!" Andrew looked pleased with himself. "Gee, I wonder who the other gentleman is?"

"Very funny."

Mead thought of all sorts of excuses: his back, his sinuses, a fridge full of moldering meat, prior commitments unbeknownst to Andrew, but he knew none would survive Evelyn's look of hurt. So they'd get through the dinner and then they could call it even. Certainly Sophie would understand the logic of that.

Early that evening Mead sent Andrew back to his room three times to find a better shirt until he realized that the boy didn't pack anything appropriate. In the end he grudgingly signed off on a dark blue T-shirt with a picture of a rabid-looking armadillo riding a skateboard off a cliff, which was only slightly less offensive than the alternatives.

"Well, what a treat!" chirped Evelyn as she opened the door. The house smelled of all sorts of delicious spices, reminding Mead of the holidays and how Sophie used to keep a pot of cider mulling on the stove. He followed Andrew in, feeling a twinge of guilt.

"I have a hoop just like that," she said, admiring Andrew's earring. Mead rolled his eyes. "I think it goes great with your highlights."

"Evelyn—"

"Let me guess, the General doesn't exactly approve."

"He hates the way I look."

"He's *sixteen,*" said Mead.

"That's just the point," said Evelyn. "If not now, when? Frankly, I wish I'd taken a million more risks when I was young." She shook her head with a smile. "I was such a prude growing up."

"I really don't think he needs any encouragement."

"I told you she's great," said Andrew, grinning.

Mead rubbed his temple, trying to recall the early warning signs of a stroke. "Would you happen to have a little bourbon around?"

"I've been waiting for someone to help me get through George's stock. God knows, I'll never drink it all." She disappeared into the kitchen.

Mead turned to Andrew. "You watch your manners, you understand?"

"Why are you so uptight?"

"I wouldn't know where to begin."

Evelyn reappeared, handing Mead a bourbon and Andrew a Coke and gesturing for them to take a seat in the living room, which was small but bright and cheery with lots of white and yellow. "So, you must be a junior?"

"Sophomore."

"I hated my sophomore year. In fact, I thought high school was a big waste of time."

"So do I!"

"For Pete's sake, Evelyn." Mead was starting to perspire, wishing he'd worn an undershirt.

"Are we bothering you?"

Mead rubbed his jaw. "Perhaps we could talk about something a bit more . . . *constructive*."

"Fine. I'd *love* to hear about your experiences in the war." She turned to Andrew. "Your grandfather is so modest you'd never know he's highly decorated."

Andrew smiled. "Yeah, I'd love to hear some stories."

"I am not *highly* decorated."

"Don't believe a word he says. You should have heard your grandmother carry on about him." Evelyn and Andrew stared at Mead, waiting.

"Some other time." He took a large slug of bourbon, wondering how he'd ever make it through dinner. "So, are those all annuals out front?" He sighed with relief as Evelyn smacked it right out of the ballpark, talking well into dinner about moisture retention and root systems and soil conditions. As she brought out dessert—pecan and raisin pie topped with whipped cream—he glanced at his watch and figured that another half hour would about do it. And yet he wasn't anxious to leave. Several times he even caught his eyes lingering on her neck, which was surprisingly smooth. He looked down at his bourbon, trying to count how many refills he'd had. Andrew and Evelyn were busy chattering like a bunch of long-lost soul mates.

"When did your husband die?" asked Andrew.

"Ten years ago this Thanksgiving. He fooled all of us right through the holiday, then collapsed just hours after our son and daughter left for the airport."

"What happened?"

"Andrew—"

"Officially it was a heart attack but I know it was stress—and probably his diet, too. He just rusted from the inside out." She folded her napkin in her lap, then spread it out and refolded it again. "George was a world-class worrywart. It wasn't so bad when he was younger; I just thought he was being responsible. But over the years he got worse and worse until he was up half the night running worst-case scenarios." She spread the napkin out again, flattening the creases with her palm. "It seems so silly; all those years wasted worrying about things and now he doesn't have a care in the world."

"So he rusted to death?"

"You'll have to excuse Andrew . . ."

But Evelyn was smiling. "In a manner of speaking."

Andrew seemed to reflect on that for a moment. "What kind of job did he have?"

"He owned a small lighting business. We were never rich but he always made enough to support us."

"So that's why it's so bright in here." Andrew squinted up at the recessed lighting.

"Andrew—"

"Is it bright?"

"I don't mind," said Andrew quickly.

"It's perfect," said Mead. He took another swig of bourbon, feeling a bit like a chaperon.

"I could turn the lights down. Everything's on a dimmer." She smiled. "George loved his dimmers. Frankly, I think he would have put me on one if he could have."

"I'm used to it now," said Andrew.

"I'll turn them down." She got up and lowered the lights. "Better?"

"Way better." Andrew smiled as Mead fired down another belt of bourbon. "So, did you work in the lighting business too?"

"I was too busy being a mother until the children were older, then I got into interior decorating—don't ask me how. My real dream was to go to cooking school and get a job as a pastry chef but George wouldn't hear of it."

"You'd make a great chef," said Andrew, who'd eaten three platefuls of curried vegetables and rice and four homemade dinner rolls.

"Why thank you." She folded her napkin again. "Your grandmother was quite a cook herself." She turned to Mead. "Andrew tells me you've kept all her things?"

Mead put down his fork. "Not all of them."

"I hung on to George's things for years. The truth is, I hadn't given up on the idea that he might come back." She took a sip of her white wine and then cupped the glass with both hands, staring into it. "It wasn't until I got rid of them that I really said good-bye."

Mead felt himself redden.

The scheming little tart.

It's just a dinner, Peanut. I got roped into it.

It's a date.

Mead stood up. "It's time for us to go."

"What?" said Andrew.

"I didn't mean to offend you," said Evelyn.

"It's getting late."

"It's only eight fifteen," said Andrew, looking at his watch.

"I said, it's *time.*"

Mead thanked Evelyn for the dinner, then hurried Andrew out the door and across the street.

"I'm sorry if I said something to upset you," Evelyn called out.

"I'm not *upset.*"

. . .

Mead was lying on his bed with his clothes on when Sharon called. She talked to Andrew briefly on the kitchen line before Mead picked up again.

"How are you, Sweetheart?"

"My car died," she moaned.

Jesus, thought Mead, what is it with some people? "That old Celica? What's wrong this time?"

"Everything. The guy says it needs a new clutch, for starters."

"How many miles does it have?"

"Just over 180,000."

"I'll buy you a new one."

"Dad, I couldn't ask you to do that."

"You didn't. Now go rent yourself something for a few days and get yourself a *Consumer Reports.* I'll ask around myself."

Long silence.

"You okay?" Mead asked, worried by the frailty in her voice. And yet her mother had had such strength.

"I think I'm going to get fired."

"But you just started."

Another long pause. "I accidentally deleted all of my boss's expense account reports. I don't know how it happened." Her voice sounded so small that Mead wondered if she was having a breakdown.

"Then you'll find another job. Or maybe you could go back to school, get your degree."

Sharon had dropped out of college after falling in love with some slick joker from Los Angeles and never went back after he dumped her, despite her parents' pleas.

"College just isn't my thing, Dad," she'd said.

"College is everybody's thing these days, Sharon. Now would you take our advice just this once?"

But she hadn't. And ever since it had pained him to see how hard she struggled, first as a receptionist, then as some sort of administrative assistant—they didn't seem to have plain old secretaries anymore—then keeping the books for some auto parts shop that promptly went out of business (no surprise there), then for some medical equipment dealer. And on top of it all trying to raise a teenager single-handedly. What sort of life was that? Nothing any girl grows up dreaming about.

The cold truth was, she never should have had the child in the first place. Not Sharon. Parenthood just wasn't for everybody. Or even most people, in Mead's opinion. Hell, nine out of ten parents were over their heads from the get-go and the children themselves rarely seemed worth the trouble, at least once they got past the cute phase, which even Mead enjoyed. (And Andrew had been cute, with big brown eyes and a sprinkling of freckles across a pug nose.)

"I don't even want to show my face tomorrow." She groaned again.

"I'm sure they'll give you another chance."

More silence.

"You still getting child support?"

"When he remembers."

"I could have him killed."

"Dad."

"I'd even do it myself. Pro bono. Think of it as community service."

"Please."

"Then let me pay for a lawyer. We'll get a court order."

"I don't want to talk about it. Listen, I've got to go. I'll let you know what happens."

From her voice Mead knew she was only hanging up to have a good cry. He never knew what to say when she got that way. Was there something I should be doing? Finally he said, "You take care of yourself, Pumpkin, you got that?"

"I'll try, Dad."

"And for crying out loud, don't worry about us."

Shortly after they hung up the phone rang again. Had she been fired already? He snatched the phone off the receiver. "Where you been hiding yourself, you old goat?" Damn. It was Harry Braxton.

"Harry."

"What do you say we play a few rounds Tuesday?"

"I'm a little busy right now."

"You? *Busy*? Who are you fooling?" Harry let out a big chuckle.

Mead ground his teeth. "My grandson's in town."

"Sharon's boy? Great! Taken him to the ballpark yet? I can get you box seats."

"He's not really much of a baseball fan."

"That's too bad. My grandson just got into Harvard Med. Did I mention that?"

"I believe you did."

"Our granddaughter's getting married in July. Great family. Eleanor's beside herself."

"Congratulations."

"Haven't seen much of you lately. You keeping any secrets?"

"I've been tied up with a few projects around the house."

"You must have added on another story by now." Harry chuckled again.

Mead glanced at his watch, then switched the phone to the other ear and stared up at the ceiling, noticing a small water stain in the corner.

Harry drew a breath. "Listen pal, I know how hard it must be for you."

"I'm doing just fine, thanks."

"But you've got to get out now and then. No use sitting around that house all day moping."

"I'm not *moping,* Harry. And like I said, I'm busy with my grandson just now, but thanks for the call."

"Hey, maybe you could bring him over for dinner next week? Eleanor would love it. Give her an excuse to make her meatballs."

Mead winced at the thought of the four of them sitting around Harry's enormous dining room table talking about Eleanor's meatballs. Granted, they were delicious. Even better than Sophie's, truth be told. (And she was always suspicious about that, probing him whenever they drove home from dinner with the Braxtons.) But not with Andrew. Not a chance. He wasn't about to take baggy butt out on the social circuit. "That's kind of you, Harry, but like I said, we're rather booked up at the moment."

"You call if you change your mind."

"Wouldn't hesitate."

After he hung up he noticed Andrew standing in the bedroom doorway. Mead raised his eyebrows.

"I was just wondering . . . when I could have my CD player back?"

"You mean *if.*"

Andrew's face sunk even further. Hard not to pity the kid, mug like that. And yet damn it, he deserved the punishment. Who did he think he was? "You'd better get back to your homework." Andrew turned and shuffled off.

•   •   •

Mead stood in the hallway outside the bathroom door the next evening waiting to intercept Andrew as he emerged. The streetlights had just come on and the neighbor's Jack Russell was having his nightly attack of hysteria, barking so incessantly that the first time Mead heard him he called the police, fearing some sort of Manson-style mass murder.

"You ever coming out of there?" Mead shouted into the door.

"Almost done."

"Christ, you take longer than your grandma and she took so long I once had to relieve myself behind the garage." Finally the door opened. "What the hell happened to your face?"

"Acne," mumbled Andrew.

"You're better off leaving those things alone." Mead thought of a soldier named Smitty, who had the worst acne in the company, like bee stings all over his face. Every spare moment Smitty would check himself in his trench mirror, groaning at the latest outbreak and blaming the K-rations. And then one day Smitty was shot in the head by a sniper and Mead remembered thinking, well, at least Smitty won't be getting any more zits.

"I was wondering if you're up to a game of backgammon?"

"I was going to read."

"You've read plenty today. Let's have a game." Mead wasn't going to give him any choice.

"I don't know how."

"Then I'll teach you."

Mead opened the hall closet and pulled down his backgammon board from the top shelf and carried it into the living room, thinking of Sophie and the games they used to play, especially double solitaire and Scrabble. He set up the board on the coffee table, then walked Andrew through the rules.

"Ready?"

"I think so."

Andrew won the first game.

"Beginner's luck," said Mead, wondering if he'd been suckered. He tried harder the next game but lost again.

"I like backgammon," said Andrew. "Play again?"

"I'm more of a card man myself," said Mead, quickly closing the board. He plucked a pencil from the holder and picked up a crossword puzzle from the side table. His grandson sat looking at him.

"You must miss Grandma," Andrew said suddenly.

Mead felt himself flush. "Of course I do." He returned to the puzzle.

"I was thinking how hard that must be, losing someone after all those years."

"Yes, it is."

"How long were you guys married?"

Mead put the puzzle down on his lap. "Fifty-one years."

"Wow."

"It's just a matter of sticking with something long enough."

"I miss her. She was really nice to me."

"She adored you." Mead noticed an embarrassed smile spread across Andrew's shiny face.

"How old were you when you first met her?"

"Seventeen. We dated for a few months before I enlisted, and then when I got back she was still waiting for me."

"You didn't think she would be?"

"I had my doubts."

A look of amusement crossed Andrew's face. "How long until you got married?"

"Four months."

"Man, that's fast."

Mead couldn't help but smile. "We just knew. People didn't need to live together for twenty years before making up their minds."

"Do you ever think of marrying again?"

"Of course not."

"How come?"

"I'm too old, for one. And besides . . ." Mead couldn't think how to finish. "Well, it wouldn't be right." He quickly returned to his crossword puzzle, feeling the boy still looking at him. And just what did he see? Mead vaguely remembered his own grandfather, who died when Mead was twelve. He seemed less a person than an institution, as old and venerable as the church. And about as much fun. Mead could see him sitting on the porch after dinner, his worn but still noble features slumped in profound thought. Sometimes he'd sit so motionless that he reminded Mead of a statue, the kind covered with pigeon droppings in the town square. As Mead got older it saddened him that he'd never had the chance to know any of his grandparents, to learn how they'd come to terms with all the losses and disappointments and most of all the horrifying realization that your turn is almost over (and you never even played your best cards when you had them).

"How come you never talk about the war?" Andrew asked suddenly.

"No need to." Mead kept his eyes on his crossword puzzle.

"Mom says it's a shame."

"Oh she does, does she? And why would she say a thing like that?"

"Because we'll never learn about your experiences. It's like, family history."

Mead put the puzzle down in his lap. "Family history?"

"That's what she says. I was going to interview you over the phone for a class project, but Mom said you wouldn't talk about the war."

"She said that?"

Andrew nodded. "Other veterans like to talk about it. You always see them on TV explaining how they attacked and what they were thinking and—"

"Some guys love to talk." Mead tapped the tip of his pencil against the puzzle.

"You took part in D-Day, right? Fighting the Germans?"

"That's right."

"Pretty cool."

"I don't think that's the word I'd use."

"Why did you call them Krauts?"

"You know, sauerkraut."

"*Sauerkraut?* I don't get it."

"Never mind." Mead returned to his puzzle.

"Mom says you were a paratrooper, that you jumped out of a plane at night."

Mead nodded.

"That is like, *intense.*"

"I don't recommend it."

"Do you think about it a lot?"

"Not so much."

"I would." Andrew bobbed his head up and down as if in thought. "What kind of weapons did you use?"

"I don't see any need to—"

"I was, just wondering if you had like, a specialty?"

"I was a rifleman."

"Did you have any grenades?"

"We all had grenades."

"And a knife?"

Mead let out a sigh. "And a knife."

Andrew stood up and walked over to the small glass case on the mantle. "What did you get these for?" He looked closely at the decorations.

"Mostly just for being there." After Sophie died Mead had put the medals in his closet, but every time he went to get a shirt or pair of pants and saw the case sitting on the shelf he heard Sophie tisk-tisking him. Finally he put the display back on the mantle and ever since he'd made a point of keeping the house just the way it was when she was alive.

"What about this purple and gold one? The heart?"

"That's for getting wounded."

"Yeah, I thought you'd been wounded. Where did they get you?" His voice was full of curiosity.

Mead arched his eyebrows. "In the buttocks."

"The butt?" Andrew let out a laugh, which he tried to stifle, causing him to make a snorting sound. "That's *bad*." He studied the decorations some more. "Are any of these for heroism?"

"Not exactly." Mead was lying. He earned the Bronze Star for crawling across a snowy field three times under fire to drag men to safety, though it wasn't courage but a sort of blind fury that guided him. But to tell anything left too much unsaid. He looked back down at his puzzle, trying to concentrate on the next clue.

"Are you going to test me on what I'm reading?"

"Hadn't thought to." Mead looked up at his grandson. "What do you think so far?"

"Some of it's interesting. Parts are actually funny."

"Funny?"

"The way they talk. But there are some sad parts, too." Andrew sat back down on the sofa and browsed through the newspaper, then looked back at Mead. "Were you in a lot of battles?"

"Enough." Mead didn't look up from his puzzle.

"Was it really like they show in *Saving Private Ryan?*"

"Never saw it."

"No kidding? Oh man, you'd go nuts. Hey, maybe we could rent it?"

"I don't think so."

Andrew paused, then said, "Mom was right."

"What's that supposed to mean?"

"That you don't like talking about it."

"Why should I?"

"I dunno."

Mead put down his puzzle. "Okay, exactly what do you want to know?"

Andrew thought for a moment. "Did you see a lot of guys get killed?"

"As a matter of fact I did."

"And was it like . . ." Andrew churned his hands in the air.

"Yes, it was."

"Wow, that's got to be harsh. You probably still hate the Germans, huh?"

"Who said I hated them?"

"I just figured that you did."

"Only some of them."

"Like Hitler?"

"Yes, like Hitler."

"I would have hated him, too."

"He was very hateable," said Mead.

"Is that really a word?"

"I'm making it a word." Sophie was always on him for making up words and cheating at his crossword puzzles but the words he used made perfect sense to him. A language, he told her, must constantly evolve.

"What about the Japs? Did you hate them?"

"I guess I did. Just about everybody did."

"More than the Germans?"

"At first."

"Because they look . . . different?"

"Because they attacked us."

"Did you hate being in the army?"

"Parts of it." Actually, Mead hated a great deal of it. Yet what else in his life had even come close?

"I know I'd hate it."

"It's good for some people. Teach 'em a little discipline."

"I'm not dying just so rich people can have enough oil. *No way.*"

"It's not always so simple."

"At least you had real bad guys to fight. They were like, *evil.*" He toyed with the tiny gold hoop in his left ear, a habit that annoyed Mead immensely. "Doesn't Hitler kind of remind you of Darth Vader?"

"Darth who?"

"Never mind." Andrew tapped his earring with his fingernail. "It must be cool being a hero."

"I never considered myself a hero."

"Really?" Andrew looked genuinely surprised.

Mead felt a rising sense of discomfort. "Look, I just did what I had to and couldn't wait to get home, okay?"

"Mom thinks you're a big hero. Even Evelyn thinks so."

"Evelyn?"

"Oh yeah." Andrew smiled.

"I'd really like to finish this puzzle."

"Sorry." Andrew got up from the couch and started toward the hallway, then hesitated. "I was just wondering . . ."

"Now what?"

"Well . . ."

"Out with it."

"Did you ever *kill* anybody?"

Mead took off his glasses and rubbed the bridge of his nose. *You killed lots of them didn't you, Father?* His father had stared back wordlessly at him, a look of deep dismay creasing his hard features—before rising from the table. He didn't return that evening. *Wasn't that the whole point, Father? Killing?*

"Good night, Andrew."

The boy stood staring at him for a moment, then turned and retreated quickly to his room.

· · ·

It was forty-eight hours after dropping into France before Mead knew for certain he'd killed his first man. He'd thought about what it would be like for months, privately dreading the moment when he'd finally find himself in the front row of the whole war effort, as if perched on the tip of a long sword that would be driven deep into the enemy. So few ever saw the front, which he imagined as a thin and jagged fault line where the continental plates collided. But he was airborne, and that's where the airborne would be. The killing zone. Would he hesitate? Or would it come naturally? Some men seemed to have the killer instinct. But not Mead. Instead, he feared he'd have to defy his instincts.

And that's what he'd done.

The Germans were trying to rush in reinforcements to cut off the beachhead and Mead and others were ordered to attack, working their way through the hedgerows and then fighting to take a cluster of heavily defended farmhouses.

"I think we should wait for tanks," said Punchy, lying on the ground next to him and waiting for the order to go forward. While everyone grumbled about army life, few made quite as much noise as Punchy, who howled in protest at every idiotic order and indignity and expended enormous energy explaining exactly how he'd do things differently. "Nothing but numbskulls running the show," he'd say. "My life is in the hands of a bunch of numbskulls." And yet despite his constant complaining, Punchy was always the first to volunteer for the most dangerous assignments, if for no other reason than to assure himself that the job would be done right. As the days went on he became almost reckless in his desire to kill as many Germans as possible and get the war over with.

Punchy popped another piece of gum into his mouth and chewed nervously. (He jumped with twenty packs of Wrigley's as well as twelve Clark bars.) "Don't you think we should wait for tanks?"

"No one's asked me."

"I'm telling you, we should wait for tanks." A few minutes later word spread that the Germans had an 88 hidden behind one of the farmhouses. Punchy was apoplectic. "Ain't this just too-fucking much?" he said, chewing loudly.

Mead had heard plenty about the 88s. They all had. But he'd never seen what they could do. The shells from the flat-trajectory gun hit before you heard them fired, and once you became the prey, there was little to do but crawl into the ground or race forward in hopes that a few survivors would get close enough to kill the gun crew.

The first shell landed to their left, nearly vaporizing two men into tiny beads of red and flaying the bodies of a dozen others. Punchy gestured at Mead to plug his ears and open his mouth to lessen the concussion. Immediately another shell struck to their right as men screamed and the air filled with debris.

"Let's go!"

Punchy was the first man up, letting out a war whoop and running madly across the field toward the farmhouses. Mead scrambled to his feet and forced himself to follow, zigzagging back and forth with his gear bouncing all around as he struggled to keep up. Soon he could see the 88 peering out from behind a barn, the barrel pointed straight at them.

Another shell landed behind him, then another as machine gun fire skipped across the ground in front. Mead found himself yelling at the top of his voice as he ran, all the fear and anger tearing at his throat, as if yelling loud enough might keep him alive. They were closer now so that Mead could see the German gunners frantically reloading and firing one last round, then blowing the breech before dashing for cover. Other Germans shot at them from behind stone walls and buildings.

Mead went through two clips, never quite certain if he'd hit anything. As more men fell to the ground writhing or in silent heaps he looked around desperately for some sign of retreat but instead they continued forward, tossing grenades through windows and kicking down doorways. He watched an American get blown backwards by a grenade as another was shot in the head, and right then he knew he'd made a horrible mistake by joining the paratroopers; that he simply didn't possess the courage—the *fight*—that the others seemed to have. But still he kept up, staying close to Punchy as they leapfrogged from building to building, slowly driving the Germans back. Twice Mead saw a German aim directly at him and fire and twice the bullets missed. But usually he had no idea where the shots were coming from. The Germans had smokeless powder, which made it easier for them to hide, while every time Mead fired his rifle let off a telltale puff of smoke. It was, he thought, like being sent into battle with a cowbell around your neck. As the months passed, Mead would seethe at the realization that the Germans had not only the best artillery piece in the war— the 88—but more powerful and heavily armored tanks and a deadlier anti-tank weapon—the *panzerfaust*—and even a better light machine gun.

And then, right up close, he'd killed his first man, or the first one he was certain of. The German was already wounded, slumped against the remains of a half-track as Mead and others rushed by in a confused assault on German reinforcements who were streaming down the road. There were dead and wounded strewn everywhere, but somehow the German on the ground to his left caught his attention.

Mead turned to look just as the German lifted a rifle that lay across his lap. *You or me.* It was that simple. Nothing to think about or consider. No courage or cunning or skill required. Mead aimed from the hip and fired three times. The first round struck the German in the stomach; the second two hit him in the face. And that was it.

"I wasn't sure you had it in you," said Punchy, offering Mead a piece of gum, which Mead declined.

Mead stared at the dead man, feeling his hands suddenly shake. Jesus, I've done it. I've killed a man. And right there by the side of the road he vomited.

"Hey, take it easy," said Punchy, patting Mead on the back. Mead waved him away, then quickly rinsed his face and mouth with water from his canteen before hurrying to catch up with the others. For the rest of the day he struggled to conceal his queasiness, feeling shame and cowardice all over his face. He was *airborne,* for Christ's sake.

He didn't get another chance for two days. Somehow he was always right on the edge of the action, taking fire but never quite getting a clear line of sight at the enemy. He'd been curious to test himself again, eager, yet terrified, too; afraid he might start shaking again or that he couldn't do it. Best to get it over with, he told himself. Just get through it and then somehow get used to it.

And then, as the Germans sent more troops in, part of Mead's platoon set up an ambush, fourteen of them hidden in the undergrowth on the side of the road. Two hours later, in the last hazy light of dusk, a German patrol came walking down the road. Mead counted twelve of them, spaced several feet apart but obviously off guard, unaware of how far the Americans had penetrated. Mead quietly aimed through the brush, first at the lead soldier, then the next, trying to pick his target and awaiting the signal. *You or me.* That's what it always came down to. But still he felt his hands tingle as he aimed at the chest of a round-faced middle-aged German, his moist finger sliding lightly up and down the trigger. What is your name? Are you married? Do you have children and pets and nieces and nephews? Were you a farmer or grocer or clerk? Are you a God-fearing man? But how could you be? He moved his rifle a few inches to the left and trained it on the next German, who was younger with narrow shoulders and a tired face. Or how about you? What are you thinking about? Your family? Some buxom fraulein? Your feet? Has it occurred to you yet that perhaps Herr Hitler has led you astray; that you and all those you love are on the losing side? And what would you think about if you knew they would be your final thoughts?

It was mesmerizing, watching the last seconds of other men's lives, feeling the godlike power to destroy them, to choose the time and place and method of their death. In the heart or the head? The tall one or the short one? Strange, as if their lives had been on a collision course since birth. A boy from Akron. A boy from Hamburg or Stuttgart or perhaps Cologne. And unexpectedly, the moment of contact had arrived.

"Now!"

Thirty seconds later twelve Germans lay dead.

"That was a damn turkey shoot," said Punchy, wolfing down a Clark bar before searching through the pockets of the dead. Mead kept to the side of the road as the others scavenged for souvenirs, trying to hold back the revulsion in his stomach.

"Hey, look at these," said Punchy, gazing through a pair of German binoculars. "I can almost see Berlin."

Mead lit a cigarette, trying not to look at the crumpled body of the young German with the narrow shoulders.

"You okay?" Punchy asked, coming over to show off the binoculars.

"Sure. Just fine."

"How many you figure you got?"

Mead shrugged. "I don't know."

"I figure I got three of them. The three toward the back. See, I was working from back to front."

Mead nodded.

"You must have got at least two of them."

"No telling."

"I'll bet you got two of them." He looked through the binoculars again, then slapped Mead on the back. "We really surprised the fuck out of them, didn't we?"

"We sure did." And despite the weakness in his legs, Mead knew he could do it again.

• • •

The next morning Mead found a small wrapped box on the front porch. Evelyn, he thought, picking it up and carrying it in. He hadn't seen her out gardening lately and wondered if perhaps he'd been a bit rude the other night.

"Open it," said Andrew, sitting on the sofa in the living room with a bowl of cereal in his lap.

"Maybe later." Mead had always hated gifts. The only time he really lost his top with Sophie was when she threw a surprise birthday party for him, all the wrong people jumping out and screaming in his face when he got home from a terrible day at work.

"Then I will." Andrew took the box, tore off the wrapping and opened it, dumping the contents on the coffee table.

Mead tried to make sense of the pile of little white squares with words on them. Some sort of puzzle?

"They're word magnets," said Andrew. "You put them on your refrigerator and you can write things. You know, like poetry and stuff."

"Poetry?"

"Sure. Lots of people have them."

"On the refrigerator?"

"I told you Evelyn was cool." He scooped up the magnets from Mead's lap and took them to the kitchen. When Mead got up to look Andrew had already returned to his room. On the refrigerator he'd written: *Thanks for not telling*.

Mead pulled off the magnets one by one and placed them in a drawer.

Chapter 5

Eleven more days. Mead lay in bed with the lights off, wondering how to make a difference with the boy in the time they had left. There'd be more talks, of course. He still had to get to the bottom of the thing, find the abscess and root it out. He wondered what book to give him next. He'd never read much about the war himself; no need to. But Sophie read a book a week and loved to rattle on about every chapter. And the librarian had been kind enough to write out a list of recommendations, saying it was her favorite era. "But then, you'd know more about it than me," she had gushed, blushing. Yes, perhaps I would. So what next? Fiction? *The Thin Red Line* or *The Winds of War*? Or stick with the facts: something about the Battle of the Bulge or Stalingrad? (It bothered Mead how few Americans understood that it was the Russians who beat the Germans; that more than eighty percent of German military casualties were inflicted on the *Eastern* Front; that Hitler fought the West with one hand tied behind his back.) He rolled over to his side, then onto his back again. Better yet, something about the Holocaust. Give him a glimpse of real horror. He remembered Sophie reading Elie Wiesel's *Night* and how she cried so hard when she finished it that they both got out of bed and went into the living room and watched the late show until she dozed off.

He rolled back onto his side, fearing that sleep would be difficult. He tried to relax himself by thinking of his father's hardware store where he spent much of his childhood, drawing his first salary at the age of fifteen. Of all the places he remembered in his life, the store was the one place he always returned to—a refuge where he could take his thoughts and feel safe. He often wondered whether it would be the last memory he would cling to in the moment of death; whether everything else would fall away and he'd be a boy again among tools and men. Even now he could still recall the pleasant and unmistakable smell: the sawdust on the floor and the hardened wooden handles of shovels and axes and hammers and the metallic scent of piping and fixtures and bolts and nails brimming from large baskets. There'd been four stores in northern Ohio until the Depression, then just the one. But the war would bring prosperity again. His father was certain of that. (And there would be war, he warned his customers.) Only, he didn't live long enough to enjoy the prosperity. Mead wondered what his father would make of Wal-Mart, to say nothing of his great-grandson. No doubt about it, the old man would have blown a gasket.

After several minutes he opened one eye and glanced at the clock, knowing he'd be up like a rooster in three hours to pee, then again three hours later, usually warming himself a cup of milk before retreating to bed. He heard the neighbor's Jack Russell hurl a few last insults at the neighborhood before retiring for the night.

Mead grew up with retrievers but Sophie had been a cat person. And so they had cats, always two of them slinking around conspiratorially and fleeing every time Mead walked into the room.

"I don't think I've even been able to touch Missy since Thanksgiving," Mead complained. "What's the point?"

"You have to be patient," Sophie responded as Missy purred in her lap.

"I'd say eight months is plenty patient. They don't like me and frankly, I don't like them."

"How can you not like Missy?" Sophie scratched Missy's neck, then held her up to her face and rubbed noses.

"It's easy, my dear."

Mead rolled onto his back again, wondering whether to turn the light on and read.

He missed going into Sophie's room. It was almost a physical craving to be among her clothes and shoes and sit in her rocking chair trying to conjure her. And now the room smelled of the boy, a sour sweaty smell that reminded Mead of the army. It would take days to air the place out. Might even have to shampoo the carpet. And then as he lay there in the dark he suddenly had the awful feeling that Sophie's smell would never come back.

.   .   .

The next day after doing his chores and calisthenics and homework Andrew got his skateboard from the garage and started playing around on the curb out front. He wasn't very good. The nearest skateboard park at home required a ride from his mom so he didn't get much practice (skateboarding was banned just about everywhere else, which drove him nuts). But he treasured his board—Zero deck, Krux trucks, Pig wheels—and the layers of worn stickers that covered the bottom and the sound it made grinding on a curb.

Evelyn came out of her house and watched him. "Very impressive," she said. Andrew smiled proudly. "Mind if I give it a try?"

Andrew's face dropped.

Evelyn let out a laugh. "That was a joke."

A few minutes later Mead emerged from the front door, a look of agitation on his face.

"Hello, General," said Evelyn.

Mead gave her a quick nod as he headed for Andrew. "Exactly what do you think you're doing?"

"He's having fun," said Evelyn.

"I was skateboarding."

"Never heard such a racket."

"Sorry."

"And what the hell are you doing to the curb?" Mead walked over and inspected it. "Look at these marks."

"It's just a curb," said Andrew.

"It's *my* curb," said Mead, grimacing.

"Don't be such a poop," said Evelyn.

"If you don't mind, I think I know how to handle my own grandson," said Mead. He turned back to Andrew. "I trust you can find a more productive way to spend your time." Then he turned and headed back inside.

"Is there a skateboard park around here?" called out Andrew.

"How should I know?" The screen door slammed.

"He does have a grouchy side," said Evelyn.

"It's the only side he has."

"He's just been living alone too long. Of course, God knows I have, too." She smiled, then pulled a small pair of cutters from her pocket and headed for her flower garden.

Andrew stood holding his skateboard, half tempted to keep grinding away, then went inside and looked through the skateboard magazine he'd packed, which had a directory of parks in the back listed by state. He turned to Southern California. Tons of places.

Summoning his courage he took the magazine into the garage where his grandfather sat at a workbench repairing a small wooden birdfeeder. "I was just wondering, are any of these places nearby?"

· · ·

Mead offered to take him to SeaWorld or the zoo instead, but Andrew seemed so eager to go to a skateboard park that Mead finally conceded. Let him have a little fun. The moment they pulled up to the graffiti-covered cement enclosure Mead regretted his decision. In and around the compound—that looked more like a prison yard, only dirtier, with litter piled in the corners—were dozens of baggy butts, each looking ready to jump the nearest bystander. Mead thought of the haunts of his own child-hood: the soupy watering hole where they swam each summer, the ravine where a boy named Joe Figora died of an asthma attack, the woods where he and Tommy Green built a two-story tree house that went up in flames when one of the hobos who passed through left a campfire burning.

Andrew was out of the car before he could stop him, so Mead sat parked next to the cyclone fence with the doors locked and kept watch, try-ing to ignore the glare from a lumpy-looking teenager who leaned against the fence smoking a cigarette with all the attitude he could muster. What a meatball. Has he ever so much as lifted a finger for his country? Does the Bill of Rights mean anything to him? Mead glared back at the boy. Just blind luck he's not freezing in a foxhole with 250,000 Germans on the move, only nobody knows it because Hitler wasn't supposed to have any punches left to throw because the German Army was supposed to be on the verge of collapse. And they just kept coming.

Mead looked over at Andrew, who kept off to one corner by himself kicking his board this way and that as though bent on breaking both ankles. Where was the nearest hospital? Not for miles.

He thought of Evelyn, feeling bad for losing his temper and then guilty for the amount of time he'd spent thinking about her lately. Why had he never really *noticed* her before? Had she had one of those makeovers? He tried to think if there was anything different about her. Did she lose weight? Was it her hair? If only she wouldn't meddle so much. Well, at least he'd put a stop to the little *thing* going on, whatever it was. When Andrew was shipped back to Chicago he wanted nothing but privacy, thank you.

He scrutinized the faces of several teenagers lurking near the entrance to the skate park, trying to gauge which posed the greatest hazard. He couldn't get over how sullen they all looked, many wearing little knit caps on their heads despite the heat, like they were going to rob a bank. No wonder the prisons were bursting. Home of the free and more than a million behind bars, Mead had recently read, which sent him right to the bourbon. And the politicians were all a bunch of blow-dried blockheads.

He decided to give Andrew an hour, but after sitting in the car stewing for thirty minutes he needed a bathroom urgently. That was another reason he didn't like to go out as much, or not without a specific plan of action. He looked over at the small green port-a-potty that sat in the far corner of the park, every inch covered with graffiti. He'd hold it. He waited ten minutes more, then got out of the car and tried to wave down Andrew, but the boy didn't see him.

"Damn," he muttered, locking the car and making his way through a small crowd of baggy butts. They don't even know what tough is, he thought, feeling himself tense as he tried to signal Andrew again.

"Old fart coming through," said a voice.

Mead felt himself blush.

"The wheelchair park's down the road," said another, causing hoots of laughter.

A tall, skinny kid whisked by on his skateboard, nearly knocking Mead over.

"You watch where you're going, young man," said Mead. Oh, to have Punchy and Jimbo with me right now. We could have brought them to their knees just by looking at them.

"Out of the way, gramps."

Would they have been so brave at the sight of a German Tiger rounding a corner, the ground shaking as the huge turret traverses back and forth? Or creeping through the snow on patrol and seeing a concealed German pillbox out of the corner of your eye, knowing they've got you?

Two more teenagers skated past, one of them grazing Mead on the shoulder. Mead held himself perfectly erect as he continued toward

Andrew, the rage making his knees wobbly. People *died* for you, he thought. Maybe even your own grandfather, ground to a pulp beneath the treads of a panzer in Belgium or drowned in the flooded holds of a sinking ship or buried in the malaria swamps of Guadalcanal. Finally Andrew saw him and hurried over. One of the teenagers nearly cut him off, then another clipped him as he passed.

Mead was sweating now, feeling the faint echo of all the power he once had. Could I still take them? Nah, too many. But if I concentrated on that fat one there . . .

"Let's go," said Andrew, a look of panic in his eyes.

"Good idea," said a teenager.

Mead remembered the first time he heard a bullet pass by his ear, how it snapped the air so that he could almost feel it brushing the hairs of his neck, reducing life to a matter of centimeters. Would the next be to the left or to the right? And no matter where they hid, it seemed like the Germans had prepared range cards for every depression in Normandy.

"Come on," said Andrew, pulling at Mead's sleeve.

Mead felt something wet hit his cheek. "Goddamn delinquents," he said, shaking a finger at the growing crowd. "Do you have any idea who you're dealing with?"

"We've *got* to go," pleaded Andrew, standing next to the car and waiting for his grandfather to get in. But Mead took his time, always keeping his eye on the closest teenager. "Your parents would be ashamed of you," he called out the window as he started the engine. An empty soda can hit the back of the car and rolled along the street. Andrew slid low in his seat, quaking.

"You shouldn't have gone in there," he said after several minutes of silence. "I should have warned you."

"I'll go where I damn well please."

"There's always a couple of jerks."

"I've been in worse places."

More silence.

As he drove with his hands gripping the wheel Mead suddenly found himself hoping that Sophie hadn't been watching. He liked to think that she usually was, somehow keeping an eye on him and laughing along at the silliness of things. (And so much of it was silly.) It gave him a secret sense of companionship, helping to make the days endurable. But not today. He had never felt so old before, so frail and humiliated. No, he hoped Sophie hadn't been watching today. Because if she had, it surely would have broken her heart.

. . .

For a brief moment, Andrew had thought his grandfather might take a swing, right there in the skateboard park. It was about the most horrifying thing he could imagine, getting into a rumble with his grandfather. Oh man, they would have been slaughtered. They might even have gotten their pictures in the paper, both lying side by side in some hospital bed, total traction.

Fuck me, that was close.

He couldn't get over the look he'd seen in the old man's eyes, not fear but something scarier. He had always had the feeling that if anybody talked that way to his grandfather they'd die on the spot, that it would not be a survivable encounter. But then, those assholes didn't know what Andrew knew about his grandfather, about the war and the medals and the gun he kept in his bedside drawer. Sarge had stood his ground all right. Still, Andrew couldn't help feeling sorry for him, suddenly seeing how vulnerable he was, being in a place he didn't belong. What the fuck was I thinking?

. . .

"Why did you do it?" Mead asked as they sat in the backyard having dinner that night. They'd hardly spoken since getting home.

"I was going to pay for it. I—"

"I'm talking about the knife. Why did you take a knife to school and pull it on a classmate?"

Andrew stared down at his plate. "I dunno."

"You don't know?"

Andrew shrugged.

"Bullshit."

The word made Andrew wince.

"I'm all ears."

"I guess I was angry."

"And where the hell would we be if we all pulled a knife every time we blew our tops?"

Andrew kept his eyes lowered and rubbed his thighs.

"So this guy picks on you?"

Andrew nodded. "And my friend."

"The one who . . ."

"Matt. He picked on Matt, too."

"I see. So in revenge, you were going to . . . disembowel him?"

Andrew looked up. "I wasn't going to do anything like that."

"Then what the hell were you going to do?"

Andrew hesitated. "I don't know. Show him he couldn't keep picking on me, I guess."

"Because if he did, you'd do what exactly?"

Andrew looked anxiously around the yard. "I didn't think it through like that."

"But you sure as hell should have, don't you think? Because once you start something like that, you better damn well know how it's going to end."

"I guess I figured he'd take me seriously."

"I see." Mead thought for a moment. "You ever seen anybody get cut up?"

"Mostly in the movies. Did you ever see—"

"That's not what I'm talking about."

"I guess I haven't," Andrew mumbled, slapping at a mosquito.

"It's not very pretty."

Andrew flicked the dead mosquito off his arm, then slapped at another one.

"You know what my father would have done if I'd pulled a stunt like that? He would have killed me."

"Really?"

"Really." Actually, Mead had no idea what his father would have done. Such behavior, and the potential consequences, were unimaginable.

"My dad doesn't care what I do."

"Your father is an ass."

Andrew winced again.

"It's bad luck, but that's the truth of it. Nothing you can do but make sure you don't turn out a thing like him."

"I don't think he's an ass."

"Of course you don't. He's your father." Mead considered how to continue. "Look, I know it hasn't been easy for you. The fact is, your grandma and I felt awfully bad about the hand you were dealt. But that's no excuse for this kind of stunt. We all have to take what we're given and make the best out of it. Why, I've known men who've pulled themselves up from circumstances you couldn't even imagine." He could see his grandson's eyes glaze over. If he only understood, Mead thought. By God, just to have both arms and legs and not be shivering and hungry. "You're excused," he said abruptly, feeling his fists tense.

"What?"

"I said, you're excused."

After Andrew went inside Mead slowly finished his steak and potato, then pushed his plate away and sat listening to the rhythmic throb of the crickets.

· · ·

He *was* going to kill Bremer. Another few moments and the big fuckhead would have been dead, slain like the Great Goblin was by Gandalf. *I got him, Matt. You can come back now because I got him.*

Andrew sat cross-legged on the bed looking down at his hands. I would have been a murderer. These would have been the hands of a murderer. He turned his palms back and forth, then imagined them wrapped around the bars of a prison cell, the years crawling by.

He still couldn't believe that he'd done it, or had tried to do it. When he started carrying the knife to school he never thought he'd actually use it; it was just exciting to know that he could, that it was there if he needed it, that he had hidden power. Then one day in the school cafeteria Bremer and several of his football buddies sat down at the corner table where Andrew was eating with Bill Humphrey and Stuart Smith and started making fun of him. He tried to ignore it at first, just letting the heat burn off his face, but then Bremer mentioned Matt. That's when Andrew felt the snapping inside, just like a piece of dry wood breaking in two.

"You really shouldn't cry too much over Shorty. The way I see it, he did everybody a favor." Bremer turned toward his friends. "Little fucker was a stalker. Did you know that? You should read the shit he wrote Megan. Fucking pathetic." Bremer pulled out a crumpled piece of paper from his pocket. "Get a load of this." He put one hand on his heart and began to read in a high-pitched voice.

Dear Megan,
Maybe you're right, maybe I am just a creep. But no matter what you think of me, I'll never regret a single word I've written to you. Sometimes the only thing that gets me through the day is knowing I

might see you (even if you hate me). In fact, I'm starting to think that maybe people like you exist to make up for people like me. Anyway, no matter what happens, at least I'll always know that this stupid world did something right.

Yours forever,
Matt

Bremer slapped his knee and then tore the letter into little pieces, letting them flutter to the ground. "Is that *too fucking much?*"

Andrew looked down at his left hand, watching it slide under the table toward his pants pocket. He didn't even ask it to go. It just went there all by itself.

"It's just a pity you little pussies didn't have some sort of suicide pact."

Andrew watched his other hand slide under the table, then felt the cold metal and heard the click as the blade locked.

"Or maybe you did and you didn't keep your promise? I'll bet that's it. Some friend you are, Sunshine."

Surprise!

Andrew lunged up at Bremer, putting the knife right up under his chin until the tip was pressed against his fleshy skin.

"Jesus Christ!"

"You killed him. You're the one who killed Matt."

"Easy, man. What the fuck are you talking about?" Bremer raised his hands into the air and tried to back off but Andrew followed him in a slow tango across the cafeteria as the crowd of shocked students quickly parted. From the corners of his eyes Andrew saw the gathered faces frozen in disbelief.

"He's got a knife!"

"Oh my God."

"Someone get a teacher."

"Call the police."

"Don't be crazy, Andy."

Crazy? But I am crazy, don't you see? *I'm insane.* He looked again at the faces, faces he'd envied for years, faces of kids who lived in houses and went to parties and dated and had cars and fathers and money. *Why not me?* Tears started rolling down his cheeks as the faces blurred. *Why not me?*

"You killed Matt. You're the one who drove him to it."

"I didn't kill anybody. You're fucking nuts."

"And I'm going to kill you."

"Hey man, calm down. I'm sorry. Let's just talk."

"Someone call the police!"

Andrew stared right into Bremer's eyes, seeing for the first time the look of absolute fear. *How does it feel?*

No matter what else happened, Andrew would always remember the expression on Bremer's face when he realized that Andrew was serious. And no matter what they did to him, he'd always know that he'd finally stood his ground. For once, Andrew was pushing back. He felt the fury building in his chest and shooting out through his arm and fist into the knife until it was shaking. *Watch this, Matt.*

Andrew briefly closed his eyes and gathered everything inside until it was all right there in his arm *push push push* when suddenly Mr. Vickers, the math teacher, grabbed him from behind, knocking the knife from his hand.

"No!"

As he was led through the cafeteria in a blur of tears he heard Megan asking Bremer if he was all right and then Bremer saying, "Sunshine just got his ugly ass expelled."

• • •

Andrew lay awake for an hour, then got up, dressed quickly and placed the fattest joint, his lighter and fifteen dollars in his pockets. Kneeling on the bed he slowly opened the sliding window, then removed the screen and gently lowered it to the ground before crawling out feetfirst and closing the window behind him. Piece of cake. He stopped to listen, hearing only the yap of a neighbor's dog, then quietly made his way through the low hedges to the sidewalk. When he was a block away he reached into his pocket and pulled out the joint, lighting it and inhaling deeply. Precisely what the doctor ordered.

He intended on smoking only half, but he felt so good at the midway mark that he couldn't resist taking his brain cells all the way to town. *Have fun, boys!* He took another deep hit, methodically scanning his central nervous system. *Demons are down 17-0 at the half with no sign of paranoia.* He paused to look into a window where a middle-aged man and woman appeared to be arguing. *She jabs him with a left, then a right . . .* Most of the houses were dark, like little tombs in the Valley of the Nobodies, though occasionally he saw the blue glow of an insomniac who had fallen asleep to the Food Channel.

It took him nearly an hour to walk to the 7-Eleven but only five minutes to convince a Mexican in a rusty pickup sagging with gardening tools to buy him some beer for a five-buck bribe. He downed two Mickey wide-mouths on the spot, then carried the rest in a paper bag, football style. By the time he reached the small park four blocks from his grandfather's house he had already peed twice in the bushes and polished off two more beers.

Cheers, Matt. He opened another beer, raised it in the air and let out a long burp. Then he re-lit the tiny roach and took a deep inhale, determined to obliterate every thought that dared to pop up in his head. *Thought-free at last. Thank God Almighty I'm thought-free at last.* Was there anything good about thinking so much? It seemed like the intelligent thing to do, and he figured he was way ahead of most people when it came to getting the *big picture,* but basically the big picture was depressing as hell. He felt another wave of thoughts approaching. *Take your positions, men. Easy now. Wait until you see the whites of their beady eyes. That's it. A little closer. And a little more. Ready? Fire!* He blasted away with a volley of smoke and beer. Ah, sweet nothingness.

After finishing off the last beer he spent several minutes staring at the street signs wondering why none of the names sounded familiar. Via Flores or Via Fernandez? What the fuck, he'd go by instinct. Once he got close it was just a matter of counting from the corner. Seven houses down on the right—depending on which direction you came from—or was it six? He looked for subtle differences as he passed each house, yet they all seemed exactly the same; white and single-story with a little putting-green of grass on one side of the driveway and maybe a row of flowers and a bush or two on the other. Somebody shoot me if I end up in a dinky little neighborhood like this. He let out another series of burps, then walked into the middle of the street and stood directly beneath the hazy yellow cone of light cast by a street lamp. *How are you all doing out there tonight?* (Deafening roar.) *All right. Got a hell of a show for you.* (Huge waves of applause.) He blew on the mic a few times, then tossed his shoulders back and started singing as he skipped from one yellow stage to the next. *An-drew! An-drew! An-drew!* Just behind the beams of light thousands of Cori

Fletcher clones were dancing and screaming and flailing their arms while panties and bras rained down on the stage. And there right in the front row was Matt sitting with his arm around Megan and giving him the thumbs-up. *This next one's for you, old buddy.* Then the flames of thousands of lighters lit up the night for as far as he could see as he twirled round and round and round from stage to stage.

He was spinning toward the next cone of light when he clipped the fender of a car with his hip, slammed into a telephone pole and flopped face first on the damp grass.

"Whoopsie-daisy."

The street was eerily still as he struggled to his knees, thinking maybe he needed to work on the final number and wondering if he'd passed his grandfather's house yet. But nope, there it was right in front of him. Bingo. Camp Sauerkraut. He tried to stand up but started laughing so hard that he had to sit down again. Jesus, it was all so fucking funny when you thought about it. Sex. Grades. Flossing. Zits. Tits. And people; oh man, people were just *too much.* As far as he could tell, there were basically two types (both miserable): the busy bees—who were terrified of sitting still long enough to give life any serious thought—and the dumb shits, who were incapable of meaningful thought. And Sarge's problemo? Essentially, the old fart was just waiting to die. Come to think of it, a lot of people were like that, killing time in the safest and easiest way possible. Pretty pathetic. He rolled onto his stomach, breathing in the moist green air and thinking that maybe he'd hump Mother Nature if he wasn't so dizzy. Not me, I'm not wasting my life. Noooooo way, José. He rolled to his side and started laughing at the sound of his laughter, which seemed almost girlish. Might just be a teensy-weensy-bit stoned. He gently slapped his cheek a few times, which only made him laugh more. Even Matt's vanishing act was kind of funny in a way because it was just so incredibly unfuckingbelievable.

He sat up and caught his breath, wishing he could pound down a couple of raisin cookies. Then he carefully stood, steadying himself against the telephone pole, and lurched toward the side of the house, plowing through a row of bushes that scratched his face, which was funny too. But fuck it was dark. He tiptoed along a walkway, alternately giggling and then shushing himself, finger to his lips. Now, which window? Eeny, meany, miney moe, my mother told me to count to ten: gotta be that one. He stepped on some plants and nearly tripped over something before reaching the sill. Christ, the window was shut. Had he shut it? Had Sarge busted him? *In the stockade, camper!* He tried to find an edge to get hold of, then pressed his palms against the glass and pushed left, then right. Gradually the window slid open. Hallelujah. First a quick pee, then sleep. He unzipped his pants and leaned against the house, thinking there was no simpler pleasure in the world. When he finished he felt around in the dark with his foot for something to stand on, then tried to peer in the window, feeling a sudden wooziness in his stomach. Uh oh, the spinsies. He grabbed onto the windowsill with both hands. *Just spring up like a panther and in we go.* He reached down and felt his pocket to make sure the roach was still there, then burped one more time before grabbing the sill again and attempting to heave himself up. *Houston, we have a problem.* On his third attempt he managed to get enough of his chest in so that he was one-third inside and two-thirds outside. Half his brain was processing urgent pain signals while the other half couldn't remember the last time anything quite so funny had happened. He tried to suppress a giggle as he kicked his legs. Couple of more inches. He kicked again and felt himself suddenly pitch forward, landing head first on something distinctly harder than a bed.

Luuuccccyy? I'm home! (His mom loved Lucy almost as much as John Denver and Andrew had memorized dozens of episodes.)

He tried to lift himself up, straining to see in the dark and trying to ignore an abrupt request from central command for permission to throw up. *Permission denied!* Beneath him the carpet swayed left, then right. Jesus, an earthquake. Or was it the pot? He giggled and burped as he curled up in a fetal position and waited for the movement to stop. Then again, it could be the pot *and* the Big One. *Ride 'em, cowboy!* He drew his knees to his chest and wrapped his hands around them. Let's see now, is it drop, stop and roll; or rock, stop and roll? Or maybe just stop, rock and roll? The carpet swung left, then right. *Surf's up!* He tried to move with it, leaning into the turns. *Whooo . . . weeeee!!!* You watching this, Matt? The carpet bucked a few times as little red phones in his brain rang off the hook. Maybe if I just close my eyes for a moment. He groped around for the bed, then gave up and lay his head down, letting the carpet take him wherever it wanted to go.

Show's over, folks.

. . .

Mead lay awake in bed that night wondering how much time had passed since he last looked at the clock. Unable to fall asleep, he decided he would at least feign sleep, hoping that every two hours of simulated rest might be worth one hour of the real thing. He still kept to the left side of the queen-size mattress as he always had, and ever since Sophie had died he never allowed his feet or arms to stray across the midline into the cool and vast empty space beside him, as if afraid of what he might find.

He talked to himself in his head for a while (the usual chatter, begun with good intentions—no major catastrophes today, health's holding up—but invariably descending into a grim interrogation, like a dental hygienist probing for sensitive spots), then he shot the breeze with Sophie—mostly listening as she critiqued his grandparenting skills and counseled patience—until finally he succumbed to the random images that flashed across the closed lids of his eyes, lulling him into a sort of drunkenness. They were rarely pleasant images. It was enough if they weren't acutely unpleasant. But tonight he knew they would be—that he no longer had the strength to hold the door closed and keep the faces at bay. And he dreaded it.

. . .

German prisoners had begun clearing the dead, using blankets when there was nothing to grab hold of. On the far side of the town shooting could still be heard. "I can't see doing this all the way to Berlin," said Punchy, lighting one cigarette from another and sidestepping around two German corpses as they marched. They were only a few miles inland from the beaches and German resistance was increasing.

Mead considered the prospect but found it incomprehensible. After three nights with little sleep he struggled to keep his eyes open.

"Someone ought to do the math on this thing, figure out just what it's going to cost per mile," said Punchy.

"I don't think anybody wants to know the answer," said Mead, who had found that he couldn't pass a dead body without looking at the face, despite the looseness in his stomach.

As they walked he kept wondering how his father had dealt with it. What did he feel when he saw the faces and how many faces did he see? Did he wonder about the people he killed or the chances of getting through each day? All his silences around the dinner table and on the porch in the evening now came to life. So that's where you were, Mead thought. You were back looking at the faces.

The sound of small-arms fire drew closer. As they passed six freshly killed Germans, Punchy and several other men stopped to quickly search through the dead men's pockets.

"What are you doing?" said Mead.

"Shopping, what else?" said Punchy, sliding his hand deep into the pants pocket of a German sprawled on his back with his mouth open.

"It's not right."

"Fuck off, Mead," said Tom Anson, a tobacco farmer's son from North Carolina who had a big mouth and short temper. "You think these Krauts care?"

Mead watched as Anson pulled off the belt buckle from the pants of one of the bodies and passed it around proudly. "My dad's gonna love this."

"I'm just telling you, it's not right," said Mead, this time just to Punchy, who was now removing a watch from a limp wrist.

"You know your problem, Mead? You're a goddamn choirboy."

Once the bodies had been stripped of all valuables the men moved on. When they reached a Y in the road marked by a large World War One memorial, two squads headed left and two veered right, everybody strung out and fingering their weapons. They passed several dead horses, a smoldering German half-track and a Panther tank, both treads separated. More gunfire, now just blocks away. Mead felt the fear in his intestines, snaking right through them.

"I hate these towns," said Punchy. "Put me in a forest anytime." They slowed their pace, cautiously aiming their rifles down each alleyway as they passed. "Why don't we just go around the towns and surround the bastards?"

"Because nobody asked us."

Punchy spat out the butt of his cigarette as a long burst of machine-gun fire erupted a few blocks ahead. "You know the problem?"

"Which one?" said Mead, aiming his rifle at a doorway, then at a bay window.

"We're completely expendable."

"Thanks for the reassurance."

"It's true. I mean, who really cares? It's not like ol' Ike's gonna run out of fodder."

"You know, Punchy, sometimes you really get on my nerves."

"Hey, I'm just talking. I feel better when I talk."

"I noticed."

Punchy started humming the melody to "Oh, What a Beautiful Mornin'" while Mead looked nervously at the upper windows of the two-story buildings on his left and right, wondering which one a sniper would choose.

It would be suicide. The sniper might get off a few shots before being killed himself. Mead had been taught that snipers generally preferred more favorable rules of engagement, carefully plotting their escape route and shooting only individual soldiers isolated from the rest. But he quickly learned that the German Army possessed a plentiful supply of men willing to face certain death in the interests of the fatherland, even if only to gain the retreating army a few minutes time. As he walked he imagined his head in the cross hairs of a rifle sight. A little to the left, a little to the right. Gently squeezing the trigger. *Now!*

"I'm telling you, Mead, we should go *around* the towns."

Mead's eyes went from window to window as rivulets of sweat ran down his face. I'm going to die, aren't I? He thought of all the bravado he had once felt, secretly assuming he had some sort of immunity. But I'm no different after all. Will he aim for my head or my chest? Soon the fear became so overwhelming that he had to struggle to control his bladder. *Please, not me.*

The first bullet struck Anson in the head, piercing his helmet. Mead dove left for the cover of a doorway when the next shot cracked. He felt it before he heard it; not pain but a smacking sensation against his gear. He crouched down and fired blindly at the windows as more gunfire erupted at the far end of the street.

Then he felt blood seeping through his pants. First a trickle then a flood of it so that he knew he'd pass out within minutes. "I'm hit!" he called to Punchy, who was crouched nearby. He fired off another round before sliding to the bottom of the doorway and curling into a ball, feeling the wetness soak through his undershorts.

Punchy crawled over, grabbed the first aid kit strapped to his helmet and looked for the wound.

"Gotta stop the bleeding," said Mead, trying not to faint.

"Where is it?"

"Down there. My waist, my crotch. Oh God, I'm not sure." Mead closed his eyes and rocked his head back and forth, knowing he wouldn't have the courage to die well. *Jesus, Sophie, I'm dying. And I knew it too. I knew I'd never make it.* He felt the blood stream down his thighs. *That must have been the deal: I could find you, Sophie, but I couldn't keep you. How could I have expected more?*

"I can't find it," said Punchy.

"What the hell do you mean, I'm soaked through," gasped Mead, desperately feeling his pants with his hand, horrified at what he might find.

Suddenly Punchy let out a burst of laughter. "I'll be damned, Mead, they shot your canteen."

"What?"

"They shot your goddamn canteen. It's water, you stupid son of a bitch! Your canteen just kicked the bucket."

"Water?" Mead sat up and stared down at his crotch in disbelief, as if time had suddenly folded back on itself. And then for the first time since he was a kid he let himself weep.

· · ·

Andrew woke to the sound of an answering machine. The telltale pause and then the beep made him think he was back home for one brief, sweet moment. Then the voice came on.

"Hi, Mom, it's me. I just got off the phone with Dr. Coleman and he says you haven't been in for *any* chemotherapy treatments. Mom, are you there? I want to know what's going on, Mom. Mom? I'm going to call you right back." Dial tone.

Andrew unglued one eye, revealing a close-up cutaway of a thick white carpet; then the second eye, which gave a slightly elevated perspective and included the animal-like legs of a dresser. Very, very interesting. It wasn't anything like the afterlife he had in mind—silk sheets, Cori at his side, ocean view—but neither was it even remotely familiar. He closed both eyes, then opened them again, hoping another click of the View Master would clear things up.

The phone rang again. "Hello, Mom? It's me again. *Please* pick up." Pause. "I just hope you know how selfish you're being." Sniffle sniffle. "This is really serious, Mom. Mom? Answer me, Mom." Dial tone.

Andrew sat up, panic now shrieking through his central nervous system.

The phone rang again. "Okay, Mom, if you won't talk then I'm going to spell it out and you can just *listen*. Without chemo you have maybe a year to live—*max*. You're only seventy-four, Mom. That's *young*. And why won't you meet with the realtor? You know we agreed that you'd have to sell the house. Did you look at the statements I sent you? You have to face *reality*, Mom. Peter blew *everything*. Those stocks are not coming back." Pause. Sniffle sniffle. "None of this would have happened if you'd listened to me."

Andrew closed his eyes and covered his ears, desperate to block out the mounting evidence suggesting that he'd been reincarnated as someone's disease-ridden mom—he always assumed that reincarnation would be a step up—when the door opened.

"What on earth are you doing here?"

Andrew opened his eyes again and saw Evelyn staring down at him. *Holy shit.* "Evelyn?"

She looked almost as surprised as he was. "Andrew. How did you get in here?"

"Well, I, uh . . . can I get back to you?"

Evelyn looked behind him at the open window, then bent down and touched his forehead. "Your poor face is all scratched and you're a muddy mess."

Andrew looked down and noticed the dirt and grass stains on the white carpet. "Sorry."

She closed the window, then got a tissue and dabbed his face. "I don't suppose you'd care to explain?"

Andrew slowly sat up, trying to ignore the sensation of blood vessels bursting in his head. "Do I have to?"

"Yes. Does your grandfather know where you are?"

"Exactly *where* am I?"

"In my study."

"Oh." Andrew looked around the room, which was so bright and uni-formly white—even the wicker chair and desk and dresser were white—that he momentarily reconsidered whether he had in fact died.

"He's going to be worried sick about you."

"He's going to kill me."

"You've been drinking."

Andrew put a hand over his mouth. "What makes you think that?"

She frowned, yet he was encouraged by the persistent kindness in her face. Time for a major charm offensive. Maybe she'd even hide him for a few weeks until things calmed down, then drop him off at the Mexican border. He slowly got up, feeling so lightheaded he thought he might tip over.

"You're going to have to be completely honest with me if you want any help," she said, steering him to a chair. Then she went out, returning with a warm hand towel and a glass of water. "So?"

Andrew guzzled down the water, then glanced over at the window. *You dumb shit.* "Well, see, I thought I'd just stop by to tell you how much my grandfather liked those poetry magnets and . . ." She crossed her arms in front of her chest and shook her head disapprovingly. "I guess I may have had one or two beers on the way."

"Aren't you a little young for that?"

"I didn't make the laws."

She put her hands on her hips and looked him over as if deciding whether or not to toss him back into the water. "You two have been having problems, haven't you?"

"It's like boot camp. The guy's a freak—but he did like the poetry magnets. I think he even wrote a poem about you."

"The General?" She laughed.

"Not a great poem, but there's definite feeling."

"Listen, Andrew, your grandfather is just a lonely old man who doesn't know how to handle a teenager, that's all. He's doing the best he can and you should be proud of him. He's a genuine hero you know."

"Don't remind me."

She kneeled down in front of him and patted his face with the warm towel. "What about you?"

"What about me?"

"I can tell a troubled soul when I see one." She put her hand on his forehead and brushed aside his hair.

"It's just that I . . ." And then without warning Andrew was spilling big hot tears all over the place.

He told her almost everything—except for stealing Matt's ashes, which seemed over the top—then turned bright red and apologized for saying anything at all. *I must be cracking up.* But the hangover had left him feeling so raw and unguarded that he hadn't been able to stop himself. And for the first time in his life he felt that someone actually wanted to listen.

"You're a real piece of work, do you know that?"said Evelyn.

"Thank you."

She sat down on the arm of his chair. "When I was about your age—maybe a few years older—I made a mistake that changed the rest of my life."

"What happened?"

She paused. "The short of it is, I got pregnant."

"Really?"

"Really. George was the father. He was just a kid too—how naïve we were!—but he was decent enough to marry me and help raise our child."

"So it worked out."

She shook her head slowly. "Yes and no."

"What do you mean?"

"I'm afraid we just didn't love each other."

Andrew sat speechless, briefly forgetting the strobe-like pulsing in his head.

"Oh, we got along all right, and I still miss him. He was a good man. But it wasn't love—at least not what I'd always dreamed of."

"You could have divorced him."

She folded her hands in her lap. "No, I couldn't have."

"Why not?"

"Because sometimes we can walk away from our mistakes and sometimes we can't." She stood and went over to the window, her back to Andrew. "Over the years I've come to think of life as this long corridor lined with doors and we only have the time and strength and good fortune to open a few. And the catch is, we never know if we opened the right ones." She turned back toward him, trying to smile. "As for the rest of them, I suppose that's what dreams and books and movies and songs are for."

"I haven't opened a good door yet."

She laughed. "Maybe your luck is about to change."

"Maybe there are no good doors." Andrew tried to ignore a bubbling sensation in his stomach.

"Or maybe there are really no bad doors." She glanced over at the answering machine, which was flashing. "I suppose you heard my darling daughter?"

"I might have heard something."

"She can be a little pushy."

"Who's Peter?"

"My son—the financial wizard." She sighed and Andrew wondered if she was going to cry. *Fuck, what a morning.* "So now we both have secrets." She held his eye a moment, then got him a glass of orange juice and a piece of toast while he went to the bathroom. He peed for several minutes before biting off an inch of Crest toothpaste and working it through his teeth. *I will never ever drink again.*

"The first thing we have to do is get you home."

"You mean you won't tell my grandfather?"

"We have to tell him something."

"He'll kill me."

"Why don't you leave this to me?" She headed him toward the front door.

"Can I have a cookie first?" No point in dying on an empty stomach, he figured, hoping to resolve some serious blood-sugar issues.

She smiled and retrieved two enormous raisin cookies from a tin, then watched with amusement as he wolfed them down. They had just reached the end of her narrow brick walkway when the door across the street opened and Mead ran out.

"Where in God's name—"

"Good morning, General," said Evelyn calmly, firing off an enormous smile that seemed to waft across the street and stop Mead in his tracks. Mead glared at Andrew while Andrew stayed close to Evelyn and averted his eyes. "Andrew was just helping me with my rosebushes out back. Poor thing got all scratched up." She pinched Andrew's cheek.

Mead's large jaw dropped open. That morning he had waited until eight to open Andrew's door, thinking he'd cut the boy a little slack. At first he thought his grandson was buried somewhere beneath the pile of sheets, skinny as he was. Then in a panic he had checked the bathroom and garage twice before charging out the front door. He looked down at his watch. "It's *eight-oh-five* in the morning. . . ."

Evelyn turned to Andrew. "I didn't mean to interrupt your morning run."

"Morning run . . ."

Andrew's sleepy-looking face—the boy looked *awful*—sprung to life. "Oh, gosh, no problem." He looked at his grandfather. "Yeah, see, I couldn't sleep so I was up early. Thought I'd get in a little exercise before breakfast, but then I bumped into Evelyn . . ." The boy smiled hopefully.

"He's quite handy in the garden," said Evelyn. "Must take after his grandfather."

"Morning run . . ."

Andrew beat back several algae-green waves of nausea as Evelyn peppered his grandfather with questions. God, she's brilliant.

"I wonder if it would be too much to ask your help in moving a planter box?"

Mead finally took his eyes off of Andrew. "Of course not."

"I'll just go clean up," said Andrew, flashing his grandfather his toothiest smile before sliding past him and dashing into the house. *Whew.* Once he got to his room he leaned out the window, picked up the screen and secured it back in place. Then he hurried to the bathroom, stripped off his clothes and got into the shower, turning the temperature up as hot as he could stand. When his body was covered with suds he burst into song, feeling giddy despite his pounding head. That was *very, very* close.

Chapter 6

Mead couldn't help notice that the amount of time he spent thinking about Evelyn was encroaching on the amount of time he spent thinking about Sophie. It was like a gala ball going on in his head and he was the only eligible dance partner.

He knew nothing about her except that she had aged remarkably well and baked and gardened with a vengeance and made his grandson laugh hysterically. He'd made a point of never asking many personal questions, not wanting any in return. But he found himself wondering more and more about her. Had she ever gone a whole day without thinking of George? Was she lonely? (But why did she always seem so damn chipper, like she'd just won the Publisher's Clearinghouse Sweepstakes?) What exactly went through her mind when she gardened? (Did she ever think of him?) And yet he resented her too, both because of the way Andrew transformed in her presence, as if she was God's gift to grandchildren, and because he knew that even his thoughts would break Sophie's heart.

Best to leave well enough alone.

And yet he found himself spending more and more time working in his front yard in hopes of seeing her. When he ran out of ways to look busy—the lawn was soon waterlogged as well as dangerously overfertilized—he even started shooting hoops, much to Andrew's horror.

"Morning, General."

"Oh, good morning, Evelyn." He jumped especially high for the next shot, but missed.

"I didn't realize you were such a late bloomer." She was grinning.

Mead blushed. "Just keeping the blood flowing."

She watched him shoot a few more baskets, none of which he made, then Andrew came outside and joined them briefly, wincing every time his grandfather took a shot.

"Why don't you two play?" asked Evelyn. "I'll cheerlead."

"What do you say?" said Mead, holding out the ball.

Andrew shrugged. "I've got a lot of homework." Then he turned and shuffled back inside, the seat of his pants positioned right behind his knees.

"He cuts quite a figure, doesn't he?" said Mead.

"He loves you very much."

"He doesn't have a lot of grandparents to choose from." Mead took another shot, missing again.

"He told me about what happened at school."

Mead picked up the ball and dribbled.

"Don't be too hard on him. He's just a very confused young man. But he's got a big heart. You should be proud of that."

"Like I said, we're doing just fine."

"Of course. Let me guess, he's Costello?"

Mead wanted to tell her to mind her own business, to just leave them be, and yet her face was full of such compassion that he actually thought of kissing it. Was she even seventy? "We may have hit a few bumps . . ."

"You know what I think he needs?"

Mead felt himself tense.

"A big hug. He's a frightened, lonely sixteen-year-old who desperately needs a little TLC right now."

"Is there anything else I should know?" Mead said testily.

Evelyn came closer and looked at him in a way he hadn't been looked at in years. "Just that you seem to need the same thing." Then she smiled and walked away.

• • •

The next morning at nine Mead left for an eye appointment, leaving Andrew alone only after he complained of a stomachache. "If you so much as step off the premises I'll have you locked up." Andrew watched from the living room window as his grandfather's car crawled down the street, then quickly went and pulled out the gun from the bed stand drawer. It seemed even heavier than before and this time Andrew carried it around the house pretending to aim at things. *Freeze!* He fingered the trigger, wondering how hard you had to squeeze and how many rounds it held. What he'd give to fire off a few. *Bam bam bam.* He'd love to see the look on Bremer's face with this jammed up his ugly nose. "What did you call Matt?"

"I was just kidding, Andrew. I promise."

"On your knees, asshole."

Andrew pretended to draw the pistol from a holster on his hip, thinking how awesome it would be to have all that power right there where you could reach it. *Better saddle that horse and ride out of town, cowboy.* Then he sat down in his grandfather's blue, overstuffed chair and held the pistol up to his face like he was about to count off paces in a duel. That's what he could do: challenge Bremer to a duel. Ten paces, then *bang!* He aimed the pistol at the dartboard, then got up and hid behind his grandfather's chair, pretending to ambush an intruder. *Bang bang!* Finally he rolled onto his back on the carpet and held the pistol up to his face, turning it this way and that and laughing to himself. Life and death right in the palm of your hand. He placed his finger gently on the trigger and aimed. *Sweet dreams, sucker.*

After carefully returning the pistol he made himself a tuna sandwich and boiled more batteries, then opened the hallway door leading to the one-car garage. There was a workbench with tools hanging neatly from a rack above it, an old-fashioned stationary bike, the manual lawn mower, a metal stepladder, a row of garden tools, and, on a large storage shelf built high on the back wall, several large, labeled boxes. Andrew took the ladder and leaned it up against the shelf, then carefully climbed until he could read the labels. *Christmas lights. Ornaments. Halloween. Cookbooks. Photographs.* He wondered if his grandfather still decorated the house for Halloween. It was hard to imagine him welcoming trick-or-treaters. *Bug off, you urchins!* Actually, it was hard to imagine any trick-or-treaters in the neighborhood.

Andrew climbed up another rung of the ladder and pushed one of the boxes aside. Behind it was another row of boxes and to the left a dark green wooden trunk. He moved another box aside and saw his grandfather's name stenciled in white on the trunk. Army stuff, he thought. This I gotta see.

He had to carry down two boxes marked *Christmas* to make enough room on the shelf to slide the trunk forward and open it. The first thing he pulled out was a folded cap that lay flat on top of a uniform. He opened the cap and looked closely at the patch sewn on the front depicting an open parachute, then tried the cap on, saluting. *Yes, sir!* Then he removed the top of a uniform, pausing to study the large patch on the left shoulder showing an eagle's head with AIRBORNE written above it in yellow. Pinned just above the left breast pocket were several colored bars and beneath them a silver badge depicting a long rifle against a light blue background. Must have been a big cheese. He unbuttoned the coat and tried it on, putting his nose into the crook of his elbow to smell the musty fabric. It was several sizes too large for him.

Next he pulled out a pair of large brown leather boots. Real combat boots. Probably even stepped in blood. He ran his fingers along the twelve pairs of eyelets and tugged at the ends of the leather thong laces, then turned the boots over and examined the worn soles, pausing to listen to the sound of a passing car. He pressed his thumbs against the reinforced toe before putting his hand inside one of the boots, surprised by how uncomfortable it felt.

After browsing through some sort of army manual, he found a small knife tucked in a white sock and a larger one in a dark green sheath lying next to it. The smaller knife was nearly identical to the one his grandfather had given him. He opened the blade and tested its sharpness. Not bad. Mead's name was engraved on the blade, just like Andrew's. Then he picked up the larger knife and drew it from its sheath, enjoying the feel of the wooden handle. Double-edged, especially for killing. He ran his thumb lightly along both blades, looking for traces of blood, then raised the knife into the air and made several jabbing motions. *Die, Jew killer.*

After placing the knives on the pile next to the trunk he removed two pairs of pants, exposing a wooden cigar box and a larger box made of metal. This is getting good. He opened the wooden box first. Inside were various medals and patches as well as his grandfather's dog tags. Very cool. He put the silver dog tags around his neck, then picked up a tarnished-looking badge in the shape of a square cross with three separate metal bars hanging from it. The top one read, "rifle," the middle one, "carbine," and the last one, "pistol." GI Joe must have been a pretty good shot. He looked at some of the other items, placing them in his palm one at a time and wondering what they meant. From the bottom of the cigar box he pulled out a small, blue cardboard box containing a medal wrapped in tissue. On one side was a woman holding a broken sword along with the words, WORLD WAR II. Turning it over he read, FREEDOM FROM FEAR AND WANT, FREEDOM OF SPEECH AND RELIGION. What about freedom from assholes? he thought, chuckling. He tested the medal with his teeth, then put it back in the box, cleared a space and placed the large, black metal box on his knees, excited by its weight.

As he lifted the lid he felt his face flush. Nazi stuff. And a fucking Luger.

Andrew didn't know much about guns but he knew what a Luger looked like. Who wouldn't recognize that distinctive, rounded handle, or whatever they called it, and the narrow barrel? Lugers were like, *the* Nazi pistol. And everybody knew that the German Army had the coolest-looking stuff. Even when he was younger and watching army shows, Andrew saw right away that the Sauerkrauts had better-looking uniforms and helmets and tougher-looking tanks and those wicked hand grenades on a stick and awesome desert cars that Rommel cruised around in. When Andrew and his friends played army with little plastic figures it was always a fight over who got to be the Germans, because even the plastic soldiers and weapons looked better. And here he was holding a fucking Luger. *You talking to me? Bamm!*

After toying with the pistol for several minutes he returned it to the metal box and searched through the other contents, first pulling out three different Nazi medals, surprised by how shiny and new they looked, the red and black colors still full of evil power. Too fucking much, he thought, holding them up to his face. And then there was a silver watch that fit loosely on Andrew's narrow wrist, a small Leica camera and a belt buckle with an eagle standing on a swastika. Next he picked up a small flat object wrapped in green felt, trying to guess what it was. No clue. Carefully unwrapping it he uncovered a piece of a fancy-looking dinner plate with a gold design along the rim. Very weird. Probably one of those decorative plates, he decided, maybe even some sort of award. That's it, and Sarge must have dropped it during the ceremony. Andrew snickered at the thought, then put it back.

At the bottom of the box, wrapped in a handkerchief, Andrew found an oval dog tag, a black leather wallet and a worn booklet of some type. He put the dog tag around his neck, then carefully opened the booklet, tensing at the sight of a face staring back at him from a black-and-white photo attached to the inside left page and partially covered with a Nazi stamp. He thumbed through the pages, which were covered with handwriting. Several came loose as he turned them. Must be some sort of army record. He turned back to the first page. Hans Mueller. Hans the Jew killer. He stared closely at the photo. The first thing that struck him was how young the face looked, practically his age, the dark hair cut extremely short on the sides with a bit more length in the front. Frankly, he didn't really look German, not in the Evil Empire way that Andrew imagined. He was actually kind of sorry-looking, with droopy ears and a large, shiny forehead, so that his eyes didn't start until halfway down his face.

So how did his grandfather get hold of this stuff? Was the guy dead? Captured? He studied the face again and decided the guy was dead; definitely something doomed about the eyes. Maybe his grandfather even killed him with the pistol he kept by his bed. Andrew tried to imagine the encounter, his grandfather sneaking up on the German sentry, then, *bang,* right between the eyes, blood and brains everywhere.

From the wallet Andrew pulled out five worn German banknotes. Nazi money. Must be worth a fortune. He put the bills back and pulled out three photos from a smaller sleeve, their edges frayed. There was mom and dad and a little girl standing in the front yard of a house, none of them smiling. Then another of just mom—a real sourpuss—and then one of a teenage girl, probably a girlfriend. Not bad looking, actually, though the hairstyle was kind of goofy, all wavy and parted way on the side. On the back were several lines of handwriting in German. He tried to imagine what the words might say. *Keep your head down? Kill a few for me? I'll always be waiting for you?* Was she still waiting?

He put the wallet down and picked up a round silver medal that hung from a red ribbon with a single thin black stripe and two white stripes running down the middle. The medal itself depicted an eagle, a swastika, a helmet and a grenade. Was it for killing Americans? Or maybe gassing Jews? *Well done, Hans, you son of a gun.* He held it up to his chest. *Heil, Hitler!* Man, if only Matt could see this stuff. He'd freak.

And then he started thinking: what if I took a few things? It wasn't like his grandfather ever looked in the trunk. Hell, he didn't even like to talk about the war. So basically, there was no way he'd notice if a few things were missing. Or when he did he'd be so old he wouldn't remember what he had in there in the first place. I could even take the medals and Nazi cash and gun to a pawn shop, get some serious money. Then maybe buy a sports car and head for Mexico. Sort of a Nazi scholarship.

He froze as a car passed, then quickly stuffed the three medals and the wallet into his pockets and grabbed the Luger before returning the rest of the stuff to the trunk, careful to fold up the coat he'd been wearing. After putting all the boxes back on the shelf, trying to remember which went where, he removed the ladder, went to his room and hid everything beneath the mattress. He was just getting out his homework when he heard his grandfather pull into the driveway.

• • •

"I thought we might go to the beach this morning," said Mead when Andrew finally emerged from the bathroom, which Mead had staked out for ten minutes.

Andrew let out a low grunt.

"Your enthusiasm is infectious." Mead hurried past to relieve himself.

"Sure, I'll go." Andrew hung in the doorway while Mead struggled with his zipper.

"Mind shutting the door?"

"Sorry."

Mead couldn't keep himself from groaning with relief. Hell, any farther than the beach and he'd need a catheter.

"You okay in there?"

"Of course I'm okay." When Mead opened the door Andrew was still standing there. "Yes?"

"Just making sure you're okay."

They were pulling out of the driveway when Andrew suddenly shouted, "Wait!"

The car lurched to a stop. "Jesus, good thing I don't have airbags."

"Sorry."

"Have you got to go again already?"

"No."

"Then what?"

Andrew looked across the street as he fiddled with his earring. "Well, I was just wondering if maybe we could ask Evelyn to come along? I'm sure she's not doing anything and she loves the ocean and—"

"How do you know she loves the ocean?"

"Because she's a nature freak." He opened the car door.

"Stop right there."

Andrew froze.

"It's awfully last-minute."

"It's *spontaneous*." He offered a big cheesy smile. "Please?"

Does the boy have a thing for older women? Granted, she certainly brought out the best in him. And wasn't that exactly what Mead had been trying to do? He looked over at Evelyn's house, thinking of her all alone with her cookies and flowers. Oh, what the hell, if it helps. "Okay, but tell her to make it snappy if she wants to join us." Andrew was already off and running across the street.

"Are you sure you don't mind me tagging along?" Evelyn asked for the second time as Mead drove.

"Of course not." He rolled down his window further, feeling disoriented by her perfume.

"Well, I'm just delighted." She gave him a quick pat on the knee.

Mead was careful to position them right in front of the lifeguard tower and this time Andrew stayed closer to shore, hovering near a cluster of girls bobbing and squealing in the surf.

"I haven't been to the beach in months," said Evelyn, sighing contentedly as she and Mead sat side by side in matching beach chairs. With her oversized sunglasses and widebrimmed straw hat she reminded Mead of Sophie, who'd been buzzing around his head for the last hour like an angry bee.

"You should have brought your suit."

"I did." She smiled as she snapped one of the shoulder straps beneath her billowy white shirt.

"Oh."

A teenage girl in a silver thong bikini paused directly in front of them and began adjusting her suit with a series of tweaks. Mead quickly turned his attention to his canvas beach bag, as if looking for something.

"Maybe I'm old-fashioned, but I always liked the idea of leaving something to the imagination," said Evelyn. "Of course, at my age there's not much left to imagine."

Mead rummaged even deeper into his bag.

"Not that there ever was." She laughed as she worked her bare feet into the sand. Mead noticed that her toes were painted, which surprised him. "What annoys me most about getting older is that I feel entirely misrepresented by my body." She swept her hands from her face down to her torso and legs. "It's like I've got on this wretched costume and the zipper's stuck."

"I hadn't thought of it quite that way." Mead shooed away a seagull that had taken an aggressive interest in his feet.

"My mother used to say that old age was like a hideous masquerade ball."

"What a pleasant thought."

Evelyn laughed, then pointed toward a passing woman who looked to be in her twenties with long shiny hair and shapely hips. "Just wait until she sees her costume."

"I'd have to say that I feel consistently old through and through," said Mead. "I guess you might say I'm evenly cooked."

"Don't you start with your weary-old-soul routine." She waved a finger at him.

"I didn't know I had a routine."

"Oh, you've got it down perfectly. Unfortunately, it's a big waste of time."

Mead felt anger rising to the surface of his skin. Who was she to keep passing judgments?

"I don't mean to be rude, it's just that, well, what's the rush?"

Mead couldn't think of how to respond. Instead he stared out over the water and tried to ignore a slight tug of melancholy. Did the ocean make other people sad?

"There's something I've been meaning to talk to you about," said Evelyn, not looking at him.

Mead tensed. Even Sophie seemed to tense.

"This isn't easy for me."

"We could skip it."

She smiled, though her face was creased with nervousness. Then she took in a loud breath. "I have an apology to make."

"You're forgiven."

She looked perplexed. "What is it you think I'm apologizing for?"

"Let's just say that teenagers are never easy to deal with."

"This has nothing to do with Andrew."

"Oh."

She took another loud breath. "Okay, here goes: I want to apologize for writing those silly poems years ago. I know it wasn't right. I guess I just—"

"What poems?"

She looked at him in surprise, her eyes shifting back and forth between his. "But you must have gotten them. I sent, I don't know, probably three or four to your office years ago. I know it was a stupid thing to do. I didn't mean any harm from it. That's why they were anonymous, though I figured you'd probably guess. I was just so . . ." She suddenly lost her composure.

Mead sank back into his beach chair. "That was you?"

"Who did you think it was?"

"I . . . well, I don't know. I mean I . . ." He felt his face turning such a deep crimson that he wanted to pull his hat down over it.

Evelyn turned back toward the ocean and kneaded her hands together. "But I thought you knew. I thought that's why . . ."

"Why what?"

"Why you've always ignored me."

Mead looked out at Andrew, who was still stalking a group of girls. *I oughta wring his little neck for setting me up like this.* And yet it was so much more pleasant to think that the poems—which had actually been rather good—had come from Evelyn rather than six-foot-three Frances in accounting. He felt a ticklish sensation on the skin of his chest and cursed himself for not saving them, wishing he could remember exactly what she had written.

"I've embarrassed you."

"No, I mean, well, it's a little . . . awkward." Sophie was now buzzing in his ear so loudly that he wondered if Evelyn could hear it.

"I had no right to send them to you."

"There's really no need to go into it."

"I must seem so pathetic to you; a married woman sending poetry to her neighbor." She slowly spun a silver bracelet she wore on her left wrist. "You see, for some reason I got it into my head that I had a talent for poetry—I must have submitted dozens to various magazines, I think I still have the rejection letters—and I just wanted someone to read them; someone who might enjoy them. Someone like . . . you."

Mead cleared his throat and adjusted his hat.

"God knows, George wasn't interested." She sighed. "Anyway, I hope you can forgive me. I was just very confused—or lonely, to tell the truth. I just had so much inside of me and I didn't know what to do with it." Her voice began to crack. "And there you were every day, right across the street. You don't know how many times I watched out the window as you came home from work or washed your car or mowed the lawn. Sometimes it felt like that street was a thousand miles wide."

Mead sat speechless.

"Well, at least I've said it." She tried to smile.

Mead started to say something when suddenly Andrew came bounding up the beach, dripping wet. "Who's going to join me?"

"Not—"

"I will," said Evelyn, standing and taking off her hat.

"If she's going in, you've got to go in," said Andrew to Mead, all smiles.

"I do?"

"If you want to be a gentleman." He winked before sprinting back into the water.

·   ·   ·

They played in the waves for an hour. Mead could hardly think straight at first, and he felt horribly self-conscious stripping down to his bathing suit in front of Evelyn. (This ought to cure her ardor, he thought, as he looked down at his pale and flaccid abdomen.) Yet soon he was immersed in the simple joy of anticipating each wave, bracing himself or diving into the soft underbelly of the larger ones and enjoying the briny taste on his lips. He made a point of trying not to look too often at Evelyn, though he quickly got the general gist. She was in surprisingly good shape with long legs and a nice little rump—for her age—yet a bit thin. He'd noticed that even her face seemed thinner lately. Not enough meat, he decided.

If only he could remember the poems. And what did she mean about him ignoring her all these years? Maybe he'd kept his distance, but hell, he'd been happily married. And then after Sophie died he was too blinded by grief to notice much of anything. But now seeing her wet and laughing as she greeted each wave like guests to a raucous party was almost more than he could bear.

"Isn't this fun?" she said, standing right next to him and springing up through a wave as it rolled past. Andrew was whooping and splashing next to her.

Mead nodded with a broad smile.

· · ·

On the way home they stopped at a surf shop where Mead bought Andrew a couple of T-shirts—"as long as they don't have Satan on them." Andrew spent forty-five minutes trying to whittle down his choices, holding them up one at a time as he posed before the mirror with Evelyn at his side. Mead enjoyed watching the excitement on the boy's face, though frankly it seemed a bit excessive. Did he really think a few overpriced T-shirts would turn the tide? Evelyn seemed to be having a grand old time putting her two cents in and telling Andrew how handsome he looked. She liked one of Andrew's choices so much—it had some sort of psychedelic dancing gecko on the front—that she got one for herself.

"The Bobsey Twins," Mead muttered under his breath.

When they got home Andrew went off with Evelyn for a snack while Mead retired to his chair, thinking he'd need at least a week of uninterrupted silence to make sense of the day. *Christ, I can't take much more.*

He thought of Frances, feeling like a heel for giving her the cold shoulder for two straight years before she finally got fired for filching office supplies. Then he thought of Evelyn's husband, George, wondering if he ever realized just how lonely his wife was. He wasn't a bad man, just dull and self-absorbed without any *umph* at all. "He's a snooze," Sophie said after they had them over for dinner one night. "I always thank my lucky stars that I didn't marry a snooze. And believe me, four out of five men are snoozes."

But why Mead? Did he really mean anything to her—and how could he?—or was it just some passing fancy that had long since faded? He tried to imagine her secretly spying on him out her window, which made him blush again.

And now what? He sat perfectly still except for the bobbing of his left knee. Now what?

When the afternoon light grew dim he got up and pulled off the dust-cover from his eight-inch Celestron Schmidt-Cassegrain telescope that stood in the corner of the living room, thinking he'd polish the lens. He hadn't gone stargazing since Sophie had died. He tried once on a moonless evening a few months after the funeral, but staring up at all that cold and infinite space made him feel so horribly lonely that he quickly dismantled the telescope, lifted it back into the trunk and hurried home.

He opened the front door and looked up. Clear skies. And just a crescent moon. He looked back at the telescope, remembering how Sophie would gasp in delight every time she peered into the eyepiece, as though it was magic. Why not?

"Only if we invite Evelyn," said Andrew when he returned, his mouth still full of food.

"Don't you think she's sick of us by now?"

"Nope."

· · ·

"I hope Andrew didn't put you up to this," Evelyn said as Mead drove east to the county park where he and Sophie always used to go, usually bringing a blanket and a picnic and sometimes even a bottle of wine.

"Not at all." Andrew sat alone in the backseat leaning forward with his head between them, an impish smile saturating his features.

Mead parked in the far corner of the empty gravel lot near the edge of a steep ravine. The hillsides were covered with cactus and chaparral. "Perfect night," he said, slipping the scope into the tripod and tightening a knob.

Two-timer, said Sophie, right into his ear.

"I can't believe the stars," said Andrew, staring straight upward. "We hardly have any in Chicago."

"That's because you've got too much light pollution," said Evelyn, wrapping a scarf around her neck and smiling at Mead.

"There's Ursa Major there—the Big Dipper—and Ursa Minor over there," said Mead, pointing.

Andrew spun slowly on his heels, head tilted back. "There must be thousands of them."

"Try hundreds of billions," said Mead, whose entire sinus cavity was now impregnated with the scent of Evelyn's perfume, producing a tickling sensation.

"You mean millions."

"I mean *billions.*"

"*Billions* of stars?"

"Actually, billions of galaxies, each containing billions of stars."

"Holy shhhhh . . . cow. How could that be?"

"Very good question."

Andrew ducked as something fluttered past. "What was that?"

"A bat," said Evelyn with a laugh.

"What kind of bat?"

"The good kind," said Mead.

"Oh." Andrew searched the air above him, then scanned the nearby brush. "Any wolves around here?"

"Just coyotes," said Mead. "And a few mountain lions."

"Mountain lions?"

"Your grandma and I actually spotted one right over on that ridge there some ten years ago, but it's rare."

"You saw a mountain lion?" Andrew glanced nervously at the darkened ridge line.

"Now don't scare the poor boy," said Evelyn, drawing closer to Andrew.

"Cities are scary," said Mead. "We're in the country." He leaned over the telescope as he tried to remember how to program the computerized motor drive. Finally he gestured toward the eyepiece. "Here, take a look."

Andrew went first. "Wow, what is it?"

"Mercury. It'll drop below the horizon in a few minutes."

"Wicked."

Mead rolled his eyes at Evelyn. A coyote howled in the distance.

"What was that?" asked Andrew.

"A lonely heart," said Evelyn.

"Seriously."

"A coyote," said Mead.

"No kidding? How big are they?"

"About like a medium-size dog," said Mead. "Now relax." He watched as Evelyn peered into the telescope.

"It's just beautiful," she said, her voice suddenly fragile-sounding. She stared into the telescope for so long that Mead coughed a few times, wondering if her back had gone out. Finally she stood up and looked at him. "Thank you," she mouthed, her eyes full of tears.

Oh, Jesus, thought Mead, nearly welling up despite himself. What the hell is it with everybody?

Andrew stepped up to the telescope again. "What does that do?" he asked, pointing to the control pad attached by a cord to the base of the scope.

Mead was glad for the question. "That programs the motor drive so you can track a particular object in the sky. The scope has to keep moving to compensate for the movement of the Earth."

Andrew looked impressed. "I didn't know you were so . . . high-tech."

"Your grandfather is a regular gadgeteer," Evelyn said as Mead let Andrew work the drive.

"I could see getting into astronomy," said Andrew, looking through the eyepiece again.

"You may need to bring up those math grades," said Mead.

"There's a lot of math?"

"It's mostly math." Mead stared skyward with his hands at his waist.

"Ah, man, you serious?"

"Don't discourage him," said Evelyn.

"Just thought a little full disclosure was in order." Mead adjusted the telescope again. "Here, look at this."

Andrew peered into the eyepiece.

"That's Polaris, the North Star. It sits at the end of the handle of the Little Dipper, more than four hundred light years away from the tip of your nose."

"No kiddin'?"

"Pretty wicked, huh?"

Andrew looked up and made a face, then squinted into the eyepiece. "I still don't get how space goes on forever."

"Neither do I," said Mead.

"My daughter's been known to go on forever," said Evelyn.

Andrew looked up at the sky, then back down into the eyepiece. "If you think about it, it doesn't make any sense."

"Most things don't," said Evelyn.

"But *forever?*"

"If it just stopped, that wouldn't make much sense either, would it?" said Mead.

Andrew puzzled for a moment. "Still, it's pretty weird. And what if there's other life out there?"

"Why not? Seems awfully roomy just for us," said Evelyn. "I just hope that whatever's out there has more smarts than we do."

"No shit," said Andrew. He quickly covered his mouth. "Sorry."

"Charming, isn't he?" said Mead.

"As a matter of fact, yes, I think he is," said Evelyn, hooking her arm in Andrew's.

Andrew smiled proudly. "Can we look at the moon?"

"Coming right up," said Mead, trying to ignore the sound of Sophie's voice in his ear. *Who does she think she is?*

"Man, I've never seen it so close up. You can actually see the craters," said Andrew, peering into the telescope. "Those guys who walked on the moon must have freaked. I mean, how do you top that?"

"You don't," said Mead.

Andrew stood up abruptly. "Did you guys hear that?"

"What?" said Mead.

"Don't ask me," said Evelyn. "Either my hearing has gone to hell or the world is a much more peaceful place than it used to be."

"In those bushes over there. That noise."

"It's night," said Mead impatiently. "It's practically rush hour for a lot of creatures."

Andrew edged closer to Evelyn. "There it is again," he said, looking back at a bush.

"I can assure you it's not a mountain lion," said Mead.

"How do you know?"

"For one, they try very hard to avoid humans. Secondly, if we *were* being stalked we wouldn't hear a thing until it was too late."

Andrew's eyes widened. "We done yet?"

"What's the rush?" asked Mead.

"Just getting a little cold."

"You want my scarf?" asked Evelyn.

"No thanks."

Mead took another look through the telescope while Andrew kept glancing nervously around. "There's nothing to be afraid of," said Evelyn.

"Who said anything about being afraid?"

"No one."

"Are you guys scared?"

"Can't say that I am," said Mead.

"Personally, I could stay out here all night," sighed Evelyn as she craned her neck and gazed skyward.

Andrew frowned, then jammed his hands into his pockets and shuffled his feet.

"Look," said Mead, "I hope you don't mind me saying this, but I've found over the years that the trick with fear is to stare it right down. You can't so much as blink."

"Is that what you did during the war?" asked Evelyn.

Mead paused. "It's what I tried to do."

"So you were still scared?" said Andrew.

"Yes, I was."

"What was the scariest part?"

"That's easy: going on patrol."

"Why?"

Mead paused. "You had to leave whatever protection you had—your foxhole, a building, whatever. And you never knew what you might run into."

"Like German machine gunners and booby traps and stuff?"

"Yes, like that."

"That would definitely scare the shit—I mean the . . . that would scare me."

"Yeah, it scared the shit out of me all right," said Mead with a laugh.

Andrew looked surprised, then smiled. "I'm just curious, did they say *shit* back then or was there some other word?"

"You two certainly have a lot to talk about," said Evelyn.

"Some of the guys said *shit* and the f-word about every other sentence."

Andrew looked over anxiously at Evelyn. "Don't worry, I'm not going to faint," she said.

"The f-word too? No kidding? I thought that was kind of a new one."

"There's not much out there that's really new, except maybe the notion that wearing your trousers around your ankles is appealing."

"Don't you start into him," said Evelyn, taking another turn at the telescope. Again she spent several minutes motionless, so that Mead wondered if maybe an eyelash was stuck.

"How come you're crying?" asked Andrew when she finished.

"I don't know," she said, trying to smile as she dabbed her eyes. "Every time I look into that silly telescope I just . . ." She waved one hand helplessly in the air.

"Is it like, an infinity thing?" asked Andrew.

"Andrew—"

"I'm not sure what it is. I guess it's just so . . . lovely."

"If you ask me, there's something kind of creepy about outer space. Everything's basically cold and dead."

"Nobody asked you," said Mead.

"Now, General."

"But I think it's really awesome that stargazing makes you cry," said Andrew.

"Why thank you."

Mead shook his head, then looked into the eyepiece one more time, losing himself briefly to the enormity of space. When he finished he replaced the lens caps and showed Andrew how to remove the telescope from the tripod before they carried it back to the car. Then all three of them leaned against the trunk, Evelyn wedged between Mead and Andrew as they looked at the sky.

"What do you think about when you're stargazing?" Evelyn asked Mead.

"I don't think."

"You must feel something?"

"To tell you the truth, I feel . . . small."

"Me too!" said Andrew.

"See, you two have more in common than you realize," said Evelyn.

"Small is a relative term," said Mead.

"Personally, I think there's something nice about feeling small," said Evelyn. "It means all our problems are small too."

"I don't know about that," said Andrew.

"Except for *your* problems, of course," she said.

"What do you think about?" Mead asked Evelyn.

She paused before answering. "I think about all the wishes people have made."

"So does it make you feel small or what?" asked Andrew.

She took a deep breath. "I guess it makes me feel . . ." But she couldn't answer.

•   •   •

They sat in silence for several minutes watching the sky, then Mead stood and stretched. "Think I'll take a quick walk."

"A walk?" said Andrew. "Are you crazy?"

"I believe it's one of those nature walks," whispered Evelyn as Mead disappeared into the darkness.

"Oh," said Andrew. Cupping his hands around his mouth he called out, "I wouldn't go too far."

"I think he can fend for himself," said Evelyn.

"I just feel sort of responsible for him."

"You're a very thoughtful grandson."

"I try."

She leaned back against the trunk of the car and looked upward. "It's a lot to think about, isn't it?"

"What is?"

"The sky."

"I guess it is. It kind of wigs me out a little."

She smiled. "Me too."

"Really?"

"Sure."

Andrew looked at Evelyn, then back up at the sky.

"I want to thank you for inviting me along tonight. I've had a wonderful time."

"No problem. In fact, I was thinking we could all do more together; maybe go back to the beach or take a road trip somewhere."

"I wouldn't want to be a—" then suddenly she let out a small gasp and shuddered, leaning hard against Andrew so that he had to grab her to keep her from falling.

"What is it?"

She clenched her eyes shut and reached out with one hand and grabbed his arm.

"I'll get my grandfather. We'll take you to the hospital. Hey Grand—"

"No no, please." She let out some air, then took another sharp breath. "Just give me a minute."

"But we gotta get help."

"I'll be okay." She took several long breaths as she tried to steady herself, still holding onto Andrew.

"We gotta tell my grandfather." Andrew looked around frantically, wondering how far he'd gone.

"No, you have to promise me you won't say a word to him."

"But why?"

"Because you have no idea what he went through those last months with your grandmother. I won't be a burden to him. Not when he's just coming back to life."

"But—"

She squeezed his arm harder. *"Promise me."*

"Okay okay, but—"

"There you are," said Evelyn, pulling away from Andrew as Mead emerged from the darkness. "We were starting to worry about you."

Mead gave them both a funny look.

"Yeah, we were getting worried," said Andrew, watching Evelyn as she tried to smile.

"Anybody getting tired?" said Mead.

"I'm afraid I am," said Evelyn.

"Yeah, me too," said Andrew, yawning dramatically.

"Let's call it a night," said Mead, walking around to the passenger side and opening the door for Evelyn.

"And a lovely night at that," she said, slipping past him and into her seat. As Mead drove she turned and looked back at Andrew, giving him a wink. All the pain was gone from her face and Andrew thought he'd never seen anyone look happier.

• • •

As soon as they pulled into the driveway Andrew jumped out of the car and headed for the house, leaving Mead and Evelyn alone in the front seat.

"I'd say you two are making progress," she said, sitting with her handbag in her lap.

"Only thanks to you. He's crazy about you."

"I'm not related. It's much easier that way."

Mead started to get out, then stopped himself. What's the hurry?

"It must be awfully hard to grow up these days," said Evelyn.

"I would have thought it was rather easy."

"You don't really believe that?"

"What the hell have they got to complain about?"

"For starters, I think the world is coming at them at about a hundred miles an hour."

"You ought to see how fast an artillery shell travels."

"I didn't mean to—"

"I'm sorry. Forget it."

They sat in silence listening to the pings and clicks of the cooling engine.

"Thank you for a wonderful day," said Evelyn, stretching her palms out over her handbag. "I just hope you can forgive me for being so foolish." She shook her head. "All these years I thought you knew . . ."

"There's nothing to forgive."

"I think there is." She laughed to herself. "If nothing else, you could forgive me for writing such lousy poetry."

"You're a fine poet."

"Nonsense."

"No really." Mead felt her looking at him as he stared straight ahead at his living room window, thinking he'd seen something move where the yellow light cut through the seam of the closed curtains.

"I'm making you uncomfortable again."

"It's been a big day."

"You've had a lot of them lately, haven't you?"

Mead sighed. "It's been an interesting week."

"You'd better get some sleep." She reached for the door handle.

"Wait."

She stopped.

"Why did you tell me about the poems?" He ran his hands along the rim of the steering wheel. "I mean, why now?"

She looked down at her hands, lacing and unlacing her fingers. "Because telling the truth seems to be the last freedom that I have." She leaned forward and kissed him on the cheek, then opened her door and headed quickly across the street to her house.

•   •   •

Is that you, Matt? Andrew was lying in bed, trying to get back to sleep after getting up to pee, when he thought he saw the rocking chair move.

Matt? If that's you man please stop because you're totally freaking me out. He slid down beneath his covers and stared at the chair. Had it really moved? Andrew strained his eyes. Couldn't have. And yet. He scooted down further. Outside the wind was up and he could see the shadow of a large branch swaying through the curtains, backlit by the yellowish glow of the streetlight.

And then he felt Matt. He couldn't say how but he just did. Right there in his grandma's room.

Matt?

How are you doing, Andy?

Jesus, Matt. Is that really you?

Who else?

Ah, Christ, I've missed you, buddy.

Me too.

Why did you have to do it? Why did you leave me?

I couldn't take anymore. I just couldn't stand it, Andy.

I would have helped you. We would have made it.

I'm not like you. I'm not that strong.

I tried to wake you up. I really tried.

Sorry, Andy. I just didn't want to be alone. I couldn't think of any other way.

I didn't mean any of that stuff I said. I didn't think you were serious. I would have stopped you. I—

I know you would have. That's why I didn't tell you.

Damn you, Matt. Andrew started to cry.

Please don't be sad.

Andrew sat up and wiped his eyes. *Did it hurt?*

Not the last part. That was the strange thing. I actually felt great. *But those last few days were a killer, knowing that I was doing everything for the last time. That's the weirdest feeling, Andy, knowing you're doing things and seeing things for the last time ever. It was like, totally sad but awesome, too, because for the first time in my life I felt invincible. Nothing could touch me. For the first time absolutely nothing could touch me.*

She's just a stupid girl, Matt. You shouldn't have wasted your life for a stupid girl.

She's much more than that, Andy. But it wasn't just her. I didn't want my life. You know that. I hated my life.

I hate my life, too. Andrew started crying again.

But you're different than me. You always have been.

I really miss you.

Yeah, I miss you, too. How are you?

I'm not so good. I tried to kill Bremer. Did you see that?

Yeah, I saw it. You were something, Andy. You were really something.

How did you like the look on his face? Andrew let out a laugh.

You really had him scared.

Andrew stared at the rocking chair, thinking maybe it had moved again. *What's it like being dead?*

Kind of quiet, really.

I'm not sure I'd like it.

It's the easiest thing in the world.

Are you happy? Matt didn't answer. *Come on, tell me. I want to know if you're happy?*

I'm free, Andy. I'm totally absolutely free.

No bullshit?

No bullshit.

Andrew laughed to himself. *I can't wait.*

Don't you hurry.

Why shouldn't I? I'm tired of the bullshit, too.

Because you've got gifts, Andy. You're a fighter.

I don't know if I can make it, Matt. Everything's so fucked up.

You've got to make it, Andy. One of us has got to make it.

I don't know. I feel so . . . And then Andrew felt a coldness on his skin that ran all the way up to his scalp. *Matt, you still here?* He stared at the rocking chair, then pulled aside the curtain and looked out the window, seeing the crescent moon blinking through the clouds just above the trees. *Matt? Don't leave me, Matt. Please don't leave me.*

• • •

"That's it, now one more set." Andrew was lifting barbells in the garage while Mead rode the stationary bike, which he'd oiled and dusted off for the first time in years, figuring he might as well set a good example.

Andrew struggled with the weights. "I can't."

"Sure you can. Soybean power, remember?"

Andrew grunted and wheezed, finally curling the barbells up to his chest three more times before collapsing onto a bench. "I'm wiped."

"They won't recognize you when you get home."

"I'll be dead before then."

"Don't you play any sports?"

"Mom made me do wrestling for a while. I hated it."

"You seem to hate a lot of things."

"I *really* hated wrestling."

"I wouldn't figure you for a wrestler." Mead picked up his pace. "Maybe a swimmer or basketball player." Actually, Mead couldn't see him as any of those things, but he wanted to say something encouraging.

"Am I done?"

"Twenty more sit-ups."

Andrew sighed loudly, then got on his back and started counting off.

"We used to run nine miles in the morning before breakfast at boot camp," said Mead. "And that was just for starters."

"But I'm not in the army," Andrew wheezed.

"Maybe you ought to consider it."

"No way. I'd hate it."

Mead grabbed the hand towel he'd hung on the handlebar and wiped down his face. "Well then, what sort of plans do you have for yourself?"

"Nothing specific."

"You must have some ideas?"

Andrew paused between sit-ups. "I suppose I wouldn't mind having something to do with making music videos, or maybe even being in a band."

"You mean like a rock band?"

Andrew nodded enthusiastically.

"What instrument? Drums? The guitar?"

"I'd sing."

"Sing?"

"It's just an idea." Andrew did one last sit-up, then stretched out on the floor, his hands resting on his stomach. "What about you, what did you want to do when you were younger?"

Mead smiled. "Hell, I just wanted to stay alive."

"Yeah, that's kind of like the way I feel."

"Well now, that shouldn't be so hard. Last I heard we were still at peace." Mead pedaled faster, then gradually slowed, trying to catch his breath.

"You don't know what it's like."

"What, being young? Sure I do. A lot of people think it's the best part."

"If this is the best part I'll . . ." He didn't finish.

"What's so bad about it?"

"Everything."

"For example?"

"Everybody's always telling you what to do."

"You're a kid. What do you expect?"

"That's what I mean."

"What else?"

"School sucks."

"And why is that?"

"It's full of jerks."

"Hell, the world's full of jerks. You've just got to pick out the good ones and ignore the rest."

Andrew sat up and wrapped his arms around his knees.

"Listen, I'm sorry about what happened to your friend," Mead said.

Andrew shrugged.

"It was a stupid thing for him to do. I hope you realize that. There's nothing stupider a person can do."

"Matt wasn't stupid."

"Well, he wasn't too smart, either." Mead hesitated, trying to think of what else to say. "You're not messing with any of those drugs, are you?"

Andrew quickly looked up. "What makes you think that?"

"I read the papers."

"No, I'm not into drugs."

"Good. You need all the brain cells you can muster in this world."

Andrew smiled.

"And I'll tell you something else: I think you boys have filled yourself with so much nonsense from television and movies that you don't know which way is up. That's what I think."

Andrew got up and put the barbells away. "Don't you like watching movies?"

"Not what passes for entertainment these days. Thank you, no."

"So what *do* you like to do?"

Mead looked taken aback.

"I mean, for fun?"

"Why, lots of things. What kind of question is that?"

Andrew shoved his hands into his pockets. "I'm just wondering what kind of stuff you're into."

Mead thought for a moment. "There's my telescope, and of course darts. I got hooked on darts in England during the war. And I play a bit of golf now and then. Hell, lots of things."

"I just thought . . ."

"What?"

"Well I . . ."

"Spit it out."

"I just thought that maybe you've been . . . well, kind of depressed since Grandma died."

"Depressed?"

"Yeah. I thought maybe, you know, that you were down."

Mead glowered. "Do I look depressed to you?"

Andrew looked at him nervously. "Well, sort of. Yeah."

"Sort of? Hell, I'm not depressed." Mead got off the bike and draped the towel around his neck. "Enough of this kind of talk, let's get some lunch."

·   ·   ·

Depressed? What the hell kind of thing was that to say to your grandfather? Mead leaned into the bathroom mirror, noticing that his face seemed a little more drawn than he remembered. Depressed?

God knows he missed her. It was like going without water. At first he didn't think he could endure it, seeing nothing but endless days stretching out toward his own death, each echoing hour like a long dark tunnel he had to crawl through. But he'd made it. He'd put one foot forward and then the other until he had some momentum again. The house was in order. He'd kept in shape. Why, he'd even learned to cook a few dishes. He ran his fingertips down the sides of his cheeks. Yes, somehow you made it, old boy. Three years in August. Three years since he'd heard that lilting voice of hers that never seemed to age. And the truth was, there'd even been some relief when she finally died because her agony was over. Seeing her fight for air those last months had about driven him insane, her body shrunken and cool to the touch and her eyes asking him to do something that he couldn't. Dear God, the helplessness of it.

"Tell me another story," she'd say, taking his hand in hers, which was permanently bruised from IVs.

"Which one?"

"Tell me the chocolate bunny story."

And so he told her again about the life-size, solid chocolate bunny displayed on a table in the waiting room where Mead sat anxiously while Sophie was in labor with Sharon on Easter morning. At first Mead nibbled at the tail when no one was looking. Just a discreet little bite. It wasn't so much hunger or a sweet tooth but nerves that drove him to it. Then he ate the little basket the bunny was holding, then the paws, and then a shoulder.

"Look Mom, that man is eating the Easter Bunny," cried a child being dragged down the hallway by his mother.

Mead quickly hid behind a newspaper.

But then he was alone again and took another bite. Then another, always keeping an eye on the big wall clock. Finally he broke off the head and ate it. After that it was a matter of getting rid of the evidence. By the time the nurse came out four hours later to tell Mead it was a girl there was nothing left of the big chocolate bunny but crumbs.

"A . . . girl?" Mead rose unsteadily to his feet, clutching at his stomach. And then right there he had passed out, all that sugar rushing to his head.

"I'll never forget when they told me you'd been admitted as a patient," said Sophie, struggling for air as she laughed. "You just about went into a sugar coma, you silly goose."

Mead blushed.

"Just how big was that bunny, anyway?"

"It was a very big bunny, my dear."

•　•　•

Andrew had just finished cleaning his room and was heading to the garage for his morning exercises when his grandfather stopped him. "I'm going to visit your grandma's grave. I'd like you to come along."

"Now?" It wasn't quite eight.

"Yes."

Andrew noticed that his grandfather was looking even more spiffy than usual, dressed in shiny brown leather shoes, perfectly pressed khaki pants and a blue sport coat. "Why so early?"

His grandfather paused, tightening his forehead. "It's the best time of day to visit," he stammered. "Nice and quiet."

Quiet? When *isn't* it quiet at a graveyard? But Andrew sensed it was no time to argue.

"And I want you to wear this," said his grandfather, extending his left hand.

Andrew stared down in horror at the shiny brown belt coiled in his grandfather's hand. "But I . . ."

"I'll meet you out front in ten minutes."

Actually, Andrew had always liked graveyards. He and Matt used to hang out in a large cemetery not far from their apartments, weaving among the long, silent rows and making up stories about how each person died. *Coronary while copulating. Cancer. Drug overdose. Asthma attack. Plane crash. Algebra overload. Broken heart.* As they walked they often made a game of competing to see who could calculate the age of the deceased first. *Sixty-two! Eighteen! Eighty-four! Nine! No wait, make that eight.* And of course, there was the inevitable question of foul play.

"Something tells me that ol' Howard C. Walker here was knocked off," said Matt, slapping a large slab of dark granite. *April 3, 1922—May 13, 1977.*

"How would you know a thing like that?"

"I just get a funny feeling."

"You and your funny feelings. So who did it?"

"His wife. Put strychnine in his pudding. She just couldn't take any more of the old gas bag."

One of the coolest things about hanging out in graveyards was that no matter how bummed you were, you always knew you had it better than anybody else in the vicinity. You could be in a cemetery of five hundred people and you were like, the only one who still had anything going for you. And Andrew found it enormously satisfying to think of all the assholes who were dead; rich arrogant assholes now sucking on worms beneath his feet. Even living in an apartment didn't seem so bad when you were walking through a cemetery because hey, at least you were topside. So what if he didn't live in a big fancy house or couldn't afford the right shoes? Everything was basically temporary as all hell. (Of course, that led right back to the essential stupidness of things, which was why it was so hard to take algebra seriously.)

"Your grandma was really something when she was younger," said his grandfather suddenly, a smile seeping through his stern features as he drove.

Andrew wasn't sure what to say. "Yeah, I bet she was."

"What I'm saying is that she wasn't always a grandma. Heck, she was practically your age when we met."

"Cool." Andrew peered over at his grandfather, trying to figure out where the conversation was going. "Was she like, popular?"

"She was no cheerleader. But she was a *doll.*"

Andrew thought of the black-and-white pictures he'd examined. Pretty, maybe, but not a doll. "Were you . . . popular?"

His grandfather let out a laugh. "God, no."

"So what kind of crowd did you like, hang out with?"

"A small one. Your grandma used to tell me that I was a bit of a square." Andrew smiled. "She was just teasing, of course."

"Of course." They continued in silence for several minutes. "Do you visit her grave a lot?"

"Now and then."

"Isn't it kind of . . . depressing?"

His grandfather didn't respond at first and Andrew wondered if he'd said the wrong thing. *Of course it's depressing, you dope. She's dead.* Finally his grandfather looked over and said, "Sometimes it makes me feel better and sometimes it makes me feel worse." Uh-oh, thought Andrew, could be a long day.

They drove through a large stone gate with a towering palm tree on each side and turned left into a newly paved parking lot. The cemetery was huge, sloping slightly uphill with grass as perfect as Astro turf and bouquets of flowers scattered here and there. Definitely upscale, thought Andrew, as he sat waiting for his grandfather to get out of the car. But Mead seemed to be looking for something in the distance, then suddenly smacked the steering wheel with his hand.

"What is it?" asked Andrew, wondering if they'd driven to the wrong cemetery. Or maybe he forgot flowers?

"Nothing." His grandfather sighed. "It's going to be a short visit. Come on."

As they wound their way through the rows of headstones Andrew spotted a large woman in purple perched in a chair and talking loudly to herself. "Who's she talking to?" he asked, but his grandfather didn't answer. As they drew closer Andrew suddenly feared that it was some sort of setup. "She's not a relative, is she?" he whispered.

His grandfather scowled as he continued toward the woman. Some-body's mood has sure soured, thought Andrew. Was it something I said? He looked down at the belt. Should the shiny side go on the inside?

They didn't stop until they were barely three feet from the woman, who looked like an immense plum and was so busy lecturing someone named Henry that she didn't seem to notice them. Andrew briefly considered whether she might be criminally insane, then looked down and saw his grandma's name etched in stone. Wow. He'd never seen the name of some-one he actually knew. Kind of creepy, he thought, wanting to touch the letters but stopping himself. He tried to think nice thoughts about Grandma but was distracted by the purple nut case blabbering next to them. This is seriously awkward.

"Who do we have here?" the woman said, turning toward Andrew and smiling like he was a delicious bonbon she was about to pop into her mouth.

"My grandson," mumbled Mead. Andrew had never heard him mum-ble before.

"What a treat! And where are you from, dear?"

"Chicago."

"*Chicago?*" She sized Andrew up so intently that he feared she might kiss him, then she looked admiringly at Mead. "You must have done some-thing right because Lord knows, none of my grandsons would be caught dead in a belt."

"He's sort of his own man," said Mead, putting his hand on Andrew's shoulder and turning them both away from her.

"Henry, the nicest boy has come to visit," she said, leaning toward the gray headstone in front of her.

Ah, so that's Henry. Andrew tried to stifle a giggle. Good thing I'm not stoned. Or maybe she's stoned? Nah, too old. But this is *weird*.

His grandfather continued to ignore the woman as he knelt down and rested both palms on the top of Sophie's thin white headstone, which came up to Andrew's waist. "I just thought you might want to see it," he said.

"It looks . . . great," said Andrew. "I like the way the letters are. You know, the style."

His grandfather lovingly patted the stone. "She adored you."

Andrew watched him closely, wondering if he was going to cry. No way. Not Sarge. Still, it was definitely intense. His grandfather kept staring silently at the grave. Andrew tried to follow his gaze. What's he looking at?

"I'm sorry you didn't know her better."

Andrew had never heard his grandfather's voice sound so soft before. "I've got really good memories," he said cheerfully.

"Hang on to them."

"Definitely."

His grandfather kept looking at the headstone while the big purple psycho ripped into Henry for failing to file three years' worth of taxes. "Well I . . . I just thought you ought to come here. Pay your respects."

"For sure."

"She would have done anything for you, you understand that?"

"Yeah."

A sad smile came over his grandfather's face. "You see, she had a way with people. Just the right touch."

Andrew nodded.

"And like I said, she adored you. She always—"

"I think it's the nicest spot in the whole place, don't you?" interrupted the woman, reaching over and tugging at Andrew's arm.

Andrew looked around, but the graves all looked pretty much identical. "Not bad," he said with a shrug.

"It's so nice of you to come. I was just telling Henry here that our granddaughter is going to be in the school play. The lead!"

Andrew nodded, then turned back to his grandfather.

"You must have been just heartbroken when she passed," continued the woman.

"Passed?"

"Yes, he was," said Mead curtly as he rose to his feet.

The woman kept staring at Andrew. "Well, don't you have anything to say to her?"

"Huh?"

She cocked her head toward the ground. "You can't come all this way and not say hello."

"We'd just like a little peace and quiet," said Mead.

Jesus, thought Andrew, this is too fucking much.

"You haven't told him, have you?" said the woman.

"Pardon me?" said Mead.

"About the conversations," she whispered, leaning forward.

"What conversations?" asked Andrew.

"Nothing," said Mead. "I think we'd better go."

"But you just got here," said the woman. "And I just happen to have some extra tickets to the theater." She reached into her purse, then waved the tickets in the air, wiggling her immense bottom in unison.

"Can't talk now," called out Mead, already heading toward the parking lot. "Got to run."

Andrew struggled to keep up. "You've really got a way with the ladies," he said when they reached the car.

"Not another word," said his grandfather.

• • •

They both saw the FOR SALE sign in front of Evelyn's house at the same time.

"Oh no," said Andrew.

Mead felt a hollowness in his stomach. Perhaps there'd been some sort of mistake. After all, why hadn't she said anything and where would she go? He vaguely recalled her having a son and daughter somewhere in the east and wondered if she was going to live with one of them. "Looks like I'll be cutting back on my cookie intake," he said as casually as he could manage.

"She doesn't *want* to move," said Andrew, his face verging on panic.

Mead parked the car in the driveway and turned off the ignition. "What makes you say that?"

"Well . . . look how nicely she keeps her garden. I mean, how could she leave that?"

It did seem surprising. "So, it's some sort of mix-up."

"It's not a mix-up. I've got to talk to her." Andrew jumped out of the car.

"Wait . . ." But Andrew was already halfway across the street. Confused and flustered, Mead headed quickly into his house, making a fist at his side to control himself.

• • •

"You can't move," said Andrew when Evelyn opened the door.

"Don't be silly," she said sadly.

"But you can't. Your garden is here, my grandfather is here—"

"Your grandfather?"

"He likes you."

She blushed.

"He really does."

"I don't think he'll even notice when I'm gone."

"Are you kidding? It'll break his heart. He's just shy, that's all. He's, well, he's sort of a nerd when it comes to girls . . . I mean ladies."

"You're very sweet but—"

"And you can't let your daughter push you around."

"I'm afraid she's right. I can't afford to live here all by myself."

"Where will you go?"

"Connecticut. That's where my daughter lives."

"*Connecticut?* But what about your garden?"

"I believe they have flowers in Connecticut."

Andrew thought for a moment. "You could move in with my grandfather. I'll be out of there soon."

Evelyn laughed. "You're quite a little matchmaker."

"You'd be perfect for him. Just look at his garden. It's *dead*. And he needs someone who's . . ."

Evelyn raised her eyebrows.

"Hip."

"Hip? My daughter would have a seizure if she knew I'd been called *hip*."

"I'll talk to him."

"Don't you dare."

Andrew shifted awkwardly in the doorway.

"Can I get you a brownie?"

"I'm not hungry."

"Would you like to come in at least?"

He shook his head. "I just want to know . . . are you doing the chemotherapy?"

"Has anyone ever told you that it's not polite to be nosy?"

"But are you?"

"As a matter of fact, no. You see, my daughter's not getting her way with everything after all."

Andrew frowned. "Maybe you ought to."

"I don't have time for that nonsense." She smiled as she reached out and pressed her palm to Andrew's cheek.

. . .

Mead spent hours circling the matter, trying to find an approach that wasn't upsetting. But no matter how he thought about it, no matter how often he reminded himself of all the little things about her that annoyed him, he couldn't keep from feeling that life was about to close in on him again.

He left his cube steak untouched. Instead he went to his bedroom, closed the door and stretched out on the bed, hands resting on his stomach. Nothing made sense anymore. Not Evelyn, not his grandson, not even his daughter. The world had gotten so confusing that he no longer felt like he knew what to do.

He was still lying in the same position a half hour later when the phone rang.

"Bad news." It was Sharon.

"Did you get fired?"

"It's worse than that." Her voice was flat with despair.

Mead put his hand to his forehead and rubbed it, waiting for her to continue.

"They've decided to hold Andrew back a year. Between his grades and the time he's missed and the incident they won't graduate him."

"They're not pressing charges?"

"Not as long as he does thirty hours of community service and gets more counseling."

"So it's good news."

"Andrew won't think so. He's going to be devastated."

"At least he's not going to jail."

"He won't look at it that way."

"Maybe he'll learn something."

Sharon was quiet for a moment, then asked, "How is he?"

"Just fine."

"Andrew is never *just fine.*"

"Then let's just say we're managing."

"He's not giving you a hard time, is he?"

"He wouldn't dare."

"I just don't want him to drive you crazy. I know how you get."

"He's my grandson."

"He's a teenager."

"Granted."

She took a deep breath. "Listen, I'd better tell him. Can you put him on?"

"You sure you're taking care of yourself?"

"I'm fine, Dad."

"You're not smoking again?"

"I *promise*."

"And what about that new car you're going to get?"

"I'm looking."

"Good. I'll go get him."

Mead was out front taking down his flag when he heard a door slam. He started to hurry inside but stopped himself, thinking maybe he'd give the boy a little space for the evening; start fresh in the morning. Everything would look better then. He unhooked the flag and folded it, then walked to the curb and looked at the FOR SALE sign across the street. Evelyn's house was dark except for a single window. He stood watching for several minutes, then headed inside, feeling more tired than he had in years.

.   .   .

After slamming down the phone Andrew ran into his room, shut the door and dove onto the bed, pounding it with his fists. A sophomore again, with all his classmates moving up? No way. *No fucking way.*

"You all right in there?"

Andrew didn't answer.

"I said, are you all right?"

"Fine."

"I'll be in the living room if you want to talk."

But Andrew stayed in his room the rest of the evening, the rage bouncing him off the walls and bed so that he finally just stood in the middle of the room with his arms wrapped around his shoulders, wanting to squeeze himself into nothingness.

"You sure you're all right in there?"

"I'm *fine*."

"You didn't eat anything."

"I'm not hungry."

There was a pause. "Well, I'm heading to bed. I'll expect to see you for breakfast."

"Good night."

"Good night."

Andrew waited for half an hour, sometimes pounding his fists into his pillow when he couldn't contain himself, then quietly opened his door and peered down the hall, making sure his grandfather's bedroom light was out. He waited another ten minutes, then crept into the living room, grabbed the bottle of bourbon from the small bar and quickly carried it back to his room.

He took a big shot at first, then sat on the bed taking small sips and listening to his CD player and tapping his feet.

No fucking way. He'd never last another year. And to be humiliated like that in front of everybody?

No way.

As he sat there drinking he started to feel better, then worse, then so good that none of it seemed to matter. In a way it was a relief, having things framed so clearly. Going back was now out of the question. He thought again of hitchhiking to Mexico, starting a whole new life for himself. That would freak everybody out. And then one day he'd show up and be way ahead of them with a car and good money and a job when they were just graduating. It would be like passing everybody by; beating the game. Maybe he could even bartend at one of those pool bars. He imagined himself tossing bottles and glasses into the air and catching them behind his back as the awestruck customers—all wearing bikinis—broke into applause. Did they have a drinking age? He wasn't sure.

He lifted the mattress and pulled out the medals, wallet and the Luger, laying them neatly on the bed. Wish Matt could see this stuff.

Was the Luger loaded? He fiddled with the handle until he managed to slide out the narrow clip. He counted five bullets. Plenty.

He took another shot of bourbon, then tried to concentrate his gaze on the rocking chair. *Hey Matt, you here? I really need to talk to you, Matt.*

Silence.

They want to keep me back a year. He kept his eyes fixed on the chair, tears coursing down his cheeks. *I won't do it, Matt. There's no way I'm staying back.*

He stood and walked slowly across the room, the gun in his left hand

and the bottle in his right. *You were right, Matt, there's just way too much bullshit.* He sat down in the rocking chair and took a long sip of the bourbon, then another. *I should have gone with you. Why didn't you let me go with you?*

He thought again of trying to run away to Mexico. Could he really do it? No, not alone. He wouldn't know where to start.

He looked down at the gun in his hand. *I can't take it anymore, Matt. I want to go with you, buddy. You hear that? I'm going with you. But Jesus, I'm scared. Weren't you scared?*

He put the bottle down on the floor, then held the pistol up in front of his face and stared at it again, wondering how many others it had killed. Then he stood in the middle of the room, trying not to sway on his feet as he raised the pistol and pointed it at his forehead, putting his thumb to the trigger. But his hand shook so bad he feared he might drop it. He went over and sat on the edge of the bed and put his headphones on, turning the music up full blast and letting the tears wash down his face. After a few minutes he picked up the German soldier's wallet, gently removed the photographs and studied them. *Hello, Hans. You're dead, aren't you? Was it bad? Were you scared? What do you miss the most? Your girlfriend? Your medals? Sex?* He looked at the German handwriting on the back of the photograph of the young woman. *Shouldn't have been a Nazi, Hans. Big mistake.* He slid the photos back into the wallet and placed it on the dresser. After switching CDs he forwarded to the third song and pressed the headphones against his ears, nodding his head up and down as the music began. Then he turned and looked at the gun, which lay next to him on the bed. *I'm coming too, Matt. Wait for me because I'm coming too.*

He started to reach for the gun, then hesitated. After taking another large swig of bourbon, grimacing to keep it down, he took off the headphones, got up and carefully opened the door, checking that his grandfather's light was still off before heading for the kitchen, weaving as he went. Might be just a tiny bit buzzed. After turning on the small light above the table he searched through the drawers until he found the bag of magnets. He emptied the bag on the table and spent several minutes trying to select the right words, then stood and steadied himself before slowly arranging them on the refrigerator, too drunk to tell if the words were straight or not. It'll do. Then he turned off the light and returned to his room, quietly closing the door before putting his headphones back on. After taking another drink from the bottle, almost gagging this time, he screwed the top back on, placed it on the floor and flopped down on the bed.

I'm really coming, Matt.

He picked up the gun.

It made him feel better knowing that he'd be with Matt again; that he wouldn't be alone anymore. And then as he lay there he realized he'd never have to worry about anything ever again. *No bullshit, right Matt?* He smiled, wiping his face with the back of his sleeve as he thought of the power he held in his hand, power to make all the problems instantly go away *forever*; power to free him from homework and tests and acne and putting up with assholes and always needing money and seeing his mom cry and meeting her latest stupid boyfriend and having to stare at Cori Fletcher knowing he'd never get to touch her and most of all just having to face the darkness alone night after night with no way to hide. Already he felt a strange sense of calm, knowing it was all over. Yeah, for the first time in his life he could let go of *everything*. It was just like Matt had said: for once, nobody can touch you.

I'm invincible.

"Jesus fuck, Matt, we'll both be virgins for eternity," he said out loud, laughing to himself as he aimed the gun first at his heart, then at his temple before putting the tip of the nozzle into his mouth, feeling his hand quake again. *Okay, Matt, I'm really coming. Just keep your eye out 'cause Andy's on his way.*

•   •   •

Mead awoke at 1:15 A.M., his bladder so full he wasn't sure he'd make it to the bathroom. After relieving himself, bracing one arm against the wall to support his weight and wincing from the pain, he headed to the kitchen to heat up a cup of milk, which usually eased the transition back to sleep. He looked up at the wall clock. The next call of nature would be between four and five.

As he reached for the refrigerator door he stopped to read the words spelled out in the small black-and-white magnetic letters. He leaned close, squinting, then finally pulled out his glasses from the pocket of his robe.

I'm sorry for everything. Tell Mom I love her.

What? Mead read the words again.

Oh, Jesus.

He ran down the hallway and burst into Andrew's room. The boy was lying on his back on the bed with his headphones on and a pistol pointed into his mouth.

"Andrew!" Mead jumped forward and snatched the gun away. "In the name of God."

His grandson looked up at him, his eyes glassy and confused, then burst into tears. Mead stood over him shaking and wondering for a moment if he would awaken from a nightmare. *This cannot be.* Unable to find any words to say, he pulled out the clip from the pistol and placed it in the pocket of his robe before setting the pistol down on the dresser. Then he stood immobile, staring at the wallet and medals, the first time he'd set eyes on them in over fifty years.

Hans Mueller.

"How dare you?" He bent over Andrew, who remained on his back crying with his hands covering his face and his knees drawn up, and took him by the shoulders and shook him. "How *dare* you!"

"I didn't mean to," Andrew cried.

"The hell you didn't." Without thinking Mead slapped the boy hard across his face. "Get up, goddamn you!"

"Please don't hit me."

"I said, *get up!*" Mead yanked Andrew to his feet, smelling the alcohol on his breath. The bottle of bourbon lay on its side on the floor. "You think you can come here and blow your goddamn brains out in your grand-mother's room? You think you can just destroy everything?"

"I don't care what you do to me. I don't care what anybody does to me." Andrew swayed on his feet, then reached for the pistol on the dresser. Mead swung and struck him again, sending Andrew reeling back onto the bed. Mead stood above him trembling and watching the blood run from a split in Andrew's lower lip.

"How did you kill him?" asked Andrew. "How did you kill that Ger-man soldier?"

"Shut up!"

"Well I don't care if you kill me." Andrew rolled onto his side and curled up, heaving.

Mead stood over him, feeling a burning sensation behind his eyes so that he had to steady himself by holding on to the dresser. Finally he took a few steps backward and slumped down in Sophie's chair, keeping his eyes on his grandson.

"Why?" Mead whispered. "Why?" But the boy wouldn't answer.

Andrew kept weeping for almost half an hour until gradually his shoulders stopped shaking and his thin frame became still. Mead listened to the boy's breathing, hearing him drift slowly and restlessly into sleep. He got up and checked on him, getting a wet washcloth to clean up the boy's lip and face, then returned to the rocking chair where he sat trying to stop the quaking in his hands and asking himself again and again what the right thing was to do.

At first he thought he'd call a doctor; let the professionals take over. Yet as he stared at his grandson's sleeping face it seemed unbearable to just hand him over, not knowing what might become of him. And how would he tell Sharon?

He looked over at the gun on the dresser. Good God, to want to kill yourself at sixteen with all of life ahead of you. How could a life barely begun be worth throwing away? Couldn't he see beyond tomorrow? Was the future really so terrifying and opaque? And yet he'd never gone to bed without a full stomach and a warm place to sleep a night in his life. He was *lucky.*

Mead slowly rocked back and forth, listening to the familiar creaking of the chair and feeling more lost and alone than he ever had in his life.

How do kids so young and pampered feel such despair? Was it the meaninglessness of the world these days, fact and fiction all blended so hopelessly by Hollywood that nobody could see straight anymore? Jane and Max Harquet had a grandson who killed himself, right out of the blue. Found him hanging from a rafter in the attic. Good grades, member of the soccer team, nice kid. No one suspected a thing. And these kids killing their classmates for the fun of it—the luckiest, most spoiled generation ever. No depression. No war. (How many young men never had the chance to grow old?) Mead would never forget reading in the paper one day that suicide rates drop during times of war and how that told him all he needed to know about human nature. My God, is peace and prosperity so tedious that people—even children—will turn on themselves in search of an adversary?

He looked over at the German soldier's belongings sitting on the dresser, beckoning. They'd been calling out to him for years, a cry that over time had gradually become muffled enough for him to ignore until he could pretend that he no longer heard it. *Have you forgotten?* After a few minutes he rose and walked over and picked up the three medals and then the wallet and carried them back to the rocking chair, beads of sweat gathering on his brow and palms. *Hans Mueller.*

He pulled out a photograph from the wallet and looked at it, then quickly put it back. *Forgiveness.* That's what the Holy Joes at church were always talking about. Anything could be forgiven, or so they promised. Absolution. Yet Mead had never felt it. Not for an instant. How could he when he could still see the look in the young German's eyes those last silent seconds, just the two of them, face-to-face, time stretching until finally it *snapped?*

Bitte.

And yet . . .

But he couldn't think of that now. He looked at his grandson still smelling of bourbon and curled up beneath the sheets that Mead had gently tucked in around him. Then he remembered striking him and felt a sense of horror.

Forgive me, Sophie.

But what should I do? Call the police? He got up and walked over to the bed again and leaned over Andrew to check on his breathing. Would they handcuff him or put him in a straitjacket? No, I can't call the police. He gently placed his hand on Andrew's forehead, which was damp. My grandson. Flesh and blood. Unrecognizable, maybe, but still a part of me. And what about Sharon? How will she cope?

He sat back down and wiped the tears from his eyes and for the first time in years he tried to pray. But he couldn't. Each time he tried, the words he flung out echoed mockingly back at him. And then when he closed his eyes tight and clenched his fists and tried to believe, all he could think was, Where were *You*? And he remembered how all those who prayed died just as easily as the rest, sometimes sooner. And Germany was covered with churches.

Then as the sun began to push through the curtains it came to him: I'll take him to Normandy. *Yes, of course.* Family history? I'll give you family history. Mead nodded slowly to himself as the idea sunk in, his fingers tapping nervously on the arms of the chair. Andrew rolled to his side and groaned. *Normandy.* He felt a prickly sensation on the skin of his forearms as he imagined the beaches and cemeteries. He swore he'd never return; not for himself. But for his grandson? He'd do anything for him. He looked over at Andrew's face, so peaceful and childlike in sleep. Would Normandy still have the power to knock sense into the boy? But it must. Even from Southern California, Mead had always felt its power, turning off the TV every time the famous images were broadcast, which seemed more and more often now that everybody was dying off like flies.

Normandy. By God, why not?

We'll stop in London first, see the sights. Mead had wonderful memories of visits to London while on leave from training at a base in Aldbourne before the invasion. As he sat there slowly rocking in Sophie's chair and watching the light gradually run beneath the curtains and pool in the folds of the sheets a smile came over his face. That's what we'll do. Just the two of us. I'll take him to the museums and show him the palace and the Tower of London and tell him about the Blitz. That's what he needs: something to think about besides himself. Does he think he's the first person to feel whipped when the game's just started; to cower with fear and want to toss in the towel? He looked over again at his grandson, watching the boy's narrow chest rise and fall beneath the sheets. Yes, I'll go back for his sake. After all, it is family history.

That afternoon he made an appointment to see a travel agent.

· · ·

"You're kidding?" said Sharon when Mead called her, not mentioning what had happened.

"It'll be good for him. And I haven't been back in years."

"Since the war! Mom said you'd never go back. She always wanted to see Europe but she said you'd never go."

"I've changed my mind."

"I can't believe it." There was a pause. "What does Andrew think?"

"I haven't told him yet."

"Oh."

"I wanted to check with you first."

Another pause. "You know, frankly, Dad, it's very generous of you but I'm not sure he'll want to go. He might be a little uncomfortable."

"Traveling with his grandfather?"

"He is a teenager."

"I can be a lot of fun."

"Your doctor didn't put you on one of those mood medications, by any chance?"

"I just want to help him. Broaden his horizons."

"But Europe will cost a fortune."

"It's my treat."

"What about passports?"

"I'll need you to send me his birth certificate. Use one of those overnight services and I'll pay you back."

"I can't believe this."

"I figure we'll be gone about eight days. I'd like to stop in London first—for old time's sake."

"You really want to take Andrew to Europe?"

"Sure. Why not?"

"I can think of a million reasons." She laughed in disbelief. "Mom would roll over in her grave."

"She would, wouldn't she?"

After he hung up Mead checked on Andrew, who was in his room reading, then went into the garage, set the medal ladder against the high shelf he'd built shortly after they moved in, and began slowly climbing. He didn't get to bed until well past midnight.

• • •

Andrew didn't talk much during the flight. Even thinking was unpleasant. Looking out the window at the clouds, he half wondered whether he wasn't dead after all and in transit to some strange new destiny. Figures I'd get a middle seat in coach.

Everything had happened so quickly. That morning when he woke up—oh fuck did his head hurt—his grandfather was sitting right there in the rocking chair staring at him. "I'm going to give you a choice," he said slowly, "and I want you to listen very carefully." Andrew rolled away from him, groaning at the realization of what he'd done, or tried to do. Would he really have done it? Oh God, his grandfather had seen everything.

"Either you come with me on a little trip and we see if you can't learn something about the value of human life—about what real misery and sacrifice is all about—or we call your mother, tell her what's happened and get you put away in a hospital. Frankly, I'd just as soon put you away myself." His grandfather impatiently drummed his fingers on the wooden armrests.

"A trip?" Andrew moaned. "Where?"

"To Normandy."

Suddenly Andrew's stomach gave way and he leaned over the edge of the bed and vomited all over the green carpet.

Part Two

London

They docked at Liverpool on an overcast afternoon after the eleven-day crossing from New York, the journey spent anxiously waiting for the wolf packs to strike, until the morning when cheers erupted at the sight of the green coast of Ireland. As Mead waited to disembark he thought of the stories he'd heard of his great grandfather, who emigrated from Manchester just before the American Civil War with only the clothes on his back and his carpentry tools. Did he also lie awake at night in fear of the unknown? Which journey required more courage: mine or his?

Mead marveled at the fairy-tale villages they passed during the trip by train and then truck to their base in Aldbourne, eighty miles west of London. The English countryside looked almost medieval and make-believe, rows of identical sheep staring blankly from behind ancient fences and old men in tweedy coats bicycling along the roadside, weaving in and out of the endless convoy.

And then, on his first weekend pass, London.

"I've already fallen completely in love three times," said Punchy as they waded through the crowds of pedestrians, many in uniform.

"We've only gone two blocks," said Mead.

"It's gonna be a long day," sighed Punchy, swiveling his head to follow a passing brunette. "God, I need a drink."

They stopped first at the American Red Cross headquarters and stood in line for an hour before reaching the information desk where they booked cheap accommodations for two nights—barracks style—along with tickets to the Winter Garden Theatre and a discounted taxi tour of the city. Punchy tried valiantly to make headway with the pretty young assistant but she blithely ignored his advances. "I think I'm a little rusty," he said as they walked out.

"Perhaps you should consider a slightly more subtle approach."

"What's wrong with my approach?"

"For starters, you might have been a little hasty when you proposed to her."

"Think so?"

Mead rolled his eyes.

"Okay, maybe I was, but I meant it. Did you see the lips on that girl and the way she tucked the upper one beneath the lower one when she was concentrating? Oh, Jesus . . ."

"You're pathetic."

"I'm Italian." Punchy shook his head. "You wouldn't understand."

"Neither would she."

After the taxi tour they spent hours walking aimlessly, trying to take in as many sights as possible, as though building a store of civilized images to counter what lay ahead. Mead couldn't believe the destruction, the first actual evidence of war that he'd seen. One building was untouched while the next was dissected in half like a playhouse with the bathroom plumbing dangling in midair. And still the city seemed incredibly dignified, Saint Paul's looming defiantly above the ruins.

"It's like the whole town's in heat," said Punchy, looking longingly at a group of nurses who were waiting for a bus. "Must be the war. I'm telling you, we could use an occasional air raid back home."

"Would you shut up?"

"Don't you feel it? I can almost smell it."

"You weren't raised in a kennel, by chance?"

Punchy made a face. "Know something, pal? You've got to start loosening up." He shook out his arms and rolled his shoulders with exaggeration. "And don't think you're fooling anybody with that Mr. Serious shit. I know a horny goat when I see one."

"You done yet?"

"Temporarily." Punchy whistled under his breath at a passing woman. "God, I love them in uniform. It's like gift wrapping."

"Mind if I ask you a personal question?"

"Fire away."

"Have you ever actually had a girlfriend?"

"What, are you kidding?" Punchy laughed out loud.

"How come you never get any mail?"

Punchy hesitated. "I'm not saying they're all college girls."

"So they're illiterate?"

"They ain't librarians."

They ate at a noisy place near Trafalgar Square—restaurants offered American servicemen dinner for a buck—and throughout the meal they both kept enviously eyeing a nearby table of GIs who wore an assortment of badges and campaign ribbons and Purple Hearts. Mead imagined himself walking up to Sophie's house with a chest full of medals and a slight limp, tears springing from her eyes as she opened the door and fell into his arms. *You made it.*

"In a way I'm looking forward to it," said Punchy, still looking over at the other soldiers. "I'm ready, you know? It's like when you're in the ring waiting for the match to start."

"Go get'em, Slugger."

Punchy wolfed down his potato and offered to finish Mead's. "I'll tell you one thing, I'm sure as hell tired of thinking about it."

"So what exactly do you think about when you think about it?"

"Easy. Getting shot in the nuts. Trust me, that's all any Italian thinks about."

"Glad you've got your priorities straight." Mead smiled, sensing from Punchy's expression that he'd already imagined hundreds of ways in which he might be grievously wounded, as though the entire Third Reich had his groin in its crosshairs.

After drinking at several pubs and making little headway with various women—all spoken for—they stumbled out into the darkened street now slick with an evening mist.

"I'm telling you, Mead, if I don't get my hands on a woman soon I'm going to have a heart attack," groaned Punchy as they approached Piccadilly Circus. "I can feel it right here." He thumped his chest. "It's like I'm gonna die."

"You're sick, you know that? You ought to see a doctor."

Just then two women emerged from a doorway. "Hey, fellas."

"Sweet mother of Jesus," gasped Punchy, who sometimes mumbled Hail Mary's in his sleep, a leftover from Catholic School. ("I'm telling you,

Sister Henrietta could whip the entire German Army," he'd say. "Built like a brick shithouse. We ought to drop her on Berlin. She'd have Hitler scrubbing toilets in no time.") "You seeing what I'm seeing?" One of the women caressed Punchy's uniform while the other worked on Mead. "Thank you, Lord!" howled Punchy, putting his arm around the woman, who was a head taller.

"I think there's a small catch," said Mead, trying to ignore the sudden stirrings in his groin. "Come on, let's get out of here."

"You kidding? I'm a pig in shit."

"You're going to be a very poor little piggy if we don't get going." Mead dragged Punchy down the sidewalk while trying to conjure up images of Sophie.

"You can't just walk away from a miracle."

"Think of it as walking away from the clap."

In the next two blocks they were accosted four more times, their first experience with the notoriously aggressive Piccadilly "Commandos" who roved the area and descended on any man in uniform (one pound for a knee-trembler, five for the night).

"I've never felt so popular in my life," said Punchy, waving at a row of women lined along a building. "Look at them. They're practically salivating."

"Must be that Italian charm." Mead struggled to extract himself from the grip of a young-looking brunette while Punchy paused to revel in the attention of two blondes. "No, no ladies, you see, it's *you* who should pay *me*," he said. "Only seeing as I'm in such good spirits tonight, I may just be willing to offer a volume discount." He put his arms around the two women, who were rapidly losing interest. "Oh, what the hell, my treat tonight—on the house—what do you say?"

"Fuck off."

"Sweethearts, aren't they?" said Punchy as they continued on. "I'm telling you, people have got the Brits all wrong."

They stopped in another pub for a final round, again eyeing men who had fought in Africa and Italy; men in their early twenties with stories that would carry them the rest of their lives.

"Do you know what I could do with a Purple Heart?" said Punchy, shaking his head. "Jesus, the gals back home would be slobbering over me."

"Not if they have to push you around in a wheelchair all day," said Mead.

Punchy sighed as he stared at the legs of the waitress passing by. "I'm going to let you in on a little secret," he said suddenly, leaning forward and lowering his voice. From his eyes Mead could see he was drunk. "I *can't* die."

"Hey, that's great. Congratulations."

"No, what I mean is . . ." he lowered his voice even more, "I haven't had nearly enough sex yet. It would be—" he groped for words "—an *injustice.*"

"You suppose God takes that into account?"

Punchy furrowed his brow in thought. "That's what's got me worried."

Half an hour later they were heading back to their hotel, weaving slightly, when the air-raid sirens sounded, wailing mournfully across the blackened city. They froze and looked up, expecting to see the silhouettes of hundreds of German bombers overhead. Should they run for a shelter? But other pedestrians continued on their way, hardly looking up. Then in the distance they heard the thump-thump of anti-aircraft fire, which lit the sky like heat lightning. After several minutes the flashes stopped.

"Must have scared them off," said Punchy.

"Guess so."

Punchy scanned the sky, struggling to keep his balance. "I was kind of hoping to see more, weren't you?"

"Maybe some other night."

"Yeah, maybe some other night." Punchy searched the sky one more time, then put his arm around Mead as they headed down the street.

·   ·   ·

Mead and Andrew took a taxi from Heathrow to their small redbrick hotel in Kensington, arriving just before lunch.

"The trick is to adapt right away to the local time schedule," said Mead, though he hadn't traveled farther than Hawaii since the war. "Don't even think about California time." He glanced at his watch, quickly doing the math. Almost four A.M.

"I'm not tired," said Andrew, eyeing the two narrow beds separated only by a small bed stand. Twin reading lamps hung from the wall, their dirty yellow shades singed by the heat of the bulbs.

"Good. We'll unpack and take a walk. Might even be able to see Westminster, Whitehall and Saint Paul's before the day is done, then maybe Buckingham and the Tower tomorrow and a few museums the day after."

Mead began to unpack, carefully placing his undergarments in the bottom two drawers of the dresser and hanging his shirts and pants. He glanced over at Andrew, who had dropped his black duffel bag in the corner and sat on the bed nearest the window, looking lost.

Should he have booked separate rooms? But he had no intention of letting his grandson out of his sight. Let the little grouch suffer a little. Mead finished unpacking, trying to ignore the weariness in his legs, then went into the cramped bathroom and washed up, pulling out his bottles of pills and trying to decide whether he should double up or skip a dose to adjust to the time change. Cheaper to skip a dose.

As he shaved he thought of Evelyn and how excited she'd been when he'd told her about his plans, slapping her hands together and talking up all the sights they'd see as if she was going herself. "I want to hear everything when you get back," she'd said, cooking up a huge batch of goodies for their flight (by the time they were airborne only a few crumbs remained). She was so happy for the two of them that he knew he couldn't possibly tell her about what had happened, even though he wanted to ask her if he was doing the right thing. And yet when he asked her why she was moving, her face seemed to freeze up. "It's for the best," she said as they sat in her living room drinking iced tea after Mead stopped in to say good-bye.

"Where will you go?"

"My daughter—ace attorney, bills at three hundred fifty an hour!—has a lovely house in Connecticut. She has plenty of room—frankly, I don't know why if she's not going to have kids—and I really don't need much. After all, why should I dust and vacuum three bedrooms?" She gestured around the house.

"I just . . . had no idea."

A sadness passed over her face like a cloud, momentarily obscuring her smile. "To tell you the truth, I didn't either."

"Is something wrong?"

She picked up her iced tea, took a sip and set it down again. "When *isn't* something wrong?" He watched as her smile fell effortlessly back into place. "But we can't let that stop us now, can we?" She got up and walked over to a small china cabinet, opening the glass door and adjusting several teacups. "George never liked this room. He thought it was too feminine." She picked up a saucer and turned it side to side. "He always wanted one of those pine-paneled rec rooms."

"I never knew him very well."

"You two were quite different." She laughed wryly. "So were we. He tried his best. We both did. We were just missing something." She closed the cabinet door. "I'm not even sure what it was, to tell the truth. There was just this big hole right in the middle of everything. Some days I was afraid it would swallow me up."

Mead adjusted himself on the floral-patterned couch, scooting closer to the edge. Again he considered telling her about Andrew. Yet how could he?

Evelyn remained standing. "I don't want you to think I feel unfortunate. I'd be a fool to waste my life thinking about what I didn't have rather than all that I did."

Mead noticed her expression give way just as she turned toward the window. He got up and walked over to her. "What is it?" he asked, putting his arm around her and noticing how thin her shoulders felt beneath her shirt. She didn't respond. "Please, tell me."

"You don't want to know."

"But I do." He held her closer, feeling scared by the sudden pain in her face. She put her head against his chest. "I have been a fool. I've been a fool all my life." Just before he kissed her he closed his eyes and asked Sophie to please forgive him.

• • •

Andrew sat on the bed watching his grandfather unpack and wondering whether he really would have killed himself if he hadn't been stopped. Every time he thought about it he felt his legs go weak. I could be dead right now. (Though he had doubts about whether he really could have pulled the trigger.) The worst part was thinking about what it must have been like for his grandfather to walk in on something like that. *Fuck*. They hadn't talked any more about it since getting on the plane but it was there between them, so that Andrew could hardly look his grandfather in the eye. And now to be sharing a room together? This *sucks*.

He had barely had time to say good-bye to Evelyn. "He wants to take me sight-seeing," he explained, sneaking outside one afternoon when he saw her gardening. (Mead had grounded him, letting him out only to get their passports.)

"So I hear," she said, leaning over a rosebush. "What's come over him?"

"Everything." Andrew looked back at the house nervously.

"I think it sounds wonderful. I always wanted to travel more myself."

"But we won't see you again."

"Of course you will. I'm not moving that fast. I'll cook a special dinner when you get back."

"But what if you need something? What if you . . ."

"I'll be just fine." She clipped off a rose and handed it to him. "For the General," she said.

He'd worried about her the whole flight over, wondering who would take care of her if she got really sick and if he should tell his grandfather and whether she was going to die soon. They never should have left her alone. (And the sparks were just starting to fly.) Yet he had to admit that it was awesome to be in *England.* He couldn't get over the accent of the taxi driver who drove them from the airport—on the wrong side of the road!—and how old the buildings looked and the fact that he was practically on the other side of the planet. If only Matt was with him.

"Aren't you going to unpack?" asked his grandfather. "I left you two drawers." He pointed toward the small dresser.

Andrew looked over at his duffel bag. "I thought I'd just keep it packed," he said. "That way I know where everything is."

"You can't keep it there. We'll be tripping over it."

"I'll put it on the floor of the closet."

"That's for our shoes."

"How about under my bed?" Andrew was already on his knees trying to cram the duffel bag beneath the bed frame.

Mead stood watching with his hands on his hips. "Okay, under the bed." He shook his head as he went back into the bathroom. Andrew listened to the weak and sporadic trickle in the toilet, wondering if his grandfather had a problem peeing, or maybe even penis cancer or whatever it was called. Getting old's gotta be a bitch.

"You ready?" His grandfather now stood by the door holding the room key in one hand and an umbrella in the other.

"Where are we going?"

"Sight-seeing." A rare smile stretched the lines of his grandfather's face.

• • •

As soon as they entered Westminster Abbey—which Andrew recognized from watching Princess Diana's funeral (his mom stayed up all night weeping hysterically)—he decided it was the *perfect* place to scatter Matt's ashes, which were rolled up in a Ziploc in his pants pocket, creating an awkward bulge that caused his pants to sag more than usual. He felt almost giddy at the brilliance of it as his grandfather eagerly pointed out various monuments and read from a guidebook. What could be more perfect? And frankly, all these kings and queens and poets and statesmen could probably use a guy like Matt to mix it up a little. Damn, buddy, who would have believed you'd get a state funeral? He tried to keep from giggling as he considered the logistics. All he'd have to do is stick his hand in his pocket, take one handful of Matt at a time and let the stuff dribble out from his fingers as he walked, maybe humming an appropriate tune. Granted, it might take some time, but he could always come back later.

"Isn't it something?" said his grandfather, pausing to stare up at the ceiling.

"It's pretty harsh."

"What?"

"It's cool."

They headed for the royal tombs. "Are they for real?" asked Andrew, casually reaching into his pocket.

"As opposed to . . ."

"I mean, are they really *in there?*"

"Last I heard." They followed a line through a small entrance into a chapel. Mead gestured toward the large tomb. "Elizabeth the First."

"The one with all the face makeup, right? I saw a movie once—"

"Right."

Andrew tried to visualize how Elizabeth looked now. Probably pretty bad. Was she buried with lots of jewelry? He imagined breaking into the church at night and cracking open her tomb and slipping big fat glittering rings off her bony fingers. Wasn't like Lizzy needed them. Then he wondered if Matt's ghost would meet Lizzy's ghost, which might be kind of a scene. Would Matt remember to bow?

By the time they reached Poet's Corner Andrew had managed to open the Ziploc using one hand. As they stood looking at a memorial to Shakespeare he carefully reached in and took a small handful. Okay, here we go. He pulled out his closed fist and let it hang discreetly at his side, feeling his eyes well up and hoping his grandfather wouldn't notice. *Good-bye, friend.* He was just loosening his fingers when he looked up and saw a janitor sweeping the floor with great big strokes. Oh, shit. The janitor flicked a little pile into a dustpan, then emptied the dustpan into a plastic garbage can and moved on. Andrew carefully put his fist back in his pocket, worked open the Ziploc and emptied the ashes back into the bag. *Whew.*

Big Ben reminded Andrew of *Peter Pan,* which had been his favorite video when he was younger. He must have watched it a hundred times, prancing around on his parents' bed with a plastic sword. *Take that, Hook!* He stared up at the clock, imagining Peter Pan perched on the large hand and waving at him. For just a moment he could almost *feel* being a kid again, diving under the bed covers with a squeal when his dad tried to tickle him. *I'll get you, Pan!*

At Saint Paul's, Andrew again considered scattering Matt's ashes, thinking maybe he'd stuff them into some nook where they'd be safe. He searched for a good hiding place as he and his grandfather toured the tombs and statues but saw none he could reach. He gently tapped his pocket. *Don't worry, Matt, I won't let you end up in the trash.*

When they reached the spiral stairs leading up to the dome Mead suggested that Andrew go up and take a look.

"You're not coming?"

"I think I'll sit awhile. You go on."

Andrew climbed quickly, mesmerized by the churning buns of a teenage girl just ahead of him. He paused at the Whispering Gallery, listening to the echoing voices and remembering just how much he hated heights, which made him feel gooey inside. Then he followed the girl up to the next level, awed by the panoramic view of London below. *What do you say, Matt?* He imagined the ashes whirling through the air and coating the city below in a fine mist. *Hard to beat that, eh buddy?* He felt for the baggie in his pocket, hoping his stomach would hold out. Of course, Matt wasn't much for heights either. He looked over the edge again, then quickly stepped back. Would Matt's ashes float down or would it be more like *plummeting?* He tried to look again but felt so queasy that he had to grab the wall. *No way, buddy, I'm not letting you plummet.* He looked over at the cute girl's butt, trying to ground himself. Much better. Taking deep breaths he slowly followed her around the dome. Much, much better. His stomach had almost recovered when she turned and gave him such a dirty look that he stopped and headed back down the stairs. When he reached the bottom his grandfather was sitting in a pew with a strange expression on his face. Was he praying? Andrew waited nearby, checking out a group of uniformed schoolgirls being lectured by their teacher. Not bad looking. Even a couple of cute ones. He tried to catch one girl's eye but instead she gazed upward as the teacher explained how the cathedral was built. Andrew looked up too, thinking that if there was a God he'd certainly be impressed by a ceiling like that. He watched the girl for a while, then looked back at his grandfather, who hadn't moved. Did he believe in God? Andrew had tried praying a few times, thinking he'd take all the help he could get in his battle against acne. One night as he lay in bed in tears from the loneliness of everything he even tried to be born again, telling Jesus that he believed *totally* and that he'd never ever wank again. But when he looked in the mirror the next morning and saw the huge new eruption centered right between his eyes he decided that either there wasn't a God or, if there was, he was an asshole just like everybody else. After applying a layer of his mother's face makeup he sat on the toilet and quickly jerked off.

He watched as his grandfather rose unsteadily to his feet.

"You okay?"

"Just fine."

Neither of them talked during the taxi ride back to the hotel.

• • •

Mead couldn't get over how different London looked, great big modern buildings—cold and sterile—towering over the old Victorians. For some reason he didn't think of London changing, at least not the architecture. And yet some parts matched his memory so closely that he half expected to see Punchy walking beside him and ogling all the girls. But it wasn't until he and Andrew were walking back to the hotel after having dinner at a nearby Italian restaurant that the biggest change hit him: he'd never seen London lit up at night. Mead paused on the sidewalk and looked at the skyline, surprised by the sudden tearing of his eyes.

"What is it?" asked Andrew.

Mead blinked a couple of times and waited until he had his breath. "I was just thinking, it used to be dark."

"Huh?"

"During the war. Everything was blacked-out. Curtains over every window."

"Really? Wow. I'd love to be in a blacked-out city. Was it spooky?"

"I never thought of it that way." Mead smiled to himself as they walked on, remembering the furtive couples that would disappear into the darkened parks and how he and Punchy accidentally urinated on a couple rolling in the bushes. "Sorry about that," said Punchy, trying to stop himself as the woman screamed. "Must have the wrong bush."

• • •

"Well, what do you think so far?" asked Mead as they lay in their beds with the lights out.

"It's all right," mumbled Andrew.

"All right?"

"Yeah, I mean it's pretty cool."

Mead smiled in the darkness. "What did you like best?"

"Definitely the tombs of the kings and queens. I've never seen serious royalty."

"It doesn't get much more serious than that."

Andrew rolled over in his bed. In the hallway two guests giggled as they passed by. "You ever imagine what they look like now?"

"Sure," said Mead. "Everybody does."

"Really?"

"Of course."

"I never knew that."

They lay in silence, both listening for sounds that the other was asleep. Then Andrew said, "I'm sorry about what happened."

Mead paused. "So am I."

"I won't do it again."

"Let's hope not."

"And thanks for bringing me here. I've never been anywhere like this."

"You're welcome."

"I know it must be really expensive."

"It's my pleasure."

The couple in the hallway laughed again, then a door opened and closed.

"Good night."

"Good night, Andrew."

• • •

After breakfast in the hotel they watched The Changing of the Guard at Buckingham Palace, which gave Mead goose bumps, particularly the rhythmic, haunting clatter of the horses' hooves on the pavement—such a majestic yet lonely sound.

"She must be *loaded*," said Andrew, straining to see over the crowd.

"Old money," said Mead.

"What's that?"

"Something you'll never have."

But Andrew wasn't listening. "Are those guys real soldiers or are they just actors?"

"A little of both."

"That's my idea of the army. I mean, how hard can it be to march around and get photographed all day?"

"Come to think of it, you'd make a hell of a Queen's Life Guard."

Andrew straightened his posture. "You think so?"

"I've never seen you smile, and that's fifty percent of the job right there."

"Very funny."

At the Tower of London Andrew was mesmerized by the Crown Jewels and medieval weaponry and prison cells, thinking how Matt would have gone nuts over some of the stuff. As they stood on Tower Green in front of the spot where Anne Boleyn lost her head he felt the bulge in his pocket. Should I scatter him in the grass? At least he wouldn't be swept up. And not every guy can say his best friend is buried at the Tower of London. Then again it wasn't a particularly cheery place (not that Matt was so cheery himself). And what if he ends up on the rack being tortured? No, better not.

" 'I heard say the executioner was very good, and I have a little neck,' " said Mead, reading from a guidebook.

"Huh?"

"Anne Boleyn's last words—or some of them."

Andrew rubbed his neck while keeping his eye on a big fat raven that seemed to be watching him. "Why'd he kill her?"

"I suppose because she was only his second wife and he had four more to go. Her daughter, by the way, was Elizabeth the First."

"The guy was worse than my dad," said Andrew.

"Oh, I don't think he was quite that bad."

•   •   •

After lunch they took a boat tour on the Thames, sitting outside on the upper deck despite the slight drizzle. As Mead looked at the wharves and buildings and passing boats he thought of Evelyn, wondering whether she'd had an offer on the house and bracing himself for her absence. He closed his eyes and remembered how it had felt to hold her—the first time in years he'd held anybody. And then without thinking he'd kissed her.

"Come to Europe with us," he'd said, nearly lifting her up off the ground in his excitement. "You said you always wanted to see more of the world and you know how much Andrew would enjoy having you along."

"I can't," she said, suddenly pulling back from him.

"Sure you can."

Her expression wavered.

"I'll take care of the ticket. You can put your house on the market when you get back. Better yet, take it off the market. You don't really want to live with your daughter, do you? And what about your garden and all the memories you have here? What about . . ." He couldn't think what else to say.

"I can't go with you. Please don't ask me to explain why. I just . . . can't."

He stood looking at her and trying to make sense of things. Had he somehow offended her? Then everything became so clear to him that he wanted to smack his head with his fist: she's not interested in you anymore. Those poems were written *years* ago. He let go of her, feeling embarrassed and confused. "I have to finish packing," he said, heading for the door.

"I'm sorry I can't go with you."

"I had no business asking."

"Actually, I'm thrilled that you asked."

He hesitated. "But why . . ."

"I just can't leave now. There are too many things I need to take care of. Please understand."

"But I—"

"*Please.*"

They stood in her doorway briefly, neither saying anything, then she leaned forward and kissed him quickly. "Have a wonderful trip," she called out as he hurried down the walkway. "And take care of that charming grandson of yours, you hear?"

Mead had gone over the scene endlessly in his head, taking apart all the pieces and carefully reassembling them, yet each time he only felt more foolish than before, then angry at having allowed himself to get so carried away. He pulled his collar up as the drizzle turned to rain. To hell with her. She only would have gotten in the way, telling him what to do and fussing over Andrew.

He looked over at the boy. Charming? No way. But he did seem to be enjoying himself. He didn't sulk once at the Tower of London and even looked downright peppy at the Crown Jewels exhibit. And yet there was so much they needed to talk about. Mead again recalled running into Sophie's room and seeing the boy with the gun in his mouth, which made his insides ache.

"How are you getting along with your mother these days?" he asked, trying to break the ice.

Andrew shrugged. "We don't really talk that much. She's, you know, busy. And she's kind of stressed."

"She's doing her best. You can't blame her for your father leaving."

"It doesn't matter."

"What does matter to you?"

Andrew watched a police boat race past.

"Tell me."

"You really want to know? Nothing matters to me."

Mead searched his grandson's face for some thread he could grab hold of. "Why are you so angry?"

"Who said I'm angry?"

"I did."

Andrew seemed to hesitate. "Everything is just so . . . stupid," he said finally.

"What the hell is that supposed to mean?"

"I can't explain it."

"Is that how your friend felt?"

"Matt?"

"The one who . . ."

"That's Matt." Andrew drained his Coke and fiddled with his earring.

"What was he like?"

A smile came over Andrew's freckled face, which glistened in the mist. "Oh, he was great. Personally, I think he was a genius, only no one knew it. And he was funny, too. He could draw just about anything."

"Did he play any sports?"

Andrew laughed. "Matt? Are you kidding? He *hated* sports."

"Not the athletic type?"

"Not exactly." Andrew laughed again. "He couldn't stand the jocks."

"What's wrong with the jocks?"

Andrew looked at Mead like he'd lost his mind. "*Everything* is wrong with them, at least at my school. They're idiots, only they think they're harsh. The fact is they don't have a clue about what's really going on."

Mead rubbed his chin for a moment as he listened. "What is really going on?"

Andrew shrugged. "You know, *stuff.* See, that was the thing about Matt, he understood exactly what was going on."

"I'm still not sure what it is exactly that's going on."

"You know," Andrew lowered his voice, "bullshit."

"Bullshit?"

"Sure, don't you think so?"

Mead hesitated. "Come to think of it, I guess there is a fair amount of bullshit."

Andrew smiled, as if his grandfather had passed a critical test and their relationship could now proceed to a whole new level. "Only, see, the jocks don't have a clue about all the bullshit that's going on because they're too busy being jocks, which is total bullshit."

"But of course you do?"

"Sure. Don't you ever think about how weird reality is? You know, when you really *think* about it?"

"I guess I'm sort of accustomed to it by now."

Andrew looked disappointed. "Matt figured we're not actually dealing with real reality, which makes a lot of sense. Society is like this PG version of the real thing because people basically can't handle real triple-X reality. It's all about faking it, only, most people don't even remember that they're faking it. And that's what sucks about school."

"Faking what?"

"You know, the stuff we're really thinking about and all the shit that's really going on in the world. Haven't you ever noticed how stupid most conversations are? I don't mean this one, but most of them?"

"You sure you're not taking drugs?"

"I'm *not* on drugs."

Mead shook his head. "You're going to drive yourself crazy with those kinds of thoughts."

"I can't help it."

"Maybe you should consider going to church. Might straighten you out."

"I don't need straightening out."

"You sure need something."

"Tell me the truth. Don't you ever think that life is kind of . . . ridiculous sometimes?"

"Of course I do. That's what laughter is for."

"But people take the stupidest things seriously. It's like what I was saying about the jocks. People are dying by the millions in Africa—have you heard about the AIDS crisis there?—and the forests are all getting chopped down and the ice caps are melting and all anybody at school cares about is what kind of shoes you're wearing and whether we're going to the championships."

Mead smiled. "Well, I suppose you can obsess about shoes and sports or whether the universe will collapse on itself. In the end, it comes down to a matter of temperament."

"Matt could explain it better. He read tons of books about what's really going on."

Mead watched a passing barge. "When I was your age I didn't have the luxury of worrying about such things."

"But you were lucky."

"Lucky?"

"I don't mean about the guys who got killed, I'm just saying that at least you got to deal with stuff that really mattered. Things were totally intense, right?"

Mead paused, not sure how to respond. "I suppose, but—"

"Well, nothing is intense at my school. Trust me."

"You have no idea how fortunate you are, do you?"

Andrew shrugged.

Mead looked out across the river, not knowing where to begin. "Why did he do it?"

Another shrug.

"You must have some idea."

"Sure I do."

"I'd be interested—if you don't mind talking about it."

Andrew looked over at Mead, as if unsure whether he was serious, then rubbed his palms across the tops of his thighs. "Well, there was this girl— I didn't think much of her, but Matt was crazy about her—and she basically told him he was a creep."

"And that's why he killed himself?"

"It wasn't just that. It was everything. See, his dad's a total loser and he got picked on a lot and he was just . . ." Mead watched as Andrew struggled to control his voice. "He was . . . he was real sensitive. He felt *everything*."

"Like you?"

Andrew quickly turned his face away.

"Things are never that bad," said Mead. "They may look that bad, but they're not. And everything passes. Everything."

"You don't understand."

"I'm trying."

"Everybody pushed him too far. They drove him to it."

"What about you?"

Andrew didn't respond.

"Please. I want to understand why you feel so . . . pushed."

"Forget it."

"Not a chance." Mead leaned toward Andrew. "Listen to me, whatever it is that's eating you up inside, it isn't worth throwing your life away for, you got that? Hell, your life will be over soon enough as it is." Mead tried to think of what else to say as the boat passed under Tower Bridge.

"I tried to wake him but I couldn't," Andrew said suddenly, his face contorting. "I really tried."

"I believe you."

"He felt so cold. I never touched anything so cold in my life."

Mead put his arm around Andrew, feeling the boy's narrow shoulders shake. "I'm sorry. I'm truly sorry."

"You don't know what it was like," Andrew whispered.

"Yes, I think maybe I do."

• • •

That Christmas in the Ardenne was the prettiest Mead had ever seen, the fields and trees and houses whitewashed with snow so that even the frozen corpses looked peaceful. It seemed ludicrous to fight a war amid such beauty, which reminded Mead of boyhood, the snowflakes twirling before his face and the tree limbs sagging beneath their crystal white carapace.

"I'm so cold I'm not even horny," said Punchy, pausing to catch his breath as they dug a foxhole in the hardened earth.

"It's not *that* cold."

"Like hell it ain't."

Three hours later they had carved out a space four feet deep, two feet wide and five feet long. After pausing to split a Clark bar and a Lucky Strike they gathered up pine needles and lay them along the bottom. Then they used a hand axe to cut down two nearby trees and section them into logs, which they placed over the top, leaving two small openings. Finally they covered the logs with branches and camouflaged the branches with snow.

"I think my dick's gonna fall off," said Punchy, curling up in a ball on the pine needles and shivering.

"It's your feet I'm worried about." Punchy's toes had begun turning a blackish blue. "Let me massage them."

"You're rather fond of them, aren't you?"

"Hurry up before I change my mind." Punchy extended his left foot and Mead placed the boot between his knees, then struggled with numb fingers to undo the laces.

"Easy," moaned Punchy as Mead pulled off the boot.

"Christ, I've never smelled anything so foul in my life."

"That's my good foot."

"Give me a dry sock." Punchy reached inside his coat and shirt and pulled out the spare pair of socks he kept around his neck. Mead quickly stripped the wet sock off and began massaging the foot, trying to knead some warmth into the cold and unresponsive flesh.

Punchy took the wet sock and placed it inside his shirt to dry, then leaned back and closed his eyes. "I've been doing some thinking," he said. "And I've come up with a lot of questions for Sister Henrietta." Whenever he was miserable, Punchy sought refuge in the Catholic teachings of his childhood, only he could never remember more than bits and pieces, most of which had to do with sitting up straight and cleaning under his fingernails. "For starters, I'd like to know what the hell I ever did to deserve this."

"I could take a wild guess," said Mead, now rubbing the toes gently, afraid the smaller ones might snap off in his hands.

"You should have heard Sister Henrietta. She had all the answers. Fact is, I'm kind of sorry I didn't pay more attention."

"Did she have any advice for frostbite?"

Punchy laughed. "She had advice for *everything.*"

Mead finished with the left foot, then began with the right, pausing briefly to stand up and listen for any movement in the woods in front of their position. As he finished his hands shook so badly that he could barely lace the boot up.

"You're going to make somebody a hell of a wife one day," said Punchy.

"Get some sleep." Mead slid his hands into his armpits trying to warm them.

Punchy was quiet for a few minutes, then said, "You ever worry that you're going to fall asleep and never wake up?"

"We should be so lucky." Mead bent down and tried to gather some of the pine needles around Punchy, making him a nest. "Sweet dreams."

"Nighty-night, darling." Punchy blew Mead a kiss, then groaned a few more times before beginning to snore.

Mead stood and surveyed the snowy woods, trying to memorize the shadows in case they moved. It began snowing again, this time thick wet flakes that stuck to his neck. He strained to hear noises from the other foxholes to his left and right and the outpost several dozen yards in front but there was only silence. What were the other men thinking of? Food? Girlfriends? God? He tried to wiggle his toes but only the two big ones seemed to move. He thought of the German *SS* prisoners he'd seen the day before, forced to stand barefoot in the snow after being captured wearing American boots. By the time they were sent to the rear they faced certain amputation. News of the massacre of GIs at Malmédy left little compassion. "Please, komerad," one had begged Mead as he passed. And yet he had felt no pity at all.

Ten minutes passed. Then twenty. The wind picked up so that Mead had to blink frequently as blowing snow stung his eyes. He tried to imagine Sophie lying in her bed; how warm and clean and soft and lovely she was. Will I ever touch her again? Such joy seemed incomprehensible. Then he thought of his brother Thomas, wondering what his last minutes were like. Was he dead before the ship went down or did he struggle in the oil-slicked water? Mead had no idea how cold the South Pacific was but figured any ocean had to be pretty damn chilly. He remembered all the warm summer afternoons they spent playing catch in the backyard, the air buggy and moist. Then he thought of the blanket forts they used to make in Thomas's bedroom and how they'd sit in the dark with their flashlights eating candy and telling ghost stories. They shared every secret, at least until Thomas got old enough to start dating, which ruined everything. Thomas was going to be a first baseman for the Red Sox while Mead was going to be an inventor or scientist. Mead smiled to himself, remembering how the future once seemed to stretch out forever like the railroad tracks near their house. Where did you go, big brother? And yet knowing that Thomas was dead somehow made his own death seem less scary, as if his brother would be there waiting for him on the other side. Whatever you can do I can do. Even that.

Suddenly Sergeant Fry appeared beside Mead's foxhole. "We're moving out. Orders."

"You're kidding?" They'd only been dug in an hour.

"Some mix-up. We're supposed to be five hundred yards south." Fry disappeared in the darkness.

Mead turned his face up to the snow, wanting to cry but feeling too tired and numb. He crouched down and nudged Punchy. "Wake up." He nudged him again, then finally gave him a gentle kick. "Rise and shine, lover boy."

Punchy moaned. "Ah Christ, three hours already? I was just getting comfortable."

Mead didn't have the heart to correct him. Besides, maybe he'd feel more rested if he didn't know. "We're in the wrong place."

"Huh?"

"Fry says we're supposed to be five hundred yards to the south." Mead began climbing out of the foxhole.

Punchy sat absorbing the implications, then slammed his fist into the side of the foxhole. "Okay, that's *it*. I don't care if they put me up for a court martial. I don't care if they shoot me. I am *not* moving from this goddamn foxhole. Understood?"

"Understood."

"I don't even give a shit if Patton himself orders me. *I am not moving from this foxhole tonight.*"

"Right-o."

"Hell, I don't care if I have to hold off an entire panzer division by myself. I am staying *put.*" Punchy curled up again in the pine needles.

"Gotcha."

Two hours later they had scratched out another foxhole five hundred yards to the south, this time only three feet deep and barely big enough for both to crouch in. They set out two land mines in front of their position, then covered the foxhole with branches before crawling in, deciding to wait until daylight to dig deeper and reinforce the roof. Punchy stood watch while Mead slipped almost instantly into a stuporous sleep. As soon as he closed his eyes he found himself crawling on his hands and knees through a warm tunnel.

"Good to see you, little brother," said Thomas, who was sitting cross-legged at the far end of the blanket fort with his face lit by a flashlight. It really was Thomas, and the fort was perfect, with three different chambers and a secret door in the rear. Mead felt so happy his face hurt from smiling. As they sat playing cards and drinking hot chocolate Mead kept looking at his brother's handsome face, wondering how he could know so much about everything and wanting to be exactly like him when he got older. Then it came roaring back at him so that he wanted to scream.

"Don't go, Thomas! If you go you're going to drown in the ocean!"

"What are you talking about, you bonehead?"

"I'm not kidding, Thomas." Mead was crying now. "If you go your ship is gonna sink and you're going to die and I'll never see you again."

"Don't be silly." Thomas flicked off the flashlight, leaving Mead alone in the dark.

"Thomas? Please turn the light on, Thomas. Thomas, *please!*"

Suddenly Mead was jolted awake by an explosion. A mine had detonated in front of their position. He was up instantly, grabbing for his rifle and then firing blindly into the dark alongside Punchy. Shooting erupted from the other foxholes as well and several men tossed grenades. After several minutes the gunfire died down.

"You see anything?" whispered Punchy.

"I can't see a thing." Mead slurred from exhaustion.

Punchy looked side to side. "How do we know our flanks are covered? Hell, I'll bet we're still in the wrong position."

Mead wiped his face and tried to shake his head clear, knowing that sleep was now out of the question. "Tell you what, you scout it out and I'll stay here and keep things warm."

They waited anxiously, but only the wind in the trees broke the silence. Punchy stuffed two pieces of gum into his mouth. "I've never been this cold in my life."

"You said that last night."

"I'm even colder than that." He smacked his gum between his teeth. "How cold do you suppose it is?"

"Let's talk about something else."

"Sure, what do you want to talk about?"

Mead figured that over the months together they'd talked about everything at least once and many subjects dozens of times, so that they could almost mouth each other's responses. He thought for a moment, then asked, "How come you wanted to be a boxer?"

Punchy chewed loudly. "You really want to know?" Mead nodded, expecting Punchy to explain how irresistible he looked in boxing shorts. "Because I had a crooked nose."

"I thought you got that in the ring?"

"That's what you're supposed to think. Truth is, I've always had a crooked nose. Boxing gave me an excuse. You know, boxers are *supposed* to have crooked noses."

"No kidding?" Mead laughed. "But you liked boxing? I mean, you were good?"

Punchy hesitated. "Not really."

"What about all those stories . . . ?"

Punchy made a sheepish expression. "Look, this stuff is just between you and me, okay?"

"Sure thing." Mead wiped the snow from his eyelids. "You know something, you're a lot more complicated than you look."

"Is that a compliment?" Punchy looked doubtful.

"Definitely."

"Thanks." Punchy rubbed his hands together. The snow was now falling so heavily that their helmets had turned white.

"So you were never really much of a boxer?" Mead was still smiling to himself.

"I don't want to talk about it anymore, okay?"

"Fine, your turn."

Punchy worked the gum around his mouth. "Remember that girl at the Red Cross desk in London? The one with the lips?"

"The one you proposed to?" Punchy smiled wistfully. "You still think of her?"

"I think about all of them." He gently knocked the snow off his rifle. "I've got every single one memorized."

"In your case that's no small feat."

"See, it's like I've got these index cards in my head with their photos on them."

"Dare I ask how many cards?"

"I don't know, maybe three hundred. Every night I just start at the top and work my way to the bottom."

"Is that why you make all those funny noises when you sleep?"

Suddenly another mine on their left exploded. Several dozen men immediately opened fire but again there was no return fire and within minutes the shooting stopped.

"You figure they're just probing our lines?" asked Mead, still staring down the barrel of his rifle and feeling dizzy from fatigue.

"Nah, they must be lost," said Punchy. "You couldn't find your own asshole out there."

They struggled to remain alert for the rest of the night, both peering into the snowy darkness and leaning against each other for warmth. The next morning just after sunrise the snow turned to icy rain, exposing the remains of two large deer that had wandered into their position. An hour later they were ordered to pack up and move out.

"All that fresh venison going to waste," grumbled Punchy, who was down to his last Clark bar. "I'm telling you, Mead, we are at the mercy of knuckleheads."

• • •

The next morning Mead supervised exercises in the hotel room before breakfast. "You're up to twenty," he said proudly as Andrew collapsed onto his face. "Keep it up and you might even make varsity next year."

"Are we done yet?"

"One more set of sit-ups."

While Andrew showered—the moment the water came on the boy began singing like a canary—Mead sat at the small corner table and wrote a postcard to Sharon telling her about all the things they'd seen so far and reminding her to buy a new car. When Andrew emerged Mead noticed skin-colored splotches on the boy's face, creating a bizarre two-tone effect. "Are you wearing . . . *makeup?*"

Andrew put his hand over his chin. "It's just cover-up."

"Cover-up?"

"For my acne."

"Oh."

"I got it from Mom."

"She teach you how to put it on?"

"Yeah."

"Figures." Mead got up and grabbed the room key while Andrew hurried back into the bathroom. When he finally came out again his face looked worse than before.

"Where to?"

Mead smiled. "The Imperial War Museum."

As soon as Mead entered the main gallery and saw the German markings on the Jagdpanther tank destroyer he felt an instinctive fear. Silly, he told himself, and yet he couldn't shake it. Andrew walked over and placed his arm through one of the three shell holes that pierced its thick armor. "Check it out," he said. "The Germans inside must have *fried.*"

Mead walked over to look at a Sherman tank while Andrew inspected a German one-man submarine and then a small wooden fishing boat used during the evacuation of Dunkirk. A V-2 rocket towered above them while a Spitfire, a Heinkel and a P-51 Mustang hung from the ceiling. Mead couldn't get over how shiny and new and toy-like everything looked. What would his grandson learn by looking at toys?

After touring the main exhibition gallery they went downstairs and turned left into the First World War exhibit, peering through the glass displays at dozens of weapons and maps and souvenirs. Mead looked at a gas mask and thought of his father, wishing he'd lived long enough to see Germany finally and utterly defeated.

"Hey Grandfather, come see this," said Andrew excitedly when they reached the entrance to a life-size recreation of a trench, complete with wounded men, sound effects and ominous red flashes in the illusionary distance. Mead cautiously followed Andrew in, remembering the foxholes of the Ardenne—always digging—and the constant smell of filth and decay, which clung to him for so many years that he used to keep a box of Altoids in his pocket.

"Was it like this?" asked Andrew, peering over the parapet across the desolation of no-man's land toward the enemy lines.

"We were usually in foxholes," said Mead. "They're much smaller." He looked at the two life-size British soldiers going over the top as voices played over hidden loudspeakers. "But you get the general idea."

"Man, I'd hate it," said Andrew.

"Yes, I bet you would."

Emerging from the trench they passed through an exhibit of Hitler's rise to power, pausing to look at large photos of jeering faces and then endless columns of soldiers and finally a wild-eyed Fuhrer lathering the people into a frenzy like a master of the hounds just before the hunt. Mead remembered sitting around the radio after dinner with his parents and thinking how comical the German language sounded.

"Why must he always shout?" his mother would ask.

"Maybe the Germans are hard of hearing," said Thomas, who'd always been much funnier and smarter than Mead.

"Well, I think it's rude."

"That fella wants war," his father would say, puffing sadly on his pipe.

"We beat them once, we can beat them again," young Mead had boasted, trying to sound tough.

His father looked over at him, taking a long drag from his pipe. "But that's where you're wrong, son." He emptied the pipe into an ashtray and began scraping the bowl with a small silver tool he kept in the pocket of his gray sweater. "You see, we never did beat them." At the time, Mead had no idea what his father meant.

As they continued through the exhibit Mead stopped to stare at a death mask of Himmler, studying the dead man's placid features. Then he paused before a white summer tunic that once belonged to Goering, feeling a sense of repulsion as he thought of the fabric clinging to the sweaty flesh of the Devil's big fat piglet. Had it been dry cleaned? Did it still smell of him? And there was Goebbels, the faithful lap dog. You little shit. Would you have traded it all for a smooth complexion and a few more inches of height? (And how was it to poison your six little children in the end?) He looked at the adoring faces of Germans lining the street as Hitler's motorcade passed. "We never did trust the Nazis," they'd insist when the war was lost and white sheets hung from every house as the American convoys streamed in. "We just want peace." And the damndest thing was, it got harder and harder to hate the German people as they busily cleaned up the rubble and hid colored eggs for the children on Easter and crowded the churches, as though an evil spell had been broken.

He looked again at his grandson, wondering if any of it meant anything to him or whether it was like looking at swords and armor in a medieval exhibit, where the striking thing is the craftsmanship.

"We've got to try this," said Andrew, getting in line for something called The Blitz Experience. After waiting ten minutes with a group of schoolchildren and two old ladies they entered a re-creation of an air-raid shelter. Soon the lights darkened and sirens wailed over the recorded chatter of voices, as if others were with them huddled beneath the city as bombs rained down above. "Just the way I remember it," said one of the ladies. "Gives me chills, it does." After the simulated attack they left the bomb shelter and walked through a life-size diorama of a city street in ruins, bricks piled everywhere and voices calling for help. "Would you look at that," said the other lady, pointing to a smashed storefront. "Dried eggs for sale!"

"That was kind of hokey," said Andrew as they emerged. Mead didn't respond as they headed toward a display for Operation Overlord. "Here's the D-Day stuff," Andrew said excitedly, as if expecting his grandfather to jump for joy.

"So it is." Mead approached slowly.

"I can't believe you were really there. That must have been *wild*."

"Sometimes I can't believe I was there either." They both stood side by side before a large map of the landing beaches.

"What's it like looking at this stuff?"

Mead turned toward a life-size mannequin of a German soldier reaching for his pistol. "A bit difficult, to tell the truth."

"I figured."

They studied the displays in silence for several minutes until Andrew suddenly asked, "Is this where you killed that German?"

"I . . . what makes you think that I killed him?"

"I figured you must have. That's why you have all his stuff. Of course, he could have been dead when you found him. I never really thought of that."

"It happened in Germany," Mead said abruptly, moving quickly to the next exhibit.

Andrew followed closely behind. "*What* happened?"

Mead stopped and turned. "Yes, I killed him. That's what happened."

"Oh."

Mead headed for the exit, pausing before a large chart tallying the death toll of the war.

"Was he coming at you? Was it like a big battle?"

Mead hesitated. "It doesn't matter anymore."

As they headed back to the hotel Mead felt he had made a terrible mistake by coming.

• • •

Andrew tried masturbating in the shower but it was way too weird knowing his grandfather was right outside the door. And fuck me, he never left the room for a minute. I'm gonna go insane, he thought, grabbing a towel. Can you die from horniness?

They were leaving for France early the next morning and he could hear his grandfather packing. He'd been quiet ever since the war museum and Andrew wondered whether he was having some sort of flashback. He'd seen a show once about Vietnam vets who went ape-shit at any loud noise, gunning down entire families. Jesus, what if Sarge wakes up in the middle of the night and thinks I'm a Sauerkraut?

After the lights were out he waited until his grandfather's breathing deepened, then reached down to his crotch and began quietly stroking himself. *C r e a k*. He tried a lighter touch, hoping to find a rhythm that would do the job without alerting the bed springs. But no matter how subtle his movements the bed acted as a highly sensitive motion detector. *Fuck*. Finally he interlaced his hands behind his head and tried to will himself into an orgasm, but that only made him want to jerk off more.

He listened to his grandfather's long, deep breaths, wondering what he was dreaming. Was he fighting Sauerkrauts? Watching a buddy get shot? Taking Grandma on their first date? Then he thought of Evelyn and how much fun she was and how unfair it was that she had to die. Was it cancer? What kind of cancer and how painful was it? He remembered the look on her face when she grabbed onto him, like someone had just punched her. *Hang on, Evelyn. You gotta hang on.* After a few minutes he rolled to his stomach, closed his eyes and tried to count all the different royal jewels and swords he'd seen. When that got boring he tried to create a perfect three-dimensional mental image of Cori Fletcher in the nude, but that left him so agitated that he had to think about staying back a year again. Then he thought of Matt and the bag of his ashes that was stashed beneath the bed in one of the zipper compartments of his luggage. *What am I going to do with you, buddy?*

Stealing Matt's remains had been surprisingly easy. Andrew had a key to Matt's place, which no one knew about, and when he found out that Matt's parents were taking the ashes to Indiana that Saturday to be buried, he figured the ashes must be somewhere in their apartment. (He hadn't been invited to the funeral. Instead, he locked himself in his room and cranked all Matt's favorite songs.)

At lunchtime on Friday he rode his bike over, circling the block to make sure their cars were gone. Then he hurried up to number 3C, put on his mother's lime green Living Hands dishwashing gloves and opened the door, locking it quickly behind him.

Jesus, this is creepy. He stood by the door listening, half expecting to hear Matt's boom box blasting from his room. He fought the desire to turn and flee. *Can't let 'em bury Matt in Indiana. Besides, Matt's ghost wouldn't hurt him . . . would it?*

"Hello?"

Silence. He flicked on a light, then walked quickly down the hall to Matt's door, which was closed. Why closed? Was it to keep things in or out? He reached for the knob, then hesitated, placing his ear to the door. Do spirits hang out in their old bedrooms? He knocked lightly. "Matt?" He turned the knob and opened the door a crack, wanting suddenly to run from the apartment. "Matt?" He opened the door further. "Don't try to freak me out, okay Matt?"

He stepped inside, surprised by how much the room still smelled like Matt. Only, it was cleaner than he'd ever seen it, the bed made perfectly and not a sock on the floor. He glanced over at the closet, which was closed. "It's me, Andrew. Please don't try to scare me, okay?"

The small white urn sat on the dresser next to Matt's bed. He carefully picked it up, then gave it a gentle shake. He thought it might be sealed but it opened easily. He took the top off and peered inside. "Jesus, what have they done to you?" He took off the Living Hands gloves, reached in and carefully picked up one of the larger chips, holding it up to his face as warm tears ran down his cheeks. *We've got to get out of the Midwest, Andrew. I'm telling you, it's all happening on the coasts.*

"Don't worry, buddy, I won't let them take you to Indiana. No fucking way."

He spent several minutes crying and looking at the ashes, thinking how they weren't really like ashes at all. Then he went into the kitchen and rummaged through the drawers before finding a box of large Ziplocs. Perfect. After transferring the ashes to one bag he sealed it and placed it inside another. Safe and sound. Then he searched through more cupboards before settling on a box of C&H granulated pure cane sugar. Different consistency, but at least it would provide some weight. After filling the urn to the brim he placed it back on the dresser, smiling to himself as he thought of Matt's asshole dad dipping his finger in and tasting it and deciding that maybe his son was a sweet kid after all.

When he finished he went back in the kitchen and liberated a bag of Oreo's, eating half on the spot and stuffing the rest in his pockets. Then he returned to Matt's bedroom and sat on the bed with the Ziploc on his lap, feeling full and depressed. He looked at the posters of Jimi Hendrix and Kurt Cobain and Bob Marley and Sid Vicious, wondering if Matt was partying with them somewhere, which made him feel lonely and left behind. He got up and looked through Matt's desk drawers until he found his drawing tablet, which was filled with sketches of houses. Picking out his favorite he tore off the page, carefully folded it and placed it in his pocket. Then he put on the gloves, grabbed the Ziploc and turned off the light, closing the door quietly behind him.

The call came from Indiana the next day. Andrew knew immediately as he watched his mom on the phone, her jaw dropping slowly to the floor as she violently stamped out a cigarette. Busted. He quickly put on the solemn face he'd been practicing in the mirror and braced himself.

"All right young man, what the hell did you do with . . ." she stood in front of him flailing her hands, "you know . . . *him?*"

"Him?"

"Matt."

"*Matt?* What are you talking about?"

She came closer and stared into his face. Uh oh, mind reading. *All hands below deck. Gamma ray shields, full power. She can't take much more, Scotty.*

"You know *exactly* what I'm talking about."

She searched his room twice, even removing the cover on the heating duct. But Matt was safely hidden in a plastic container in the forest preserve. "Maybe the mortuary screwed up," Andrew suggested after the second search. "You read those kind of stories all the time."

"It was *sugar.*"

"No kidding? You know he always did have a serious sweet tooth."

Matt's parents briefly threatened legal action and the dad even came close to clocking Andrew during one particularly ugly visit. But the whole incident was so awkward that everybody seemed more concerned with avoiding publicity than finding out what happened to Matt.

After Andrew's mom finally gave up her search Andrew dug up the Ziploc baggie from the forest preserve and began carrying it to school each day in his backpack, feeling like he needed all the companionship he could get. And then one afternoon while he was sitting in English class looking at Megan Wynn and wondering what Matt ever saw in her, it came to him. The next morning he arrived in class early and hurried over to the front row left section where Megan always sat in one of two chairs. But which one? He hesitated before selecting the chair on the right. Reaching into his pocket for the small baggie containing a portion of Matt's ashes—which he'd divvied up for this mission—he took a pinch and sprinkled it on the seat, careful to monitor the classroom door. After making sure the ashes weren't too visible he quickly took his spot in the back of the room and waited. *You're gonna love this, Matt.*

Just before the bell rang Megan walked in. She gave the class her customary smile, running one hand through her hair to make sure everyone noticed just how unbelievably perfect it was, then headed for the front left section, hips swiveling. Both seats were still empty. Andrew gritted his teeth as he tried to will her into the chair on the right. *Please please please.* She paused before the chair containing Matt's ashes, then slid into the adjacent seat. *Damn!* The bell rang. At least Matt would be safe. But just as the teacher began the lecture the door opened again and Bill Humphrey lumbered in. *Oh, no.* But Humphrey wouldn't dare sit next to Megan Wynn. It was unthinkable. Humphrey stood scanning the room, a helpless expression flooding his sweaty, red face. *What's he waiting for?* Then

Andrew understood. Humphrey couldn't get to the other two available desks, not without plowing down narrow aisles clogged with legs and book bags. Slowly and sheepishly, he headed for the seat next to Megan, who recoiled in horror. Andrew closed his eyes as Humphrey lowered himself onto Matt's remains.

Courage, Matt.

Andrew made three more attempts, but each time Megan selected the other chair, leaving Matt to suffer a variety of unspeakable fates. Finally on the fourth try Matt got his girl. *We have touchdown.* Andrew could hardly contain himself as he watched Megan settle in right on top of Matt's remains, rubbing her butt left and right as she got comfortable. *Go Matt, go!*

"Is something wrong, Andrew?" asked the teacher as Andrew squirmed in his seat.

"Everything's just great," he said. "Really, really great."

Normandy

They arrived in Caen at dusk after taking the ferry from Portsmouth. Andrew was bored and queasy during the six-hour crossing and spent most of the time listening to his headphones and asking how much longer. Mead sat quietly, walking out on the deck now and then to look out over the rough ocean and then at the Normandy coast coming into view. After disembarking they rented a car—the smallest Andrew had ever seen—and headed for their hotel, stopping to ask three different people for directions, including a cute young French girl who looked at Andrew like he was the biggest tourist nerd in the world.

"I could really go for a bean burrito," said Andrew after they checked in to their narrow room, which was on the third floor overlooking a side street. "Do you suppose they have a Taco Bell around here?"

"Over my dead body," said Mead.

They ended up at a bright and nearly empty café where Mead struggled to translate the menu with a guidebook while the short balding waiter looked on with disdain.

"Sheep brains?" said Andrew.

"I thought that might get a rise out of you." Mead continued down the list. "Perhaps you'd prefer the chicken gizzards?"

"I'm gonna throw up."

"Now, what's the word for frog?"

Andrew looked ill as he sank into his seat. "Is there anything the French *won't* eat?"

"Not if it moves."

Andrew finally settled on a triple order of fries while Mead had a steak.

After they finished Mead pulled out a map, laid it across the table and tried to explain the military situation in Europe just prior to the landings.

"Did guys really piss in their pants from fear?"

"You're not listening."

"I was just wondering. You read about it but I thought maybe it was one of those things like people's hair turning white from fright."

Mead frowned. "As a matter of fact, yes, they did."

"Did—"

"Once."

"Wow. I can't imagine being that scared. Did you ever see anybody's hair—"

"Back to the map." Mead pushed it toward Andrew. "These are the main invasion beaches. The British and Canadian sectors were over here while the Americans landed here and here. The 101st and 82nd Airborne jump zones were in these areas and I landed somewhere around here," he jabbed the map with his finger, "though I couldn't tell you precisely where."

"Why not?"

"It was dark, for one."

Andrew studied the map. "And where were the Germans?"

Mead smiled. "Everywhere."

"No wonder you guys were pissing in your pants."

"So were the Germans. Anyway, I figure we'll start here and drive past Sword, Juno and Gold beaches tomorrow on our way to Omaha Beach. We may even make it to Pointe de Hoc. Then the next day I thought we might drive through Carentan and Ste.-Mère-Église, then tour the jump zones before stopping at Utah Beach."

"Sounds cool."

"I don't suppose you have another way of indicating your enthusiasm?"

"Interesting. It sounds interesting."

Mead sat back in his chair. "How far have you gotten in *The Longest Day*?"

"I've been so tired at night . . ."

"I'd like you to read at least an hour before bed. You'll get a lot more out of this trip if you know a bit about what happened."

Andrew sighed as Mead signaled for the check.

· · ·

Mead hardly said a word when they got to the room. Instead he sat in a corner chair and stared out the window before changing into his light blue pajamas and getting into bed.

"Are you mad at me?" asked Andrew.

"What gave you that idea?"

"You just seem kind of upset."

"No, I'm not mad at you." Mead rolled to his side. "Good night."

"Good night."

Andrew stayed awake for another half hour reading and listening to his headphones—it made the battle scenes much more dramatic—then turned off his light, crawled low in the sheets and attempted to masturbate. Creak. Oh God, I can't take it anymore. He put his finger on his pulse, wondering if he was having a nervous breakdown. He'd never last until he got home. It was like walking around with a loaded gun with a hair trigger, safety off; only it was more like a huge naval cannon on one of those destroyers, the kind that can lob a VW Beetle twenty miles. The slightest provocation and *Kaboom!*, he'd swamp all of Normandy with a tidal wave of lust. He forced himself to think of the five most embarrassing moments of his life. The list soon swelled to over twenty as the fever in his groin broke, replaced by a hotness in his cheeks. When he finally fell asleep he dreamed that he and Matt were seagulls flying high above a beautiful white beach, looping through the air and swooping down to shit on the jocks and peer into the bikinis of the girls.

·   ·   ·

Mead lay listening to the creaks in the bed next to him, wondering if his grandson was just restless or upset. Eventually the noises subsided and he heard the telltale rhythmic breaths, which had a childlike tone. And he was still a child; a confused and angry boy. Then he thought of Evelyn, allowing his imagination to briefly roam along the contours of her smile and cheeks and neck before retreating in bitter sadness. What was he thinking, that he could simply start all over again? That Sophie could be replaced? At least Evelyn had had more sense. In a way it was better that she was moving. God knows he needed the chance to clear his head and get back on his feet. It wouldn't be easy at first, not when he'd be reminded of her every time he stepped out his front door, but he'd survive. He always had.

That's what you are, old man: a survivor. He thought of Jimbo and

Rokowski and Punchy, wondering why he'd been allowed to live. Was it just dumb luck? Or was he spared for some purpose he never discovered? Even after so many years he still felt singed by guilt, thinking that any one of them would have made more of their lives. Was it really so long ago? He tried to recall how different his body felt back then, hard and agile, like driving a sports car. What would the boys think if they could see him now? He smiled to himself as he lay in the dark, eyes open and staring at the ceiling. *That you, Mead? Jesus, you look like shit.* He tried to imagine how they would have aged but he couldn't. That was the one thing they had on him: eternal youth, dying at the top of their game. And here he was more than half a century older than they'd ever be, old enough even to be their grandfather. How absurd.

· · ·

"We'll begin at Sword Beach and then drive along the coast to Omaha," said Mead as they pulled out of the hotel parking lot the next morning after a quick breakfast, which he left untouched. All morning he'd felt nervous, fearful of what might come howling back at him. Andrew seemed excited, like a kid going to the circus. "If you open the map I'll show you our route."

But Andrew was too busy staring out the window. "Hey, check out the cemetery," he said, pointing to a sign. Mead decided to stop. Best to plunge right in.

After parking they entered the small and neatly tended cemetery and walked slowly among the British, Canadian and German graves. Okay, I can handle this. And yet he couldn't shake the feeling that he was being stalked, that at any moment something—he dared not imagine what— might pounce on him.

"Don't you think it's cool the way the British graves have sayings on them from the families?" said Andrew.

Mead nodded as he stood before the grave of E. G. Winter, killed July 8, 1944, age 21:

OF THE WORLD
HE WAS JUST A PART,
TO HIS MOTHER
HE WAS ALL THE WORLD.

And nearby, J. H. Norman, killed July 22, 1944, age 24:

CAN WE E'ER FORGET
THAT FOOTSTEP
AND THAT SWEET FAMILIAR FACE.

And R. B. Vinall, killed July 22, 1944, age 17:

MANY A SILENT HEARTACHE
OFTEN A SILENT TEAR.
GONE BUT NOT FORGOTTEN
MUM AND DAD

"I wonder if any of these guys killed each other?" said Andrew as he headed over to the German section.

"They seem to be getting along pretty well now," said Mead, who had to stop reading the British headstones in order to maintain his composure. He thought of the simple marker for his brother Thomas that his parents had placed in the small graveyard six blocks from their home. He spent hours sitting on the grass looking at his brother's name and wishing he hadn't been lost at sea, which made him seem even farther away. He made his way to the German graves, which bore only names and dates. Nineteen-twenty-five, what a year to be born. He watched as Andrew hurried from headstone to headstone reading each one, then he stood back and looked up at the trees, which were dense with new leaves. Maybe time alone really is enough, though he had his doubts.

They stopped next at Pegasus Bridge on the Orne Canal. Mead explained how it was captured by British paratroopers but Andrew was more interested in a Cromwell tank on display.

"Did you fight around here?"

"I told you, we're in the British and Canadian sector," Mead said impatiently, already sensing that his grandson wouldn't really understand at all; that he might as well have taken him to Yorktown or the Alamo. Mead decided to skip the small museum and continue on to the coast.

"So these are like, *the beaches?*" Andrew asked as the ocean came in sight.

Mead nodded, surprised by how ordinary everything looked, well-kept but modest houses and apartments strung along the peaceful shoreline. "This is Sword Beach. Next is Juno, then Gold, and beyond that Omaha and Utah, which were the American sectors."

"Where's that Point Huck place?"

"Pointe *du Hoc*. It's near Omaha."

Andrew looked at Mead closely. "Does it creep you out being here?"

Mead thought for a moment, knowing there was no way to describe the sensation. "Let's just say that seeing you here is a little weird," he said, wishing he'd insisted that Andrew wash the yellow dye out of his hair.

They parked near the harbor at Juno Beach and walked down to the shoreline before inspecting a restored Sherman tank that had been salvaged from the sea, then Andrew ran over to a nearby German anti-tank gun, fingering the shrapnel holes in the armor plating. "They must have nailed these dudes," he said.

Mead spent several minutes looking over the gun before hurrying into a nearby gift shop to use the restroom. After buying several postcards they drove further down the coast, stopping to look at the battered remains of German bunkers and a large cross marking the spot where Churchill, Montgomery and de Gaulle came ashore. At the coastal town of Arromanches they examined the remains of the Mulberry harbor before visiting the Musée du Débarquement, where they studied dioramas and working models of the landings.

So far so good, thought Mead as he stared at the black-and-white faces of anxious young soldiers. His stomach felt unsteady and at times he had a slight burning sensation in the back of his throat, yet it was manageable. He had control. He even felt a certain pride in how well he was holding up. He glanced over at Andrew, who was looking closely at a photo of bodies strewn across the sand. The important thing was to make an impression on him; to teach the boy something.

"This may interest you," Mead said as they pulled up at the German battery at Longues-sur-Mer, where four enormous 155-mm cannons sat back from the bluff, each housed in a thick concrete casemate heavily scarred by shelling.

"Awesome." Andrew hopped out of the car and headed for the nearest casemate. "Look, you can tell exactly where the bombs landed." He ran his hands along the battered concrete and the exposed steel reinforcing bars, which were gnarled like bramble bush.

Mead stared at the rusting cannon, surprised by how old it looked, like some relic from the Spanish Armada. He glanced down at his hands. You too, he thought.

"These guns were still working on D-Day despite massive bombardment by our forces," he explained. "It took a few direct hits from the big naval guns to finally silence them."

Andrew stood behind one of the guns, his face taut with concentration. "You've got to admit the Germans were pretty brave."

"I admitted that a long time ago." Mead pulled out a disposable camera from his pocket and took several pictures of Andrew, then asked an elderly British tourist to take their picture together beside the long barrel of one of the guns.

"Mom will never believe it," said Andrew, leaning against Mead and smiling at the camera.

"That's why I'm collecting proof."

After exploring all four guns they walked along a trail to the heavily fortified observation bunker that sat on the edge of the bluff a thousand feet away. Andrew slid down a muddy path and climbed a metal railing to the top, then crawled inside. Mead was out of breath by the time he caught up.

"You gotta check this out," said Andrew, looking through a concrete slit toward the ocean.

"The men stationed here were the eyes for the guns," Mead said, wondering what the German troops would have made of his grandson, yellow hair and all. "They relayed targeting information using communication wires buried underground."

"They must have been kissing their asses good-bye big time when they saw all those ships approaching."

Mead imagined the young men awakening to their certain destruction and felt an unexpected sense of pity. Rotten luck to be born German in the first half of the twentieth century. And it all came down to chance, a roll of the biological dice that made one child a German and the other American; one an Aryan and the next a Jew. Would I have faced the firing squad rather than fight in Hitler's armies? He'd asked himself that question over and over and the answer was always the same: I wouldn't have had the courage not to fight. Not even close. And that's the horror, isn't it; that all over the world people still kill and die for causes they inherit by mere happenstance, accidents of birth that make one a Serb or Croat, Hindu or Muslim, Arab or Jew, Hutu or Tutsi. Why must it be so? *Why?*

As he and Andrew stood staring silently out at the ocean far below Mead resisted a momentary impulse to put his arm around the boy. Instead he took Andrew's picture before they headed back to the car and continued on to Omaha Beach.

· · ·

This would be the most difficult part, thought Mead, sitting in the car in the parking lot of the American Military Cemetery after turning off the ignition. How many names would he recognize? Would Jimbo and Rokowski be there? He had no idea if their remains were interred in France or repatriated home. He looked over at Andrew, who seemed uncertain of what to do.

"I want you to take your earring off."

"What?"

"It's not respectful."

"*Respectful?* It's just an earring."

"Just do what I say." Mead was surprised by the force of his own voice.

Andrew hesitated, as if debating his options. Slowly he reached up to his left earlobe and removed the earring, placing it on the dashboard. "Satisfied?"

"No, but it's a start. Now let's go."

As they entered the main gate they paused to take in the long rows of white marble crosses and stars of David. "This place is huge," whispered Andrew. "Did all these guys die on the beach?"

Mead didn't respond.

"Are you okay?"

Mead cleared his throat. "Fine. Why don't we start at the beach first?" Mead hurried across the cemetery toward the bluff.

"Sure thing."

They stopped at the top of the stairs that led down to the beach and examined an orientation table that depicted the landing operations. "Look, you can still see things sunken in the water," said Andrew, pointing to several long shadows offshore. "You suppose there are still bodies trapped inside?"

"Nothing you'd recognize."

Mead was surprised by how clean and desolate the beach looked, thankful that it wasn't developed. He looked over at Andrew, wondering what the boy was thinking. Did he feel anything? Did he have any understanding at all? Fifteen minutes later they reached the water's edge. Mead bent down and picked up a smooth wet stone, placing it in his pocket.

"I wish I had a metal detector," said Andrew, digging into the sand with his foot. "I bet you could find all sorts of cool stuff."

Mead thought of Punchy, his pockets so weighed down with souvenirs that he couldn't carry any more without getting rid of something first. "This is torture," he'd complain, sorting through his collection.

"What you need is a wheelbarrow," said Mead, whose own collection of German pistols, medals, watches and military belt buckles had begun to weigh him down (only to be stolen from him several weeks later).

Mead turned and looked back toward the bluff, pointing out some of the German bunkers and pillboxes. "They could cover every inch of this beach. A lot of guys never even made it to shore." He could see his grandson working to bring the violence to life. "They weren't much older than you."

Andrew squatted down and dug in the sand with his fingers. "Did you ever feel like you were going to die?"

"Lots of times."

"What's that like?"

Mead paused. "I couldn't say."

"Did your life really pass before your eyes?"

Mead smiled. "Just the highlights." He started down the beach.

"It feels kind of lonely here, don't you think?" said Andrew, following close behind.

"It ought to."

"I mean like, haunted."

"I hadn't thought of it."

"Do you believe that places can be haunted; that people—spirits—can come back?"

Mead thought of Sophie and how he often felt her presence in the space just behind his right ear. "It seems rather unlikely."

"I know it doesn't make sense scientifically, but when people have a lot of like, life force, I don't get how it could all just . . . vanish."

"It takes a little getting used to."

They walked on for another ten minutes, then turned and headed back toward the winding path that led up the bluff to the cemetery.

"I feel like my life is boring compared to yours," said Andrew, coming alongside Mead.

"We weren't exactly having a rip-roaring time."

"I know, but still you experienced amazing things. I can't think of anything I've done that's even a little bit amazing."

"You have a whole lifetime to do amazing things."

Andrew made a grunting noise. "I've been thinking about quitting school."

Mead stopped. *"What?"*

Andrew looked at him nervously. "I could get a real job. Make some money."

Mead could feel his face redden with anger. "How could you stand on *this beach* and talk about quitting school?"

"It doesn't have anything to do with this beach."

Mead jabbed a finger toward Andrew. "And you're going to college too, you got that?" A group of passing tourists stared.

"College?"

"You're damn right." Mead started up the path again.

"But I hate school. It's a total waste of time."

"I'm not going to talk about it right now."

"You don't know what it's like."

"I said, I'm not going to talk about it."

When they reached the top of the bluff Mead sat down to catch his breath. How dare he say such a thing. Andrew stood squirming in his baggie pants and black T-shirt, which had some sort of dragon's head on it.

"I'm going to walk around a bit," said Mead. *"Alone.* I'll meet you at the car in half an hour."

"I'm sorry."

"And no funny stuff, got that?"

"Okay."

Mead headed for the large semicircular colonnade inscribed with battle maps, trying to calm himself. He noted the other veterans in the crowd, silently attempting to guess their service and rank and hoping none would approach him. He couldn't believe how old they all looked, even a bit comical in their baseball caps and blue vests covered with pins and patches. After walking through the Garden of the Missing he wandered among the rows of headstones, half fearing he'd recognize a name. Finally he went to the Visitor's Building where a staff member showed him how to search the registers.

Roy Rokowski.

He clenched his fists as he approached the grave, trying to keep the sadness from reaching his face. Left here then eight down. He counted off the crosses as he passed. And there he was: *June 6, 1944.*

Mead crouched down beside the headstone, resting one hand on the smooth white marble. *Hey, Roy, it's me, Mead.*

Well, it's about time. What took you so long?

It's hard to explain. Somehow the years kind of slipped by and, well, the truth is I'm not so good at these kinds of things.

Hell, you've got the easy part.

Mead smiled to himself. *I sure miss you.*

Seems like yesterday, doesn't it? And all the time I was thinking I was going to land in the water and drown.

Mead tightened his jaw. *I tried to get him off of you. I should have shot him but I couldn't think straight and I was worried about hitting you and there was no time.*

Don't worry about it.

I'm so sorry, Roy.

We sure as hell showed them, didn't we?

You're damn right we did. We showed the whole world, Roy. Mead gripped the headstone with both hands.

Ever get up to that little spot I told you about in Michigan? Best fishing you'll ever find.

Not yet. But come to think of it, I just may one of these days.

The fishing's never been better.

You mean you've been . . . fishing?

What else?

I don't know, I just thought . . . Mead looked up and saw Andrew watching from a distance.

Is that your boy?

My grandson.

No kidding? I thought you looked a little gray around the temples.

Oh hell, even my insides are gray.

How come his pants are falling off?

Don't get me started, Roy.

"Did you know him?" Andrew asked softly as he approached. Mead nodded. "Was he like, a friend?"

"As a matter of fact he was."

Andrew stared down at the grave. "How did he die?"

"Grenade."

Mead could see Andrew waiting for further details. "Did you see it?" Mead nodded again. "Wow." Andrew reached out and touched the headstone.

You take care of yourself, Mead.

I'm trying, Roy. I'm really trying.

Mead stood up, hearing his knees crack. "A lot of these guys would have had grandchildren your age by now." Andrew looked around as if doing the math. "What I'm trying to say is that I was lucky, which means that you're lucky. Very lucky."

Andrew nodded, but Mead could see that he didn't really feel it. *How foolish I was to think that bringing him here would change anything.* "I'd like to be alone for a few minutes," he said.

"Sure," said Andrew, backing off. "I'll meet you at the car."

•   •   •

It was another hedgerow, identical to the one they'd just taken. Germans dug in across the meadow; a machine gun in one or both corners. No Shermans available to spray down the bushes. And yet when the order came to attack Mead felt his legs go. He tried to shake them but they wouldn't respond.

"Ready, men?"

Helmets nodded. Mead reached down and slapped his thighs but felt nothing. He slapped them again, harder.

"Now."

Mead watched helplessly as Punchy and five others scrambled out of the bushes and charged, tossing grenades as they ran. He struggled twice to lift himself, then tried to claw forward with his hands but his lifeless legs held him back. *Coward.* Punchy turned and waved him forward, then ran back and tried to pull him to his feet. "Come on, you son of a bitch!"

"I can't!"

"Like hell you can't!"

Finally Punchy let go and ran off without him. Mead screamed for his legs to move but still they refused. The others were now halfway across the meadow when the Germans opened up. Mead watched them go down one by one, feeling his mouth move but not making a sound. Punchy was the last to fall, almost reaching the German position and tossing a grenade just before he fell forward on his face, his helmet bouncing off. And then it was quiet.

Mead lay immobile for several minutes. *Why weren't the Germans coming for me? Were they dead? Had they retreated? Please come for me.* He looked at the crumpled figures sprawled across the meadow, then made a fist and began pounding it against his thigh as hard as he could, tears streaming down his face.

"Mead!"

He looked up and saw Punchy struggling to his feet. Quickly grabbing his rifle Mead fired several rounds into the far bushes as Punchy staggered back across the meadow and collapsed on the ground next to him, blood streaming from his forehead. Mead pulled out his first-aid kit and leaned over him. "Looks like just a scratch," he said as he cleaned the wound. "Jesus, I thought you were dead."

"Yeah, me too," said Punchy, still breathing hard. He never said a word about what had happened.

· · ·

Andrew was standing by the car waiting as Mead approached. Neither spoke as they got in and buckled their seat belts.

"I brought you here for a reason," said Mead, one hand on the ignition.

"I know," said Andrew quietly.

"But I think I was mistaken."

"Sorry."

"Stop saying you're sorry."

"Okay."

Mead sighed. "I thought maybe this would make a difference to you; that you'd understand how lucky you are not to have to go through what all those boys went through."

"I really appreciate what you and your friends did."

"But it really means nothing to you, does it?"

"Look, I'm sorry for all the guys who died but it doesn't change my life."

"Please tell me what's so goddamn bad about your life? I seem to be missing something."

Andrew sank lower in his seat. "Everything."

"You're an ungrateful little son of a bitch, you know that?" Mead was quaking now.

"You don't have to get so mad."

"Well I am. Don't you think any one of those boys under those headstones would have given his right arm to switch places with you?"

"I'll switch places. I don't care."

"Goddamn you!" Mead leaned over and slapped Andrew across the face.

"You expect everybody to be like you, don't you?" shouted Andrew. "Well I don't want to be like you!"

"Shut up!"

"Why would anybody want to be like you? You don't have any friends, you don't do anything all day, you don't even have the guts to ask Evelyn out. All you've got are your stupid medals and your stupid secret memories about stuff that happened *decades* ago."

Mead sat frozen in his seat while Andrew continued. "You're just as scared as I am, you know that? Ever since Grandma died you've been scared of even leaving your house. Well, I don't want to turn out like you. I'd rather *die*." He reached for the earring which sat on the dashboard and put it on. "And I'm never taking my earring off again no matter what you say. Ever." He wiped the tears from his cheeks with his sleeve and turned his face toward the window.

Neither moved for several minutes. In the sharp silence Mead felt something give way inside like scaffolding collapsing to the ground. "I'll take you home," he whispered as he started the car. A fine rain blurred the windshield as he drove, hands sticky on the wheel. In the rearview mirror he saw a growing caravan of cars pressing him on.

"I don't want to go home yet," said Andrew softly. "I mean, since we're here we might as well see the rest of it, don't you think?"

Mead drove on another mile, uncertain what to do, then pulled into a driveway, turned around and headed for Ponte du Hoc.

. . .

Andrew was in bed pretending to read while his grandfather sat in the corner writing a postcard. Andrew watched him out of one eye, wondering if it was the dull light from the dinky lampshades that made him look so old. Exactly how old was he anyway? Would he get sick and die in a few years? He tried to imagine his grandfather lying in a coffin or being slid into the furnace at a crematorium. Then he thought of Evelyn, wondering if she was all right and whether she'd sold the house yet. How soon would she die and should he tell his grandfather? He'd been sworn to secrecy, and yet . . .

"I'm sorry about the things I said."

His grandfather didn't look up. "You were right."

Andrew's face widened. "No I wasn't. Well, maybe about Evelyn."

His grandfather put down his pen and pushed aside the faded yellow curtain to look out on the street below. Rain streamed down the window panes. "After your grandma died I figured that was it for me. I didn't want to go on another single hour." He let out a long breath. "We'd spent fifty-one years together."

"I was just angry."

"But somehow I got through that first day, and then the next, and that's what I've been doing ever since." He let go of the curtain. "You see, I thought that was enough. It never occurred to me to try to . . . enjoy them."

"I'm sorry, Grandpa."

"No need to be." His grandfather picked up his pen and held it over the postcard.

"Are you writing Mom?"

His grandfather nodded.

"I bet Evelyn would love a postcard."

His grandfather looked up, raising an eyebrow.

"Grandma's been dead for three years," Andrew said gently.

"What's that got to do with anything?"

"What I'm saying is that she wouldn't be mad at you."

"Andrew—"

"And she wouldn't want you to be lonely. I know she wouldn't."

"Who said I was lonely?"

"I did, and I think it's time you started dating again."

His grandfather shook his head. "I'm a little old for that."

"Bullshit. And Evelyn's definitely got the hots for you."

"That's where you're wrong."

"Give me a break. She's all over you. What does a girl have to do?"

"She's just a friend."

Andrew laughed. "I've heard that one before. Now me personally, I'd date her just for her cookies."

"I don't *like* her cookies."

"Have you tried her pecan brownies?"

"Andrew—"

"Be honest, don't you kind of like her?"

His grandfather hesitated. "She's my *neighbor.*" He looked down at the postcard and tapped his pen against the table.

"So? Your generation didn't date neighbors?"

"What I mean is that . . ." His grandfather raised his hands, then dropped them.

Andrew sat up and pointed a finger at him. "You like her. I can tell."

"I did not say that I like her."

"But you do. And she really is in pretty good shape—for her age. She doesn't even need a walker."

"Andrew."

"So you'll ask her out?"

"No."

"But you'll think about it?"

"You don't understand."

"What's to understand?" Then it dawned on Andrew. "Oh jeez, do you have like, a medical problem? Because there's this new—"

"For Pete's sake . . ."

"Then why won't you ask her out?"

"I'm telling you, she's not interested."

"Well I'm telling you that she is—and there's not much time left."

His grandfather rubbed his forehead, looking confused. "What makes you so sure she's . . . interested?"

"What am I, blind?"

"It's occurred to me. Besides, why would I want to get involved with a woman who's moving to the other side of the country?"

"That's just it. She wouldn't have to move. You guys could . . . consolidate."

"Whoa there."

"One date. That's all I'm asking."

"I told you—"

"*Please.* At least consider it."

His grandfather sighed and rolled his eyes. "I'll consider it."

Andrew clenched his fist victoriously in the air. *"Yes."*

· · ·

Mead hardly slept that night. Instead he tried to keep within the safe perimeter of consciousness like a man by a campfire in a forest full of wolves. And yet as the fire grew dimmer he could hear the rustling in the woods, and then he could see shadows against the trees and he could smell the salty stench of sweat and urine. He drew closer to the fire, bending down to breathe air into the dwindling embers as the sounds in the forest grew closer. But there was no more wood and gradually, very gradually, the last flames died out.

· · ·

Andy?

Is that you, Matt?

Who else?

Jesus, you scared me. Andrew sat up in bed and looked around the darkened room. *You gotta be quiet, Matt. My grandfather's sleeping.*

That's what you think.

Andrew looked over at the adjacent bed, straining to make out the silhouette of his grandfather, who lay with his back to Andrew. *He's awake?*

Let's just say he's got visitors.

Visitors? What kind of visitors?

All kinds.

Andrew slid down beneath his sheets. *You mean like, ghosts?*

Call them whatever you want.

You're just joking, right?

Nope.

Andrew looked again at his grandfather's silhouette. *You're freaking me out, Matt.*

Sorry.

Where are you? I mean, how come I can't see you?

It's just the way it is.

Are you a . . . ghost?

What do you think?

I don't know. Andrew slid down even further into his bed. *I gotta talk to you about something. Something serious.*

Shoot.

It's about this woman I met.

You got a girlfriend?

Not exactly. She's like, old.

You're dating a senior?

I mean, really old. A senior citizen."

"*Citizen?*"

"*And we're* not *dating. But she's really nice. I never met anybody so nice. And the thing I want to talk about is, she's dying. She's got some sort of a disease and she's gonna die soon.*

I'm sorry.

And I just thought that maybe . . . well I thought maybe you could keep an eye out for her. You know, make her feel welcome. Show her around or whatever.

Matt laughed.

What's so funny?

It doesn't work that way.

How does it work?

I can't say.

Come on, we tell each other everything, remember?

Things have changed.

I don't like the way they've changed. In fact I hate it. Andrew felt his eyes watering.

Then let me go.

What do you mean?

You should let me go, buddy.

Why?

You don't want to end up like him, do you?

Andrew looked over again at his grandfather, who hadn't moved. *What are you talking about, Matt?*

You know what I'm talking about. I can't help you anymore.

Andrew's throat grew so tight it felt like he was hanging from a rope. *But you're my best friend. You're the only one who understands.*

I'm dead, Andy. I didn't wake up.

Don't say that.

You've gotta go on without me. There's no other way.

Andrew buried his face into his pillow and stifled a sob. *I don't want to. I don't want to be alone anymore.*

You're going to make it, Andy. I know you will. Don't let anybody ever tell you that you're not good enough, you got that? You're better than any of them.

I'm too scared.

Good-bye, Andy.

No wait! Andrew sat up. *Matt? Don't go, Matt. Please don't leave me alone. Matt? Matt? Matt?*

· · ·

The next morning Mead and Andrew ate croissants in the car and reached Carentan by ten. Mead was surprised by how familiar the buildings and intersections looked, only cleaner and unmolested. "They called this Purple Heart Lane," he said as they crossed over the long causeway. "The Germans flooded the whole area. It was a big swamp on either side of the road. A lot of men who landed here the night of the jump drowned." Mead could see Andrew straining to find the drama in the passing scenery, which offered no assistance.

They stopped several times to read roadside plaques and memorials and as Mead drove he imagined where the Germans might lay an ambush, half expecting to see flared gray helmets protruding from the bushes. When they reached Ste.-Mère-Église they parked in front of the church where a dummy paratrooper hung from the steeple.

"I read about that guy," said Andrew excitedly.

"He played dead but the Germans eventually cut him down and took him prisoner," explained Mead.

"That definitely would have sucked."

"Worse even than staying back a year?"

"Close."

They stopped briefly in the church, where Mead studied the stained-glass windows commemorating the paratroopers while Andrew pointed out the bullet marks that still scarred the walls, then headed for the Airborne Museum across the street. "You get free admission," Andrew noted proudly, insisting that Mead sign the Book of Honor for veterans. "You're practically a celebrity."

"Enough."

Mead did feel a certain pride. Yet there was so much sadness and shame mixed in that all the pleasure was taken away, leaving him with an acute sense of fatigue. He glanced over at some of the other veterans. What about them? Did they see faces too? And what were their secrets? Certainly they must have secrets. Or had they managed to put their secrets to rest? (And how?)

Together they wandered among the displays and military gear for an hour, Andrew asking lots of questions and Mead fumbling for answers. "Wow, you actually jumped out of one of those?" Andrew asked as they stood looking up at a restored C-47, which loomed above everything else.

"That's it."

Andrew looked at the plane, then back at his grandfather, as if trying to put the two together. "It's kind of hard to imagine you jumping out of a plane."

Mead smiled. "Trust me, it's even harder to imagine *you* jumping out of a plane."

They circled it one more time. "I wouldn't even feel safe flying in something so. . . ."

"Old? Well, it wasn't old when I flew in it."

"Still."

Mead put his hand on Andrew's shoulder. "Sometimes I'd give my right leg to live long enough to see you reach my age—if you ever get there."

Andrew frowned.

They walked around the town reading various plaques posted on walls and trees and browsing in an army surplus store before stopping at a café for lunch. Mead pulled out a map and explained how the 101st was assigned to secure the exits from Utah Beach, knock out German coastal batteries and guard the southern flank before taking Carentan itself and holding off a furious German counterattack by an *SS* panzer division. As he talked he noticed the middle-aged waitress smiling at him. "You should tell her who you are," said Andrew. "I bet she'll give you a free dessert."

"I don't need a free dessert."

"I'd eat it."

Mead rolled his eyes and signaled for the check.

"Where to next?" Andrew's face still showed excitement, which made Mead glad. He'd been worried that his grandson would quickly grow bored.

"I thought we might drive through some of the surrounding country-side a bit, see some of the jump zones, then head to Utah Beach."

"Excellent." Andrew drummed his palms on his thighs like a bongo player. "I still don't get how you jumped out of a plane at night. How could you see the ground coming?"

"You couldn't."

"Weren't you freaking out about whether you'd land on something . . . sharp?"

"As a matter of fact, I was."

"Did you wear a cup?"

Mead smiled, thinking of Punchy. "They weren't offered, but if they were I think every man would have worn one."

When they reached the car Mead studied his map a moment, then put it aside and decided to work from memory.

"Is it like you remember?" asked Andrew as they drove.

"It's a bit more peaceful," said Mead, who was pleasantly surprised by how little the landscape had changed. He looked closely at a meadow as they passed. Could that be where Jimbo bled to death? And what about that old tree there? Could it be where he saw Louie's lifeless body dangling from his parachute? He looked for familiar landmarks but saw none. Yet in a way it was all familiar—the narrow sunken roads and hedgerows and farmhouses and lush pastures, each landscape rekindling a long-suppressed memory until sounds and smells and faces seemed to crowd around him.

"So those are the hedgerows?" asked Andrew as they drove down a road bordered on either side by dense growth.

"That's them." Mead felt a tingling sensation in his legs. "Our intelligence failed to mention anything about them before the attack. Apparently they don't look quite so formidable from the air."

"So maybe you fought right in those bushes?"

"I suppose it's possible."

"That's *intense*."

"The Battle of Normandy was almost a stalemate the first few days. The Germans had all the roads and intersections and hiding places pre-sited by their artillery. It was hell making any progress."

"But then you guys kicked butt."

Mead winced. "After seven weeks of fighting we were no farther than a few dozen miles inland at most—and that's with complete air superiority."

"But I read that we were bombing the shit out of Germany, like, leveling the place."

"We were. I can remember looking up and seeing the sky darken with B-17 heavy bombers flying overhead in formation like a school of silver minnows—and no sight made us happier." Andrew looked up. "But even so, the Germans produced more weapons during the fall of 1944 than at any time during the war." Mead remembered the gaunt faces of slave laborers who begged them for food and kissed their hands.

"You really gotta see *Star Wars,*" said Andrew. "It's all about fighting the Dark Side."

"I've seen enough of the dark side."

Andrew began drumming on his thighs again as if fueled by several cups of espresso. "So what's up with the Germans? Are they just like, total assholes?"

"I wouldn't know where to start. And watch your language."

"Sorry."

Mead turned down a small lane and parked.

"What are we doing?" Andrew looked suddenly anxious.

"Time to take some prisoners." Mead got out of the car.

"What?"

"That's a joke. I thought you might like to see a hedgerow up close."

"Oh." Andrew let out a big breath and opened his door.

"How'd you like to try and crawl through that?" Mead asked as they walked along the dense bushes, stopping to peer into the dark entanglements.

"No way."

"Ideal if you're playing defense, not so good for offense."

Andrew reached in with one hand.

"Careful."

"Do you suppose there's still, like, bones and old grenades around?"

"You never know."

"I'd give anything to find a souvenir."

Mead started to say something but stopped himself. "Come on, we've got lots more to see."

By the time they reached Utah Beach Mead was desperate for a restroom. Andrew followed him in, taking the adjacent urinal and glancing over occasionally, so that Mead had to remind himself not to wince. (And it hadn't really occurred to him how much he did wince.)

They started in the museum where they watched old footage and looked at landing craft and artifacts and scale models of the invasion before going outside to examine the memorials and remaining fortifications. Mead felt a sweeping sense of loneliness as he looked out over the beach, which seemed impossibly quiet and barren, as if impervious to even the mightiest human achievements. Looking at the ocean he thought of the men who were dropped prematurely. No fate could be worse.

"You still haven't told me how you got wounded in the butt," said Andrew as they reached the waterline. The surf was rough and the wind stirred small sandstorms at their feet. Mead noticed Andrew struggling not to smile.

"We were in Holland. Fall of '44."

"I didn't know you fought in Holland."

"It was a hell of a mess. Anyway, one day I got hit by a little shrapnel."

"Ouch. How'd it happen?"

"Nothing to tell, really. One minute we were sitting around eating and the next a shell from an 88 landed and my butt started hurting something awful."

"Did you think you were going to die?"

"I wasn't sure I'd ever sit down again."

"Then what?"

"I was bandaged up and eventually evacuated to a hospital in England."

"At least you didn't have to fight anymore."

"What gave you that impression?"

"You mean they sent you back?"

"Damn right." Mead remembered the Purple Heart ceremony on the grounds of the American Hospital in Coventry, then cleaning the Cosmoline off his new rifle as he got refitted. Three weeks later he rejoined the company, overjoyed to see that Punchy was still alive. "Only the dead and disabled went home."

"That doesn't seem fair."

"Nothing was fair. Hell, even after Germany was defeated we figured we'd be sent to fight Japan. We weren't expecting to live until the end of the war."

"I bet you went wild when you got home."

"I ate a lot of ice cream."

Andrew shook his head in disappointment. "I would have gone a lot wilder than that."

"Seems like you already have."

Andrew grew quiet. "I know you think I'm a total loser."

"I certainly do not. But I think you've got some real problems."

Andrew stopped, hands shoved deep into his pockets. "Yeah, well you do, too."

"What?"

Andrew cleared his throat. "I said, you do, too. You're just as messed up as I am."

"Oh really?"

"Sure. You just hide it better. I mean, you still haven't told me basically anything about what happened to you during the war or why you're so secretive about it. Why did we come all this way if you're not even going to tell me anything?"

"Maybe it's none of your goddamn business."

"Why are you so afraid to talk about it? Everybody else talks about it."

Mead watched the whitecaps that stretched toward the horizon, then took out a handkerchief from his pocket and wiped his forehead. "You want a story, is that it?"

"I want to know what you experienced. Like Mom says, it's family history."

Mead carefully refolded the handkerchief, then put it back in his pocket and started walking again. "All right then, I'll give you a little family history."

•   •   •

Punchy's death was the last one that Mead fully felt. After that a heavy sort of numbness descended on him until at times his surroundings seemed almost dreamlike, as if he were a child in bed with a fever, untethered from the passing world. And besides, more and more of the men were replacements, many of whom would soon be replaced themselves. But Punchy's death was different. For years Mead wondered what Punchy's family had been told. Certainly not the truth, because the truth wouldn't do at all.

Eighteen of them had been on patrol in the Ardenne—twelve rifles and two three-man BAR teams—when Bruce McCullum stepped on a Schü mine, blowing off his left foot. Moments later a Bouncing Betty sprang up and exploded at waist height right in front of Mark Foley and Jay Goldberg, filling their groins and abdomens with steel balls. As the rest tried to retrace their steps another mine detonated, then another. The survivors dashed for the woods as a German machine gun opened up.

Mead and Punchy dove behind a tree and lay prone in the snow, firing blindly into the thick forest beyond the clearing. They watched as Foley tried to rise to his knees and was shot dead. Goldberg lay on his back with one arm extended, calling out for help until several more shots silenced him. (Only recently Mead had begun to suspect that Goldberg was one of those soldiers who, despite their bluster, never shoot to kill, hoping to emerge from the war with a clean conscience.) Then mortar rounds began falling, killing a Texan named Walt Slocum. Bark flew into Mead's face as bullets struck the nearby trees.

"Pull back," yelled Tom Duncan, the squad sergeant. Another mortar round landed, killing him instantly. Small-arms fire now came from several directions and Mead could hear German voices approaching.

"Let's get out of here," yelled Punchy, who took off running. Mead followed behind, tripping twice in the heavy snow. They zigzagged through the woods, then dropped down into a ravine, waded through an icy stream and climbed up the other side, grabbing on to branches to pull themselves up the snowy hillside. Mead paused to turn and fire, emptying his clip, then reloaded and took off again after Punchy.

"Which way?" asked Mead, breathing hard as they rested against a tree.

Punchy looked uncertain. "The road we came up on should be this direction," he said.

"You sure?"

"It's more an intuition."

They crossed two more deep ravines, then skirted the edge of a large clearing. As they reached the top of a ridge they finally saw the road down below. It was clogged with German troops heading west.

"Son of a bitch," said Punchy. Crouching in the bushes they watched four Tiger tanks rumble past. They tried to backtrack and loop around to the north, but an hour later they nearly ran into another German force. By nightfall they realized the German lines had swept over them.

"Okay, we know we're fucked," said Punchy, pulling his coat around his neck and stomping his feet. "The question is whether we are permanently fucked."

Mead tried to think but the cold made his head hurt. Hungry and tired, he had an overwhelming urge to sit down and cry.

Punchy lit a cigarette and offered it to him. "Either we can try to reach our lines in the morning or wait until the sons of bitches are pushed back where they came from."

"I say we try to reach our lines," said Mead, taking in a deep drag of the cigarette. "The question is, what do we do now?"

"We find ourselves a warm place to sleep."

"I don't suppose you made reservations anywhere?"

"I'm working on it."

The first farmhouse they approached had two German half-tracks parked out front. The windows were brightly lit and a thin strand of white smoke curled from the chimney, reminding Mead of a Christmas card. "I know what you're thinking and I'm not doing it," he said.

"It would make a hell of a story," said Punchy. "We could each have our own."

"*No.*"

Moments later two German soldiers emerged from the house and leaned against one of the half-tracks, talking and laughing.

"Damn," muttered Punchy.

They quietly retreated, then followed a narrow road until they reached the ruins of another house. Smoke still rose from the ashes and the carcass of a dog lay in the snow nearby. They watched from the nearby woods before cautiously approaching and warming their hands in the embers, which cast an orange glow on their faces. The heat made Mead long for sleep.

Once warm they continued toward the distant lights of another farmhouse across a wide field. As they crept closer, finally dropping to their stomachs and crawling, they could see three German soldiers eating at a table. A lone soldier stood on the front porch with his rifle over his shoulder and his hands stuffed into his armpits.

"We can take them," whispered Punchy, which is exactly what Mead feared he would say. "You get that one and I'll get the three inside."

"There could be more upstairs."

"Then we'll get them, too."

Mead looked around. "I don't like it."

"You want to stay out here all night?"

"Given the choices? Sure."

"Not me. I'm not freezing my balls off. Besides, I'm feeling lucky."

"Well I'm not." Mead watched as the German on the porch lit a cigarette. Four against two. They'd certainly have the opening advantage. And Punchy was a great shot. Mead imagined filling himself with warm food and then crawling into a soft bed. "What about the barn?" He gestured toward the dark structure silhouetted behind the house.

"You stay here, I'll check it out." Before Mead could stop him Punchy had crawled off, working his way around the back of the house. Minutes later he returned.

"It's empty."

"Maybe we could sleep there?"

"When a warm fire and food beckon? Forget it." It occurred to Mead that Punchy was little more than a collection of urges. "So, you with me?"

Mead nodded slowly.

"Let the show begin." They crawled closer until they could hear laughter coming from the house. Punchy glanced over at Mead. "Ready?"

Mead nodded and aimed.

"Now."

Mead hit the German on the porch with the first shot, then fired two more rounds before aiming through the window, where a single remaining soldier staggered from the table. Punchy and Mead both fired simultaneously and the figure dropped from view.

"You got the other two?"

" 'Course I did." Punchy smiled, then pulled out a grenade and ran for the door, stepping over the body of the German. Mead followed close behind, leveling his rifle at the three soldiers sprawled on the floor while Punchy bounded up the stairs.

"Just a couple of warm beds," Punchy said as he came back down.

"These two are alive," said Mead, gesturing with his rifle. One German was groaning softly while the other simply looked at Mead with eyes full of fear. Before Mead could say anything Punchy walked over and shot each one in the head.

"Jesus Christ, what the hell did you have to do that for?"

"They were goners. I was doing them a favor." Punchy bent over one of the bodies and relieved it of a shiny new Schmeisser MP-40 machine pistol. "Hey, look at this beauty," he said, holding it up.

Mead turned away, feeling sick.

"What exactly did you think we were going to do, take them with us? Come on, let's eat." He pulled up a wooden chair and sat down, quickly finishing off the remaining cheese and bread on the half-eaten plates.

Mead walked over to the shattered window and looked out at the pale, snow-covered yard, which glowed from the moonlight. Closing his eyes he filled his lungs with the cool damp air.

"Aren't you gonna eat?" Punchy held out a plate.

"You're a goddamn pig, you know that?"

Punchy smiled, then stuffed another piece of bread into his mouth.

Suddenly there was a light knock on the door. Mead and Punchy grabbed their rifles and dove behind a small sofa.

"Americans?" a voice called out. "You are Americans?" Mead and Punchy kept silent, rifles pointed at the door. "Please don't shoot. We are Belgian." The door slowly opened, revealing an elderly man and his wife, both wrapped in heavy coats and shivering. "Welcome," said the man, extending his hand and smiling.

"This is your home?" asked Mead, rising cautiously to his feet.

The man smiled while the woman stared down silently at the bodies of the Germans. "We were hiding in the barn. My wife is very cold."

"Please, come on in," said Mead. "We were just . . ." He couldn't think how to finish.

The old man gently pushed his wife forward, then quickly closed the door behind him, took off his hat and wiped his brow. "You must be very careful," he said. "The Germans are everywhere."

"We noticed," said Punchy.

"They came in yesterday. All the roads are full." The woman kept staring down at the bodies, her small wrinkled face expressionless.

Punchy looked at Mead and signaled him, then bent down over one of the Germans and took hold of the arms. Mead put down his rifle and took the feet. A few minutes later all four corpses lay side by side in the snow.

"Tonight we will hide them behind the wood pile," said the old man. "Then tomorrow we must bury them in the woods."

When they returned to the house the old woman was on her hands and knees scrubbing the blood from the wooden floor. "Sorry about the mess," said Punchy. The woman didn't respond. Mead wondered if she could be trusted.

"She doesn't speak English," said the old man. "Actually, she doesn't speak much at all. But then, what's to talk about after fifty years, eh?" He laughed to himself as he stoked the fire that still burned in the small hearth. "I would offer you our beds but you wouldn't be safe. Germans have been coming through all day and night."

Punchy frowned. "You got any other ideas?"

The man smiled again, as if enjoying himself, then took a lantern off a hook, lit it and motioned for them to follow. Crossing the hardening snow, which crunched beneath their feet, he led them to the small barn. "They took all my animals," he said as they entered.

"Hell, it's freezing in here," said Punchy, sizing up a mound of straw in one corner.

The old man held up a finger, then handed the lantern to Mead, took a few steps and pointed toward the worn wooden floor, which was made of mismatched boards of varying lengths and widths, like a quilt. "Do you see it?"

Mead guessed he was looking for some sort of trapdoor but saw nothing. Punchy tapped the toe of his boot in different spots, trying to find a hollow sound.

The old man watched with amusement, then dropped to his knees, dug his fingernails into a narrow crack and lifted a small panel, exposing a larger metal handle which he yanked hard, revealing a heavy trapdoor. "Good, eh? My father built it for the last war," he said, showing them how thick the door was. "He was a carpenter."

Punchy and Mead looked at each other, then climbed one at a time down the narrow ladder into a small-but-deep cellar, which had a wood floor, two plank beds and a shelf stocked with candles, a round of cheese, a deck of cards and three jugs of water. A shotgun rested in the corner and there was a large blanket on each bed. The air was damp and fetid. Mead glanced over at a bucket in the corner, which was partially filled with human waste.

"We hid for three nights," said the old man apologetically, taking the bucket. "Please make yourselves comfortable and I'll get you some hot soup."

"You expect us to sleep down here?" asked Punchy.

"Of course!"

After the old man left Mead stretched out on one of the beds, placing his hands behind his head. "Can't beat the privacy," he said.

Punchy stared up at the ceiling, which was supported by four wood beams. "I'm claustrophobic."

"Gee, that's unfortunate."

"You don't understand." Punchy's unshaven face glistened. "See, when I was a kid my older brother locked me in a trunk. Two fucking hours I was in there."

"So this must feel roomy."

Punchy loosened his collar and paced around the cellar. "Don't you think it's kind of hard to breathe in here?"

"Not until you mentioned it."

Punchy's breathing grew louder. "No way, I'm not staying down here."

"You got anything better in mind?"

"The barn," he said, starting for the ladder.

"Wait." Mead sat up.

"What?"

"Listen."

Soon the sound of an approaching tank was unmistakable. German.

Punchy climbed partway up the ladder and stuck his head out the trap-door. "Must be at least two of them."

"Get back down here."

"Hell no, let's run for it."

Mead grabbed his rifle and followed Punchy up the ladder. After climbing out the trapdoor he hesitated, wondering whether to close it or leave it open for the old couple. Where were they?

"Let's go," said Punchy, standing by the barn door. The tanks were so close now that it was hard to hear anything else. Together they opened the door a crack and peered out. Dozens of approaching German infantrymen were silhouetted by the moonlight.

"We can't make it," said Mead.

"Sure we can."

"Not a chance." Mead ran for the trapdoor and crawled in feetfirst, leaving his head and arms exposed and gesturing frantically to Punchy.

"Come on!" Punchy hesitated as the ground began to vibrate. *"Now!"*

Finally Punchy turned and sprang for the opening, nearly falling on top of Mead. "Close it!" Punchy scrambled back up the ladder and pulled the trapdoor shut. Mead blew out the lantern and they both stood motionless in the pitch blackness.

"I can't breathe," whispered Punchy.

"Shut up."

"I'm gonna make a run for it."

Mead heard Punchy stumble around the cellar searching for the ladder. "You want to get us killed?"

"I can't breathe!"

Bits of earth began falling from the ceiling and Mead could hear the grinding of tank gears.

"It's gonna cave in!" cried Punchy, his voice hysterical.

The tanks suddenly stopped. Mead groped around the room for the ladder, then climbed up halfway and listened. Thank God they'd hidden the bodies. Yet they'd see the blood in the snow and the shattered windows. Where was the old couple? Moments later he heard a woman's screams. Oh, Jesus.

"They're going to tell them about the cellar," said Punchy. "We're going to die down here."

"Quiet."

"I'd rather die fighting."

The screams grew louder. Were they torturing her, or was she watching them torture her husband? Mead clenched his teeth as the screams continued. Surely the old man would tell. Who wouldn't? Punchy had been right, they should have run for it.

He flinched at the report of a single gunshot. A second shot quickly followed. He looked up in the darkness, imagining the door opening and hand grenades dropping down on them. Or would they simply burn the barn down? He heard Germans shouting, then footsteps on the wood planks above him. Mead froze on the ladder, his head just inches beneath the trapdoor. Down below, Punchy's breathing grew shallow and rapid. There was a distant tapping sound above, then another, this time closer. Finally he heard footsteps directly above, then a pause followed by more tapping.

Mead closed his eyes and prayed. There was another tap, then voices. Mead bit into his lip until he felt blood run down his chin. *Good-bye, Sophie.* Another tap, followed by a long silence. Then gradually the tapping grew more distant. Tears filled Mead's eyes. The old man was right to be proud of his father. When the sounds stopped completely Mead quietly climbed down the ladder, then found one of the beds and sat on it. "You okay?" he whispered.

No answer.

"You okay, Punchy?"

"I don't want to die down here."

"You won't. I promise."

An hour passed. Then another. Mead lay on his back listening, unsure whether his eyes were open or closed. He wondered whether Punchy had fallen asleep. Several times he heard footsteps above, but no more tapping.

"We wouldn't have made it," said Punchy suddenly.

"What?"

"If we had tried to run for it we wouldn't have made it."

"I know."

"But we're going to die down here. We're going to run out of air."

Mead had thought of that too. If the cellar was airtight, wouldn't they suffocate? And yet the old man had said they'd hidden for three nights. Mead took another breath, trying to taste the air. Was he getting enough oxygen? He did feel sort of light-headed and the more he thought about it the harder it was to breathe. "For God's sake, don't talk about it."

"It's like being dead," said Punchy. "Just like a coffin."

"Jesus Christ, would you shut up?"

Punchy's raspy breathing filled the silence. "The truth is, I'm scared to death of dying."

"Me too."

"I can't even stand thinking about it."

"Then don't."

"I can't help it."

"Get some sleep."

Mead placed his fingers on his eyelids to make sure they were closed, still concentrating on every breath until he felt dizzy. *Am I dying? Is the air almost gone?* He gulped down several rapid breaths, his chest rising and falling uncontrollably as he fought off the impulse to rush for the trap door. He felt his eyelids again, then thought of Sophie, trying to recall as many of their dates as he could in chronological order. Still struggling for air, he tried to recall the prices of the items in his father's hardware store. He saw the rows of hammers and the bags of nails and the snow shovels in winter and then he heard his father's voice and the chime of the door. He bent down and picked up a handful of sawdust, holding it up to his nose and thinking how good it was to be back. Maybe he and Thomas would even have time for a game of catch after work. He let the sawdust run through his fingers as he gradually made his way to the stockroom, making sure to smile at the customers. Closing the door behind him he poured a glass of lemonade from the pitcher his mother kept on a table next to a bowl of apples, then curled up on an old sofa, thinking he just needed a few minutes rest.

He couldn't figure out why the sofa started shaking but soon everything on the stockroom shelves began falling to the floor. Father? Thomas? He tried to open his eyes but he couldn't. Where's the light? The noise was deafening now. *Father!*

"We're gonna be crushed to death!" cried Punchy as large chunks of earth fell from the cellar roof. Over the roar and screech of a tank Mead heard the splintering of wood. Seconds later the tank was directly overhead, the treads grinding the wood and causing more dirt to fall. Mead crouched against a wall in terror as he waited for the cellar to collapse.

"We're going to die!" screamed Punchy, his voice nearly drowned out by the noise. He's going for the door, thought Mead, jumping up and reaching around in the darkness. Finally he found the ladder and felt Punchy's legs partway up. "We're going to die!"

"No!" Mead grabbed at Punchy's legs and tried to pry him off the ladder until a sharp blow to his face knocked him backwards. Above, the screeching of wood and metal grew louder. "Let me out!" cried Punchy, now banging against the door. Mead crawled around on his knees feeling for his rifle, then rose to his feet and searched for the ladder. When he felt Punchy's feet he aimed high and swung the butt of the rifle.

"We're going to die!"

"Get down!" Mead swung again, harder. He heard Punchy groan, then the sound of his body hitting the floor. Mead froze as the tank passed overhead one more time before slowly driving away. Thank God. He waited until the tank was out of earshot, then felt around until he found Punchy.

"You all right?"

Punchy let out another groan. "I'm dead, aren't I?"

"Not yet." Mead began searching for the ladder. When he found it he climbed to the top and listened.

"What makes you so sure I'm not dead?"

"This." Mead pushed open the trapdoor a crack, letting in a stream of blinding white light. He listened, then opened the door a few more inches and looked out. The roof of the barn was gone and only a portion of one wall remained standing. Across the yard long wind-whipped flames rose from the house.

"Let me out of here," said Punchy, pushing against him from underneath.

As they crawled cautiously out of the cellar they gulped down the crisp cold air, shielding their eyes from the light. Mead dabbed blood from his lip while a thin red trickle ran from Punchy's hairline down his forehead.

"They didn't talk," said Punchy, gesturing toward a large tree in the center of the yard. Mead looked up and saw the old man and his wife, both bleeding from the head and strung by their necks from two short ropes. Nearby four fresh graves were marked by helmets suspended from simple wooden crosses. Mead and Punchy cut the bodies down but were too tired to bury them. Instead they covered the elderly couple with a thin layer of snow, then returned to the cellar and filled up on cheese and water before heading off in search of the American lines.

• • •

They spent the rest of the day walking and hiding, twice watching German patrols pass close by. By evening Punchy could barely hobble.

"Let me look at them," said Mead as they crouched in a small foxhole they had dug behind a large bush set back from the road.

"You're not taking these boots off."

"Yes I am." Mead struggled with the laces, then finally pulled off the left boot as Punchy let out a cry. Gently peeling off the sock, he held the foot up to the moonlight. The toes were now black while the rest of the foot was bluish white.

"I can't feel your hands," said Punchy.

"Just relax." Mead slowly rubbed the heel and sole but avoided touching the toes.

"I'm going to lose them, aren't I?"

"I don't know."

"I don't care about the little ones. What the hell do they do? But I don't want to lose my big toes. Who wants to marry a guy without big toes?"

Mead cautiously touched the big toe, then began massaging it gently. When he got the sock and boot back on Punchy offered him the other foot. "I'll do that one in the morning," said Mead, whose fingers could no longer move.

They reached an American roadblock the next afternoon, Punchy limping with his arm around Mead. As they approached two sentries leveled their rifles and ordered them to drop their weapons.

"We're Americans, you idiot," said Punchy.

"I said, *drop them.*" Behind the sentries a third GI manned a jeep-mounted machine gun.

Mead placed his rifle on the ground and raised his hands, offering a smile. Punchy hesitated. "I've hardly eaten in two fucking days, I'm tired and my toes are falling off. Now cut the—"

"Now."

"Jesus, a couple of cowboys." Punchy placed his rifle on the ground, keeping the Schmeisser strapped to his back.

"And the other one."

With a curse Punchy took the German machine pistol off and placed it next to his rifle. The two sentries eyed each other. "Don't even *think* of stealing it from me," said Punchy.

"The password?"

"A few days ago it was mayflower or maypole or . . ."

The taller sentry cut Mead off. "Wrong."

"How the fuck are we supposed to know the password?" said Punchy.

"We're with the 101st," Mead explained quickly. "Our patrol was ambushed and we've been trying to get back for two days." He listed the name of every officer he could think of.

The sentries conferred. "I still don't trust 'em," said one to the other. "What are they doing with a goddamned Schmeisser and how the hell did they get through the German lines?"

"We went *under* their tanks," said Punchy, starting forward again. "It's a nifty trick. Ever been under a Tiger before?"

"Halt right there!"

"Do what he says," said Mead.

"I'm in no mood for this," said Punchy, stopping.

"Hands up."

"I'm from the *Bronx,* you dumb fuck."

"I said, *hands up!*"

Punchy raised his hands.

"It could be an ambush," said the shorter sentry, looking nervously down the road behind Mead and Punchy.

"An ambush?" said Mead with a laugh. "Listen guys, I'm from—"

"We got orders to shoot anybody who doesn't know the password."

"Akron, Ohio. I went to Millfield High and my father owns a hardware store and I went to basic at Camp Toccoa and jumped in Normandy and Holland and if you'd like I can probably recite some of the Pledge of Allegiance."

The taller sentry aimed his rifle at Punchy. "How many home runs did Gehrig hit with bases loaded?"

"Hell, I don't even know the answer to that one," said the shorter sentry.

The taller sentry furrowed his brow. "Okay then, how many career runs did Cobb get? Ballpark figure."

"Frankly, I don't give a fuck," said Punchy.

"Can't say I know that one either," said the shorter sentry.

"Fine. You try," said the taller sentry, tilting his head and spitting angrily to the side.

The shorter sentry thought for a moment. "Got it. Name the seven dwarves."

"The seven dwarves?" asked Punchy in disgust.

"Go ahead," said Mead.

"I'm looking at two of them right now," said Punchy.

Mead jumped in. "There's Doc and Sleepy and—"

"I think they're Krauts," said the taller sentry.

"Look, fellows, we've had a long couple of days," said Mead.

"They caught three Krauts yesterday wearing our uniforms and driving a stolen jeep. Spoke perfect English. Besides, I don't like the looks of this one." The sentry gestured toward Punchy with his rifle.

"You wise-ass son of a bitch," said Punchy, stepping forward and reaching out to swat the sentry's rifle out of the way.

"No!" cried Mead.

The soldier fired, hitting Punchy in the chest. Punchy took another step, then collapsed to the ground. Mead crouched over him. "Get a medic!"

"You are Krauts, aren't you?"

Mead pulled out his medical kit, removed a morphine syrette and jabbed it into Punchy's arm. Then he ripped open Punchy's coat and shirt and undershirt, took out a compress and gently held it against the wound, which made a gurgling sound.

"You can't tell 'em I died like this," cried Punchy, his lips quivering.

"You're staying right with me. Right here with Mead."

"I don't think he's a Kraut," said the shorter sentry nervously.

"Then why'd he rush me like that?"

"Get a goddamn medic!" screamed Mead.

The shorter sentry turned and ran back toward the jeep while the taller one stood staring down at Punchy, a look of fear in his eyes.

Suddenly Punchy reached up and grabbed Mead by the collars. "Don't tell anybody I died like this, you understand me?"

"Shhh," said Mead, placing the palm of his hand against Punchy's cheek.

"I didn't mean to shoot him. Honest to God I didn't."

"Shut up!" said Mead.

Punchy's lips were moving but Mead couldn't hear him. He leaned closer, straining to make out the words. "I was right," whispered Punchy. Mead waited for him to continue. "I knew I was dead. You said I wasn't but I knew I was."

"You're going to be okay."

Spasms shook Punchy's body. "You tell them the truth: you tell them how Punchy died under that Tiger tank."

"I'll tell them."

"I can't breathe down here."

"The sun's out, ol' buddy. Take a look."

But Punchy didn't seem to hear him. "Sweet Mother of Jesus, don't leave me down here. Please, anywhere but down here . . ."

When the medic arrived Punchy was dead.

. . .

Andrew was silent when his grandfather finished, trying to pretend he didn't notice the tears in the old man's eyes or the way his voice changed pitch near the end. Something about seeing his grandfather—*Sarge*—get choked up made Andrew feel prickly inside, like nothing in the world was really solid. He focused his attention on a seagull that had been circling above their heads. It landed and took a few steps toward him, turning its head to one side as if waiting for him to say something. *Is that you, Matt?* The seagull came closer, sinking its head low in its feathers, which were remarkably white. *Matt?* It would make perfect sense. What better way to hang out on the beach? And in a way it kind of looked like Matt, a bit cocky around the eyes. As Andrew knelt in the sand the seagull flapped its wings and rose high in the air, then swooped down and skimmed low over the waves. Andrew watched it until it disappeared against the gray horizon. *Come back, Matt.*

"I have his ashes."

"What?"

"Matt's ashes. They were going to bury him in Indiana and so I stole them, or him."

"You're pulling my leg?" Mead looked at Andrew hopefully.

"Nope." Andrew braced himself. "Please don't get mad."

"Jesus Christ."

"Sorry."

"You *stole* them?"

Andrew nodded slowly, watching the skin on his grandfather's face start to twitch in anger.

"What the hell did you bring them *here* for?"

"I've been trying to figure out where to bury him." He swallowed, then continued quickly. "At first I figured I'd bury him in California, like at the beach, because Matt always wanted to live on a beach in a place like California, but then when you said we were going to Europe I thought he might like that better. He'd never been to Europe."

"Are you out of your mind?"

"I couldn't let them take him to Indiana."

His grandfather slapped his palm against his forehead. "For God's sake, you even took them through customs."

"I was a little nervous about that." He tapped the large bulge in his pants pocket.

Mead looked down at Andrew's pants in disbelief. "He's in your *pocket?*"

"Most of him. I spilled some in this forest preserve back in Chicago when I was—"

"I cannot believe this."

"Sorry."

"Give them to me." Mead held out his hand.

Andrew's face reddened. "No, please."

"We are *not* carrying . . . *ashes* . . . around Europe."

"You can't just throw them out." Andrew's voice was breaking now as he covered his pocket with both hands.

Mead started toward him, then hesitated, muttering to himself. "Exactly what did you have in mind?"

"I dunno. I was gonna scatter them in Westminster Abbey. It seemed like, *perfect.* But then I saw this guy sweeping the floor and that totally freaked me out. Then I thought maybe I'd sprinkle them around the Tower of London—you've got to admit it beats Indiana—but then I started worrying that maybe the place was haunted by all those people who got their heads chopped off."

"I see." The skin on Mead's face began twitching again.

"And yesterday I was going to scatter them at Omaha Beach—it seemed pretty intense, and Matt was a totally intense guy—but then it just seemed too depressing. So actually, I was thinking of taking them back to California and sprinkling them on that beach you took me to. He would have loved that beach."

His grandfather stood rubbing his forehead.

"Please don't take them."

"Let's go to the car."

. . .

As Mead stormed down the beach with his arms stiff at his sides he imagined the search in customs, then trying to explain why his grandson was returning to the States with the stolen ashes of a friend who killed himself in Illinois and should have been buried in Indiana. Of course, the story was so implausible that it just might stand.

Jesus.

He thought of his big blue chair back home, wishing he could sit for a minute and work on a crossword puzzle. Yes, everything would be better when he got home. He imagined a nice, thick porterhouse on the grill, then his evening walk just as the light softened, the air quickly cooling. What the hell was he thinking coming here? Did he really believe that his own past—that the sheer unspeakable enormity of what he'd witnessed—somehow held the key to his grandson's salvation? What an old fool I am. And what had he achieved but to stir up memories that now threatened to engulf him; dozens of soiled young faces drawing closer and closer, their sad, imploring eyes filled with questions he could not answer; and sounds too, sounds of shouting and gunfire and explosions and the animal-like shriek of the wounded and always the angry staccato of German phrases, which still produced a dense fear low in his gut. He looked over at his grandson, hating his sullen arrogance and his yellow-streaked hair and his earring and the mousy way that he carried himself, like some sort of underfed stray. It's all his damn fault. But soon he'd be back in Chicago and Mead would have his house all to himself again. (And Sophie's room.) What would he tell Sharon? He had no idea. Perhaps he could pay for a shrink or get the boy into the army. He pulled out his handkerchief again and wiped down his face, walking faster despite a weakness in his legs. If only I could sit for a minute.

But he couldn't go home. Not yet; not when the thing he dreaded most was so close he could feel its moist breath on his neck. *You wouldn't, would you?* Somehow he always knew that it would come to this, that eventually he would no longer have the strength to keep it at bay. *(All those years.)* It wasn't enough that he'd been a decent man; that he'd been faithful to his wife and honest at work and generous with the church. Because no matter what he did or how many years he safely tucked away, the accusation stood, the charges ringing louder and louder in his ears until it had become hard to hear anything else. *Murderer.* And now there was nothing left to do but to stop running and hold his ground and try to stare right into the face of his accuser—to confront the very thing that had ruined him—and say, *I'm sorry. Now please leave an old man be.*

There was no other choice.

"Are we going back to the hotel?" Andrew asked nervously when they reached the car.

Mead opened his map and studied it before starting the engine. "Not yet."

. . .

"What's this?" asked Andrew, looking at the sign. *Cimetière Militaire Allemand.*

"A German cemetery."

"No kidding?" Andrew looked at his grandfather, who seemed distracted. "Are we going in?"

"Yep."

After stopping in the modern visitor's center they walked through the stone archway and entered the burial grounds, which didn't look like any cemetery Andrew had ever seen. Clusters of small decorative crosses, each roughly chiseled from dark stone, were scattered at regular intervals while the graves themselves were identified only by small flat markers. In the center, atop a large earthen mound surrounded by flowers, stood a tall stone cross and the sculptured figures of a man and a woman, heads bowed in grief. Parents.

"The American cemetery is much prettier," said Andrew.

"This is all the sorrow without the pride," said Mead.

"I think it's kind of creepy." Andrew looked down at the names on the markers as they walked, trying to pronounce them. "How come they have more than one name on them?"

"Comradeship in death."

"What?"

"It's a nice way of saying they had to economize."

"Oh." He followed behind Mead, reading more names and wondering how each died. "There's really 21,000 Germans buried here?"

"Just a drop in the bucket."

Andrew tried to visualize the entire student body at Montrose, then multiplied it by seven. Holy shit. And the weird thing was thinking they'd all been killed; 21,000 *violent* deaths. He tried to imagine the worst pain he'd ever felt—the time he cracked a tooth trying to pry open a beer bottle with his teeth—then having it get worse and worse until you die. Fuck me. And then to die for the losing side. Hard to put a good spin on that. He looked down at the grass, wondering if some of the skeletons were wearing medals like the ones his grandfather had. Be amazing to dig the place up.

He heard people speaking German on his left and turned and watched as a small group slowly walked down several rows, turned right, then left, then stopped at a small marker, gathering around it. Wow, the family. He stared at a teenager his age, looking away quickly when the boy caught his eye. So that would have been the enemy. Him or me. *Bang!*

He watched the family a few more minutes, feeling unexpectedly sad and thinking how glad he was that he wasn't a Sauerkraut, then looked around for his grandfather. He finally found him standing off by himself on the far side of the large grassy mound. Andrew approached slowly from behind, thinking he shouldn't disturb him. Maybe he killed some of these guys with his bare hands; maybe even the German whose family was visiting.

Suddenly his grandfather reached into his shoulder bag and pulled out several objects, laying them one at a time on a stone ledge. Andrew squinted, then took a few steps closer. Jesus, he brought the dead German's stuff. I can't believe this. He watched as his grandfather dropped down on his knees. Is he having some sort of heart attack? Andrew started to approach, then decided to wait. His grandfather's lips seemed to be moving but from the distance Andrew couldn't hear anything. God, I hope he's not freaking out. Andrew looked around to see if anyone else was watching but the cemetery was now deserted. He looked back at his grandfather, who was now staring up at the two large stone sculptures. Please don't let him have a heart attack. Finally his grandfather rose to his feet and straightened himself. So he's gonna leave the stuff. Andrew debated trying to grab the things without being noticed. But then, just as his grandfather seemed about to walk away he hesitated, knelt down and gathered up the belongings, placing them back in his shoulder bag.

"How would you like to go to Germany?" he said as he walked quickly past.

Andrew followed behind. "Germany? Why Germany?"

"Because there's something I have to do."

This is getting too weird. "When?"

"Tomorrow."

"*Tomorrow?* You're kidding, aren't you?"

"Not at all." His grandfather continued toward the parking lot.

"Why? Are you going to return his things?"

His grandfather slowed. "I'm going to try."

"To . . . who?"

"I don't know yet. There's an address among his papers. We'll start there and see where it leads us." He turned to Andrew as if gauging his reaction. "You didn't have any other plans this summer, did you?"

"Not exactly, but—"

"Good." His grandfather hurried on to the car.

Germany

They caught a train to Paris early the next morning, then took a taxi from Gare St-Lazare to Gare de l'Est, where they loaded up on food and sodas at a concession stand before boarding a train to Germany.

"So he's from Stuttgart?" asked Andrew, finishing his second croissant as the train pulled out of the station.

"According to my map he's from a little town nearby. We'll transfer to a local line when we get there."

"Maybe the town was bombed to smithereens during the war and never rebuilt."

"Maybe."

"Maybe everyone in his family died or moved away years ago."

"Maybe."

Andrew leaned left, then right in his seat. "My butt's already killing me. How come we didn't fly?"

"Because I wanted to take the train. Good enough?"

"Just asking."

They sat across from each other, both next to the window. Andrew patted the large lump in his pants pocket, where Matt's ashes were stuffed in the Ziploc. Would they be searched at the German border? He imagined snarling German shepherds and Dobermans sniffing at his pants. *Maybe I should hide Matt under the seat or in my bag. What if they confiscate him?*

He looked over again at his grandfather, who stared out the window, his leather bag on the floor between his feet. *So basically, we're both carrying the remains of dead people: a murdered Nazi Sauerkraut and a short,* green-haired teenager from Chicago who killed himself. What a family. Are other people's families this weird?

"How long do you think we'll be in Germany?" he asked.

"As long as it takes."

"Does that mean like, days or months?"

"I'm paying the bills, aren't I?"

"This could get expensive."

"I'll manage."

Andrew listened to his headphones for a while, wishing he'd bought more batteries, then ate another croissant. His grandfather remained almost motionless, face turned toward the window. Andrew couldn't believe how bad the old man looked, like he'd gotten hammered and slept on his face all night. Must be some serious shit going on in his head. "Are you nervous?" he asked, regretting the question immediately. His grandfather glanced over at him without responding, then returned his gaze to the window. "I'm just saying that I'd be nervous, that's all."

"Yes, as a matter of fact I am a little nervous."

Andrew pulled out his notebook, thinking maybe he'd write some lyrics. He jotted down a few lines but kept returning to the story his grandfather had told him about how Punchy had died. Was that worse than waking up next to your best friend's dead body in the forest preserve? Tough call. He looked at his grandfather again, trying to imagine how he killed the German and why it was such a big deal—it *was* war—but too afraid to ask. He wrote a few more lyrics, tinkering with a long song he was writing for Matt, then closed the notebook and lay his head back, quickly lulled into a deep sleep by the gentle motion of the train. Within minutes he was dreaming that drooling Dobermans were snapping at his pants. When he awoke his grandfather was staring at him, looking even worse than before. "Welcome to Germany."

• • •

The first thing Mead noticed as U.S. troops entered the concentration camp at Landsberg in Bavaria at the foot of the Alps was the smell, a smell he could recall for years after. Once inside they stared in stupefaction at the bodies, stacked row upon row, barely human. And then Mead struggled with a sense of repulsion as dozens of inmates surrounded him and kissed and hugged him, their bodies filthy and lice-ridden.

So the stories were true.

Mead couldn't stop himself from retching, and then later that day behind a barn he and another GI watched in horrified fascination as a pack of prisoners cornered a guard, spitting and kicking at him, then tearing him apart like piranhas. Neither of them dared intervene. It seemed like such a *private* matter.

And then, in a barrack filled with those who could not move, they passed out candy and rations, trying again to ignore the suffocating smell. Mead knelt next to a young boy with huge dark eyes. "What's your name?" he asked, placing his hand gently on the boy's forehead. The boy said something in a language Mead didn't recognize. An older prisoner on the wooden bed just above translated.

"His name is Grzegorz. Gregory. Polish. He says he wants to go with you to America; that he's a good worker."

"He can go home. He's free."

The inmate translated again. "He says he doesn't have a home."

"How long has he been here?"

The translator and the boy talked back and forth for some time. "Two months. He was working for a wealthy German family—a household slave—before they were forced to flee the approaching front. He says that he knows where they buried their silver. Very expensive things, he says. He will take you there if you promise to teach him English and take him to America."

Mead smiled. "First we have to fatten him up." He pulled out a bar of chocolate and broke off a piece, placing it in the boy's mouth. Suddenly the boy lifted his hand and snatched the rest of the bar from Mead, stuffing it into his mouth and chewing greedily. Mead laughed. "Easy there."

"Jesus, don't feed them any solid food," said a medic, entering the barrack. But it was too late. Within minutes the boy went into convulsions. Mead stood by helplessly as the frail body rocked and heaved, the face turning beet red and the big brown eyes bulging. Five minutes later the boy was dead. As Mead left the barrack two other prisoners had begun convulsing.

· · ·

They checked into a hotel near the train station, eating dinner in the small dining room off the lobby, which smelled to Andrew like a butcher shop. He couldn't look at anybody in the face without thinking of Nazis, especially the creep in *Saving Private Ryan* who knifed the Jewish guy. He nibbled at his bread while eyeing the other diners warily. It's like being on the Death Star. Definitely should have packed a knife.

When they got up to the room Mead polished his shoes and ironed his slacks, then changed into his pajamas, brushed his teeth and climbed into bed.

"You going to sleep already?" Andrew didn't feel like being alone.

"I'm tired."

Andrew wondered if his grandfather was having flashbacks. And what would happen tomorrow? Just thinking about it made him jumpy. "Mind if I stay up a bit?"

"Not as long as you get some reading in."

Andrew forced himself through ten pages but couldn't concentrate. He got up and peed, then tried to finish the chapter but kept losing his place. He looked over at his grandfather, who had his back to him. Was he dreaming of the war? Was he killing that German right at that very moment?

He put down *The Longest Day* and began browsing through the photographs in one of the guidebooks they'd purchased in Normandy: first three dead bodies by a burning tank; then a wounded German with his hands up, eyes round with fear; then more bodies, some in strange, inexplicable positions; then two muddy-faced GIs carrying ammo and wincing from exhaustion. He tried to imagine his grandfather being so dirty but it was incomprehensible. Mr. Tidy must have gone nuts. Finally he reached for the small bedside lamp and flicked off the light. Immediately he felt the silence closing in on him until his ears ached like he was at the bottom of a deep pool. Was there enough air in the room for two people or was he just breathing in his grandfather's exhales? He rolled to one side, then the other. What I'd give for a big fat joint and a couple of beers. He tried to visualize Cori taking a bubble bath, thinking he'd rather be horny than paranoid. Yet no matter how hard he tried he couldn't assemble her in his mind. Bad sign.

He was sweating now, wanting to kick off the last sheet but afraid to be naked. In the darkness his thoughts began swooping down and clawing at him like hundreds of bats, wings flapping in his face. He thought of the day his father left home and how for weeks he ran to the front door every time he heard a car door slam, certain that Dad had come back. He thought of the color of Matt's cold lips and how peaceful he looked and then of his mother's endless tears and all the faces at school jeering at him. He thought of his grandfather and the awful things he'd been through; the killing and destruction and seeing his buddies die and then losing his wife and having nothing left but his ghosts. He thought of Evelyn dying in some house in Connecticut without even her flowers to keep her company and how all she wanted was a chance to love a grumpy old man without hurting him. And then he thought that maybe everybody was lonely; that perhaps loneliness was the unspoken reason for everything else: for music and sex and getting high and gardening and his mother's tears and Matt's suicide and even God. So they were all lost: his mother and father and grandfather and Evelyn and even his teachers and Cori Fletcher and ass-holes like Kevin Bremer. Every single one of them was lost and alone and yet nobody had the courage to admit it; loneliness was the dirty little secret that nobody dared talk about. And that, he realized, was what he hated above all else. It wasn't the loneliness, it was the silence. The infinite unbreakable silence. He ran his hands through his scalp and pulled at his hair, feeling so much fury for the way things were that he wanted to smash something. *It was the silence that killed you, wasn't it, Matt?*

When he opened his eyes he saw a pale moon peeking through the curtain. *I always thought the man in the moon would be smiling.* Andrew pulled the sheet aside, got up and tiptoed to the window, his thin frame shaking with fear. He glanced at his grandfather, then quietly pulled the curtain aside a few inches and looked up, squinting.

Jesus, Matt was right. The man in the moon wasn't smiling. Not if you looked hard enough. Andrew pressed his face against the pane. He even looked like Matt, cold and pale and so far away. Anger swelled in Andrew's throat. Why did people say he was smiling? Couldn't they even be honest about that? He clenched his fists in rage as he stood in the darkness looking up at the saddest face he'd ever seen; a face that stared down at the Earth night after night and couldn't bear what it saw; a face that understood the awful, cold, lonely truth of everything. When he got back into bed he wrapped himself around his pillow and rocked slowly back and forth. God, what was the point of even being born?

"Evelyn's dying," he blurted out.

His grandfather's breathing stopped.

"I'm not supposed to say anything but it's true. She's *dying*." He let out a sob. "I overheard her daughter. She won't do chemotherapy and she's broke and that's why she has to sell the house and she's going to die soon."

The room was so silent that Andrew thought he could hear the moon inching across the sky. Then he heard the adjacent bed creak and felt his grandfather's large warm hand on top of his.

"It's true. I swear it's true. She made me promise not to tell you because she doesn't want to hurt you. You gotta believe me."

"I believe you, Andrew."

"I just hate it. I hate everything." He couldn't control himself now. All the anger and pain rushed out of his eyes and nose and dribbled down his chin as he cried.

"Sometimes, so do I." Andrew felt the roughness of his grandfather's cheek press briefly against his. The hand remained until the last terrifying thought flew away in the night.

· · ·

His grandfather said nothing the next morning over breakfast. Instead they ate in silence and then Andrew sat in the lobby while his grandfather talked to a middle-aged man who worked at the front desk. After a few minutes the German, who had a round red face and wore small wire-framed glasses, invited Mead and Andrew into a back room. "There wasn't much damage to our town during the war, thank God. Nothing worth bombing." He pulled out a telephone directory. "Now, what did you say the name was?"

"Mueller," said Mead.

"Do you have an address?"

"It's here." Mead pulled out the wallet from his shoulder bag. Andrew watched as the German's eyes widened.

"Are you an . . . investigator?" the man asked warily. Andrew tried to imagine him doing the *Heil Hitler* thing. And yet he seemed friendly enough.

"Oh, no," said Mead. "I just . . . I have some things. I'd like to find the family. It's personal."

"I see." The German studied the wallet for a moment, then looked carefully at Mead again. When he seemed satisfied he opened the directory and began slowly turning the pages, making little noises as he carefully traced his thick forefinger along the columns. Then he picked up the phone and dialed.

Oh great, thought Andrew, he's alerting his neo-Sauerkraut skinhead buddies.

But after the third call the German hung up and smiled, looking pleased with himself. "We have three Muellers listed—it's a common name—and I'm afraid none are at the address you have. I managed to reach one of them and the man doesn't know a Hans from the war. That leaves two, and neither seem to be home at the moment."

"Well, thank you for your help," said Mead.

Phew, thought Andrew, wishing he could put his headphones on, close his eyes and leave Hitlerland far behind.

"Ah, but the good news is that one of our Muellers lives very close to the address you have. Maybe three, four blocks away. Same neighborhood. The other Mueller lives in a new development across town. Ugly buildings, if I may say."

Mead stiffened.

"Perhaps I could try later?"

Mead was silent for so long that Andrew gave him a little nudge. Finally he said, "May I have that address—the one in the same neighborhood?"

"Of course." The German jotted it down on a piece of paper and handed it to Mead.

"Is there somewhere around here I can rent a car?"

"Three blocks down, right across from the train station. Come to the front desk and I'll get you a map."

Andrew was desperate to ask questions as they walked to the rental car agency but his grandfather was so tense that he didn't dare. This has got to be the vacation from hell. Once they got in the car—a Mercedes with leather seats, which was the most promising development in days—he couldn't stand it any longer. "So we're just going to knock on the door?" he asked, working the powered seat back and forth.

"Actually, I thought I'd have you knock."

Andrew's face whitened. "You're kidding?"

"Yes." His grandfather glanced over at him and smiled, though his face was colorless. He drove so slowly that Andrew could see a convoy of impatient drivers in the side-view mirror, which made him cringe.

"I like the car," he said. "Nice and roomy. Probably goes real fast too— if you give her a little gas."

"It's a bit fancy for my tastes, but it's all they had."

Andrew looked into the side-view mirror again, wondering if they were being followed. "Maybe they save it for veterans. Kind of a courtesy car. It's the least they could do." He powered his seat forward again.

"I rather doubt it." For the second time his grandfather pulled over to study the map, then finally turned down a small residential street lined with drab brick row houses, each with a small patch of green out front.

"This is it?"

His grandfather looked down at the piece of paper given him by the hotel clerk, then rolled down his window and slowed the car. "We're look- ing for number twenty-two."

Andrew counted down the houses. "It should be that one." He pointed to a plain two-story house, the upper-floor curtains closed and the brick darkened with age. Red and yellow flowers filled two small flower boxes on each side of the front door.

His grandfather continued on to the end of the street before parking. "Well, here we are," he said, unbuckling his seat belt and reaching into the backseat for his leather bag.

The dead German's stuff, thought Andrew anxiously. "They probably won't even know who we're talking about, right? I mean, it was so long ago?"

"Only one way to find out."

"But then again, the whole block could be filled with relatives. Are you sure they won't be . . . mad?"

"I'm not sure of anything."

Andrew watched a tall, heavyset German teenager walk past, hair cropped close and feet embedded in big, black shit-kickers. Definitely a storm trooper. "Maybe we should call first, or we could e-mail them? I know all about computers."

His grandfather took a deep breath and opened his door. "Come on." He walked quickly down the sidewalk and through the little gate to num- ber twenty-two, hesitating briefly at the door before ringing the bell. Andrew stood back a few feet, ready to bolt. Good, nobody home. But then the door opened a crack and an elderly woman peered out. Oh, shit.

"Do you speak English?" asked Mead.

"Nein."

"I'm American."

She opened the door a few more inches, looking puzzled, then shook her head and began to close the door.

"No English?"

"Nein."

"Wait." Mead pulled the German military ID from his bag and held it up. "Do you know him? Hans Mueller?"

The woman's eyes widened. Uh oh, thought Andrew, taking another step back and scanning the street. Slowly she opened the door all the way and reached for the ID, her gnarled hand visibly shaking. Andrew braced himself for screams as she stared at the photograph, holding it close to her face. But instead she just let out a small cry as she pressed it to her chest. Andrew looked at his grandfather, who stood frozen, a look of anguish on his face. Jesus, this is too fucking much.

"I have more," his grandfather said, reaching into his bag and pulling out the wallet and then the medals.

With both hands the woman grabbed at her wiry gray hair, her eyes fixed on the objects. Then she lowered her hands and carefully took the wallet and ran her crooked fingers over the smooth black leather before opening it, slowly shaking her head back and forth.

A young man emerged from a house two doors down and looked curiously at them. Uh oh, backup. He said something in German to the woman, who answered him back, pointing at Andrew's grandfather. Andrew tensed. If only I had a light sword.

"You're American?" asked the young German, staring at the medals.

"Yes, you speak English?" The man nodded. "Wonderful. I . . ." Mead gestured toward the wallet but seemed at a loss for words. "I . . ."

The woman interrupted, saying something to her neighbor.

"She wants you to come in. She asks please. I will translate."

Mead turned and looked briefly back at Andrew before following the old woman into the house. Andrew held back a moment, then quickly followed. Can't leave Sarge alone in a house full of Sauerkrauts.

The woman led them into a small living room with two low chairs and a sofa covered with a frayed vanilla-colored cloth. Andrew figured he'd just stand but the woman caught his eye and gestured toward one of the chairs. His grandfather sat in the other. A series of small landscapes—

mostly of mountain lakes—hung on the walls and a small dusty cupboard was filled with glasses and china. Andrew wondered if all German homes were so dark and depressing.

"She would like to know what she can bring you to drink?"

"I'm fine, thanks," said Mead.

"I'm fine too," said Andrew, half-tempted to ask for a big shot of Southern Comfort.

The woman frowned, then disappeared down the hallway.

"She hasn't been well lately," said the neighbor, watching her walk away. "I try to check in on her." Mead nodded. "She was a tailor until a few years ago. She has trouble with her—how do you say?—balance."

Mead nodded again, rubbing his palms along the arms of his chair.

"You knew her husband?"

"Not exactly."

Andrew squirmed in his seat.

"I always feel sorry for all the women who lost their husbands. There were millions of them, including my own grandmother. There were no men to marry after the war."

No men? Andrew tried to imagine an entire generation of men being killed. Then he thought of the huge German cemetery in Normandy. How many others were there?

"So what brings you to Germany?"

Mead reached into his leather bag and pulled out the German dog tags and wristwatch, adding them to the medals, wallet and pay book that lay on the coffee table. "These," he said.

"You came all this way just to . . . return them?"

Mead nodded.

The German looked at Mead appreciatively, as if letting it sink in. Andrew guessed he was in his mid-twenties. "And this is your grandson?"

"Yes, I'm sorry. This is Andrew."

The German leaned forward and shook Andrew's hand. "You are very lucky. I always wished I had known my grandfathers. They were both killed on the Eastern Front."

Jesus, thought Andrew, the whole country's a fricking morgue.

When the elderly woman returned she offered milk to Andrew and coffee to Mead, then placed a plate of sliced cheeses and meats and cookies on the table. After easing herself onto the sofa she stared at

Mead for several moments, then leaned toward her neighbor and said something.

"She says she remembers many young American soldiers. She says that you were very kind and she thanks you." He paused as the woman continued, then translated again. "Not like the Russians, she says."

Andrew watched as his grandfather picked up his coffee cup, spilling several times as he tried to bring it to his lips.

"She asks if you are long in Germany?"

"Just a few days," said Mead, putting the cup down with a loud clatter.

"She says you have a very handsome grandson; that you are lucky."

"Thank you."

The woman continued to stare at Mead, her creased features now alert and animated. "She would like to know if you have a large family?"

"Rather small, actually."

"Very small," added Andrew meekly, holding his thumb and forefinger a few inches apart. He reached for a cookie and popped it into his mouth, hoping it might ease his anxiety.

The neighbor continued to translate as the woman talked. "She says you must have been very young in the war. She thinks you have lived a good and healthy life."

"He's in great shape," said Andrew proudly. "He's kind of an exercise freak."

The woman pointed to her knees and then tapped her chest as she spoke. "She says that she has many problems; that old age is, how should I say . . . ridiculous." The woman interrupted. "But she thinks that maybe there is something worse than growing old."

"Tell her I think she is right," said Mead.

Andrew popped another cookie into his mouth, then tried to catch his grandfather's eye, thinking it might be a good time to go. But no one moved. Then the woman began talking again as her neighbor tried to keep up. "She says her husband was a very good man but a terrible soldier." The old woman laughed and Andrew saw that she was missing two teeth. "She says he was in trouble many times for being, what is the word? A funny man. Too many jokes."

Andrew thought of the black-and-white photograph of Hans, trying to imagine the droopy young face cracking a joke. What could possibly be funny about being a Nazi?

"He planned to be a schoolteacher like his father. English and geography, that's what he wanted to teach. She says he was very smart, but she warned him that his students would never learn anything because they'd always be laughing. She thinks he would have gotten into trouble, just like in the army." The neighbor couldn't keep from smiling as he translated.

"I'm starting to like this guy," said Andrew, thinking he'd chip in now and then. He kept his eye on his grandfather, who listened without looking directly at the woman.

"She says she last heard from her husband in a letter two weeks before the war ended. He said he was coming home." Now the old woman's features constricted into a large knot. "She says she waited and waited . . . but he never came." The neighbor put a hand on the woman's thigh as she rubbed her lower lip with her fingers and blinked rapidly.

"Does she know what happened?" asked Andrew without thinking. Mead's eyes flashed at him.

The German man translated. "She thinks maybe he died in prison. He was sick many times in the army. Bad lungs." The neighbor added, "We had many many missing in action, especially on the Eastern Front."

Mead started to say something when suddenly the old woman rose and gestured for them to wait.

"She wants to show you something."

Andrew polished off three more cookies before the woman returned. She held a small, dark green photo album, which she placed gently in Mead's lap. Then she stood beside him and opened it to the first page, pointing. Andrew leaned over to look.

Holy shit, it's the Sauerkraut. The woman turned to a wedding photograph. Hans Mueller stood proudly in a Nazi uniform with a pretty young woman in a simple white dress at his side. Andrew looked at the young woman's face, then at the old woman. Unbelievable. The woman was now full of excitement as she turned the pages and tapped her crooked finger on the photographs. Andrew looked over at his grandfather, whose face was gray and sweaty, like he was going to get sick. What if he had a heart attack or stroke? Oh man, don't croak on me now, Sarge.

"I killed him," Mead said suddenly, pushing the book away.

The woman looked confused while the neighbor stared at Mead, his expression uncertain.

"Tell her I killed him."

"Maybe it's better—"

"Tell her."

The woman said something to her neighbor, apparently asking what was being said. The man hesitated, then spoke several sentences in German. Andrew sat gripping his chair, his eyes darting back and forth between the woman and his grandfather. A look of confusion crossed the woman's face, then she walked over to the sofa and sat down, her hands folded in her lap. Finally she spoke again in German, her voice small and dry.

"She says it was war. You are not to be blamed."

Mead sat trembling. "No, you don't understand. You see ..." He stopped and wiped his forehead with his sleeve. "You see, I ... I murdered him."

"But—"

"He was unarmed." Mead turned to the woman. "Your husband was unarmed."

The young German waited a moment before translating. The woman sat stunned, staring at Mead. Finally she turned and whispered something to her neighbor.

"She doesn't understand why you are telling her this?"

Andrew sat on the edge of his seat, wide-eyed. His grandfather raised his hands slowly in the air and then dropped them, a look of helplessness on his face. "I don't understand either." He wiped his face again with the back of his hand, then leaned toward the coffee table, gently picked up one of the medals and placed it in his palm. "Maybe it's because I have to." He glanced briefly at Andrew, his eyes red and unfocused, then looked back down at the medal and slowly closed his fist as he began to talk.

• • •

In the final weeks of the war Allied intelligence feared that Hitler would create a last redoubt in the rugged Alpine mountains of Bavaria and Austria, using the radio to rally resistance from his heavily fortified mountaintop retreat above Berchtesgaden. Though the German Army was in a state of collapse, remnants of the *Waffen SS* and the *Hitler Jugend* were expected to put up a costly fight while small bands of commandos called Werewolves had been instructed to retreat into the countryside and begin guerrilla warfare.

Allied forces moved quickly to seize potential Alpine strongholds. The 101st was transported in open rail cars and then trucks from the Ruhr

pocket to Bavaria, the men marveling at the destruction caused by years of
Allied bombing. On May 5th, American troops drove unopposed into
Berchtesgaden, once the luxurious retreat of the Nazi elite, and quickly
made their way up to Hitler's beloved Berghof, perched at three thousand
feet with sweeping views of the snow-capped Alps. Though largely
destroyed by British bombers, Hitler's home and compound were a souvenir hunter's dream. Soon drunken GIs were taking joyrides in the
Fuhrer's long black Mercedes staff cars, testing the bulletproof windows
with point-blank shots from their rifles. Others fanned out to search the
remains of nearby villas owned by Martin Bormann and Hermann Goering as well as officers' quarters, *SS* barracks, warehouses and a series of
underground bunkers. At Goering's Officers' Quarters and Club, troops
discovered a huge wine cellar stuffed with thousands of bottles of Europe's
finest vintages. For men who had lived for months in foxholes eating
K-rations, the opulence was stupefying.

While some high-ranking German officers sought to disguise themselves and others headed for the hills, most Germans quickly laid down
their arms, relieved that for them the war was finally over. The Third
Reich would survive only two more days until delegates signed the uncon-
ditional surrender at Allied headquarters in Reims. Yet for some combat-
ants, the transition from war to peace would prove simply too difficult,
causing unnecessary tragedies on both sides.

Mead wandered the streets in a sort of exhausted stupor, stunned into
silence by the beauty of the surrounding Alps, which seemed almost
incomprehensible after months of warfare. And yet he remained haunted
by what he'd seen at Landsberg; by the pleading eyes and weakened cries
of starved prisoners and the stench of rotting corpses, which not even the
crisp mountain air could flush from his nostrils. As he looked at the well-
fed German civilians and the large gingerbread houses and the fancy cars
and stocks of goods he felt a building fury inside until he could just barely
contain himself. *How dare they.*

He took some satisfaction from the pained look on the faces of German
soldiers and citizens as American troops swiftly stripped them of their
valuables. Serves them right, he thought, wishing that the inmates he'd
seen at Landsberg could take part in the looting. Eager for a few souvenirs
of his own, he tried several houses but found them empty. He watched
with envy as GIs loaded down with fur coats, Nazi flags, cameras,

watches, artwork and liquor caroused through the town in liberated Schwimmwagens and half-tracks and motorcycles and luxury cars, as if Berchtesgaden was a giant piñata that had been busted open. Gradually, as the looting continued, he felt almost a sense of panic, like a child during musical chairs when the music stops and all the seats are taken. What about me?

"Look what I got for my girl," said a short GI from New Jersey named Joey Ovito, holding up a set of silverware with Hitler's initials on them. "And Phil got himself a couple of the Fuhrer's personal photo albums!"

Prevented from reaching the Berghof by MPs, Mead hitched a ride back down into town, where he searched through several more houses but found nothing except a pair of lace curtains, which he soon tired of carrying. Weary and frustrated, he headed toward a brown and white chalet nestled into the hillside, hoping at least to find a comfortable bed and thinking that maybe after some rest he'd have better luck.

The door was unlocked. He entered warily, rifle at waist height. Months of battle had worn down all the elasticity of his nerves so that he was perpetually on edge. He closed the door behind him and locked it, desperate for a few hours of privacy and maybe even a bath. After crossing a short hallway he entered a large living room with polished hardwood floors. Two couches and several chairs were covered in rich brown leather and several large landscapes and two pairs of snowshoes hung from the walls. Pairs of skis and poles were stacked in a corner. He paused to take in the panoramic mountain views out the floor-to-ceiling window. So this is how they lived. Is evil easier from such a distance?

On a long dining room table he noticed two silver candelabra, making a note to take them if they weren't too heavy. He stopped to listen for sounds, then walked over to the large fireplace, blackened with soot. The ornate, mahogany-colored mantle was covered with silver picture frames. He picked one up and stared into the fleshy face of a beaming German officer who stood with his arm around a tall and attractive woman. In another photo the same officer—now in battle gear—stood proudly in front of a tank while in another he shook hands with Himmler. Old chums. He put the photograph back, then rested his rifle against the side of the fireplace and drew his pistol before heading down another hallway into a dark, wood-paneled den. He gazed at the leather-bound books that lined the recessed shelves before pulling out several at random, trying to

guess at the titles. He thought of his mother, who was on the library com-
mittee and always said that books were the foundations of civilization.

He was heading down the hallway toward the stairs when he heard a
creak in the floorboards above him. Then another. He quickly stepped
back around the corner, pistol ready. Soon he heard hobnailed boots—
German—on the stairs. He pressed against a wall and waited as the sound
drew closer. There was a pause at the bottom of the stairs, then the footsteps started slowly down the hallway, pausing again, then coming closer
until Mead could hear shallow breathing. He waited another second, then
swiveled around the corner with his pistol leveled at chest height.

"Don't shoot!" cried a boyish-looking German soldier, who stood holding a suitcase in one hand while clutching a small bundle in the other.

"*Hände hoch!*" shouted Mead.

The German dropped the suitcase, then squatted and carefully placed
the bundle on the floor by his feet before standing and raising his hands
into the air. "Welcome, komerad," he said in good English, offering a nervous smile. Several inches shorter than Mead, he had narrow shoulders, a
soft face, a large forehead and a slight droop about his brown eyes, which
made him look permanently sad. His uniform was dirty and frayed and his
brown hair was matted on the top of his head. Only the dregs are still
alive, Mead thought.

"Step back."

The German retreated two paces. "I was just leaving," he said.

"Where did you learn to speak English?"

"My grandmother was British."

Mead looked for a weapon but saw none. "I don't suppose this is your
house?"

The German laughed. "Do I look like a general?"

"What does the German Army do to soldiers who steal from officers'
homes?"

"There is no more German Army."

Mead looked down at the suitcase, which was expensive-looking.
"What's in there?"

"My things."

"I didn't realize the Wehrmacht traveled so well."

The German shrugged. "I will leave you alone." He started to reach for
the suitcase and bundle.

"Hands up."

"But—"

"Now."

"Okay, *komerad*."

They stood staring at each other.

"Open it," Mead said, gesturing toward the suitcase.

"The house is all yours. These are just my things."

"I said, *open it*."

The German hesitated, then bent over the suitcase, placed it flat on the floor and clicked open the two latches. The he stood and stepped back.

Mead crouched down, keeping his pistol pointed at the German, and lifted the lid. Pushing aside a fur shawl he saw silverware, two ceremonial knives with *SS* markings, a new pair of men's leather boots, three pairs of women's dress shoes, a Luger, two clips of ammunition and several dresses.

"You travel well."

The German didn't respond.

"What's in there?" Mead pointed toward the towel-wrapped bundle on the floor beside the suitcase.

The German's face tensed. "It's nothing. Just a . . . plate."

"A plate?" Mead carefully picked it up and unwrapped it, pulling out a gold-rimmed china dinner plate with an eagle and swastika emblazoned on the top and the initials A.H. on the bottom. As he stared at it he felt a sudden giddy sense of excitement like a child discovering hidden treasure. Pay dirt.

"A.H., huh?" Mead smiled as he held the plate up to the light, the pistol still in his other hand. "Rings a bell."

"I had five others, but the rest were taken from me."

"The Fuhrer wouldn't be too happy with you now, would he?"

"The Fuhrer is dead."

Mead ran his fingers along the rim. "Come to think of it, I could use a plate like this. Great conversation piece at Thanksgiving. Probably worth something too, wouldn't you say?" Mead could already see all the neighbors back home gathered around and then the front page photo in the local paper. *Hometown boy cleans Hitler's plate.*

"I'll sell it to you," said the German.

"Sell it?" Mead laughed. "You greedy son of a bitch."

"I have a wife and—"

"You don't seem to understand. You lost."

"The war's over," said the German, trying to smile. "We can all go home."

Mead felt a rush of anger as he thought of the German machine gunners who would wait until they ran out of ammunition before offering to surrender, emerging from their pillboxes with friendly smiles for their American *komerads* and explaining that they had relatives in Milwaukee. "You think it's that easy?"

The German shrugged his shoulders again. "I didn't start the war."

"But you fought it, didn't you?"

"I had no choice. I'm just a common soldier."

Mead took a step closer. "I've seen what you common soldiers can do."

"I'm not a Nazi."

"Suddenly no one's a Nazi." Mead looked down at the plate in his hand, trying to imagine Hitler feeding from it, his appetite fueled by his latest conquest. Then he remembered the souvenirs from the Great War that his father kept in his closet: a German Iron Cross 1st Class, a helmet, a watch and a knife, but nothing like this. Not even close.

"Have you been to a place called Landsberg, by any chance? Near Munich?"

"I don't know what you're talking about."

"Bullshit."

"You can have everything in the suitcase. Take it."

"But you want the plate?"

"I found it."

"Where?"

"At the Berghof."

Mead studied the German's face closely, trying to see beyond the uniform. "You weren't at Normandy, by any chance? Or Bastogne?"

"I was on the Eastern Front."

Mead looked down at the plate again, feeling suddenly overwhelmed by the thought that the war really was over. Why did he survive? Was it a certain calculated cowardice that improved his odds? Had he really done his part? And yet, wasn't he secretly relieved—glad, even—every time it was somebody else's turn to die, as though the gods would be appeased until their next feeding?

"I had a friend named Rokowski," Mead said slowly. "Meat packer from Chicago. Shy kid, but a hell of a skater. You should have seen him on the ice." Mead smiled to himself. "Drove the English girls crazy, and I'm telling you, Roy was no ladies' man." He paused. "A German prisoner blew him up with a grenade. Damndest thing."

"I too lost many friends."

"Ol' Jimbo never even saw the sun come up in France." Mead shook his head. "Poor son of a bitch died right after he landed. Bled to death. And Punchy, well, there wasn't anyone quite like Punchy."

"Perhaps we could find some Schnapps in the kitchen." The German gestured down the hallway.

"Schnapps?" Mead laughed out loud.

"I find it helps." The German began to move.

"Don't you dare."

They remained motionless, each staring warily at the other. Mead held up the plate. "What exactly would a *common* German soldier do with a plate from Hitler's dining room?"

"Sell it."

"Of course."

"Please, my family has no —"

"Do you expect my pity?"

"I expect nothing."

"But you expected to win. That was the idea, wasn't it?"

"I was never asked what I expected."

Mead nodded slowly, feeling his palms sweat. "It's not so much fun when the tables are turned, is it?"

"Come, let's have some Schnapps. We are both tired of this war."

"To hell with you," said Mead, feeling the anger building in his temples so that he wanted to close his eyes and rub them. He blinked a few times, fighting the exhaustion in his limbs and a sense of awful sadness that swept over him. Ah, to sleep for a month and never dream. That's all he needed. Yet—to have a plate from the Berghof. He felt the adrenaline rolling back into his veins. He could just see the look on his father's face. And Sophie, what would she think? But if only Punchy were here.

Mead caught himself lowering his pistol and raised it again. The German's eyes darted toward it.

"My father fought in the Great War," Mead said.

"And mine, too," said the German, smiling hopefully. "You see, we are not so different. Are you married?"

"My father was right: we should have finished you off when we had you." The German waited nervously.

"What's wrong with you people?" Mead felt his arms quaking.

"I don't know what—"

"There was a bully on my street when I was growing up. Picked on everybody smaller than him. Used to beat the bejesus out of me."

"I don't understand."

"And then one day this kid named Scotty—used to be a scrawny little thing, always getting whopped—well, one day he realized that he'd grown taller than the bully only no one had noticed because bullies always look bigger than everybody else. So you know what he does? He waits until the next time the bully starts teasing him at the bus stop and then he just hauls off and pops him in the face, breaking his nose." Mead laughed while the German's expression grew more anxious.

"Go ahead, take the suitcase," said the German. "It's yours."

"So how did he do it?"

"Who?"

"Hitler. How did a madman get so far?"

"I'm only a soldier."

"Or maybe you're all mad. Yes, that must be it." Mead wiped the sweat from his brow, wondering if he had a fever. "A whole goddamn country full of bullies."

"The war is finished, we can go home now." The German's voice was almost childlike now, which annoyed Mead. What did he sound like when he was winning? And how would this meeting end if *he* held the cards? Mead remembered seeing a Belgian family shot with their hands tied behind their backs and left in a frozen heap in front of their ruined home, the children on top. The German started to move again but Mead waved his pistol.

"There was this Polish boy at Landsberg. Gregory. Just a skeleton. Sweetest eyes. I tried to feed him some chocolate . . ." Mead couldn't continue.

"You don't look well. Would you like some food? I have—"

"I'm perfectly well, goddamn it. We won, didn't we?"

"So I'll go."

"Tell me, how does it feel to lose?" The German glanced down again at Mead's pistol. "Please, I want to know."

"Why so many questions?"

"Because I need some goddamn answers." Mead wiped his face again. "Ever since I set foot on German soil I've been wondering how it feels to lose a war."

The German didn't respond.

"Then I'll tell you what I think. I think it feels like shit. I mean, you stupid Krauts really bet the bank." Mead laughed out loud, a cold, mocking laugh.

"Are you going to kill me?" The German's voice was soft and reedy.

Mead smiled, thinking how pleasant it was to see fear, even submission, on a German soldier's face. No, he wouldn't kill him. But in a way it was tempting. After all, why should he get to go home to his family when so many others never would? What justice was there in that?

"It would be murder."

"Murder?" Mead spit out the word. "You've got a lot of goddamn nerve."

"May I show you a picture of my wife? We only got married a few—"

"Shut up!" Mead tightened his grip on the pistol.

"What are you going to do?" The German's smooth young face—was he even eighteen?—looked pathetic now, like one of the raccoons Mead used to catch in a trap by the chicken house, guilty as could be.

Mead looked back at the plate in his left hand when suddenly the German reached out and snatched it from him.

"You son of a bitch."

The German held the plate out to one side, arm extended. "If you shoot me, I'll drop it."

Mead raised his pistol, straightening his arm. "Give it to me. *Now.*"

The German's large brown eyes swelled with fear. "You can't shoot an unarmed man."

"Like hell I can't." Mead's limbs shook with anger. "What about the Americans at Malmédy? Or the slaves you starved to death at Landsberg? How many of them had a fighting chance?"

"I don't know what you're talking about."

"Oh, I think you do."

"I told you, I'm a simple soldier. You can't blame me."

"Then who can I blame?" screamed Mead. "Tell me, *who?*"

"Please, you must calm down."

"Give me the goddamn plate."

"But if I do you'll shoot me."

"I'll shoot you if you don't."

"I will trade. You turn me over to an American officer and I will give you the plate."

Mead saw the sudden defiance in the German's eyes, which infuriated him. And yet he felt confused too, not knowing quite how he had suddenly found himself on the brink, face to face with the enemy yet wavering between war and the vague expectation of peace. Sweat from his palm gathered on the pistol grip and his mouth felt so dry that he had trouble swallowing. He looked longingly at the shiny gold rim of the plate clutched in the German's small hand, suddenly wanting it more than anything, as if it were the prize he'd been fighting for all these months, a trophy that would pass down through generations of his family with stories of his deeds. And it was for Punchy too, and Jimbo and Rokowski. All of them. They'd paid for it with their *blood*.

"A deal?" Mead lunged for the plate with his free hand but the German was quick and managed to sidestep him. Mead lunged again and this time managed to get a grasp of the plate. They struggled briefly before it slipped from their hands and fell to the floor, shattering.

They both froze, staring down mutely at the pieces.

"There, now neither of us can have it," said the German, a smile spreading across his long and dirty face. The smile quickly vanished as Mead raised his pistol.

You wouldn't, would you?

Oh yes, but I would.

But it's cold-blooded murder.

No, you see, it's only war.

Mead pulled the trigger.

The first shot hit the German in the upper chest just as his face sank in disbelief. As he fell backward the second shot struck him in the shoulder and the third ripped open his cheek.

Then silence.

Mead stood over the body for a moment, pistol still in hand, then put the gun back into its holster and quickly rifled through the German's pockets, pulling out a wallet, a military pay book and three medals before removing the dead man's dog tags and wristwatch. Then he reached into the suitcase and grabbed the Luger.

He was rising to his feet when two GIs burst through a side door, rifles at the ready. "What happened?"

"He . . . he tried to take my gun away," said Mead, stepping back.

"You all right?"

Mead nodded slowly.

"Hey, look at this stuff," said one of the soldiers, crouching by the open suitcase. The other soldier headed for the candelabra while Mead bent down and picked up the largest piece of the plate.

"Mind if we help ourselves?"

"Be my guest," said Mead, trying to avoid the face of the dead German, who looked like a mere boy with his eyes closed. He slipped the piece of plate into his pocket, then turned and headed for the door.

· · ·

When Mead finished he sat in silence, eyes unfocused and face stricken so that just looking at him made Andrew want to cry. No one spoke.

"I came to say I'm sorry," Mead said finally, looking up at the German widow, who was wiping tears from her eyes. "And I wanted you to have his things. They never belonged to me." He rose unsteadily to his feet and walked over to the woman. She took his hand and patted it but stayed seated. Mead looked as if he might say something else, then abruptly turned and headed for the door, shoulders slightly stooped. Andrew followed quickly behind.

"She says she's sorry, too," said the young German, standing by the woman with his hand on her shoulder. "It was a terrible time."

Mead paused, then bowed his head slightly before continuing out the door and down the sidewalk. Andrew stayed right behind him, not daring to look back.

After Mead slid the key into the ignition he seemed to hesitate.

Andrew glanced over at him, surprised by how different he looked, smaller and more fragile, which made Andrew feel that maybe he wasn't really so alone after all. "What are we going to do now?" he asked gently as he buckled his seat belt.

"We're going to give your friend a proper burial." Mead started the engine.

"We're going to Indiana?"

"We're going to California."

Andrew felt a spreading sensation of warmth in his chest as his grandfather drove in silence, both hands high on the wheel. After several blocks he suddenly pulled over to the side of the road, turned off the ignition and sat back in his seat.

"I've been doing some thinking," he said, letting out a long breath and keeping his gaze fixed straight ahead.

Andrew waited nervously for him to continue.

"Well, I thought perhaps that maybe—with the way things are going with your mother lately—well, I thought . . ."

"What?"

Mead turned and looked at Andrew, then stared straight ahead again. "I thought perhaps you might consider staying in California for a year. You could enroll in the local high school; see how it goes. It's a good one, I hear. Anyway, you can't beat the weather. Maybe you could even learn to surf. And then there's Evelyn, who's going to be needing our help. You could visit your mother anytime—heck, maybe we could even get her to move out, too. Of course, if you'd rather not . . ."

"Really?"

"Really."

Andrew could only smile before quickly turning his face away and concentrating his watery gaze on a small German boy peddling by, wondering if by any chance it was Matt.

Home

They took turns sleeping on the couch in the living room to keep Evelyn company at the end. Some nights, as Mead stared wearily through the darkness at the green glow of the monitors, he was almost convinced it was Sophie's shallow breaths he heard coming from the bed beside him. In a way it no longer mattered, not so long as one breath followed the other until the sun crept beneath the curtains and he could search Evelyn's face for the defiant smile he'd grown to love. He preferred to lie on his back so that he could easily reach through the metal railing to take her hand, always shocked that even those who give off the most warmth can turn so cold. When they tired of talking he would patiently await the responsive squeeze of her fingers until finally sleep eased her pain. Then he would follow along with each tentative breath, gently coaxing them on one after the other until morning. If the silence became unbearable he would get up and lean over her bed and put his ear to her mouth, reminding himself of his promise that this time there would be no ambulance.

She had just finished transplanting the last of her flowers into Sophie's old garden when Mead and Andrew returned from the airport. Mead was so startled by the sight that he drove right on down the street, thinking he must have made a wrong turn. When he finally pulled into his driveway he sat staring out the window as Andrew jumped out and pounced on Evelyn, nearly lifting her off the ground as he hugged her.

"Well, what do you think?" she said, taking off her leather work gloves and gesturing toward the flower bed when Mead finally emerged from the car.

He could only nod.

That evening she cooked up a huge vegetarian feast in their honor and peppered them with questions until well past midnight. "Don't leave out *anything,*" she said, sitting between them at Mead's dining room table and ladling food onto their plates. To her delight, Andrew set a new record by consuming seven macadamia nut and raisin rolls while even Mead admitted that it was the best meal he'd had in days.

"I don't think I've ever had such so much fun," she said as Mead walked her home. "And I didn't even go anywhere."

"I wish you'd come," said Mead, stopping as they reached her walkway.

"So do I," she said softly. "But Andrew needed time with you. And anyway, I've been so busy since the offer on the house and—"

Before she could finish Mead took her by the shoulders and kissed her firmly on the lips.

"We need to talk," he said, still holding her.

"Actually, I'm happy to talk later," she said with a smile as she kissed him again. "Any chance you want to come in?"

"You mean . . . now?"

"I mean right now."

Mead called Sharon the next morning.

"I've been worried sick about you two," she said just before she accidentally dropped the phone, causing Mead to wince as the receiver bounced across a hard surface. "Sorry. So don't tell me, it was a disaster."

"Not at all."

"What happened?"

"We got along just fine."

"And?"

"And it was . . . very educational."

"Educational? For you or for him?"

"For both of us. He's a great traveler. I'd take him anywhere."

"I want whatever your doctor's got you on."

Mead heard a telltale inhalation on the other end. "Are you smoking a cigarette?"

There was a pause. "Jesus, Dad, how do you do that?"

"I'm a parent."

"You ought to work for one of those psychic networks. But don't worry,

I'm stopping tomorrow. Promise. I've even got a patch ready. It's just been crazy lately."

"Were you fired?"

"Well, actually, things have taken a rather interesting twist."

Mead cradled the receiver with his shoulder and lay back on his bed rubbing his forehead. "What happened?"

"I'm not sure you want to know."

"Of course I do."

"He asked me to dinner."

"Who did?"

"My boss."

"The one whose expense accounts you deleted?"

"That one."

"You said no."

Another pause. "Actually, we've had a couple of dates."

"Sharon."

"I know, I know. But it turns out he's really a nice guy."

"He's not a guy, he's a boss."

"I'm a big girl, Dad."

Mead looked over at the photograph of Sophie taken on the balcony of their hotel in Hawaii. "There's something I want to talk about."

"You're going to lecture me."

"Tempting, but no, it's about Andrew."

"I can come get—"

"I want him to live with me."

"What?"

"Just for a semester. See how it goes. It's a good high school and he could use a change, and besides, I could use a hand around here now and then— and I thought you could use a break or maybe you could even join us."

"You're kidding?"

"Of course not."

There was a long silence before she started crying. "You're really serious?"

"He needs a fresh start, Pumpkin. Frankly, I think you do, too, but if you won't join us you can always visit. We could just try one semester and see how it goes."

More sniffling. "What does Andrew think?"

"He's game. I think he's sort of taken to Southern California. You know, the beaches and all."

"I can't believe this." Mead heard a quick inhale, followed by a long exhale. "I want to talk to him."

"Of course. And then why don't you think it over and we'll talk again tomorrow, okay, Sweetheart? Just consider it."

"Mom wouldn't believe this."

"There are a few things she wouldn't believe."

Another big exhale. "I don't know what to say. I mean, you've thought this through?"

"Yep."

"But aren't you a little old to be raising a teenager?"

"Oh hell, I'm just hitting my stride."

Once Andrew was on the line Mead headed out front, turned on the hose and began watering the flowers.

· · ·

The following Sunday Andrew, Mead and Evelyn drove to the beach and held a small sunset service for Matt, the three of them standing in a small circle around the Ziploc bag at their feet. Mead had argued for a more dignified means of transport but Andrew wouldn't hear of it, saying that Matt didn't give a hoot about appearances, and besides, the Ziploc had seen more of the world than most people. Even so, Mead insisted on wearing a suit and tie while Evelyn wore an elegant black dress that completely undermined Mead's efforts to think morbid thoughts. After several aborted attempts Andrew managed to get through a song he'd written for the occasion, which made Evelyn cry so hard that the service had to be stopped twice so that she could collect herself. "Sorry," she squeaked, dabbing her eyes. They finished with a moment of silence, which was actually quite noisy, and then Andrew reached into the bag and took out a small handful of Matt's remains, hesitating briefly before sweeping his arm through the air and tossing them to the wind. Then he took another handful and let the ashes gradually slip between his fingers as he headed down the beach and along the water's edge, first walking and then running as fast as he could while his best friend trailed out behind him.

Evelyn declined quickly after that. As soon as her house sold Mead and Andrew moved her in with them, first into Mead's bedroom—which gave Andrew the heebie-jeebies, even though he approved in principle—and then onto a hospital bed they set up in the living room. "It doesn't get any better than this," she liked to say as she worked the automatic bed recliner and gazed out the window at her flowers, the bedsheets littered with recipe clippings that she was determined to finish pasting into one of three enormous books.

"You're kidding, aren't you?" Andrew finally said one afternoon when he got home from school.

"Actually, not at all."

"But how can you say that? I mean, we both know it gets *a lot* better." His chin was trembling.

"Only if you imagine yourself in someone else's shoes."

Mead wanted to sleep on the couch every night but Andrew insisted on taking turns, sometimes finishing his homework by flashlight. He had promised his grandfather to wake him if anything happened and not to call 911 under any circumstances. But secretly Andrew still hoped that nothing would happen, not so long as he remained awake to watch over her.

"Tell me again about the look on your grandfather's face when he saw the beaches at Normandy," she said one night as they lay talking in the dark.

"Oh man, I thought he was going to freak. I was like, *tiptoeing.*"

"I can't imagine what he felt."

"How do you think *I* felt? I already had Matt's ashes to worry about, and now it's looking like the General's about to stroke out on some beach in *France*. Jeeze, I could have been stranded."

Evelyn let out a laugh. "Now that would have made a story."

"But the scariest part was being around all those Sauerkrauts."

"I believe the correct word was *Kraut,* and it's just a bit outdated."

"No, you see Kraut is just short for Sauerkraut. They're Sauerkrauts."

"Never mind."

"Anyway, when we got to the widow's house I figured we were goners. To tell you the truth, I was prepared to fight my way out."

"All the way to the border?"

"At least to the train station."

"That would have been some fight."

"No kidding. The place is crawling with storm troopers."

"But not in uniform?"

"No, that's the thing. The whole country's gone undercover. But you can just feel it."

"I see."

"You should have been there when he started telling the woman about how he killed her husband. I could almost hear him sweat."

"I'm surprised *you* didn't have a stroke."

"Yeah, me too, but I figured at least one of us needed to be in control."

"Good thinking."

. . .

Andrew talked about the trip almost every time it was his turn to sleep on the couch, telling Evelyn all about the Crown Jewels and Elizabeth's tomb and the fortifications at Normandy and the rows of white crosses and how there's hardly a thing worth eating in all of France. Sometimes he kept talking even after he knew she was asleep because at least that way he figured he could keep himself awake. And when he did finally drift off he would wake with a start, afraid of what he would see when he opened his eyes.

It was his turn the night Evelyn died.

"I'd like you to sing at my funeral," she said after he turned out the lights.

"I couldn't do that," Andrew said nervously.

"Of course you can. And you have a wonderful voice. Anyway, you have no choice. It's a dying woman's request."

"Don't talk like that."

"I'm done."

He looked over at her, trying to make out her silhouette in the darkness and wondering if maybe there were things she needed to talk about. Finally he asked, "Are you afraid?"

"I have my moments." She let out a hoarse sigh. "I just keep telling myself that a path this well traveled has got to lead somewhere interesting."

"You really think so?"

"The truth is, I'm not entirely convinced." She coughed several times, then made a soft moaning sound that Andrew had come to dread.

"Are you okay?"

"No . . . but it'll have to do."

"You want me to get another one of those blue pills?"

"If I get any more schnockered I'm liable to start dancing on the tables."

"I'll get you some more water." He quickly got up, turned on his flashlight and refilled her glass, holding it to her lips.

"At least I'm flying first-class," she whispered, resting her head back on her pillow.

When Andrew returned to the couch he pulled the blankets up to his chin, keeping his eyes wide open as he waited for her to fall asleep. But every time her breathing seemed to ease into a pattern she would let out a sudden gasp and her breaths would quicken again.

"I hate this," he said, clenching his fists at his side.

"Me too," she whispered.

"What can I *do?*"

"Just keep your head up and promise me you'll look after the General. He's had about enough of this nonsense."

"He's a lot tougher than he looks."

"No one's that tough."

"I'll keep him out of trouble. Promise."

"And make sure he gets plenty of air. After your grandmother died he sat in that chair of his so long I was afraid he'd turn to stone."

In the silence Andrew wondered whether maybe stones didn't have it easier. "Want to talk some more?" he asked.

"I'd rather have you rest up for school."

"I don't need much sleep. Really. Let's talk."

"Okay then, what shall we talk about?"

"I don't know. I've been wondering what kind of stuff you think about. I mean, is it mostly old stuff or new stuff?"

She tried to laugh but her voice was dry and thin. "A bit of both. That's one of the few pleasures of old age. You have an enormous catalog to choose from." Her bed creaked as she turned to her side. "The real truth is, I'm bursting with advice but I don't think you really need any of it."

"Advice about what?"

"Oh goodness, all sorts of things. Dating, work, gardening, the best way to remove red wine stains from fabric. That's the silly thing about getting old: you start feeling like a how-to manual that nobody's going to bother to read." She coughed again. "But I promised myself that I wouldn't start telling you how to run your life."

"It probably wouldn't make any difference. Matt used to say that everyone has to . . . screw up their lives in their own special way."

"Oh really? Well, he just may have been on to something."

"He was basically a genius, only no one listened to him."

"You must miss him terribly."

"I wish you could have met him."

"So do I."

Andrew felt his throat closing. "See, he believed that everybody has to put up with some major bullshit—sorry—sooner or later, and that it's just a question of when. So he figured that we were just getting it out of the way early, and then we'd be in good shape."

"Sort of like clearing the decks; work before play."

"*Exactly*. Only . . ." Andrew couldn't finish.

"I'm sorry."

They were both silent until Evelyn spoke again. "You know what I think the real trick is?—and I've only just figured this out."

"What?"

"You have to have some momentum in life. That's what gets you through the tough times." Andrew listened as she tried to catch her breath. "Come to think of it, that's what this feels like."

"What what feels like?"

"Dying."

"Don't say that."

"But it's true. After years of rolling along I'm afraid I'm finally running out of momentum."

"Maybe I could give you a push."

He heard a rustling of sheets and then felt her hand sliding across his cheek. "But don't you see? You already did."

Epilogue

Evelyn was cremated according to her wishes and her two children agreed to hold a small service in California before taking her remains to Connecticut for interment. Mead spent hours working on a eulogy, sitting up late in his blue chair with a cup full of sharpened pencils and pausing now and then to run his hands over Evelyn's old gardening gloves, which he kept on the table next to him. But once he reached the lectern and looked down at his grandson and daughter watching him he knew he'd never be able to say what he wanted to say, not with all the voices filling his head. He tried once more to speak, then stared down helplessly at his notes, feeling the full weight of his life pressing down on him. He was just about to return to his seat when his grandson stood up.

Andrew looked at his grandfather, then nervously surveyed the other mourners. "Hang on to your hats, folks, because there's something I have to do." He coughed, then took a deep breath. "I wrote it myself." Then he clutched the pew in front of him with both hands and began to sing.

He started softly at first, his cheeks flushed red and his voice quivering. When it looked like he wouldn't be able to continue Mead figured they'd both be booed right out of the church. *Sorry, Evelyn.* But gradually the boy's voice grew in volume until finally at the end he was singing with his fists clenched and his eyes squeezed shut. When he finished there was a moment of stunned silence before the church filled with applause.

"I have nothing to add," said Mead proudly as he stepped from the lectern.

It wasn't until the following week that Evelyn's children discovered that their mother's ashes were missing, replaced by a substance that tasted remarkably like sugar. (Her son did the tasting, using his moistened pinkie when nobody was looking.) Despite investigations by both the police and the funeral parlor, the remains were never found and no charges were filed.

That spring, Sophie's garden had never looked quite so good.

F
HULL

Hull, Jonathan.

The distance from
Normandy.

DATE			